CW01018889

ISBN: 978-0-993371-48-6

Heaven is a Donut

Heaven is a Donut
by
H.J. Brown
ISBN: 978-0-9933714-8-6

Published by

i2i Publishing. Manchester.
www.i2ipublishing.co.uk ·

Heaven is a Donut

DEDICATION:

To Mike Somerset

The man who inspired the character of Chris.

If you love and get hurt, love more. If you love more and hurt more, love even more. If you love even more and get hurt even more, love some more until it hurts no more.

- William Shakespeare

Life

There once was a time when I knew best; I think it was when I was born.
Before the cuts of existence began, my heart oft wounded and torn.

Too soon the pattern of life emerged; conceived to decorate the soul
Grief and sorrow jostle at will; beckon the mind's shadowy hole.

Regret and remorse live side by side in a person shrunk to fit,
With desolate walls of assumption, encouraged to absorb the hit.

The soundless scream of abandonment, that all others never shall hear.
Hollow vict'ry for neglected child, whose survival is not held dear.

There is a way to heal the pain: become unfettered and be free.
Make a choice: Drift and blame? Or lift the veil, so we can see?

To all I say, if you want to hear, to all of you I can state,
I am not alone, I need not say I, but We! We no longer wait.

See who we are, bathe precious spirit - in a promise of clear, sweet light.
Become who we are, in an act of love; have faith in our strength and might.

Heaven is a Donut

At last to be, who we're meant to be: a force, a guiding power.
With brave new choices for a future bold, enriching our ev'ry hour.

Then being the best that we can be, with faith and trust in our force,
Blessings will come to reward us so well, with love our richest source.

Have Faith. Have Hope. Have trust in Above. But most of all - have Love.

I dedicate this poem to my dear friend, Jackie Fitch.
(1959-2015)

Heaven is a Donut

Contents

Heaven is a Donut

Chapter 1

Cloth Ears & the Edge of Insanity

In the Beginning was the word
and the word was with God
and the word was God.
St John chapter 1.1

And for the moment the word was ..... silent.
(not St John chapter 1.1 or any other scripture)

"Cloth Ears? Nothing but a cloth ears," she muttered, but the thought aroused interest.

"Hey Cloth Ears?" Amelia raised her volume and angled her head vaguely in the direction she thought God might be residing: all seeing, all disapproving - as usual.

"Cloth Ears? Are you there? Are you at home today or are you too busy?" she sang with eyes fixed upward, appearing to jeer at her exasperated eyebrows as the word 'busy' looped out of her mouth and evolved into a delicate, but somewhat surprised, wine flavoured hiccup.

"Oops, pardon me. Are you on vacation somewhere?" Amelia entertained herself with this new idea. God's gone looking for God, A God holiday; God is in need of a break. Her errant voice oozed satirical indignity at the wooden Sheila Maid, heavy with her washing, hanging from the ceiling of her old-fashioned kitchen. As her chaotic alcoholic thoughts tumbled from mildly iniquitous amusement to panic-stricken trepidation of such profanity again (surely it is bordering on outright wickedness to heckle God as much as she had taken to, of late?) she stood frozen, poised, and waiting. Will the much-feared threat of a thunderbolt from God strike her down today?

Amelia felt a surge of electric anger shoot through her, seeping into her core like water into a sponge. "Ooh, I'm a sponge," she gushed to her silent God, "and I need wringing out," she giggled as she visualised the idea. "God, I don't want to be a sponge," she pouted, "I'm overflowing with mel...melun...coh...lee." Amelia shrugged, abandoning the word melancholy to a contented fizzle in her wine-blanket tongue, her tipsy incoherent mouth struggling to cope with multiple syllables.

"Clean me up, wring me out, starch me free of mis-a-ree, hang me out to dry-ee," she sang, "I'll be all nice and clean again then."

Her words stultified, "arlbeallniceancleanagainthen. Ssshh..." she shrunk her neck into her shoulders and held a finger to her lips in an attempt to block the thought process of necessary cleansing and hush herself back into the moment. "I wish it were that easy."

She ended the discourse with flat acceptance that it was not that easy or even possible to re-start life without the irrevocable stain or blemish that being alive brings upon us all. "I'm a blemished sponge and that's it. I'm a blotted, well-used piece of blotting paper; I've certainly blotted my copybook, God's not going to clean me up with a fresh start, bleached free of sin."

Unshackling her thoughts from the improbable cleaning duty she had batted God's way, she attended the present. Thankfully, Amelia was pleased to note, she discovered a glass of mollycoddle-inducing alcohol in her hand. "Oooh, that's nice," she said in awe, convinced the glass had jumped its way into her hand when she was not looking.

She took two gulps bigger than her mouth could hold, in an attempt to ease the discomfort of life and grabbed at the bottle to top up her glass, not bearing to see it empty; this being, a worthy bottle of precious Bordeaux she was shamefully throwing down an unappreciative neck. The concentration necessary to keep clutched bottle safe in a pulsing fist had successfully postponed the affect of the inevitable wobbles, resulting from alcohol hitting base.

Unremittingly, the smooth red decided on a brief detour, travelling beyond her squeamish disapproving stomach, which, having already pre-empted worse was to come, belched a bagful of wind both ends in protest, causing Amelia to wrinkle her nose in contempt at her body's loose conduct.

In a boldness only alcohol can command, the Bordeaux surged its way with single-minded determination past base camp, to the intended temporary resting place - Amelia's ankles - where hungry wave-like gestures momentarily settled to gather momentum before beginning gleeful redeploy. Sloshing and splashing, coating every orifice as it licked and slurped the journey of a lifetime, purposefully retracing joyous steps, making the most of every cloying moment back to Amelia's quivering gut awaiting its fate; thrusting upwards, past the knees, swirling around the thighs, twice around the block and bang – hitting, collywobbling, tummy lurching heaven.

At least .... that's how it felt to Amelia.

Some moments still from losing all feeling in most of her body, she found herself with a second or two to contemplate the rather confusing effect of out-of-control limbs. Having developed a will of their own, they rebelliously disassociated themselves from the convulsing head that temporarily bore little resemblance to Amelia. This, although not obvious, was Amelia attempting to sing and dance simultaneously to Beethoven's Ave Maria, which had just for some inexplicable reason, popped into her head. Not the wisest of moves, but then drunks are not particularly noted for their wisdom but rather the more common, 'it seemed like a good idea at the time' philosophy.

As she cast delirious shadows manically pummelling the walls, her arms and legs concluded the time had come to deliver their final blow to her dignity. Bendy, boneless and buckling, she found herself no match for their callous proclamation that, much as the rest of the world, her human frailty against the affects of alcohol was astounding. Unable to remain an upright citizen of great esteem, she succumbed to the clanging of her brain cells. Her internal loudspeaker broadcast victoriously the jousting tournament about to begin inside her skull, once again reminding her as every other inch of her body had done so cruelly, that she wasn't quite - in full compos mentis.

She reached for her phone. "I will call Lulu....shall even....I shall call Lulu. God? I'm... going... to... speak... to... my friend Lucinda." Amelia spoke primly into the heavens, accentuating her words to carefully hide her drunken state. Proud with success in the knowledge there was absolutely no way God would suspect she was a smidgen under the influence, she catapulted towards her next sentence, "ash you not shpeaking to me. See, losht your chance. Losht your opp....toonitee for nother convert. Hah. Lulu? LuluLululu...lululu ... sfunny name ishnt it.........LuluLuluLooooo."

Having experienced a long day at work, and it being two-of-the-clock in the morning, Lucinda's gentle snores indicated she was pleasantly occupied elsewhere, as Amelia breathed ardent, 'LuluLuluLooos' into her unresponsive phone.

Nonetheless, desperate to hear her friend Lucinda's gentle American lilt, Amelia spewed five minutes of drunken garble in response to the answer service before tossing the unhelpful phone aside in disgust. She reluctantly surrendered to her jitterbugging head atop a violently swaying body, whilst a dawning revelation of how her preoccupation for the coming thunderbolt from God launched in her direction loitered on the edge of obsession. Snapping to attention, her remaining functioning memory cell alerted her to the fact it contained one piece of information only - the insult she had just enthusiastically propelled towards her Maker.

"I'll try an apology and repent – forthwith, forthwith. Maybe that will stop the fear of God nipping, snipping, snapping at me." Amelia's left hand teased her nose with a nip, snip, snapping motion, imitating a crocodile preparing for lunch. "You're always snapping at me," she grouched into her crocodile-conscience hand.

"Sorry God; I'm drunk! (hic).... Are you listening Cloth Ears? Sorry I called you Cloth Ears." Amelia 'tee-heed' at her own audacity, until interrupted by an audibly spiteful thought crawling its slimy way obstinately from her bad side whilst leaving an all-consuming trail of evil-infested gloop in its wake. On this particular occasion, *bad side* was gleefully preparing to rip shreds into Amelia's re-born interest in God.

Her *bad side* was a thing to behold. *Bad side* could not but laugh uncontrollably at the expense of others: Bad Amelia loved nothing better than to witness loss of dignity when someone trips over something, (especially if it's one's own feet, this, always generating more chagrin to the luckless individual than an obvious obstacle) preferably supplemented by a hurried glance around to see who has spotted such ineptitude – and stirring sound effects, such as an embarrassed groan or a pathetic little whimper, either could be equally amusing.

Bad Amelia would argue relentlessly, needing to be right at all times, regularly featuring a, "I've only been wrong once and that was when I said I couldn't be right about everything," statement. Amelia's *bad side* gave recurrent use to every foul-mouthed profanity known to mankind – albeit mostly inside her head.

Bad side would rob a bank without any conscience whatsoever if she thought she could get away with it; would start a fight and laugh tempting them to, "come and get it," taunting them with, "that didn't hurt," as she is floored by a thump in the face. Amelia's *bad side* was a very large, damaged and needy self-destruct button – painted bright red to make sure it would not go unnoticed. Her *bad side* was the drunkard lying face down in the gutter; her *bad side* had the morals of an alley cat.

In short, her *bad side* was an insufferable pain in the butt, deliberately procuring more trouble over the years than she dared think about. Oh yes, she had a very bad side, creating a veritable cesspool of evil life within her head.

Bad side, being an evil toe-rag, had often given her cause to speculate how on earth, she of all people had managed to gain a respectable degree in psychology when the last thing she was capable of doing was understanding her own fragmented personality, bowing to the opinion she was (as once described,) 'completely off her stump.'

'Whatever makes me think I can grasp the functioning mind of others with any sort of helpful comprehension is beyond all reason, surely.' she lambasted herself. 'With boring regularity I throw all caution to the wind, behave like an impetuous idiot with no thought of consequence to self or others whatsoever and make the most ridiculous, appallingly defective decisions in the history of the universe - numerously. I can't even spell the word psychologist for heaven's sake,' she lamented.

Mind you, that is how it came to pass; her intention being, to gain a degree in physiology. 'Learn how the body works, maybe that will help me find the meaning of normal as heretofore, *normal* has enigmatically skirted over my head, repetitively escaping my hold on life.'

Despite the passage of time, she remained clueless. Her dyslexic self had led her to the university library, poring over information on psychology courses and becoming so drawn in by a magnetising attraction before she realised her mix-up, her interest had locked into a fascination that took root. From that moment on, her fate was determined by a blunder. 'Story of my life,' she decided. In step with her routine coping strategy, she made her career error easy for herself by timorously surrendering to the acceptance of her, 'my life is made up of a series of bungles' theory, in which indulging proved delightfully helpful, giving her permission to end each failure or mistake with a 'story of my life' proclamation.

Somehow, acquiescence to lack of responsibility taking was made tolerable by a stark, simple truth - how could she ever change anything, when the story of her life was already written?

However, as much as she enjoyed her gaffe, a problem lingered; long aggrieved that her profession was represented by one of those ridiculous words with a stupid 'sike' or 'fizz' type pronunciation going on, she oft pondered, 'Why couldn't it be a regular word like teapot or buttock, easy to say, easy to spell?' Life would be so much easier.

Amelia relaxed into a kitchen chair to indulge a sudden wave of nostalgia for her Uncle Billy's dreary

cocktail parties. Her initial impatience to be grown up enough to attend had quickly worn thin, causing Amelia to disappear into her bedroom until the last of the boring guests had departed. She refigured her distant memory.......
"Hello, come and meet my niece Amelia, she's studying to be a Senior Teapot in the city."
"Really, tell me, it must be quite stressful holding down the position of Senior Teapot these days, especially in the city, how do you anticipate coping with the strain?"
Or,
"How do you do. You must be Bill's niece Amelia, and what is your line of work?"
"Hello how nice to meet you, actually I'm a Buttock."
"A Buttock? Oh how interesting, I've heard it's a meticulous, time-consuming job. Tell me, is it an advantage in that particular field if one is anally retentive?"
Teapot or Buttock would have saved her a fortune on business cards that were solely for the purpose of stuffing into every pocket, bag, purse, car door, open hand or any other useful orifice, mindful of situations in which she found herself requiring to write down her chosen occupation. No matter how often she tore out her hair trying to stamp the word Psychologist into her brain, it would skip its merry little way through her head, teasingly dally a while before playfully exiting, pausing to give her the one finger tribute as it disappeared, turning right at her left eardrum and departing onto the highway of life outside Amelia, never to be seen again.
Her dyslexia had plagued her throughout life in an interesting variety of collective discomfitures. One such terrible recollection always to make her squirm with a creeping, blotchy, red-necking embarrassment, was the heart stopping second when after submitting her thesis,

(which to her had been an extremely well researched, well written piece,) she was to discover an awful truth. She had taken her time over this most precious testament of her intelligence, knowing it would forever silence her critics. This will stand as her *tour de force*. She had clapped her hands with satisfaction in the knowledge the invisible unnamed *they* would become flabbergasted by her cleverness.

'Never again will I be labelled, Dumb-Blonde or Dimbo-Bimbo, or cringe in shame as my self-esteem is battered and squashed with taunts of, "Amelly-Welly with the big fat Belly." No, I will be looked upon with reverence and respect, curbing any references to being stupid and foiling all attempts to disparage my body dysmorphia, for….absolutely….well…...ever! People will look up to me and come to me for help and advice with their problems. I will get a fantastic job earning loads of money and will be the envy of everyone. This will show them what I'm capable of.' She knew this with great certainty.

She worked hard in her resolve to make her fantasy of achieving a first-class honours degree become reality. She believed in herself and had written at length with great self-confidence, only to discover with a stomach lurching sickness that her masterpiece was despoiled by - a typing error. How could this happen? It was easy to see what she meant to say - even if it did look a bit weird.

"Amelia?" Her tutor had spoken her name with a little tiredness she felt. "Amelia, it was going well up to the point when, in your thesis, you began discussing, and I quote, *…the merits of group therapy within a counselling environment for experiencing, as some case studies had described, 'lemons' in their head. Statistics were emerging that demonstrated those facing up to their 'lemons' found great benefit from the group support they received whilst in treatment…."*

When confronted with the wretched truth of her slapdash workmanship, Amelia had stared at this typo in disbelief, willing it to disappear.

Why oh why?' she thought despondently. Angry fat tears scorched her cheek, espying terra-firma in the lap of the truth-telling piece of paper, which, no longer a tribute to her ability, fast became a sodden indictment of her inane stupidity. Her clumsy fingers had mistyped, it becoming cruelly clear; her dyslexic eyes had lied to her, lied! They had seen what they knew *should* be there - demons.

So near and yet so far, only one letter out. 'Why oh why didn't I accept Lucinda's offer to proofread instead of jealously hugging it suspiciously in case the temptation to plagiarise, such was its brilliance, overcame Lulu? Or, she carelessly left it lying around for someone to steal. Why oh why?'

Backwards, she should have written it backwards, she realised too late - snomed. 'See, that's so much easier. Why didn't I think of it before?' She paused to consider how long it would take to write a 10 thousand-word thesis backwards? Deciding that gaining a degree at 96 years old would not be as helpful to her as in her twenties, she had set aside this idea, although conceding the point that she did manage to spell words with more success when she started at the end of them rather than at the beginning. 'Star….. Bugger, I'm doing it again,' she thought, 'I mean Rats….not Star! Gosh, life is hard sometimes.'

Chapter 2

The Delinquent at Work.

(What doesn't kill us makes us stronger - *Friedrich Wilhelm Nietzsche*)

Back to the drunken moment and Amelia's shallow attempt at contrition, true to character, her own demon and home-grown sorcerer, her inner *bad side* enjoying all things evil, had deduced it was quite good fun to mock God and her growing fixation with Him, so began whispering devil's nonsense in her ear.

'That's what happens when you find God,' sneered Lemon, *'you spend every waking moment waiting to be punished for some misdemeanour or another, real or imagined. Then you take to the bottle in your disappointment and disillusionment when you don't get any of the so called good stuff happening; like a miracle here and there just to keep you going. Not much of a life is it really? And don't think anybody would be fooled by your half-baked insincere apology either.'*

Enough to woo the faculties of the most bibulous of drunks, Amelia scrutinised her satanic demon child, henceforth since university days known as Lemon, managing a valorous attempt at talking to herself, bringing her current lack of clear headedness into the equation. 'Oh, there you are Lemon,' Amelia confronted her personal demon with an alcoholic dribble. 'I wondered when you'd put in an appearance, not like you to miss out on any fun involving my torment. You've been remarkably quiet up to now.'

'I thought you were doing a very good hatchet job all by yourself,' chortled her Lemon in reply. *'You clearly don't always need me to dig that hole for you. Anyway, you haven't*

*really found God have you? Where is He? He doesn't even blink
an eye when you call Him Cloth Ears. Any self-respecting God
would soon put a stop to that dissent Amelia. Listen!'*
Amelia listened.
*'Do you get the drift? No thunderbolt. Oops, don't
think He's there. Hah, don't think He exists.'* Lemon taunted
with recalcitrant superiority.

Amelia wanted to stamp on Lemon's head, to
drown her, kill her; 'how can I destroy the evil living inside
me?' she questioned grimly, clapping her hands to her ears
in an effort to drown out the evil voice in her head.

But it was too strong for her, too clever to die; a
High Priestess living in a particularly virulent corner of her
clouded mentality. She hated the badness inside her all the
more when spurred on by the compulsory demands of
alcohol. 'Oh shut up you spiteful swamp,' Amelia spat at
her demon Lemon with heartfelt loathing.

The visible silence was broken by a calm
authoritative voice, hitherto unheard by Amelia.

"Are you telling me to shut up Amelia?" The voice
spoke quietly but firmly.

She jumped nervously, "Oh My God." 'Stop it,
don't blaspheme, straighten up, stop dribbling, keep still,
I'm jigging about like a three year old needing to pee – God
is speaking – What? Yes, God is talking to…Me - sober up
for God's sa …. I mean, for goodness sake.'

Swallowing back the rising bile, she ventured
bravely forth. "Is that really you God? Are you there? Are
you really there? You are there. I thought you were…."
Amelia wasn't sure how to confess this one.

"On God vacation?" God helpfully prompted. "Or,
do not exist?"He gently chided.

"Sorry God."

"What is it you want Amelia?"

"Urm, I can't remember," she stuttered. "I think I'm in shock."

"What is shocking you Amelia?"

"That you've answered me of course."

"Why is that so shocking for you?"

"It's shocking because you've ignored me for years."

"Amelia, am I missing something? Am I truly a Cloth Ears?"

She winced.

God continued. "This is the first I have heard from you in a very long time – blasphemy aside."

God had spoken a truth she found hard to face. 'He is *so deffo* going to give me The Thunderbolt now.' She understood that one as fact. Having systematically disregarded, ignored or anathematised God, she had just verbally abused Him whilst drunk as a galloping Lord. She gulped noisily at the realisation. Having established her lack of common courtesy, she used the back of her hand to assist a hearty sniff and tried bravely to bring her disordered thoughts back to the immediate dilemma of how to answer God. He was ahead of her.

"What can I help you with Amelia?"

"What?"

"Would you like to start again Amelia?"

"Yes please." she sighed with relief that He had noticed her disarray. "I didn't think you existed." Her shoulders hunched inadvertently in expectation of the ever-present threat of the You Know What bolt.

"I thought you were the figment of a deluded population's imagination." She spread her arms widely for added drama. "Or that perhaps you do exist, but had gone away; you'd left us all alone on the planet, in disgust. Or maybe it was just me you'd given up on. Either way, I stopped believing in you. Now you're here asking me what I want and how can you help me? Well I'm sorry God but it's all a bit overwhelming to be honest. I'm not sure I can come up with anything right now. I'll have to get back to you on this... and ... and maybe sober up a little," she added as a quiet afterthought; a glimmer of hope her inebriated plight had remained unnoticed, clinging pessimistically. "I know, I'll jot down a few notes for you; write a list of wants and don't wants. How's that?"

Silence.

"God?"

Silence.

"Are You really there? Or am I pretending? I do occasionally. You know the sort of thing. Especially me, I'm always pretending something or other. In fact, you wouldn't want to know what goes on in my head - it would scare the living daylights out of you. Are you my new fantasy friend? You are, aren't you? It's all in my mind as usual."

"What would convince you Amelia that I am really here listening to you?" God spoke at last.

"A sign," she said emphatically.

"A sign?" God replied, "What sort of sign?"

"You should know. You're far more experienced in all this sort of stuff than me. For goodness sake, how many times in history have people asked you for a sign of Your existence? We can't *see* You, you know," she informed him helpfully in case being invisible was news to God. "So it stands to reason. How about something along the lines of what you've done before? That would be easy for you then and you won't need to go and look it up in a God-Spell book - your own personal, My Book of God Miracles," she giggled wine juice through her teeth at this amusing thought. "I know, how about the tried and tested good old Burning Bush trick - or something of that biblical ilk?"

"You want a Burning Bush in the middle of your kitchen Amelia?" spoken with God-like patience.

"What?" Amelia's fuzzy head scrambled to focus on the words she had just heard. Thus managed, being a mini miracle in itself, she found herself surprised by His response. She stood in her lonely patch of isolation, concentrated thinking provoking her head into persistent shaking, producing a swimming throb to her temples. She clutched at the pulsating sides of her face in realisation that she was getting far too carried away once more with her thoughts.

She wondered if she needed sedating - again. 'Now, is it I'm pissed as a fart and am hearing more voices than usual in my head, or WOW, maybe I am having a conversation with God; that I am lucid, and sober, enough to hear God and this is really happening?' Her head voices lowered in religious respect at this one, forcing her to apologise at once for the uncouth words *pissed* and *fart*. "Sorry God."

'*He's patient on this occasion,*' Lemon concluded, '*bet He'll bolt you if you carry on testing him.*'

"God?" The silence ignored her. "Are you there God, or am I talking to myself?" she voiced her doubts, "Come on, you can tell me, I'm a reasonable human being you know." she slurred.

'*Reasonable? Now that's something you wouldn't be able to recognise sober or not, reasoned thinking isn't exactly part of your remit is it.*' Lemon ridiculed her.

The miracle that was truly happening for Amelia unravelled gracefully, like a beautiful bespangled magic carpet at her feet, offering up all manner of jewel-like promises. Alas, she was being far too human to greet the blessing.

The voice of God returned. "I am here talking to you right now Amelia. Why do you need a show of proof?" God spoke with resolute charm and fortitude.

"Because I don't think it's happening, I think I'm dreaming. Give me something to prove I'm not; something I'll remember. Something I can look at when I'm sober and know you really did talk to me. I need a sign God. Give me a sign please. No one ever takes me seriously, or listens to me. I don't believe you'll help me - I'm the original Doubting Thomas."

Silence.

'Told you – you mindless fool. God doesn't want to know!'

Chapter 3

The Ego and the Salubrious

(Perhaps misguided moral passion is better than confused
indifference - *Iris Murdoch*)

On cue, just as Amelia's humbling disorientation could
degrade her no further, she felt her ego twitch. Her ego
reminded her of a stress ball you roll and squeeze in your
hand to relieve tension; they fascinated her. When she held
one, pressing hard, it seemed to Amelia, for all the world,
like a squidgy fat face poking up through her fingers, and
no amount of pushing could force submission without it
popping up gleefully elsewhere, as unrestrained and
disobedient as ever, hidden out of sight, laying in wait
inside a hot sweaty palm ready to pounce. How like my ego
she thought.

Despairingly, no matter how hard she strove to
stifle and control her ego, it squidged up through her
fingers on many an occasion. *'Hey up,'* it would cry,
bafflingly reminiscent of someone she had once met, but
could recall little beyond his name - Reg. A likeable enough
fellow, Reg had discarded greetings of norm such as
"hello," preferring to announce his presence with a call of
"Hey up." How, where and when she knew Reg, mystified
Amelia, 'How do these things happen; someone stays in
one's subconscious long enough only to imprint a *something*
into memory – sometimes a like or a dislike of some sort.'

In the particular case of forgettable but possibly
pleasant Reg, it was the expression "Hey up" that fixed it
for Amelia; with no particular identity to make a claim, no
face chaperoning the expression, it had inexplicably
attached itself as her ego. Amelia could not remember

when it happened, but for quite some time when battling with her ego, she often sensed a '*Hey up*' coming on.

Perhaps it eased her fractious, troubled mind to be one step removed and disassociated from the part of her that was demanding and selfish, finding a third-person self so much easier to bear - as with all her voices. '*Hey up*,' her ego would shout at the world on any occasion initiating an act of self-interest.

Sniffing disrespect in the air from Amelia's unheard self-pitying plea, her ego blew himself up and squidged a fat smiley-smug face through her slender fingers.

'*Hey up*,' said Reg. '*I'm talking to You God! You need to listen. And it's nothing to do with you, Lemon, so stop smirking like that. You're not invited to be part of this conversation. Get it? Sod off.*'

Status quo: Squidgy ego Reg persists with vociferous intent, despite alcohol poisoning.

Uninhibited by Reg's arousal, Lemon squashed him with a carefree wave, '*Get back in your cell Reg - you insignificant turd.*' Lemon's hackneyed dismissal of ego Reg was brutal; '*It's my turn and I'm having fun.*'

Feasting on the joy of sabotaging a fledgling Faith, Lemon twisted her evil eyes back to Amelia. '*So you're having a conversation with God, demanding a sign He exists? Have you got any idea how bizarre that is and how preposterous you sound? You asked for a sign - which you haven't had By-The-Way! Where is it then? You do know that it was all in your head, as everything is? You've got more chance of striking up a tête-à-tête with the ferret next door than your supposed Higher Being. You were not talking to God. He was not talking to you. Let's face it, you're not right in the head and He does not exist. Is that clear enough for you?*'

Lemon was right. Reg swapped allegiance and agreed. *'Who needs God anyway, we certainly don't?'* he squidged.

Amelia didn't know whom she hated most at that moment: Lemon and Reg for destroying her hopes and dreams of finding true happiness, or God for not existing. Her little flame extinguished with one spit from Lemon's sharp vitriolic poison. After hours of discussion about God with her friend Chris, the little seed he had generously handed to her and so delicately planted - stamped upon. 'What a thin veneer of Faith I have,' she thought with bitter disappointment. 'My hopes have turned to ashes in a heartbeat.'

She rested, breathing in slowly – bringing once more a change of heart that resurrected her curiosity and suppressed desire that God truly did exist, and that for her, true happiness could be found through this Belief. "God?" she called. "God, where are you?" 'He's having a rest from urgent business.' she gathered. 'Probably needs it after a few minutes of me,' she had to concede, 'I've been told it often enough - I am rather gruelling and tiresome.'

Her ego Reg baulked at this, *'Hey up, you just said this could be important to finding happiness, what could be more urgent than that?'*

'Well, I think you'll find a lot more compelling things going on in the world that would be more important than us - like most things really,' Lemon reminded Reg and Amelia pithily.

Self-pity welling inside Reg's inflated bombastic head, released a fleeting recollection that with indolent confidence oozed itself insidiously from the edges of the memory box inside Amelia's chest where her heart toiled vainly to dwell. Elusive and slithery, unable to grasp and hold without sliding away: *You remember happy don't you, it*

29

whispered snidely, *but it always slips through your fingers, you can't do it Amelia, you'll never be happy.*

'Dangerous territory Amelia,' she scolded herself for her outlandish pessimism, 'of course I know what happiness is. Of course I've had happy times. For goodness sake, positive thoughts, come on, positive thoughts. La, la, la la. Where's my positive good side when I need her?'

Amelia's *good side* had evolved from the badness of Lemon and the arrogance of Reg to counteract all her internal caustic clutter. It was all things good; all things sweet; all things nice. In an effort to make it true, and assert herself as a nice person, Amelia would chant the nursery rhythm to spring good into action and block out evil and ego. *"What are little girls made of? What are little girls made of? Sugar and spice and everything nice, that's what little girls are made of."*

Regrettably, as bad as Lemon proved to be, as self-important as Reg could only be, Amelia's *good side* had no option but to counterbalance in the opposite direction. Consisting of nothing but honourable intention, when in full reign Amelia's *good side* was more than a tad irksome, especially to her friends and colleagues.

On many an occasion they would urge, "go for it, tell us what you really think? It's okay for you to say it out loud; we know you're thinking it. You think she's fat/ugly/gross whatever. You think she's a bitch and want to shove her under a bus. We know what you're really thinking - look at the state of that, what on earth is she wearing? Talk about mutton and lamb. What about him? You think he's a waste of space; you think he's hateful; Gorgeous but stupid; Rubbish in bed…. whatever. You think he's an arrogant, pretentious, misogynistic shit. *Whatever* - just go for it Amelia and stop being so Goddamn nice."

Heaven is a Donut

On no account could anyone persuade Amelia's *good side* to "go for it and stop being so Goddamn nice." She was made of honey, how could she not be sweet? She did not have a bad bone in her body. She was a sugar lump; a syrupy sweet, sticky mass of sickly good, living in a golden garden of air-headed illusion in Amelia's well-behaved, well brought-up, polite Pollyanna head.

'Oh Amsy dearest,' said Sugarplum, Amelia's good side, *'I've had an idea; it may explain why God has stopped talking to you at the moment. Perhaps He's busy. There you go. That's it, God is busy and let's face it, there's bound to be a war going on somewhere or other for him to suppress – which He will of course,'* she squeaked enthusiastically.

'Or instigate,' Lemon farted suggestively.

'No, no.' squealed Sugarplum, covering her ears in sweet childlike innocence.

Amelia ignored the taunt from Lemon and concentrated on Sugarplum. 'Yes, yes, you're right Sugarplum, He's busy. I'll try again later.'

She reassembled her rubber legs, flexed her surprised muscles and tightened her grasp, creating a vice-like grip with one hand on her bottle of consolation. With the other, she splayed her fingers in an overstated, dainty gesture to assist the transportation of her glass of dwindling wine. Cautiously balancing herself she vacillated, as if walking a high wire, towards the sanctity of her much loved squashy sofa, long ago christened 'Old Faithful', loyally waiting in her sitting room to give her the comfort and cuddles she desperately required. Old Faithful held its breath - she made it. Just. The long wait began......

"God? God? God?" She had dozed as she waited in solitary confinement; she could wait no longer. "How much of a rest does a God need?" She shouted now at the silence. "Please give me a sign." The exciting hope of

31

inaugurated faith had been sliced apart by an expert executioner. The shattered remains forsaken in an ignominious and humiliating grave, squirming whilst in the throes of slow death, buried alive with Lemon and Reg dancing atop. This now delivered with a hammer-force blow, a double dose - Doubt and Fear. Doubt and fear merged as one to rise like an evil phoenix from the ashes, promising to bring harm to those daring to strike it down. Taking on a new and malignant life force, this virus of abomination slowly rose in her throat like a disease threatening to close off her oxygen supply to the world forever. This, far worse than when she could laugh at those who believe in God; beyond when she could mock those who build a life of faith and obedience on something they could not even see.

She sank to her knees, the desperation she had managed to stave off for so long now, fast creeping, growing like an unstoppable cancer. All her renewed hopes that God, Jesus and the Angels really existed, tussled on the threshold of defeat.

"God please show me a sign that you're here," her words echoed around the room. Falling short of the finish line, they trailed pathetically into oblivion.

The atmosphere was stinging with palpable silence. She searched frantically with her eyes, rooted to the spot where she had fallen. Nothing. No Burning Bush. No unexplained breeze. No white feather nestling reassuringly in an unexpected hiding place. Not even a voice in her head, 'and I usually get plenty of those,' she admitted to herself. She waited. No sound. No movement except the tears expertly mapping her cheeks, effortlessly routing the disenchanted contours of her face.

Her voices returned to fill the void; '*Try calling someone again,*' Sugarplum urged, '*you need help.*'

Heaven is a Donut

Lemon sneered, *'They've all gone; you haven't seen pudding-brain Tristan for months. He says he loves you? Pah, where is he in your hour of need? Uncle Billy won't help you anymore. Where are your other, so-called, best friends Lucinda and Greg? Coten loves you but thinks you're ga-ga. Where's your soul-friend Chris? Ridiculous term, soul-friend; where's he, your soul-friend? He got you into this mess, with all his 'God-talk', where is he now? Not frigging here that's for sure. Face it; you're all alone with me, your bad side and your overinflated ego, turnip-ears Reg. Don't look to Sugarplum to help you out, we're far stronger than that snow-white syllabub.'*

Amelia pleaded with herself, 'Oh for once in your life Amelia, stop listening to the negative self-talk churning relentlessly around your stupid head. Come on, focus, you're sober now; you can control this, stop the morbid ruminations.' She inhaled, slowly bracing herself to try again.

"God, please don't desert me now, just as I had my hopes raised that maybe you really were here. Surely all my conversations with Chris weren't in vain. He's so certain in his own belief. Jesus, Angels, Guides, they're all here for him. He believes. He even knows all their names for goodness sake."

Chris had brought Amelia, kicking and screaming, out of her isolated scepticism. He had encouraged her to reopen a door called Faith. A door she had long ago firmly bolted and locked; then double locked; then put the chain on; then kicked (twice) in disgust before she walked away; as she had thought at the time, forever. Having helped her open the door to glimpse beyond, Chris had then wisely left her to make a choice, her own choice. She had chosen to take a long look through the doorway at the view on the other side.

She remained on the threshold for some time, savouring the sight before her, soaking up its truth. There it was, still surviving after all these years, the view of heaven on earth, Heaven for those who believe in God, who have faith. She resolved to walk slowly and hesitantly back through that door to reacquaint herself with faith in God.

'But I'm lost' she thought to herself, 'I don't recognise this unfamiliar place called "Faith in God." I see a beautiful view, but life isn't beautiful, it's cruel and ugly, this place is all too good to be true.' This place of God and Faith that she had decided to step into and explore unnerved her. Lemon and Reg didn't belong in this place, nor did Sugarplum; they were not necessary. She could feel them all jittering inside her, worrying they would die here. This frightened her - what would she be without them?

She wanted to go back to the safety of her blockade, her fortress of denial. But she was frozen now, rendered powerless by the pain of hope to be normal crumpling away. For a tiniest fragment of time she had held a growing belief that God would help her to live an ordinary life. Her inner child gradually exposed as nothing more than Pandora's box.

As she stood on the edge of this new insanity, her anarchic thoughts raised old taunts, "You'll never be mature enough to hold down a proper relationship, you're too damaged, you're just a flawed needy freak," the voice of past convinced her; the voice belonging to the man to whom she turned after the first heart-breaking spilt from her fiancé, Tristan.

'Too right!' Lemon had hissed in her ear at the time, not wanting to help her, not knowing how to help her. Sugarplum, scared by the possibility of a deadly and chilling axiom – the damage was irreversible.

God had been her last hope; so reluctant for release, she clung to the cremated dust that had once been her dream. At last, she gave in to the urgent need to lie down on the floor and curl into the familiar and comfortable foetal pose she knew so well. Through the grey hours, she lay - a dying ghost haunting the hazy place of night and day. Every ticking moment quietly cutting into her raw flesh, becoming fractured, and diminishing to nothingness.

As Amelia haemorrhaged self-pity, she castigated God for causing her pain.

Panting for life, Reg sent a curse heavenwards, *'Damn you God. Damn You.'*

"No," cried Amelia, foolhardily defying her voices, as she turned to God. "I don't mean it. I take that back, I don't damn you. I will prove You do exist - somehow."

Reg regained control, in desperate need of negative attention. *'You're just pretending to disappear aren't you God? You want to teach me a lesson - some God you are.'*

"Well, I'll show you!" Amelia cried into the harsh unforgiving eyes of twilight.

THREE YEARS EARLIER...

Chapter 4

When Amelia met Chris

(Friendship? Yes please! - *Charles Dickens*)

Amelia pushed open the heavy door to the office, grumbling as she blinked hello at Judy the receptionist. "Oh, so yet again, I'm working with someone I've never even met."

'Good isn't it! Cohesive, seamless, best practice - NOT.' Lemon spat at Amelia's brain cells, pulling her features into churlish malcontent.

She ignored Lemon and paused for breath, heavy with the unwanted regret Sugarplum was heaping upon her for placing the receptionist at the receiving end of her ill-humoured mood.

"Sorry Judy, you don't need to hear my moans and groans do you?" she teased her mouth into a hint of a smile.

Judy acknowledged Amelia's presence by smiling back her greeting whilst adding, "It's you Amelia."

'How observant, so bright this woman - that's why she's made it as far as the signing-in book in reception and no further,' tweaked Lemon evilly in Amelia's head, *'surprised she's made it that far.'*

Sugarplum looked on the positive side. *'It's true Amelia has never met her colleague Chris before, but we've heard he's a good trainer and counsellor and besides, whose fault is it anyway that we are so short-staffed and constantly re-jigging the schedule, certainly not Chris's or poor Judy's - that would be the Judy with the Masters in Business Studies by the way,'* she gently reminded Amelia.

'Yes, shame on you Ameel-ee-ah,' Lemon spoofed, *'for being so obnoxious about our Nudy-Judy.'*

37

Amelia had often felt Judy looked somewhat naked due a curious lack of eyebrows. Without the conviction to ask, she had concluded it was the result of over-plucking. The outcome undoubtedly being, by everyone after a quick double take, that something rather vital was absent from an otherwise pretty face.

Lemon of course, never failed an opportunity to implant name-calling in Amelia's head. *'Rude-Jude doesn't need to know about your problems now does she? And she's much cleverer than you,'* she added, jumping on the bandwagon Sugarplum inadvertently let loose when reminding Amelia of Judy's superior qualifications. *'All that short-staffed overworked stuff is such an old chestnut,'* mocked Lemon, *'get a grip and work harder.'*

'Get a grip? Oh why do I turn into Greg every time I'm feeling stressed at work,' thought Amelia, tiredly referring to her close friend Greg, aka Grip the Quip. 'Go away, Lemon, you're annoying me you irritating twit, don't bother me at work.' Thankfully Lemon appeared to do as she was instructed. 'Hopefully I'll get some peace.' Amelia told herself, knowing instinctively that whilst at work Lemon must behave herself.

'Or is she? No, she's planning something, I can feel it. Oh God, am I going to say something out of order again and get into hot water,' she moaned secretly. 'Last time, Lemon made me say aloud, "I don't give a stuff about Targets." By God did that get me into trouble. I'll swear that's why I didn't get the promotion I was after.' Greg had been overjoyed when she recounted her indiscretion. "Welcome to the ranks of the rebels my pretty pariah," he praised her gleefully.

Judy heard Amelia sigh heavily.

Amelia had often puzzled over the voices in her head, not fully understanding the personalities to whom she was giving houseroom - much to Lemon's perverted sport. She knew one thing; their recent proliferation was worrying.

'How doesn't she get it - the Ditz,' Lemon laughed. *'It's such fun to square sickly fondant Sugarplum up against mighty-maggot Reg, and throw into the pot an occasional acerbic lemon drop of evil, with Amelia as referee, running manically back and forth between the three of us trying vainly to appease and make sense of the situation.'*

Lemon would then just sit back and enjoy the show. The interesting thing for Lemon was that Sugarplum, being all things good, was quite predictable. But as for Reg, fortunately for Lemon, he was another issue entirely, therefore providing hours of merriment. Self-venerate, with an equal measure of wretched abasing inferiority, our Reg was a complete and utter loose cannon.

Amelia was constantly trying to subdue her ego into some kind of reasonable behaviour, more often than not, unsuccessfully. No one could ever predict which way Reg was going to squidge; from which finger he would thrust his fat squidgy face, his trumping hot air of, *'Hey up, what about me,'* lingering unhealthily. Will he be preening with self-importance and feeding his greedy squirrel cheeks, or sullenly slamming doors in Amelia's bruised head, with poor-me venom?

This target of dreamy revelry, skipping with delightedly high spirits down the path of laughter, is what had temporarily captivated Lemon for a quiet second in Amelia's brain cells. Not any semblance of conscience or remorse bringing on a 'be nice to Amelia because she's at work' resolve, allowing her a crumb of peaceful mind with a dash of sanity; oh no.

However, as a result of Lemon engrossed in scripting a trouser dropping comedy-farce on her personal stage, Amelia was able to give free reign to Sugarplum's influence, basking in good, positive thoughts; 'something I'm never allowed to do when Lemon is around, not without her spiteful interference.' she moaned indulgently. 'On the bright side' she convinced herself, 'Lemon appears to have dozed off momentarily.'

Sugarplum's cursory reign sweetened the climate, *'How inspirational that the psychologists, mediators, counsellors and trainers have been taught to undertake this work in a multi-agency capacity.'* she dwelled, causing a sugary smile to dance a tune on Amelia's face.

With Sugarplum's finest efforts leaving her wanting to address the balance following her whingeing, Amelia spoke again to the long suffering and bemused receptionist, Nudy-Judy, "Oh well, I'm sure it will be alright, I've heard good things said about Chris."

"Yes," she replied, "me too. He's already here by the way."

"Thanks sweetie," Amelia proffered Sugarplum's most angelic expression in an effort to unburden Judy from her earlier gripes and prove to herself that corrupting Judy's name in her head did not make her a bad person; only if she did it out loud - and behind Judy's back. "I'll go search him out. By the way, I'm thinking of getting my eyebrows done, back in fashion you know, thick heavy eyebrows – what do you think?" Amelia congratulated herself for her skilful introduction of a friendly hint as she obligingly lifted her hair from her face, to assist full eyebrow scrutiny.

"Amelia, you'll look good whatever you do darling."

Thwarted in her attempt to be helpful in a discreet sort of way, Amelia smiled at her colleague, wondering what on earth it would take for Judy to realise what the rest of the world could clearly see, 'something is missing – on your face there.' She allowed her eyes to linger gently on the empty place just above Judy's eyes, before sweeping out the office in frustration at the blank unawareness of the significance of her gaze that Judy's returning happy aura suggested, and headed towards the suite of offices. She stepped into the sweltering training room, pausing to turn on the air-con, then walked towards the nearest desk to dump her bag, files and folders down heavily, turning her head towards the door as she heard it open.

"Hello," a cheery voice said. "I was told to look for a pretty lady wearing a green dress and when I find her - that would be Amelia and therefore, my co-trainer for the day."

Amelia noted the mop of untidy, slightly greying, hair and the warm smile on the stranger's pleasant face, whilst Reg began to glow with the compliment Amelia had just received.

Reg squidged happily in response, *'How I love being called pretty.'* causing Amelia to unconsciously flick her hair nonchalantly once more off her face.

"You must be Chris."

'Rather unnecessary, who else is he going to be?' Lemon, stretched as she emerged stealthily to the forefront, idly mouthing the silent words, sensing fun could be had.

Amelia managed to return the smile despite Lemon's rude intrusion on her pleasantness.

Chris and Amelia spent the next hour discussing the coming day's training and allocating the workload. Apart from the occasional, *'we're doing more than him,'* from

Lemon; and a, *'no we're not,'* counter attack from Sugarplum; with interjections from Reg, *'make sure it's fair, no one's taking advantage of me,'* her voices, in general, behaved themselves.

"We can go through each of the participant's history and detailed analysis, then discuss their progress and ....." Having glanced up as she spoke, Amelia noticed a certain look on Chris's face, a look she recognised only too well. The look that says, I hope the next thing you utter is, 'shall we have a coffee break?'

"Shall we have a coffee break?" she queried brightly. This abrupt change of subject startled him momentarily. With admirable powers of recovery, a broad smile spread across his face.

"How did you know? I'm parched."

"I'd know that look anywhere," she smiled back, "it practically lives on my face." They hurriedly scuttled out the room towards the upstairs canteen; hopeful they would find biscuits to go with their coffee.

Many hours later, after an exhausting day's training, they were faltering with the unremitting onslaught of the post training paperwork. She always struggled to remember who said what, why and when. She rubbed her forehead feeling thoroughly tired and fed up. "Chris," she wailed, "It's seven thirty in the evening and my brain is turning to cotton wool."

"I think I might remember a bit better in the morning after a good night's sleep," he rescued.

"Alright then," she agreed with the magnanimous air of Reg wanting to be seen doing Chris a favour. "We'll share the work out between the two of us and exchange by email. There aren't any urgent issues so it can wait until tomorrow." They swiftly gathered all their belongings and made a beeline for the door. Everything off; lights out;

Heaven is a Donut

alarm on. "Out we go quickly before we have a moment of conscientious *jobs worth* that makes one of us change our mind." they grinned.

'Just get the hell out of here' sighed Lemon, *'I'm bored now, you're being too nice and it's making me feel slightly nauseous.'*

"Chris, it's been so good to meet you at last and a pleasure to work with you today," Sugarplum, rising bravely above Lemon, prompted Amelia to speak. Amelia knew this to be a genuine statement because of the silence in her head; she found herself pleased with the non-appearance of Lemon or Reg to contradict her.

"I feel exactly the same," he said, "and I'm looking forward to next week."

They said their goodbyes and drove off in their differing directions to make their way home. As she turned her thoughts to Tristan, who had taken to popping round to see her when she had been working late, she allowed herself some pleasure in the knowledge that a comforting ear and either a takeaway meal bought by Tristan or a home-cooked meal by Uncle Billy, would be waiting for her at home. 'Dear Tris,' she thought fondly, they had been getting on so well again lately following his divorce from Bella the previous year.

Some years ago, when Tristan and Bella's wedding was announced, their mutual friends Greg and Lucinda informed her with alacrity that his subsequent marriage was a "rebound thing" because Amelia had jilted a heartbroken Tristan, calling off their engagement. "How the hell is that supposed to make me feel better!" she thundered at the time. But then, it was not. It was designed to urge her to go all out to get him back before nuptials could take place. But no, much to their concern and puzzlement, she stood by and watched it happen.

43

Amelia had known Greg and Lucinda since university days and Tristan years longer; they were all close friends and Amelia became Godmother to Lucinda's daughter, Catherine, who was five years old when the three of them, Amelia, Greg and Lucinda, started their university course. It had been hard for Lucinda, a single mother deciding at the age of twenty-two to become a mature student. Born in England, Lucinda had spent most of her childhood in America. Following the unexpected and tragic death of her parents in a car accident, at the age of sixteen she found herself pregnant - initiating an impromptu marriage. Once their excitement had worn off, opposition from the young husband's prominent family bore down the two teenagers.

Under pressure to have an abortion and fearing how far they would go in their verbal bullying, she fled to England - where Catherine was subsequently born to a scared but defiant seventeen year old Lucinda. Her family scattered, she knew not where, she was alone in the world with her baby until she met Greg, Amelia and Tristan.

Amelia and Greg, both younger with no added responsibilities, were able to concentrate on their studies. Acknowledging that, by comparison, their task was easy; they resolved to do what they could to help Lucinda through the difficult times of raising a child. As did Tristan, who at twenty-one was also studying and working hard: all of them uniting in their love for this fatherless little one and her young mother, becoming their family. Amelia and Catherine especially had a very close relationship; playfully discovering they had much in common and adoring each other's company.

Enjoying the freedom to unwind and release her thoughts of work, Amelia smiled as she steered her car homewards, reliving the early years of friendship with

Heaven is a Donut

Lucinda and her daughter. 'My God,' she mulled, 'was it really ten years ago when we all met; where's the time gone?'

Shortly after meeting, Amelia was dubbed Millie by Catherine who, delighting in Amelia's company was frequently to be heard crying joyously, "Silly Millie." amid one game or another. Amelia therefore felt it only fair to return the gift of name and repaid the compliment by calling her "Kitten" - so sweet and tactile was the child with bundles of energy, personality and affection. The enthralled Catherine insisted everyone used her new name of Kitten, even at school.

Until that is, she grew to the excitingly grown up age of eight, whereupon she avowed fervently to her Mother that Kitten was now far too babyish and she would not answer to the name any longer. Momentarily relieved, secretly thinking that what is cute for a five year old may have slightly different connotations once beyond puberty, Lucinda agreed that using her daughter's given name before hitting double figures should be encouraged.

"Catherine is a beautiful name or Cathy. Which one would you like to be known as?"

"Don't like Catherine or Cathy. I've already decided and Auntie Millie helped me."

Why were alarm bells ringing, Lucinda frowned, "Aunt Millie helped you?"

"Yes, remember when she was helping me with my embroidery – sewing my name on a pillow? Well, Silly Millie got muddled up and said, "pass me the Kitten please cotton." That's very funny isn't it Mummy."

"Yes darling, very funny." Knowing how contrary her eight-year-old could be, Lucinda wasn't sure she liked where this conversation was going.

"Yes, we laughed for ages. So that's my new name."

"What, Ages?" said a bemused Mummy.

"No, Cotton."

"No, no, no. Definitely, finally, NO!"

"Yes, yes, yes Mummy, definitely, finally, yes …. and Millie showed me how to spell it, look."

Lucinda peered down at the piece of paper where her strong-willed daughter had written the word in childish, but legible, handwriting – Coten.

"But darling, that's not how you spell cotton, I think you should stick with Cathy, it's much prettier."

"No. Anyway, it must be how you spell cotton, Millie said so."

After a heated exchange with her truculent daughter, Lucinda capitulated and called her friend, inwardly cursing Amelia's worsening dyslexia as she stabbed at her name on the phone.

"Amelia?" Amelia knew it was serious when Lucinda used her full name.

"Hello to you too. What's up?"

"Get over here now and put this right. She's decided she wants to be called Cotton and it's entirely your fault – you can't even spell it properly. I can't cope with the intractable histrionics she uses to enforce her ideas. You know what she's like once she's made up her mind, only you can talk her out of it."

"Not my fault I can't spell," Amelia guardedly defended her dyslexia, "don't you think she'll just grow out of it - like she has kitten?" Aunt Millie suggested half-heartedly, not managing to hide her growing amusement.

"It's no joke. She's started using it at school apparently and her teachers think her imagination is vivid and lively; they tell me to encourage her creativity, not quell it. Creativity my bum! It's not going to happen."

"What's wrong with the name Cotton? You're usually more easy going about such things."

"Not with her surname."

"Watson? What's wrong with Cotton Watson? Sounds rather pretty, certainly different." Amelia's barely suppressed frivolity was not helping.

"To remind you, Watson is MY surname – I reverted to my maiden-name when I divorced, after she was born. Catherine's surname is Budd. BUDD. Are you still there – you're not laughing are you – you're so dead if you are."

"Oh, it's just, I don't think I knew that." Amelia recovered sufficiently to mumble.

"Well now you do." was the sharp reply.

"You never objected to everyone calling me Silly Millie," (echoes of Catherine's childish truculence).

"You are thirteen years older than Catherine – although sometimes you'd never know it. Come on, come over now and sort it out."

Hours later a defeated Amelia emerged from Catherine's bedroom to find a posse waiting anxiously. "What are you two doing here?" she demanded accusingly to her boyfriend Tristan and friend Greg, both standing implacably by Lucinda's side. "No need for a summit conference you know – it's not life or death, nor is it my fault."

"Well?" Lucinda ignored Amelia's rising paranoia.

"She's sticking with it."

"Have you explained that she'll be a laughing stock with the name Cotton Budd?" Lucinda cringed as she mouthed the name.

"Yes, at great length. She's sticking with it, and don't forget, it's big C, o.t.e.n, not c.o.tt.o.n, get it right Mummy!"

"You're so on thin ice right now Amelia. Did you go into the last resort *Dutch Aunt* routine?"

"Yes – the best face frown and strictest tone of voice I could pull off. Didn't work."

"Oh bollocks."

"Yes, afraid so."

And so it came to pass.

Young Coten Budd grew into a beautiful, creative, talented teenager with adoring adults all around her. Greg - resembling a madcap exciting young Uncle; Tristan - the reliable Father figure; Auntie Millie - the loving older sister and friend. Coten Budd remained Coten Budd. Lucinda, having withstood a few years of disapproving looks that said, "how could you do that to your own child," magnanimously grew to forget the whole thing wasn't her idea and yes, how expressive and striking is her daughter's name.

Amelia was destined to remain a combination: Amelia - when important or in trouble; Ams or Amsy as an intimate endearment - mainly by Tristan but occasionally by the others when feeling particularly tender towards her; Millie on all other occasions, with several variations depending upon Greg's mood of the day.

In turn, Greg and Lucinda became matchmaker to Tristan and Amelia knowing they were made for each other. The infelicity being, one half of the couple made for each other seemed not to recognise such an obvious fact. In truth, Amelia increasingly wrestled with the concept that she was made for anybody as her voices covertly implanted doubts of norm.

Nonetheless, on the day when Amelia met Chris, her relationship with Tristan was in a good place. His ex-wife Bella was happily moving on, Tristan had regular contact with Jules his baby son. Amelia, being prodigiously pleased she had Tristan to herself once more, was the derivation of him currently experiencing a brief idyll of supreme happiness in life, which of course, was not going to last, not if Lemon had anything to do with it.

Tristan loved arriving at her house in time for long heartfelt discussions with Amelia's Uncle Billy on all matters of importance (or trivia), whilst both awaiting her return from work with open arms and open hearts. They would all chat about their day, their worries about their families, friends and world peace, as they enjoyed a late supper. Tristan and Amelia would then retire to bed, snuggling up to each other, blissfully content.

If only they could have peeked into the future and witness Amelia's meltdown of destruction, her destitution, yet to come, three years later. Could they have sidestepped the annihilation of their budding love and trust in each other? Or was it yet again, "story of my life" predestined fate?

As with all, or maybe most, the future was an unknown quantity for Amelia as she made her way home that night.

With stomach satisfyingly teased into pleasant anticipation and armed with complacent knowledge that Tristan and Uncle Billy were waiting for her, she breathed her pleasant daydreams of the past to an end and returned to reflecting upon the day as she drove her car expertly towards her loved ones. She realised there was something exceptional about Chris. She could not quite put her finger on it. 'I think I've just met someone likely to become very special to me; a genuine friend.' She mused thoughtfully over the word platonic, 'yes that was it, a special platonic friendship.'

Lemon had been waiting for an opening to rudely punctuate her reverie; *'Never met a man yet who can do platonic,'* she taunted with a jaundiced grumble, *'What makes him so different?'*

'They're not all the same you know,' Amelia chided her Lemon with Reg's opinionated voice.

'No they're not,' urged Sugarplum, *'shame on you Lemon.'*

'Hah,' Lemon barked in retort, clearly feeling a one-syllable non-word quite sufficient.

'No, I mean it, I think this is the start of a very special friendship; I can feel it in my bones.' Amelia stood her ground.

'Well your bones have gone soft then.' Lemon congratulated herself for her wit.

There it began - a friendship with Chris that was to change her life. But in true curved-ball fashion, as serendipity awarded her Chris, life delivered a blow so cruel she was thrown into a seizure of excruciatingly raw misery that scarred her very existence.

Several messages left on the house phone were awaiting her arrival. Three from Tristan; one to say he wouldn't be able to make it that evening because he'd been called away on business; the second, to confirm she had received the first message, the third was to moan lightly and query why her mobile phone had been switched off all day yet again - and to tell her he missed her, "and by the way, have I told you today, I love you Ams? See you tomorrow my love, sleep well."

Tristan's confirmation of love was destined to remain unacknowledged.

One chilling never-to-be forgotten message was also marking time, '…..please call us on…..,' the solicitous voice spoke quietly. '…local hospital, we received a call this morning to attend….'

Amelia struggled to make sense of the message as she wondered why the house was in darkness. The stranger knew why, the stranger's voice held inescapable and heartrending news. That morning…. after she had left for work, Uncle Billy, her beloved hero of childhood, had been rushed to hospital. That morning…., only that very morning; after she had popped into his room leaving a cup of his favourite breakfast tea on his bedside table, swiftly kissing his forehead as he stirred and sleepily returned her smile: That morning, after she had left for work.

That morning Uncle Billy had passed away; her anchor, her support, her mentor and confidante – gone.

For the last few minutes of oblivion, before one of life's most savage of bombshells sadistically struck her down and dismantled her, Amelia had managed to block out the irritating presence of Lemon by engrossing herself in the music and singing along to Elton John at the top of her voice as she wended her way home. 'Don't let the sun gohooo down …..' Before she knew it, she was pulling into the country lane where she lived with her Uncle Billy, having to quieten it down so as not to frighten the neighbours with her excruciatingly tuneless performance.

'Sorry Elton, just massacred your song,' smiling, she shouted her apology as deafening as her neighbourly concern would allow whilst swinging through the gates and into her accustomed parking spot on the driveway.

THREE YEARS LATER:
(BACK TO THE DEBACLE CAUSING THE CLOTH EARS INCIDENT)

Chapter 5

Faith, How it all started

*(I sometimes think that God, in creating man, somewhat
overestimated his ability - Oscar Wilde).*

As Amelia sucked her breath brusquely in silent horror,
Lemon and Reg's internal screech signified they too were
equally disturbed by the comment - for once in perfect
sync. Sugarplum sallied forth with a squeal of excitement,
prancing in circles, flapping and waving her hands,
resembling a demented monkey on speed. Despite the calm
exterior, World War Three had just been declared inside
Amelia's head. She was worried that Chris, who was
standing nearby looking at her in expectation of a reply to
his observation, would hear the bombs dropping and the
quick succession of gunfire ricocheting around the walls of
her skull.

She felt an urgent need to sit ... immediately…
before her legs gave way underneath her. 'What an absurd
sensation; why are legs, which are so important considering
the fact they hold us up for like…all of our lives,
pathetically stupid at times and completely unreliable.'

She allowed Lemon free reign to Speakers
Corner and the announcement came through painfully
clear, *'Much like the rest of your body,'* boomed Lemon with
noticeable delight, immediately forgetting her earlier
disquiet.

This fuelled Reg into a much-favoured moan. *'Hey
up, why is it, just when you need your limbs the absolute most,
they let you down – literally, in moments of distress. Just like
when you need your dignity, a quiet but refractory little trump*

*rumbles down from your belly and skips out with a disingenuous
apology – whoops, pardon me.'*

Congratulating Reg on his impressive words,
Lemon was secretly convinced he had been furtively
poking around her word-memory-bank again, knowing
"refractory" and "disingenuous" were far too grand for Reg
to use of his own accord. Denied the fun of being able to
prove such heinous larceny, Lemon returned to the current
sport of baiting Amelia; so took up the baton and, after
giving Reg a hearty poke in the ribs, mounted her clichéd
grandstand.

*'Yes Amelia, just when you need to sound intelligent,
hiccups strike and you dribble like a loony. Just when you need to
write important instructions on the flipchart in the presence of all
your colleagues - dyslexia takes over and you write complete
garbage and look like a retard. Just when you need to be calm and
steady, your bladder swells up like a balloon and you start
clamping your muscles together in order to maintain a dry state -
mostly unsuccessfully, much to the amusement of anyone who
spots you hopping about from foot to foot like a spaspot making a
quick exit to the nearest loo.'*

Lemon came to this heart-wrenching conclusion
and much more, as Amelia vainly attempted to steady
herself on an unruly chair designed to swivel easily for the
user's convenience.

*'Oh for God's sake, get a grip of this chair will you - you
Bozo,'* sniped Lemon, *'you're making us all bilious.'*

*'But it's made that way, it's supposed to turn around
like that,'* squeaked Sugarplum trying to find the
equilibrium she craved, *'for a diligent office worker probably,'*
she suggested sweetly.

'Or a porker too fat to balance properly,' sniggered
Lemon dryly.

As Sugarplum withdrew to prepare a counter-argument on all she had just heard, one thing was for sure, this chair was definitely not designed to administer comfort and security to one with wobbly legs induced by high conflict warfare, which then, without convalescence time, quickly descends into the aftermath of great shock. Such as Amelia was now encountering. 'Post traumatic stress disorder,' she moaned, 'that's what this is. Thanks to Chris, I've experienced the trauma of great shock and the resulting stress of it - all in one hit.'

To add to Amelia's growing loss of control, Sugarplum began to gently but urgently issue an 'Objectives to Work On' list with regard to Amelia's relapse into anti political-correctness and lack of perspective taking.

'Firstly, Amelia, it would be prudent to consider how someone with learning difficulties, or physical disabilities, would feel at the words you've used to describe a situation we all may face at some time or another, when nervous or stressed, or tired. It can happen to anyone. How would they feel? How would their family feel? And don't think your reference to weight-challenged people has gone unnoticed either.'

'Ok, Ok. Even though it was clearly Lemon's fault, I'm sorry. They'd feel like shit and want to slap me; I'd slap them back and then get fired. I get it and I'm sorry. But I only said it in my head, in fact you're the only one upset, Lemon and Reg are laughing. At least it cheered them up and took their mind off things – which is good. Not to mention, no one outside *me* heard. That makes it a lapse not a relapse. I only *thought* it when under duress, I didn't *say* it.'

'That's not the point dear,' Sugarplum said unwaveringly, nodding wisely. *'You thought it. The thinking*

was there and therefore it demonstrates how you view people and quite frankly Amelia, it's not pleasant to witness.'

This upbraiding, wrapped in oozing sickly honeyed niceness was enough to send Amelia into frenzy. 'No one did witness it, ask Chris, he was standing right next to me and heard nothing. Who do you think you are?' she ranted at Sugarplum, 'The Thought Police? It's what I say and do that counts; not what I think.'

Sugarplum sighed kindly as she patiently explained in simple terms to Amelia; *'The premise of your work is helping people to challenge their thinking.'*

'Yes yes,' Amelia was on the verge of screaming now, 'I know what I do for a living,' she accentuated the word *living.* 'I help them challenge their *own* thinking because they want to change – but you can't go stomping around inside someone's head armed with a machine gun, telling them what to think, punishing them by lining their thoughts up against their ear drum and mowing them down gangster style if they get it wrong. They have to come to these conclusions by themselves, for themselves; they make the effort to think things through and want to change.'

Following a crisp silence, Sugarplum had no option but to state the obvious, much to Lemon and Reg's delight, as they stood engulfed with laughter at this exchange.

'But I am inside your head dearest Amelia, I live here remember, and I am challenging your thinking,' Sugarplum smiled sweetly, *'in other words Amelia dear, you are challenging your own thinking.'*

'Therefore, methinks,' stated Lemon suppressing the giggles in order to be heard, and using her microphone voice, *'this is your conscience speaking,'* she added, *'and this, is your maladjusted delinquent speaking; you feel guilty, you said*

the word "retard"among others! Haha, that's hilarious – saddo.'
Lemon relished the contrast with much enthusiasm.

'Only because it gate-crashed my head, I don't usually think about people in that way.'

Noticing how ineffectual her insistence that she's intrinsically good towards all, she swiftly reverted to Lemon-style attack.

'Oh go boil your noggin – both of you. Make a syrup, a lemon syrup - you treacle tart. And I didn't say it, I thought it,' she reiterated, childishly maintaining her innocence. At this, she suddenly remembered Lemon and Reg's discomfort of only moments ago, when they had begun shouting and railing against Chris's words. This powerful ammunition fiendishly redressed the balance. 'Anyway, you've all got something much more important to think about now, you're heading for disaster, you're accelerating towards extinction if Chris's got anything to do with it – with *my* help,' her words impaled the air.

'*Oh bloody Hell,*' groaned Lemon and Reg, '*yes, yes, yes – we are in trouble, how could we have been so distracted. What was it Chris had just said, oh yes that was it - oh no, what could be worse than the turn this particular God-Talk had just taken?*' Feeling in 'back up against the wall' fashion and spinning out of control, Lemon, more than a little bemused by this previously unheard of situation in her lifetime, had no option but to return to the repellent suggestion that Amelia was cogitating upon life without her.

'*What on earth is he going on about? You, believing in God? What God? It's nonsense. Get thee behind me Satan and all that,*' Lemon shouted hotly into Amelia's unlucky ear, having returned swiftly to the issue she was facing. Lemon's hackles were up, she knew instinctively this was serious and had to be addressed. '*We've got to nip this in the bud; we can't have thoughts of God bandied about, not unless it's to laugh at the idiots who believe all that nonsense.'*

She nudged Reg who had begun squidging in fear at what would become of them if Amelia were to turn to the good side. *'Good people aren't supposed to have inflated, fat egos are they,'* he blubbed, *'or for that matter, nasty evil demons like you Lemon.'*

'Heavens above,' responded Lemon, *'can you imagine Sugarplum rampaging around the place on a 24/7 basis? We've got to stop this nincompoop Chris from talking and dimwit Amelia from listening. We must do something.'* Lemon's enmity rose and Reg began to tremble violently, emitting foul gases into Amelia's brain chamber. The repulsion at such a calamity does not bear thinking about. Should this fate befall them – they were done for. *'Done for, God damn it!'*

'This is what we do. We Reg, listen then,' Lemon said shaking him; *'we are going to war. This is our war to end all wars and we fight for our lives.'* Lemon accelerated her powers of persuasion with an antagonistic argument on survival. *'For God sake Reg, stop being such a constipated cowpat. What sort of ego are you anyway, just sitting there all aquiver, where's your amour-propre?'*

'I am wearing proper armour,' Reg retorted, licking himself with enraptured gratification as he rubbed up and down Lemon's leg.

'Urgh, don't touch me, and stop that disgusting habit. I'm talking about 'self-respect' not you getting above yourself, you turgid, self-absorbed polyp. You've got to assist me, not swagger around smelling like blown up entrails. No, I'm in charge and you're second-in-command. From now on, call me Chief. Chief Lemon.'

'Of course I'm self-absorbed; I'm Amelia's ego. What else am I going to be you dense Doppelgänger and what a stupid name - Chief Lemon, who's going to take you seriously with a

name like that?' discharged Reg with conceited superiority at the glorious prospect of having stolen the magnificent sounding word Doppelgänger from Lemon's cache - he could now use it against her, even though he had no idea of its meaning.

'Well I'll be Colonel-in-Chief then, no let's keep it simple and classy, Commander Lemon. There you go, Commander Lemon. Commander Lemon to the rescue. You can be Private Reg.'

'It's not my real name you know.'

'What? Private?'

'No, Reg - you fool. Reg is what she calls me,' said Reg waving at the inside of Amelia's head.

'So what is it then? Haemorrhoid? That'll work nicely, Private Haemorrhoid. Come along Private Haemorrhoid, stop hanging about being such a bleeding nuisance.' Lemon was beside herself with mirth, having once more forgotten her urgent "fight for survival" speech. *'You'll have to be cauterized if you don't shape up, mind you, that would give you a promotion wouldn't it. You could become a Lance Corporal then, or should I say - Lanced.'* Lemon was in danger of swallowing her own epiglottis such was the ensuing choking on her bitter acid as she convulsed in a paroxysm of nefarious laughter.

'Oh aren't we funny. No actually,' Reg spasmed haughtily, *'my name if you please, is not Haemorrhoid, ha-ha, no actually, it's Eye. My name is Eye,'* repeated Reg grandly.

'What? I've never heard of anything so stupid. Of course your name isn't Eye.'

'Yes it is. I heard Amelia talking about it. She said ego is of Self and therefore Eye.'

'That's 'I' you blubbering boaster. 'I' not Eye as in E.Y.E. Ego is of Self and therefore, I.'

'*Oh.*' Reg deflated with an embarrassing whinny; paranoia setting in, as so often the case with Amelia's ego. '*Why are you persecuting me again,*' he shook. He hastily checked his reflection to restore status quo and fall back in love with his image. '*Ah yes,*' he breathed in deeply, '*Reg is back. I'm still gorgeous, still wonderful. 'Eye' is back. Hey up.*'

'*You spermatic buffoon. Shape up and take a look at yourself.*'

'*Just have. I'm perfect. I love myself, I love myself.*'

'*Oh*' groaned Lemon. '*What have I done to deserve living with an egotistical douche bag like you? Well okay then Mr Perfect Plonker, are you concentrating? Private Pipsqueak, are you ready to go to war? Come along, stay close, no not that close, you smell; here, that's it.*' Lemon squared up stiffly in line, showing Reg his standing place, '*Ready, steady, aim ......let battle commence.*'

They lasted less than a second before being shot down. In one swoop, Amelia managed to have them under control, figuring divide and conquer would doubtless work. 'SIT.' Reg obeyed, swishing his wagging tail, enjoying the spotlight.

'*You traitor, you turncoat, I'll have you court marshalled for this,*' whispered Lemon hoarsely.

'I can hear you Lemon, just calm down will you and zip it.' Amelia breathed silently to her two needy selves, endeavouring to maintain a dignified appearance whilst hoping against hope that Chris would not notice her lips mouthing the words. She attempted to comfort her other selves back to some kind of respectable decorum rather than the farcical black comedy being played out behind her eyes. 'They need help; after all, they're just doing their job, which is to be the other side or sides, of me,' Amelia explained to Sugarplum, whose sweet levels, at Chris's words, had risen to stomach churning niceness, causing Reg to start gagging.

'We can all pull together. There is strength in numbers don't you know.' She finished wistfully, not quite maintaining the confident air she was trying to achieve.

But it was good enough for Sugarplum. With uncontained rapture, she oozed, *'You mean like a ..like a .. oh my goodness, like a Higher Self?'* She was dizzy with exhilaration. Firstly, Chris had spoken about Amelia and God like they were the hottest new couple on the block, sending thrills of pleasure running up and down her spine; and now Amelia was there reassuring her that Lemon and Reg were able to behave themselves, despite all evidence to the contrary. To co-exist without the constant bickering and without relentlessly waving swords at life's windmills in true Don Quixote-esque fashion.

She quivered with gleeful anticipation as she pictured her prevailing battleground becoming a haven of peace and joy, a place of integrity and calm as befitting a Higher Self. *'Now where shall I start? Ah yes - Lemon. Lemon dear,'* she began, *'you really will have to stop criticising everyone Amelia meets, after all, most people are truly virtuous and do not deserve the names you give Amelia to call them; not at all. Yes I know it's you planting all things horrible in her psyche. It will have to stop. Where's my list?'*

Lemon's answer to Sugarplum was flamboyant retching joining in unison with Reg's sick-burps in a cacophony of agonising wretchedness.

Amelia, dangling on tenterhooks whilst struggling with her resident lunatics, slid, freefalling into a comic strip of tragedy. 'Chris will think I'm talking to myself – in front of him.' Which, of course, she was and therefore in danger of resembling an extremely disturbed individual at the very least. It was all his fault; Amelia and her voices blamed him fully; he'd ruffled Lemon and Reg's feathers to anarchic proportions and stimulated Sugarplum into a toffee-apple on heat. Amelia was in a state of horrified melt down that was not going to dissipate quickly.

Ignoring Chris's increasing scrutiny, Amelia retraced her thoughts, sensing a useful grenade of argument. She found a careful homily inside the regions of her opaque cortex. 'Lemon, let me address your contradiction when you said, Get thee behind me Satan.'

I know what I said,' Lemon seethed sharply.

'If you don't believe in God, then you can't believe in Satan either, it stands to reason,' Amelia lectured. 'They're cut from the same cloth; two sides of the same coin; can't have one without the other.' A jarring, cadenced performance of the old Sinatra classic Love & Marriage arose despite the highly inappropriate timing, leaving her abstractedly inquisitive if what was going on inside her head was also visible from the outside.

'What a screwball I must look,' she deliberated; her mind fascinated with the thought of swaying from side to side on a defective chair; head fluctuating as if too heavy for her neck, in peril of unscrewing itself from its flimsy attachment, to tumble poetically to the floor in a refined, but clearly possessed, kind of way. Sinatra's voice would be echoing around a barn-dancing, vacuous skull, leaking into expectant silence, inhabiting the room.

'Wouldn't it be funny if, as it fell off and bounced onto the floor (she felt there was reasonable argument to suggest that her head would surely bounce as there never appeared to be a brain of any substance to give it weight), the strain of Love & Marriage were to resonate around the walls, whereupon languidly morph into … *and did it, My Way…,'* Amelia indulged in the imagery.

The sensation of being alone in her head with a psychopath for hours, spurred her to wearily continue, 'Lemon, you can't go quoting the Bible - Hello - The BIBLE, if you don't believe in God. Secondly, All Chris said was, he thinks I'm a very spiritual person. Not exactly the reason to give me the headache you're all causing in my cranium's frontal lobe is it? I've got a brass band practicing the Funeral March in there now. My lobes are done for - they've been scrubbed and polished, ready for inspection and probably in a dish right now on their way to be dissected; which will, I'm totally aware, take all of two seconds. My head is all disjointed and unconnected and you and Reg are talking mass genocide – get a grip.'

Friend Greg would be so pleased to note her patronage of his favourite expression.

Lemon shrank back in horror as if being assaulted by a grotesque harridan. 'Which she is of course,' Reg thought with a small amount of vain, but self-destroying, satisfaction.

'What masochistic pleasure do I find by torturing myself this way? Maybe I can change. Chris can see something in me.' Amelia parried wistfully.

'Don't keep saying that,' Amelia's voices whispered.

'What? Keep saying what? That I'm a very spiritual person?' Amelia enjoyed repeating the word spiritual, rolling it around her tongue like forbidden ambrosial chocolate melting in her mouth. Spi..riT....Yuu......Aaul. Oh what pleasure it gave her to curl the syllables slowly and poetically into the nether realms of her brain with which to leave Lemon and Reg suffocating in the aroma of higher cognitive insight.

Amelia suddenly remembered Chris had no idea of the controversy raging in the secrecy of her mind, goading her multifarious nature to widen even further, and that he was indeed the very instigator of her disparity, albeit inadvertently.

Despite the fact that all of this had taken a mere second or two to unfold in her head, Chris had been waiting for a response a little longer than good manners dictate. His smile had frozen and become a little fixed space where his mouth had once been. She was immediately filled with concern that she had so worried him. 'Oh my God, Chris, poor Chris.' She gathered herself together and reunited her fragmented self.

"Chris," she smiled reassuringly back at him to display her normalness. "Do you really think so? Do you really think I'm a spiritual person? I'm not sure what you see in me. I thought all that had long since dried up and shrivelled to nothing." Amelia's initially false smile had slowly adopted a genuinely wistful air.

Chris's smile re-entered instantly, his inner calm restored. "It's definitely in you Amelia. It shines out of you. Maybe it's just different to what you expect or what you're used to. Being spiritual doesn't have to mean you subscribe to a religion or go to Church every Sunday."

"Shines out of me?" An out-of-tune rendition of a Frank Sinatra song was what had really been shining out of me - along with a good old-fashioned dose of split personality, Amelia corrected her thoughts.

She faltered, perhaps Chris was right? She was confused and a little scared by this. If it did not mean being self-righteous and piously proving to the world what a good person you are by penitent prayer and going to Church, then what did it mean? What does spirituality look like? The only insight gradually dawning on her was that his comment and observation had actually (not to mention unexpectedly) begun to please her.

As they parted to go their separate ways home after work that day, she recollected the conversation she'd had with Chris. Truth be told, the warmth of dawning understanding remained with her, despite the rocky road to finding answers. What does my spirituality look like? She worried at the time, unaware that this little seed of love he gave her was destined to carry her through many an anxious moment.

For those early days of contemplation, Amelia lived with fear and pessimism. This kernel of truth lying so deeply inside, she had ignored and neglected for so long. It frightened her. She knew it had once been such a powerful force; she had lived her whole childhood by it. Surely, she argued with herself, she could not risk that happening again. That was too awful to contemplate.

There it lay; a belief and spirituality, she thought dead and buried for many years. 'I should have laughed in his face surely? Chided him for his nonsense,' she remembered thinking at the time. But her reaction was diametrically opposite: She took this manifestation home with her: over the weeks that followed, she looked at it; studied it; by so doing, learned to love it. Gradually a glimmer of light was allowed to rest after a long darkness, learning to grow, unrecognisable for some time, but undeniably there. The first embryonic waterfall of love and light provided by Chris's annotation, installed him forever in her heart as her soul-friend from that moment on. He helped her find life. He helped her find love and strength in Faith - eventually.

Faith she came to identify was about belief in self. Therein lay her biggest dilemma….. 'Having now found it, what do I do with it? I don't have to go to Church. OK, got that bit. I don't have to study other religions if I don't want to, or try them out (certainly not feeling that one). So how will this potentially wonderful gift grow and benefit me if I don't do anything with it?'

This quandary gave her many a sleepless night with Lemon constantly dripping her poisonous suspicions in her ear and Reg niggling with worry about his survival. Despite the growing excitement she began to feel, her other selves were not prepared to relinquish the state of power too readily. As for Sugarplum, she was impossible to live with; such was her sanguine disposition that Amelia was ready to dissolve her with butter and turn her into a pudding.

Lemon and Reg joined forces against Amelia, doing their best to alienate Sugarplum.

Lemon spoke for them both, *'Don't take any notice of that rubbish; you've been there before, done that, and been hurt by it. People telling you what to do; how to do it; how to live your life; you're better off without it. You turned your back on all this religious nonsense when you were fifteen years old and have never regretted it. What are you doing, you stupid cow, starting all this up again? Look at the state the world is in today. Sort yourself out and shape up. If there was such a thing as God, He's not doing a very good job of it is He? Frankly, if I was God, I'd be embarrassed at the mess I'd made of it. Face it, there is no God! Doesn't exist. Never has, never will.'*

Amelia was taking her first steps on the road to breaking point. 'Lemon's got it all wrong. God does exist and He knows what He's doing – but how can I prove it?' The resulting conflict became immeasurable.

Chapter 6

Sunshine

(Nobody can hurt me without my permission – *Mahatma Gandhi*)

'*HOOOOAaa... Hey Up.*' Reg's sonorous call echoed through the corridors of Amelia's cortex sending Lemon and Sugarplum scuttling to find the cause of such discontent.

'*Now look what's happened.*' Reg quivered as he pointed to the wretched specimen laying in obscurity, shivering in agony.

'*All this God–talk going on for so long has driven Sunshine into a frenzy.*' He puffed.

'*The poor little thing,*' said Sugarplum.

They were all very fond of this little one. The little one in sufferance before them was Amelia's 6th sense. This creature was an HSP, a highly sensitive person. It would seem she had come into being without an outer layer of skin for protection. Every noise, jar and bump stung with pain. Every nuance of negativity caused her to shrink in discomfort.

Reg remembered the first time he was aware of her and all his longing to be needed and helpful, a Knight in shining armour, rose to the forefront of his large squidgy body; and how, much like today, the sight of her moved him to pity. Reg had found her, that first time, a child still, trembling plaintively, trying to ease herself into the walls for comfort; not wanting to live and yet knowing she cannot *not* live.

She was the one who had activated the process of divided temperament. That was her misery, her mantle. She took sole responsibility for Amelia's sphere. She was too sensitive to live but had to live. If she did not, she believed Amelia would die. Without doubt, 6th sense had to subsist.

From the onset of his awareness of '6th sense', Reg had risen to the battle cry. *'Hey up,'* he wheezed, *'what's this? Is someone being nasty to you? How dare they! Come on little one, smile; let's see some sunshine.'*

As Reg had bent down to clumsily chuck and tease the lugubrious creature under her chin, he squidged with pride realising he had just appointed upon her a beautiful name, Sunshine.

6th sense did not speak, but relaxed at the loving touch and smiled – and the sun did come out, lighting all the inner depths of Amelia. To this day, each time Sunshine's warmth floods through her, Amelia may smile suddenly, a secretive happy smile, charmingly unaware of why it is on her face. "What a lovely day," she will inexplicably exclaim to no one in particular, causing heads to turn warily.

'There we go, I'll look after you,' Reg had put a fat sticky arm around Sunshine as he pledged to always be there for her. He had lectured her on how to answer back when the bullies at school started picking on Amelia. *'You're far better than them,'* he said loftily, *'let them know you think they're idiots and way beneath you. Watch, turn your nose up and look down on them, like this – see?'*

Sunshine had shaken her head sadly, although it had helped cheer her with a smattering of courage. The result of which had emboldened the young Amelia to bravely retort, "go away you smelly pig," or, "stop teasing me or I'll tell."

Reg could not control anyone outside of Amelia but he could help Sunshine through the pain they made her feel. He had enlisted the help of Sugarplum, who immediately fell in love with Sunshine - as she does with everyone. Although concerned that Lemon would touch her with her nasty ways, causing Sunshine to lose her innocence, Reg had felt it was worth the risk asking Lemon to help toughen her up, 'stick up for herself.' He need not have worried, Lemon did not want to hurt little Sunshine - possibly the only creature in the world she didn't want to hurt, Reg discovered.

Lemon knew instinctively that Sunshine understood her bitterness: would never interfere with her.

'*Unlike saintly Pavlova-head Sugarplum always nagging,*' Lemon's habit of growling insults at the thought of sucrose Sugarplum, was reserved for when out of earshot of Sunshine, so as not to cause upset. No, it was Sunshine's pain that fuelled Lemon; that motivated her to all manner of malicious vengeful behaviour throughout Amelia's life. It was Lemon's job to be all things bad, to administer revenge, to seek retribution, to start arguments, to raise an insolent finger at religion and civilization in general, revelling in shameful activities.

This was Lemon's function. Her influence was not too obvious when Amelia was still a child, but as she grew, her unsettled fractious behaviour changed her. Lemon was never able to toughen Sunshine enough to help Amelia shrug away the effect of negative, jealous people. However, she managed quite spectacularly to install a mask. A mask so effective, not many could penetrate. This indurate mask instilled the proficiency of negative action. To quash an individual with one cruel sarcastic comment; to laugh and mock in the way she too had been mocked; to respond aggressively like a trapped animal biting the hand that stretches out to befriend.

This was why some people chose to shun Amelia, thinking her a cold, spiteful ice-maiden.

Sunshine would never have power over her lifelong responses to hurtful people. She was not equipped to deal with, as Lemon described it, *'the outside world.'* Amelia had been ridiculed for not being like them: her hesitancy to take the lead in matters in case she was ridiculed or misunderstood – was taken as laziness. Her aloofness, for fear she was not wanted - taken as supercilious hauteur. Her sensitivity, labelled forever as weakness by others too different.

Amelia's 6th sense, Sunshine was acutely aware of when people were laughing at her, even when not obvious to others – but then that marks the success of subversive coercion, she knew.

Sunshine knew all these things. She knew she processed things differently: forever aware of the subtleties of human make-up; forever knowing when others were being cruel or flippant and feeling so bruised by it; forever knowing when others were hurting and she could only respond with such empathy their grief would be heaped upon her, weighing her down with unbearable burdens - forever. It rendered her unable to protect Amelia, unable to respond with a light-hearted abandonment to the cruel side of human life.

Resulting from her failure, the gradual emergence of Lemon, Reg and Sugarplum took place throughout Amelia's childhood. They chained each other down into Amelia's innermost being to stand before all things negative, all things painful and hurtful, swearing to protect Sunshine. How else would Amelia endure? How else would Amelia have pulled through the terrible events of *that* winter, when she was only fifteen years old? That is why Sunshine loved them so fervidly. As for them, they returned her love, aware only of a primitive, protective devotion causing them to vow to annihilate, or in true Sugarplum fashion rise above, all whom dare hurt her - hurt Amelia.

As sweet and good as Sunshine, Sugarplum was a different quantity. Sugarplum chose goodness, responded to goodness, because she could recognise the opposite; chose love, because she knew the outcome of fear. She understood badness and always strove to bring positive love and light to a situation rather than witness negative forces at work. Some battles she won, some she lost. It bothered her to lose and witness Amelia in frequent trouble, but she was never cowed, never intimidated. She would always bounce back.

This was her function: to provide Amelia with the goodness of humanity. She knew she was stronger than Lemon and Reg put together, but she did not know - would not know, how to stop being Sugarplum – sweet and good at all times; this was coincidently her strength and Amelia's Achilles Heel.

This was why some people would describe Amelia as a prissy, two-faced goody-goody.

Reg had no idea of course that his existence, just like the others, was due to Sunshine. They were all born from the need to protect her. Reg could not bear it when Amelia was belittled. His, *'How dare he! How dare she! How dare they!'* being so entrenched in her subconscious, she found herself repeating his favoured phrase with all the self-righteous air of one damned without due cause; one whose ego would not allow perpetrators of image-bashing to continue without self-important egotistical confrontation.

This was why some people thought of Amelia as a conceited egocentric bighead.

Oh how her internal personas got it so wrong at times. When they turned on Amelia to enforce their own way: when they shuffled and pushed, vying with each other for position, delivering Amelia such bewilderment. They misdirected her constantly to shoddy decisions and behaviour that induced more heartache and trouble.

And so, on this particular day, as resident pincushion living deep inside Amelia's psyche, permanently on alert for the little darting arrows of pain being thrown Amelia's way, (by others and of course, by Amelia herself), Sunshine was suffering greatly from this new onslaught. How can Amelia deal with this latest predicament? Will she survive the torment of believing she can resurrect her faith and belief in God, as Chris had suggested, or will she succumb to the impossibly high demands she places upon herself in her search for human perfection?

As Reg and the others had sensed, Sunshine's latest cause of concern was not without due reason.

Amelia's belief in God and manmade religion all those years ago had brought her to her knees, trying to meet the demands of adults. As a child, instilled, by the adults surrounding her, that she knew better than other children of her own age owing to her Bible teachings, the true meaning of the Bible, God's word, therefore, unlike them, she was "in the Truth." One day, she discovered that many religions had similar beliefs. They were, The Way; The Truth; The One and The Only. Their interpretation of God's Word – was the correct version.

That was the day her internal house started to crumble. She had tried so hard to be good. The day she gave up trying, brought the greatest relief; so she also gave up on God. Life became so much easier, and as Lemon infused, far more interesting. But it had left such an empty space inside of her; hollowed out like a pumpkin ready for Halloween. Mere remnants of guilt were left decaying, clinging to the edges of her soul that she could not reach with her internal vacuum cleaner.

Amelia's quandary deepened; part of her strongly warming to Chris's confidence that she could find peace and love by belief in God with its promise to fill her empty corners. The space, the cavern in her soul, remained alone and forlorn, neglected and forgotten. A very large space in Amelia's heart, had been set aside for her faith to occupy, but had gathered nothing but dust and despair for many a year.

Aware of her inner wasteland, her strong voices wore her down into inextricable confrontation, "What's so good about this," she challenged God. "What's so good about having Faith and Belief in You? Show me, what's in it for me? Prove to me you're there," she demanded of Him.

I'll pray, she thought.

'If you can remember how,' her Lemon scoffed.

'This is important,' Amelia reminded her primly.

'You'll live to regret it,' Lemon warned gravely.

'Gosh, was Lemon being singularly emotive? Her tone of voice suggested she just may.'

Regardless of Lemon and Reg, Amelia prayed: She prayed every night; She prayed every day; She tried praying to God; to Jesus; to the Angels; She prayed to her Guides – not that she knew if she had any, but Chris told her that his Guides, "guide him regularly," which made her feel outright jealousy rather than any higher form of wondrous goodness. However, a strong-willed if slightly battle-weary Amelia persisted; she prayed for specific things such as Faith, Belief, Strength. Then she tried a general sort of praying - for direction, for the *right* thing. She prayed to the birds, because they flew in the sky and therefore might be a little closer to Him. Nothing. Nothing.

Weeks later, lost in time and space and on the brink of sleep-crazed deprivation, she called Chris, oblivious to the fact it was three am.

"Amelia, whatever is wrong?" A concerned, if rather sleepy Chris, murmured groggily into the phone.

"Chris, help me, I can't find Him!"

"What? Who? Sorry Amelia, are you saying someone has gone missing?"

"Yes."

"Who? What's going on Millie, we'll come over, have you called the police yet?"

"Yes. No."

"Which is it? Ams, what's going on, you sound in a bad way."

"I am. I can't find Him…. God. I can't find God!"

Her lacerated statement was met with a silence she wasn't used to receiving from Chris, but one she recognised only too well when coming from other quarters. The silence that said, 'You've woken me up at three in-the-morning for this crap?? Sort your bloody head out woman!'

She could hear Chris's wife, Gail, in the background and Chris apologising for waking her. She thought she heard a soft groan from Gail when she heard him say, "It's Amelia," - but couldn't be sure.

"I'm sorry Chris. I've woken you up – both of you probably. Please apologise to Gail for me. I'm all right, just couldn't sleep, then I did…sleep that is… but then I had a nightmare. Now I'm awake again, well I guess you know that. Just feeling a bit, you know, slimsy. I'll be fine now, sorry. Sorry Chris, sorry Gail, go back to sleep. Good night, night-night, night-night. Don't let the bedbugs bite. Night-

night. Sleep right, I mean tight, sleep tight, whatever that means." Helmless, her voice trailed into cryptic-cliché.

Gail whispered hoarsely, "She's feeling what?"

Chris twisted his head away from the phone to murmur, "Slimsy, her word for frail," he then returned to Amelia, "Are you sure you don't need us to come over? We will you know, no problem."

"Sounds drunk to me," muttered Gail, shaking her head as she sought her favourite sleeping position in a defiant response to her husband's offer for them both to gallop over in the middle of the night and rescue a maiden in distress. "Yes, that too probably," Chris smiled at his wife as he mouthed an apology and tenderly stroked her hair as she settled back into the blissful comfort of her downy pillows.

Amelia spoke again, "I love you both but no, it's no big deal. I'm a bit confused just now and it's affecting my sleep patterns. I'm so sorry I've interrupted yours."

"Ok honey. Listen, I can come over in the morning. We need to talk. You can't go on like this. It'll be fine, honestly it will. Carry on praying, reach out to Him and He'll hear you. Then try some of the meditation and relaxation techniques I showed you. Whatever you do, don't despair, everything will be all right, it always is, you know, you just have to give it time. I'll see you in the morning. OK? OK?" He sought reassurance in the absence of an immediate reply.

"Yes. Thanks Chris, thank you for caring. See you in the morning. Sorry again. Sorry Gail. Good night. Erm... sleep well."

Amelia snapped her mobile phone shut and hurled it across the bedroom, in a wave of self-indulgent antipathy, shouting, "It's all your fault God, if You'd answered me straight away, I wouldn't have disturbed them and made a fool of myself – again."

She angrily punched her pillows, and, attempting a yoga-like posture, sat up, placing her palms together, she pointed her fingers heavenwards. Taking some moments to successfully adjust her features from devilish-poltergeist, to one emitting angelic-virtue, she settled down to pray once more. She stared out of the window and told the black sky her problems – it took some time.

After a good deal of praying into nothingness, her glimpse into paradise had begun its slow shift, the terrain had changed, and her view returned to the known aspect, the familiar no-man's-land. Dead, barren ground where no spirit could lift high a head and thank God, in sheer joy, for the pleasure of existing. This was the land of the no–hopers, the land of the living-dead.

Hours later, shunning Chris as he spent some considerable time on her door-step ringing her doorbell, and then trying to contact her on the phone thereafter, a pummelled-into-submission Amelia began, once more, to spend her days simmering in spiteful and bitter disappointment.

One late afternoon, after being stood up on a lunch date (*'how dare he,'* smouldered Reg) and returning home very disgruntled with the world, she peered hard into the mirror, 'Don't look at me with that smug look on your face you two,' she raged at Lemon and Reg, as she opened a bottle of wine with the great gusto of a phenomenally angry individual.

'Like that'll help you find God – or your blind-date,' they rebuffed Amelia, nodding at the bottle.

'Well at least it's an instant comfort,' Amelia said, dribbling the rather good red she was slurping back far too quickly. 'Not left waiting, hanging around for someone or something I can't even see deign to answer me.' How like Lemon, alcohol always makes me sound, she deliberated as she poured another glass.

'You know what Lemon?'

'*What?*'

'God's deaf.'

Having decided this new theory was more than a mere possibility, she proclaimed again, 'God is deaf,' with increasing conviction.

Lemon growled at her, '*what are you mumbling about now, you drunken spigot-legs? Didn't take you long. You've never been able to take your drink – lightweight spaz.*' Lemon and Reg waltzed a victory dance upon the floor of Amelia's head. '*Well, despite a promising start, she didn't put up much of a fight did she,*' they cackled, '*we won the war, we won the war, will we be evicted? No we won't. Will we be evicted? No we won't,*' they chanted victoriously. '*There's no way Amelia's going to get all God-like now, she didn't even clear the first hurdle. Where is He?*' they sung, '*where is He? Is God listening? No he isn't. Hah!*'

'Stands to reason,' Amelia slurred merrily. 'He can't hear me, He's deaf. God Is Deaf. Not a thing. Not a whisper.' Enamoured by her diagnosis of deafness for God she smirked to herself as she mopped up yet another renegade dribble of wine deserting her mouth to explore her chin. 'Now there's a predicament, now what are we all going to do? We didn't bank on that little impasse did we? Oh no. How many people in the world praying like mad to have their sorry little souls saved?' (That was proving rather difficult to say under current alcoholic restrictions, involving a degree of spitting).

'AND GUESS WHAT YOU SORRY LITTLE SOULS?' She shouted to the invisibles as spit, dribble and more spit accessorised by, what would have embarrassed Amelia greatly had she been sober, a stubborn splat as spittle hit York stone floor. As it turned out, she did not give a tinker's cuss. 'GOD CAN'T HEAR YOU! God is deaf. God has cloth ears.' She asserted as impertinently as she dare, bearing in mind, if He really did exist and he really was deaf - He really may do Thunderbolts.

Sunshine shook tremulously and Amelia challenged her God.

"Cloth Ears? Hey Cloth Ears?.............."

Chapter 7

Proving there is a God – and He's not deaf either.

(Healthy discontent is the prelude to progress – *Mahatma Gandhi*).

After her night of God Damning, Amelia roused herself from the depths of the floor; circumspectly discovering her mislaid feet. She sensed her limbs and torso had been welded to the spot with high tech skin glue, by an invisible mischievous sprite in the impish early hours, from which a clean-cut extrication would present an insurmountable problem. Once belonging to her rug, adorning so handsomely, sprouts of wool had changed ownership and now firmly embellished her stale, sticky-wine chin like a concussed threadbare goatee. To complement the ensemble, there was a perfectly imprinted indent of the highly textured rug tattooing her face.

'Temporary,' she decreed, thankfully smothering the visual – until Reg noticed. *'No matter how depressed or upset I am about something, I always manage to maintain pride in my appearance, and look at the state of it,'* Reg nodded at Amelia's reflection haughtily.

'You know what pride comes before don't you?' said Lemon, relentless in her persecution of Amelia.

'What is it with you and quoting the Bible at me, you just can't help yourself can you Bitter-Lemon,' Amelia spewed as she, on cue, promptly tripped on the rug and fell over.

'We told you.' Lemon and Reg rubbed themselves better as they sanctimoniously watched Amelia fall and then felt the blow. They echoed like evil twins, *'You know*

you've racked up a whole shed load of bad karma after last night's performance don't you?'

Amelia picked herself up from her ungainly collapse and sat down heavily once again on the floor. 'If I was a Catholic I'd be able to say Hail Mary or whatever it is and I'd be forgiven, apparently. What does that mean exactly?' thought Amelia. 'Hail Mary. Hail Mary what? Can't be a cab, although it's the only thing I can think of that one hails.

'Idiot,' Lemon muttered.

'Oh and I suppose *you* know all about it don't you Missy Know-it-All?'

Lemon opened her chest sourly, *'It's not difficult to work out is it. Hail can also mean acclaim, salute, affirm.'*

'Exactly.' seconded Reg, without being entirely sure if Lemon was correct or not, but felt it necessary to join in with the puffing up.

'Alright don't go on,' Amelia nursed her hangover head as she spoke. She was not in any mood to cope with their superior tone. She was roused though, interested enough to ignore the war of dehydration vibrating through her body. 'So what are they doing then? Worshipping Mary?'

'Yes,' her voices acceded firmly.

'What are they doing that for, she's not God is she?'

'No idea. It doesn't make any sense to us either,' they answered unhelpfully, *'maybe to get noticed?'* Reg suggested, his interest growing.

'But how does saying 'Hail Mary' absolve you from sin then?'

Lemon puzzled, *'How should I know, it's all a little bit odd if you ask me. You do something terrible, some sin or another, and then just say "Hail Mary" and it's suddenly all right? The sin has gone away; slate clean; all cleansed and ready to commit another one. Why would anyone want a boring old clean slate anyway?'*

Lemon's frustration was infectious. 'Well I've never heard the like,' retorted Amelia, 'that can't be right, that's so unfair. My sins have chased me around for EVER!' Once again, Amelia was beginning to feel cheated by life somehow. 'I've clearly missed out on the *how to deal with guilt* philosophy,' she thought.

'They're all like that.' Reg's spiel was backed by the sudden realisation he could execute any format of guru-babble; it being abundantly clear that on this subject, Amelia knew nothing.

'Who are? Who's the *they*?' Amelia queried.

'Religions of the world, they're 'the they.' They've all got a 'Get Out of Jail free' card.'

'Really? So why haven't I got one?'

'I *don't know,*' chimed in Lemon, *'perhaps you're too far gone to be saved.'*

'Oh great, thanks a bunch. Face it Lemon, you know nothing about religion either - other than the one you/we/me ran away from years ago that is, so you're talking out of your skinny little derriere.' Amelia wasn't happy. This was all too much. She had spent the last few hours relentlessly rebuking God for his - wait for it - non-existence. There was not one shred of consideration for the incongruity of this thinking and her voices were driving her crazy. 'How can you rebuke someone who doesn't exist - how can you say anything to someone who doesn't exist?'

'That's a point.' piped up Lemon with insinuated intelligence. *'How can you curse him if you think He doesn't exist? Come back on you big time that will.'*

Amelia groaned, 'Alright, alright, I do think He exists. OK? GOT IT? He just doesn't like me very much, that's all. He's ignoring me.'

'Can't blame him really can you? You know you've delivered Him a challenge, don't you?'

'I really must learn not to drink so much,' Amelia thought with wise but pointless hindsight. 'Now what have I done? Isn't that the worst, waking up in the morning not knowing what has happened and to whom one must apologise.'

'You're well practised at that one' smirked Lemon.

The growing awareness that looming on the horizon was an apology to God Himself, has got to be pushing the fight against her self-destruct gene beyond any chance of redemption, surely.

Amelia groaned again. 'What did I do?'

'You said, you would prove to him that He did exist,' Lemon replied flatly.

'Don't be ridiculous, that makes no sense at all.'

'Quite.' Lemon's tone was even flatter.

Amelia waned as she laboured through the minefield she had created for herself. 'But if He exists, then he knows He exists so there is little point in trying to prove it to Him is there? And, erm... what's my point? Oh yes, and… if I did still want to try and prove it to him, even though He already knows it - how can I do it? How can I prove something to someone who already knows it, but knows I'm proving it to Him?'

'What a little pickle you find yourself in; I don't suppose God's too pleased with you this morning. How's your hangover by the way? Amelia? Well?'

'What do you want Lemon?' She answered gruffly.

'Have you given up yet?'

'NO. GO AWAY.'

'*Give it up, just apologise.*'

'Apologise? Am I hearing things?' Lemon has never apologised in her life and she's telling me to apologise. Apologise to God. Right, come on then. Amelia sat up quickly, with immediate regret as her insides heaved in protest of fast movements, her stomach's dubious contents sloshing brutally in great waves of threatening vomit. 'Wooah, I really don't want to see that lot again; okay then, sore head and fluctuating tummy dictates I take it a little slower, but I'm still going.'

Amelia sprang into life - sort of, almost.

'*Where?*' Lemon, Reg and Sugarplum were greedy to know.

'Into town.'

'*Into town? To enjoy a shopping jolly? Goodho. Nothing like the old retail therapy to lighten the conscience is there.*'

Amelia examined her other selves; 'I can't really blame them, I've been a terrible pain to live with just lately. Just as well it's only me I live with then.' Amelia wisecracked sorrowfully to herself. As she gazed intently, Lemon, Reg, Sugarplum, Sunshine and Amelia ephemerally merged into the 'one' they were supposed to be.

She felt a wave of unexpected warmth lap around her as she sympathised with the parts of her she generally found difficult with which to come to terms. 'Oh who'd have thought; so this is what it's like to feel at ease with oneself, to feel safe and grounded. Sure of one's self, I guess. When did I ever feel sure of myself, outside of work that is - that's the only place I feel grounded and reasonably secure in my ability to hold my job down with any shred of competence.'

Lemon temporarily disconnected herself from the others to elicit a smirk of disbelief at that one. Noticing, as

Lemon knew she would, Amelia doubted herself, 'Although that's open to debate, one or two colleagues may take a different view.' she judged herself harshly with a barrage of habitual gross self-deprecation.

'Oh bollocks,' she groaned, 'perhaps I need to start being nice to myself for a change? Now there's a thing.' Amelia managed a small smile at the thought.

'No, I need to find it,' she finally decided.

'*Find what?*' They queried with the faintest undertone of sardonic parody, again not unnoticed by Amelia, prompting her to take note that the apparent truce may be over as quickly as it began.

'The answer,' she replied to her voices aloud, as her commonplace ritual.

'*To what?*'

'Are you being deliberately facetious?'

'*About what?*'

'Yes, you are, of course you are. About who or what is the answer. Who or what will sort me out. Who or what will help me sort my life out.'

'*Hmm, you'll be lucky, who'd want to take you/us on? Tristan has tried and given up a few times, stupid numskull. Hello - just a reminder if you need it - he's currently on a rather long Amelia-sabbatical, after his few months of cosy evenings in the "Stepford" household you tried to create,*' jeered Lemon.

'I don't know, but I don't think I'll find the answer by sitting at home blaming everyone else for my woes and drinking myself silly when life gets too much to bear, so don't bring Tris into this. I'm going into town for inspiration. Something tells me I'll find it, today, right now, today.'

'*You can find anything you want in town, even that pair of red shoes you saw in a magazine. There's a shop that stocks them.*' urged Lemon.

'Really? No, stop it, you can't distract me that easily. The answer is there. To get the proof I just need to read the signs.'

'You and your signs.'

Much to the amazement of her doubting selves, Amelia did indeed read the signs and find an answer.

Chapter 8

Reading the Signs

(Open your eyes, look within. Are you satisfied with the life you are living? – *Bob Marley*)

Ignoring phone messages and her lunch date with Lucinda, and, most of all, the bitter delight in her life called Lemon, Amelia would like to say she marched off into the ancient town centre with a firm step. However, this would be something of a lie. She groggily shook herself, like a flea-bitten arthritic old dog attempting to cock its leg in anticipation of the relief that ancient memory reassured was certain to come. Amelia's slapdash positioning of her sunglasses suggested one renegade ear had, in a carefree life of defiance, decided to reside completely independent of the other.

The sun, on this occasion, being an instrument of torture as it bayoneted its way, cutting Zorro-like initials into her brain, carving it into grey sponge mincemeat. This persecution she also ignored. 'There you go, one step at a time. Small steps, soon feel better, hangovers don't last forever and the fresh air will do me good. Whom exactly am I kidding?' She was not really sure what she was looking for but she knew she would find something. Something that gave her the answer she craved.

For the rest of the world, the day had begun quite intelligently. It was a hectic Saturday morning with the lively market in full swing. Behind delicious pearly-clouds bobbing in the cornflower sky, the sun played peek-a-boo with the crowds as they jostled to find the bargains, Amelia squinted, and after pausing to take three slow deep breaths, she smiled her hangover into the rubbish bin left in the corner by the market stallholders. She passed by, waving at the remnants of misery in the bin as she went.

She suddenly felt alive and surprisingly well. She wanted to gather up a whole armful of life and hold it close, feeling it beating in unison with her own childlike expectant heart. She remembered the feeling when she was three years old and splashing in puddles; oh the sheer joy of it as the cold water splashed delightfully down the side of her Wellington boots. The challenge of making it greet her little toes was to remind them of what a chilly pleasure it was to be alive without soaking them to the uncomfortable bone, and freezing them into forgetting they existed.

She stopped to admire her surroundings. She had always loved this place. "One of the finest examples of an ancient stone town England has to offer." The brochure boasted proudly.

To her left stood the grand Church, imposing over the people hurrying about their business, a credit to 13th century religion. She scanned the beautiful sights before her, as if noticing them with any seriousness for the first time. She thought about the townsfolk alive all those centuries ago. 'Did they realise their handiwork would remain admired all these years on, into a very different future? A future they would never be able to imagine. What would they make of this world we now inhabit? Probably scare them to death. It would me; well, modern day living does anyway, if I think about it too much. What would they make of that plane droning by and that pizza house over there'

But the town is still beautiful. Look at it. Really look at it.'

So she looked. She didn't care about the small glances from the passersby as they casually queried what the rather dishevelled-looking woman was playing at? What could she see that they couldn't? They idly conjectured, before scampering on with the importance of living.

Amelia could see. 'That's the meaning of it all.' she told herself. 'I'm looking at the world and seeing the beauty, not the ugliness, experiencing how good life is and not how nasty it can be.'

'Not another I'm so happy I'm going to hug a tree and save a ladybird moment for Miss Goody-Two-Shoes surely? Who are you being today? Amelia? Or the sugar & spice 'Motorised-Honeypot' called Sugarplum?'

'There you are Lemon, come and look at this.'

'*What?*' Lemon's pseudo boredom didn't work. She was noticeably interested and beginning to enjoy the delights of the day. '*It is all rather nice.*' Venturing as far as the 'nice' word was quite touching for Lemon.

More than nice, what is happening? Could it be that changes to Amelia's true self were afoot?

'Over there.' Amelia beckoned with such gusto she nearly swiped the head of an elderly woman labouring past her with two rapacious pop-eyed shopping bags, one in each hand, bulging like hungry bugs devouring their delicious hard-won fare.

"So sorry," Amelia carelessly dispensed her apology to the ravenous shopping bags rather than their carrier who initially advanced with brave caution, whilst recouping from the onslaught of an unexpected (and at first glance one would have judged relatively harmless source) but realised on further inspection this may not be the case, so quickened her pace thinking beyond nothing more than making an extremely hasty flight from the real threat of attack by a deranged woman.

Heaven is a Donut

The demented woman (the shopping bag carrier noted) was standing in the middle of the pavement, throwing her arms wildly in the path of those who, trying to approach life with sanity were then being thrown off balance into the passing traffic by someone who had appeared to have left all form of rationality behind some time ago, and was quite obviously happy to publicly and openly talk to herself - at full volume.

'How peculiar,' puzzled Amelia as she stooped to pick up the pack of pork sausages that had expedited their escape from the jaws of the carnivorous bag and cast themselves at her merciful feet. Defying her age, the woman, ducking and diving like a berserk gazelle, ran to safety as Amelia gave chase, shouting and frantically waving the sausages at the disappearing figure, in what was to be a well intended but futile attempt to return lost goods. 'Some people do behave oddly.' Puffing to a stop, sausages hanging limply in her hand, Amelia meandered from pondering the eccentricities of people, to the merits of pork.

'That's another thing; some people don't eat pork do they, what's that about?'

'*It's a religious thing,*' said font-of-all-knowledge from the back of her head. '*It's something to do with being unclean.*'

'No, they're fine, the wrapping has survived the fall, still intact.'

'*Idiot.*'

'I was only joking Lemon, where's your sense of humour gone?'

'*Had a lobotomy don't you remember – recognised anything I found to be mildly funny as an abnormal growth threatening my life source so had it cut out before it smothered me,*' growled Lemon with great conviction.

Undaunted, Amelia enthusiastically returned to her brand new, 'I'm in a wonderful mood and nothing will spoil it's modus operandi. 'Look over there Lemon you blind git, and you Reg, go on, look at the view for goodness sake. Come on Sugarplum, you can see it can't you.'

'*I'm looking,*' said an ill-tempered Lemon reluctantly, silently cursing the feel-good factor currently beginning to take hold throughout Amelia's body.

'*I'm looking,*' squidged Reg happily, in a wanting to please mood.

'*Of course I'm looking,*' squealed Sugarplum ecstatically. '*Oh yes, yes,*' she breathed with over-the-top enthusiasm, '*it is stunning.*'

The view was truly marvellous and subdued Amelia into heart-stopping silence. A 12th century priory with little left to recognise but still surviving amid the flurry of contemporary life. Beyond that, a well-known Hotel thought to date possibly as far back as the 10th century and famous for apparently providing important guests over the years, such as Charles Ist, William III and Sir Walter Scott, with warm and comfortable rooms in which to rest after a long day.

Over a pretty stone built bridge ahead of her, she could just make out the landscaped grounds where the summer season of Outdoor Shakespeare was located, which boosted tourists to the area every year. The lovely gardens were a picturesque haven of tranquillity where visitors could enjoy leisurely picnics.

Amelia swung around to soak in the view across the green, where she had heard the Spring Fair had been held for over a thousand years. To outlast the age of shopping malls, cinemas and sophisticated electronic gadgets of all descriptions, it had evolved into an annual Fun Fair to entertain the visitors with old-fashioned fun, helping to fund the town's needs by bringing in pleasure-seeking families.

'Have you ever for one minute stopped to think how lucky you are to live in such a beautiful place as this?' Amelia asked herself.

'NO.' Lemon countered before Sugarplum managed to sanctimoniously squeak with inevitable goodness. 'Why the hell should I?' Lemon continued grumpily.

'Well it's about time you did.' The reaction was to be expected really, Amelia had predicted the response from inside her cave-brain and answered swiftly without surprise. With that, she turned rapidly and walked doggedly towards the main shopping area. As she approached the street the most delectable aroma of donuts seduced her senses, making her alive with scrumptious expectancy. She spied the little stall with the cheery red and white bunting, home to donuts of every description. She salivated helplessly, whilst Lemon teased her.

'What happened to the hangover then?'

"Gone, gone, gone," she oscillated her happy answer to Lemon's sarcasm with a loud voice towards the people around her, swinging her arms back and forth in tune. This gave rise once more to much consternation amidst the surrounding Saturday crowds, milling hopefully for their preferred donut before they sold out. They shrewdly parted to make way for the Mad Lady, deciding it best policy to allow her to outrank them and be served first. "Just in case, you never know, you can't be too careful. She might start brandishing a knife around or something."

Amelia, brandishing her sausages, oblivious that she was the cause of it, saw the opening in the small crowd and dived in, signalling delightedly when she spotted her beloved above all other donuts; a donut amongst donuts, glistening and twinkling at her.

"That one, please." She gave the stallholder her money without even a glance in his direction, eyes for no one and no thing other than the piece of sheer heavenly bliss she was about to experience. She smiled at it lovingly before thrusting it into her watering mouth oozing with anticipation, not noticing nor bothered by the people watching her with increasing unease, as the icing sugar happily settled into its new home. New home being, halfway around her face and just ever so slightly up her nostrils, making her look even more suspect than before. She wasn't just a knife brandishing, sausage-eating madwoman. Oh no, but a knife brandishing, sausage-eating madwoman on crack.

'*Make you fat.*' Lemon squeezed an insult in an attempt to spoil the day.

Amelia was not listening. Amelia had found joy. She had found comfort. 'How have I done that? Surely not from one donut – good gracious, whatever have they put in it?

She realised the donuts had always been there but she wouldn't or couldn't let herself enjoy them. The grace and charm of creation had always been there, but she wouldn't or couldn't be part of it. The pleasure of life came from within. This morning she had looked around her and for the first time in a long time, had seen the goodness of life and the beauty mankind can create.

'I think this is a sign.'

Happily spurred on, she wandered around the narrow medieval streets forking off in every direction from the market square, pausing to savour another fabulous smell; the coffee was out of this world, even more sumptuous than the donuts had been. It enticed her, without any effort, to stop and buy one to drink as she sauntered through the town. The coffee thankfully began to resettle the icing sugar, resulting in Amelia appearing a little more normal and therefore no longer attracting the glances of scared adults and derisory children. She stopped suddenly, mouth open mid sip, causing rivulets of coffee to slide inelegantly from the corners of her gaping lips as she came upon a little shop full of wonders. The shop had old fashioned 17th century-style bow windows with leaded glass winking in the sunlight; these were to be found either side of a low blue door forcing those of average height and above to dip down to enter. A merry bell greeted them as they walked in, and sang a cheery goodbye as they walked out. The window displays were crowded with candles and incense, crystals and all things that sparkle and cry out, "Come in and look at me."

Amelia went in and looked at them.

"Can I help you?" Amelia turned and, being human, made an assumption - a wrong assumption, as it joyfully turned out. She saw an overweight spotty-faced young woman with greasy looking hair, of indeterminate colour, tied tightly back from her face, making her features look harsh, consuming a very large hamburger.

"No thank you," was her immediate, prim response. What on earth would she know about finding God, Amelia relapsed into her own personal hypothesis, "and you've got some tomato sauce on your chin," Amelia added as she waved distastefully with the abstracted air of a superior being whose etiquette would never let such a thing happen in public (or allow icing sugar up her nose, or coffee stains down her crumpled tee-shirt, or manage to convince a whole population that she was stark raving mad within the impressive time of one half of one hour).

The girl behind the counter rewarded her with such a warm and honest smile as she gently rubbed her chin free of the offensive ketchup, that Amelia felt quick remorse for being such a prig. She baulked at the thought that if *she* had realised her own judgemental attitude so quickly then surely the young woman on the receiving end had also noticed. Amelia began to backtrack to prove she was able to be nice, but genuinely could not be helped at this juncture.

"You see," she explained, "I don't know what I'm looking for." That sounds a bit lame she thought, or crazy maybe?

"Until you see it?" suggested the young woman knowingly.

She now had Amelia's full attention. "Why yes, that's exactly it, until I see it. How did you know?"

"I can see it in you, feel it. Come over here, I can help you." This time there was something in her tone that calmed Amelia into believing her without hesitation. She edged towards the counter with as much care as her naturally maladroit self could muster – it took great effort. The shop was bursting with goodies that glitter and her eyes darted about her as she passed the groaning shelves buckling under the weight of semi-precious gems, glass angels and colourful stones as she gingerly passed. Holding her breath she crept slowly forth. She stood before the young woman, who was still smiling at her with mystical warmth.

"How about some of these?" The woman gestured towards the tarot cards lined along the shelf above her head.

"Oh, I don't know, I don't know anything about them. There are so many different types. I don't know which to choose."

"Don't worry about that, they'll choose you. I have open packs so you can look through them; take your time, you'll know which ones are for you, they will make sure of it."

Amelia was intrigued if somewhat amused by the young woman's assured belief in silly bits of card with fanciful pictures, being able to communicate.

"OK then, I'll have a quick look through them," she conceded magnanimously. To her great surprise, within a very short time, a pack of cards had chosen Amelia.

"It's these," she said with quiet disbelief, "these are the ones I want to buy." Amelia had picked up an unopened pack.

"Those are the ones that want you," corrected the young woman. "I don't have a pack already open, but I'll open them for you if you want to look first before you buy."

"No thank you, I don't need you to do that for me. I can hardly believe it, but out of all these, I know without doubt which ones to buy."

"Yes, it's always like that if you allow it to be," replied the woman whose special smile transformed her face into a thing of benign beauty.

Amelia smiled back hoping her smile could perhaps be a fraction as lovely as the one upon which she now gazed. After paying for the cards and promising to let her know how she fared with them, Amelia left the shop with a growing sense of excitement. She was impatient to get home and inspect them properly. I think this is it; this is what I've been looking for - the sign. My sign. My sign from God, she thought. Or am I being too self-important? No, why shouldn't I have a sign from God, other people do, why shouldn't I? She smiled again.

The long walk home no longer tempting her, after buying a few necessary items - the inspiring coffee, six more heavenly donuts and a packet of acid relief stomach pills, she grabbed a taxi to hasten her journey, this time oblivious to the beauty around her that had previously marvelled and lifted her spirits. On her return, she thrust open her front door as quickly as the stubborn lock would allow and entered, throwing her few purchases down belligerently. She rummaged through the bag looking for the cards. 'Here they are, Uncle Billy,' (Amelia included Uncle Billy in many of her mono!ogues despite his death three years previously) she cried exultantly to herself like a child, clasping them to her chest as if they threatened to fly away without her consent.

Skipping to the sitting room, where only hours before she had spent the night in self-imposed misery, she sat on the floor cross-legged and cautiously opened the pack, slowly spreading the cards out before her.

'To whom can I turn? Who is here for me? What is the answer?' After reading the instructions on how to use them, Amelia picked up the cards, without reading their messages, and shuffled them thoroughly and asked her questions one more time. She carefully made sure she could not see the faces of the cards and only the backs were showing as she fanned them out. She controlled her breathing to give her instincts a chance to perceive their message. 'To whom do I turn? What is the answer?' From the many cards in her hand with all their differing messages, messages she could not yet see, whilst still looking at their backs, she picked the card that she imagined had spoken, the card that said, 'Look at me.'

She looked at it. She then slowly turned the card over.

There was just one word at the top of the card, one word …. GOD. The card said GOD. Amelia closed her eyes tightly after devouring the short message underneath the word God, telling her to have faith in God and tune into her Higher Self. Whatever Higher Self tells her - is the word of God.

Amelia's life was about to change forever.

Chapter 9

The 1ˢᵗ Lesson

(I do not feel obliged to believe that the same God who has endowed us with sense, reason and intellect has intended us to forgo their use. – Galileo Galilei)

"Dear God?"

"Yes Amelia?" God responded as she had hoped.

"Tell me more about Higher Self?" Amelia spoke quietly with her eyes still closed, feeling confident that she would not need to see God, nor a sign, to know He was there and would answer her.

"Your higher self is the self within you that thinks first before acting. Higher self thinks in a positive and constructive way. To that end, Higher Self represents good in the world. Higher Self examines consequences. Higher Self is enlightenment. As higher self is within all people, enlightenment is for all. Therefore, you have seen the truth of God. This truth I have given to all of your species."

"Gosh. But so many of us don't use it, I certainly don't."

"It is now that is important. NOW is the present and that is all there is. What can you do with the past Amelia, can you change it?" God waited patiently for her response.

"No. But it can change me; it has changed me."

"What can you change about the way you think about your past?"

"I can try not to be trapped by it, I mean, try not to stay feeling negative about it; I suppose I'm talking about learning, my learning. I can choose to stay in my own misery or I can learn by it and pick out positives."

"Give me an example of that Amelia."

"Well, most of us have no choice as to the culture or religion we are raised within, but although I don't think I have been so far, thinking about it now, I can be more tolerant of other people's beliefs and values, even if they differ from mine."

"Not all religious experiences are negative Amelia. You have been affected by your past and have carried a burden. How can you cope with that now?"

"By remembering there are aspects that can make me a better person. Realising how childhood experiences can affect people, helps to understand them, really seeing the point of view of others. What's the famous quote, 'Do not judge me until you have walked a thousand miles in my shoes,' or something along those lines. I thought I knew all about that because of my upbringing, but I didn't know it at all. What I was taught - was how to sell, how to sell a religion, a theory. When still a child, I was quite good at it. To do that you have to learn to read people and touch their inner thoughts, but it wasn't empathy, I know that now, it's using their vulnerabilities to your own end."

Amelia continued, "I was shocked when I first realised that's what I was doing, it never brought true contentment or comfort and I certainly didn't like myself for it, so I gradually sought quick-fix ways to console myself - alcohol for one. I think my self-esteem hit rock bottom just by thinking I wasn't a very good or nice person. Self-defeating consequences to be honest."

"What about now?" God queried gently.

"Can I come back to you on that one?"

"You are not ready to forgive yourself yet Amelia. Change is a process, not a quick-relief painkiller. What else is there that you can look back at now and find positive?"

"My parents really loved me - love me," she corrected her usage of tense, her parents were still very much alive, albeit neglected by Amelia of late. "They did what they thought was right and what they believe in. They won't be very pleased with me for calling you Cloth Ears that's for sure - not to mention all the other thunderbolt invoking moments over the years, I must go and see them, let them know I love them."

"Would you like to talk about your thunderbolt theory Amelia?" God changed the focus slightly in accordance with her angst.

"You're not planning one are you?"

"I do not do thunderbolts. I never have and I never will."

"Wow, good, that's a great relief." She contemplated on how she was going to relieve herself of the habit of ducking like a feverishly demented chicken expecting speedy castigation at every desecration pouring from her Godless potty mouth. God believes in freedom of speech, who would have thought? Uncertainty lingering as to whether she could believe Him or not, she stoically reverted from pulverising lightening flashes of heavenly just deserts, to her favoured topic of conversation.

"Getting back to the subject - which is me and I'm rather enjoying this -there's something else, something to add: I think I'm quite strong as a result of some of my experiences. I know what it feels like to be laughed at and bullied. I try my best to stand up to it and have a strong sense of justice. I don't like seeing people upset or hurt by bigotry or prejudices - believe it or not – even though I do have my fair share of both."

"Amelia, the conversation was about Higher Self if you remember. You have just given a very good illustration of your higher self."

"Have I?" She felt impressed with herself at the suggestion.

"Yes, along with a vivid example of when you were not using higher self to make decisions – your quick-fix solutions?" God prompted.

"Oh." Amelia deflated.

"Amelia, you are only just learning – do not be so hard on yourself. Think about it, and tell me your conclusions?"

"That we all have a higher self? That I have a choice, I can either base my thinking and decision making process using higher self or choose to not use it. That is the difference between positive and negative; right or wrong; good or bad."

"Amelia, think Higher Self in all things and the rest will come naturally. It is a start and without a start there is no 'now', no 'present', only the past. God is the Higher Self and is within everybody. Therefore, You are higher self. Some choose not to listen, but when they do, the world will change. Your own personal world will change. If you act to reacquaint with Higher Self, you reacquaint with God. This will bring you joy. This joy is available for all mankind if they choose to see."

The wave of emotion surged through her like electricity, cleansing her spirit. She had forgotten she was going to have sausages for supper, free sausages with at least two donuts for dessert, ('Have a stab at all six,' Lemon had goaded, 'If you're in binge-mode, you can always throw it all up afterwards.') without caring about calories for a change. She no longer cared if people thought she was a weak, feeble individual needing a crutch to get through life. They were wrong. Faith is strength, not weakness. She felt strong, she felt able. She felt whole. She felt exhausted. She fell asleep.

Chapter 10

The Aftermath

(The problem with making assumptions is that we believe
they are the truth – *don Miguel Ruiz*)

Yes it's official. 'What does that actually mean though?'
Amelia wondered. 'I'm publicly stating I have found God.
Had someone put it in a box somewhere and there it sat on
the shelf, tidily stored, labelled the 'Amelia has found God'
box. Or maybe it's merely official because I've just said it,'
she deliberated. Having given this thought enough time,
she ended the controversy by deciding that indeed, just
saying it legitimised a charter and therefore official enough
as far as she was concerned. She made the point of
repeating this firmly to her evil side Lemon and her ego
Reg, with a determined nod for authenticity. "I HAVE
FOUND GOD."

 'Where did you find him?' Lemon quipped, *'Behind
Old Faithful? Skulking in the cupboard under the stairs? Maybe
He was laying in wait somewhere, waiting to jump out at you;
ooh, under the bed with the bogey-man perhaps?'* She chortled
cleverly.

 'Hey' Amelia shouted, 'you've got to stop mocking
like that now I've found God. He wouldn't like it.'

 *'Really, how do you know what He would like? What's
going to happen then if you displease him? Will He take himself
off on another mammoth sabbatical?'* challenged Lemon,
refusing to die quietly.

 This worried Amelia, having been Godless since
she was a rebellious fifteen-year-old, she wondered what
needed to be done to stop Him wandering off again? She

drifted to images of being handcuffed to God so she didn't lose Him again - or even worse, she thought, He lost me.

'Right Lemon, you listen to me,' Amelia stated firmly, managing to enlist the services of Reg, who had been increasingly concerned about his lack of status of late and had taken to shaking with tremors of anxiety whilst awaiting to reassert himself. His time had come; he dribbled as he licked his lips and wobbled with anticipation. She therefore allowed Reg to speak on her behalf.

'*Firstly, I... we...that is God and I.... well not like a royal We or anything of course, I'm not up there with Him.....*' Believing he looked adorable, Reg gave Amelia a cheeky grin, the sign of grins to come. Now temporarily a thrall to her ego as his puppet, Amelia was feeling rather revved up with the subject and beginning to enjoy the images Reg had implanted of herself floating about in space somewhere next to her new best friend.

Amelia carried on where Reg left off, 'I assume God will feel exactly the same way as I do,' she paused, commandeering Reg's very best superior air, which, she decided, rather suited her – how good it felt to give full reign to her ego. 'God will certainly not disappear, He promised. Furthermore, Lemon, WE do not appreciate your sarcasm and impiety,' she ordained self-righteously, causing Reg to brake wind in complete ecstasy.

'*Well, excuse me.*' Her evil-side Lemon's tone and delivery of this sentence was a masterpiece in itself, with an implacable 'WELL', a rather elongated 'EEXXCUUUZZE', ending with a crescendo of resentful and misunderstood 'MEEEE'. Added to this was a performance of astonishingly expressive head and finger movements to further enhance her pique.

To good effect - Amelia sat up and took notice. Reg shivered in dread of the scorn about to be heaped upon Amelia's head by Lemon, knowing full well she would surely sooner or later succumb to her demon's viciousness.

'*Well, excuse me,*' Lemon repeated unnecessarily, '*who are you to assume what God thinks? And another point I'd like to make,*' the fantasy spectre jabbed her finger dangerously close to Amelia's nose, '*who are you to say He won't like criticism. Isn't he supposed to feel nothing but love and can forgive the human race of ALL sin, including your pathetically smug self-satisfaction? Which I have no doubt whatsoever God has seen many times before. So he's not going to be phased by the little bit of irreverence coming from this quarter is he?*'

By this time, she was so acutely irritating, Amelia had to suppress the urge to do her serious damage. Mind you, she reluctantly had to admit to herself, as much as it pained her to say so, she's got a point. Amelia talked silently to herself, 'If God is what Lemon just said, all loving and all forgiving, He surely can cope with a bit of piety. That makes me well and truly (her heart sank) in the wrong about this - star. I mean rats,' she said to herself, adding, 'I hate being wrong *and* I've got to get the better of this backwards thing before it gets the better of me. – I simply must stop reversing my words.'

'Anyway,' she said brushing aside all things backwards, 'thinking about it, of all things to make assumptions about, I'm making assumptions about God....... Oh My God.' OMG. OMG. She retracted her profanations hastily, "Sorry God."

'I'm really in a state of flux now. I've only just joined up to all this Godliness stuff and I think I've sinned already. Now what's going to become of me? I'll pray.'

"Dear God,"

"Yes Amelia?"

"I have sinned."

"What would you like to tell me Amelia?"

"I've made assumptions. I'm worried you might leave me again as I'm not getting it."

"Amelia?"

"Yes God?"

"I never leave anyone. I am exactly where I have always been. It is impossible for me to be upset with or by anyone. What have you learned from this?"

"Oh I like this," she told Him. "You're being a proper God now, asking about my learning and stuff. Well God," she continued as Reg began pulsating with pleasure at the joy of being noticed by someone as important as God, "I've learned I should get all my facts straight, as much as I can. Think things through." She hesitated again. "Erm, how about, check it out with you first as well?"

"Do you think that is a good start Amelia?"

"Yes God, I do." she stated very firmly. "If I check it out with you first, I'm more likely to get it right aren't I. Hang on a minute though God. Are you saying that pain in the 'you know what' Lemon, was right? I hate it when she's right. She's pretty bad stuff you know, very flawed. Nasty. Repugnant. Downright evil."

"An observation: Talk it over with her and make it up with her."

"God, have you got any idea what you're asking of me? She's despicable. Got me into all sorts of trouble over the years."

"I am aware."

"It's alright for you to say, but this is going to be hard. I've hated myself for so long now, I don't know how to be nice to myself. I want you to just kill her off and be done with her."

"Amelia, this is why it is important for you to deal with this. She is part of you, and you need to come to terms with that and find where she fits within you. She cannot be killed off, but she can be controlled."

"That's difficult to believe. I'll try and think about it." she said begrudgingly. "If you say so."

Silence.

"Are you grinning at me God?" Amelia asked suspiciously.

"There is nothing wrong with a grin Amelia."

"God?"

"Yes Amelia?"

"Do you promise you won't leave me? Everybody else does," she added mendaciously but with such pathos she believed it to be true.

"I never leave anyone Amelia."

"God?"

"Yes Amelia?"

"Just testing."

"You are welcome Amelia."

"Will You....."

"Yes, I will always be here."

"Thank you God."

"You are welcome Amelia."

The morning after her discussion with God, Amelia awoke feeling unsettled and anxious. Why did she carry a heavy air of perpetual longing to be left alone with her thoughts at every moment? Why would she have such revolutionary dialogue with God, leaving her marvelling at what would come next, only for her exalted mood to be chased away with a crashing reality that would plunge into her heart, slamming her into crisis?

Everything she remembered about talking to God was mesmerising. Last night was the ultimate so far. God lets her speak to Him any way she chooses and still listens.

Why would God talk to her anyway? Why wouldn't he talk to her? She was confused, thrilled one minute and in a deep black hole of despairing failure the next.

She pounced on her cards. She saw them as a way of communicating directly to God and His Angels, and Jesus. She loved inhabiting this world, with increasing resentment towards anyone or anything that even briefly stole her attention. Receding into an environment of meditation, peace, quiet and solitude felt miraculous. It felt wonderful – it was dangerous. Dangerous because she wasn't ready for miracles, she wasn't ready for peace. She was heading extemporarily for the pinnacle of perturbation and for the alienation of all those around her.

She was entering a void and was fighting it every step of the way. Internal conflict was alive and kicking - ferociously.

Chapter 11

The Grin

(It is the certainty that they possess the truth that makes men cruel – Anatole France)

"Hey, cheer up, it may never happen – moody cow."
   "It's my normal face, this is how I always look when resting my features. Look at it, see, normal-face, you moron."
   Oddly enough, explaining to her unknown verbal assailant that her normal-face was indeed, pretty damn miserable, did not improve her bristling indignation over his comment. 'Do you realise,' thought Amelia, as if revealing a fact hitherto concealed, 'if I had a pound for every time I had that said to me, I'd be a wealthy woman. Well, actually that's not strictly true. It's been said maybe two or three times in my life, which at best puts me £3 better off as the result of possessing a miserable mug-shot.'
   Either way, the aspersion levied as she walked along the street one day shortly after she had found God, she confessed to herself, had been gnawing away at her ever since. 'I don't look like someone who is spiritual and enjoying inner peace. Surely by now I should have a sort of happy aura about me. An, 'I *know* what Jesus would do,' look on my face, without having to wear a bracelet reminding me to ask. But oh no, I just look like a *'moody cow,'* chronically depressed, that's me. Where's my, 'I've found God,' look?'
   'Well,' she said stridently to Lemon, Reg and Sugarplum, 'that will never do.'
   Sunshine began to quiver.

Heaven is a Donut

Sunshine was a beautiful being, who, in the natural scheme of things, should have evolved wearing an overcoat. Sadly for Amelia, little Sunshine was scantily clad. Some, those who have managed to grow a protective layer as they turn from child to adult, have an emotional strength that safeguards their sanity. Amelia's friend Lucinda was a good example. Grounded and sensible, Lucinda was able to stall all attempts to damage or hurt her when brought on by other people's inadequacies. "Whatever their problem is Amelia," she spoke with volubility, "really isn't mine. If they choose to let envy or some other ill-perceived resentment stand in the way of the genuine friendship I offer, it's their loss and I'm certainly not going to lose any sleep over it."

Amelia could only admire this attitude and never understood why she couldn't be like it herself. Common sense told her she was always going to suffer if she didn't toughen up by stop expecting the world to be good, and puzzling and hurting over why it wasn't. But that was because she was not particularly aware of Sunshine.

She was aware of the gathering ache that resonated as a result of a sorrow that came from deep inside and never left her. But she did not know a Highly Sensitive Person dwelled within. If she did, she would have had greater insight, not only of herself, but also of others. All she knew was the perpetual sadness with which she lived, and the distress she felt over things that she really should be able to tolerate.

Such is the life of highly sensitive people. In Amelia's case, her sensitive side had evolved into a separate little being, her other selves called Sunshine, that lived amongst them. Good, Bad, Ego and oversensitive 6th Sense. Sunshine knew that Lemon and Reg would forever fight their claim, like despots in a country holding onto ill-gotten power. And like all wars, there would be large and small battles, with peaks and troughs of quiet and calm within.

But Sunshine could not look in the bright light of Hell, as Sugarplum was able, it hurt too much. She needed calm and quiet; she needed peace. She was no stoic Sugarplum, steadfastly believing in her stance of good above evil and challenging the very face of Satan. Sunshine could not bear to witness the evil in the world, crying out silently in pain every time she heard Sugarplum defy it so courageously.

Ergo, Amelia's declaration of, 'That will never do,' impelled Sunshine to consternation. Another battle was looming - no surprises then, that there were times when this lived so visibly upon Amelia's face.

"For goodness sake," her friend Greg would say, "Millie, get a grip. You're not responsible. You're asking why you look scarily fed up half the time? Well that's why, you carry the world's misery of guilt on your shoulders."

Amelia recalled one occasion when Greg had spotted the look on her face when she appeared to be deep in her own thoughts, "Caught you" he pounced.

"What? What's wrong?" she jumped warily like a naughty child trying desperately to cover up the broken pieces of glass that until recently had been Mother's best vase.

"You're worrying about something aren't you? I know that look, it's the look that says, 'oh no, there's been an earthquake in Japan; must be my fault. The children in Africa are starving; it's my fault. My best friend's just broken a nail; it's all my fault.'" Greg turned to hold her lapels in each hand and gently shook a giggle out of her as he looked her in the eye and said, "You left him; must be your fault. Actually my little Leibchen, let's look at reality:

you left him because he's a pig. He let you down, not the other way round. It's not your fault; he was a pig. Got it? Got it?"

Amelia had laughed, "Yes, yes, I've got it. Who are we talking about now by the way, who's the pig?" laughter fading with her mournful afterthought.

"Take your pick. You usually go for the one syllable guys, Dave, Ben, Tim, Matt - must be a correlation to their brain cells, maybe they can only manage shortened versions of their own name."

"Ha bloody ha. Don't you dare add Chris and Tris to your list, they're precious friends and not to be put in the same category of 'Those who Come & Go'. Anyway, you can talk, Greg... or...ree." Amelia laughed again as she elongated Greg's name for effect.

"Point taken Mon Cherie."

"Have you decided yet whether to be German or French, or are we going to be treated to a mix of both all day? Don't answer that, I'd prefer to stay on the topic of me for a moment and you still haven't answered my first question Greg. Why is it I always look so wretchedly sad? Sometimes, I feel wretchedly sad and I don't know why. I'm supposed to be a convert for goodness sake, and *they* always look sickeningly cheerful."

"I have answered your question Amelia, you're not listening. Nota bene little buttercup, and act upon my words; everything hurts you. You look blooming miserable because you *are* blooming miserable. Personally, thinking of oneself as a convert is enough to make anyone suicidally miserable if you ask me. What is going on with you Millie-Moo? Why do you feel so much and hurt so much? Why do you blame yourself for everything? There'll be a reason for it you know, and once you know it, it's more likely to go away."

"Really? I don't know why. Do I? Perhaps I do."
But still she puzzled. Her life should be good. She should be happy.

They knew why of course: Sugarplum, Reg and Lemon. They knew Amelia's little HSP Sunshine was the nucleus and so did Sunshine. Sunshine did have her happy moments; when she could forget all the things in the world that brought undue suffering to her senses; when Amelia's health was good and Sunshine was not rocking back and forth with pain rattling through her frail little body. They tried so hard to help her and she loved them so much for it.

But even being loved hurt Sunshine. Depleting her, sucking her dry.

'*Come on,*' they would say as they gathered around her protectively, '*come and dance for us.*' At this, Amelia would become aware of a lifting of her spirits, quite out of the blue she would smile and feel strong, peaceful even, and the sun truly did come out.

Therein lay the true solution and not even Greg with all his perception would have figured this one out easily. The acknowledged shivering Amelia could not account for, as her gnawing persisted. She did not want to appear to the world like a "moody cow" as her verbal thug fashioned it. She wanted her belief in God to shine forth like a beacon. She wanted to put all the tragedies of the past behind her.

The heart-wrenching part being - in no way was she ready. Lemon grew in her determination not to be extinguished; Reg's caterwauling of '*what about me*' grew louder; Sugarplum's squeals of anticipation echoed resiliently around the cavities of Amelia's soul; and Sunshine shook violently at the prospect that the little pinpricks of everyday life would grow into spears of anger and hatred, ripping and clawing her apart.

As for Amelia? She thought it would be easy. Be good not bad; positive not negative; happy not sad; forgiving not vengeful. How could she guess that, within, she was facing a raging battle, one that would unravel her irrevocably? Oh no, this was not going to be easy. This was not a simple case of, 'what you know - you do.' The conflict of interest was crushing.

Little wonder Sunshine was worried. She braced herself for the onslaught of pins. 'That will never do.'

'What are you going on about now?' Her voices chorused.

'How will people know I've found God if I look miserable?' Amelia inquired with a frown.

'You'll stay like that,' said Lemon garrulously. *'Stop frowning.'*

'Only if you start listening for a change,' Amelia retorted.

'Hey up,' Reg squidged up squidgily. *'You can't go pulling faces that make you look ugly.'*

'Oh so what, what does it matter what people think?' shrugged Lemon. *'Anyway, it doesn't make her look ugly, it makes her look like a simpleton.'*

Reg squidged uneasily again, unable to decide which would be worse, looking ugly or looking stupid.

'Now you're worrying me with all this. You've become a convert, and that in my book is not only terribly boring but also extremely dangerous - that's if one can be boring and dangerous at the same time. What do you think?' Lemon caught her prey.

'That's interesting Lemon, can one be simultaneously boring and dangerous? Dangerous, by the very sense of the word surely implies …….. huh, penny's dropped. Okay Missy Clever Clogs, I know your game. Don't try to the change the subject.' Amelia responded.

'I *just did, and with great success actually.*' Lemon feigned insouciance as she yawned her hissed words to indicate her returned lethargy in a pathetic effort to demonstrate her superiority in all matters.

'Why are you saying converts are boring and danger...,' thinking it best to eschew the boring versus dangerous wrangle, Amelia stopped mid-sentence to simplify the contest. 'What's wrong with converts?'

'*They are overenthusiastic; arrogant; don't just think they're right they know they're right and they can't wait to make sure you know they're right; they invariably kid themselves into believing they are nobly saving your life - when in fact you don't want your life to be saved, especially as the significance of their fancy words laced with false concern is that they're preaching the so called benefits of living in eternal boredom with them; they're like vultures who feed off your guilt or your grief or whatever other terrible negative emotion life has so far dumped upon you.*'

Goodness me, Amelia thought, her apparent indifference was quite false, Lemon feels very strongly about this, she hasn't drawn breath yet.

'*Hear, hear,*' cried Reg imperiously, in agreement with Lemon, from the safety of the backbenches.

Lemon continued loquaciously, '*They don't care a jot that whilst being held verbally captive on the doorstep, the dinner's burnt and the baby has drowned in the bath. Or that behind their fake smiles, as they preach from their chosen platform, they're plotting how best to relieve you of your hard earned cash, why do you think so many religions are so wealthy?*'

'*Or, they're deliberating which guns to bless in a war. "Oh well" they shrug, "let's cover all options and bless both and all sides. Unless one side is really rich or possesses something we all want and need – like OIL - in that case we'll stick with them."*
... And a newly metamorphosed convert is the worst of the worst.

In short, the best thing to do with a convert is to steer clear at all costs. They transmute into nauseatingly enthusiastic zealots, capable of inflicting lasting damage on some unsuspecting victim!'

Finally, Lemon breathed to position her succinct finale, mouthing the words slowly.

'So, you dangerous convert you, to respond to your statement, "they need to know", I say, Fuck-a-de-Piddle. Nobody needs to know anything. Just mind your own business.'

'That's a very impassioned speech there, Lemon. Well done, I'm impressed. But you haven't *converted* me to your way of thinking.' Lemon recoiled at Amelia's play on words. 'Actually no, I'm not impressed,' Amelia persisted. 'I think you've gone too far there. Have a little respect will you.'

'Respect, for people like that - or anyone else with a grandiose idea of what God wants? They think or pretend they are doing God's will and all they're doing is ruining people's lives. Don't you understand? It isn't just about trying to control people's lives one way or another – which is bad enough, you of all people know that; it's also about some fanatics somewhere planting bombs and blowing children to smithereens, it's about controlling people into fearfully thinking they can't have blood or medicine; It's about isolating them from their families; It's about cover-ups; It's about thinking they know best for you … and it's all done in God's name. Not only that, they think they're better than anyone else along the way. They have truly convinced themselves that they are right and God will reward them. Reward? For murder? For instilling fear? Do you know how serious that is?'

'I know it's wrong to kill anyone under any circumstance, specially when lying to oneself by believing it's what God wants, I agree, of course I do, but they are a minority. The others? No. For people choosing to preach and educate? People who pray and go to Church and worship God? I think they do it because they genuinely believe it's what God wants them to do, and they're entitled to their belief, as are you... we... me... I mean. Anyway, forget the converts, as I was saying, they need to know.'

'*Who the hell are 'they' anyway?*'

'People. The masses. Everyone I know. Everyone I meet. Everyone who crosses my path.' Amelia declared sweepingly.

'*God help them. God Help Them!*' Despite the flat tone she attempted to use, Lemon the atheist, couldn't help feeling a hint of 'holier-than-thou' tiptoeing into her voice and enjoying this Pun of Puns, believing it to be particularly appropriate at this juncture.

Lemon surveyed the scene. '*Now I get it. This is Reg's doing isn't it? He's showing off again, on an ego trip...again. You want everyone to look at you and say, "She walks with God, isn't she wonderful? Ah, Saint Amelia!" Well in that case, I know exactly what you need to do. You need to devise some sort of code, a way for them to recognise your, erm... goodliness.*'

'Don't you mean Godliness,' Amelia snarled in a very unGodlike way.

Lemon dismissed this with a swift, '*I'm not sure. Anyway, if they recognise you as someone who has found God as soon as they lay eyes on you, they can therefore....,*' she paused for emphasis, '*ask you how you found God, and ask you to help them find God.*'

'Exactly,' Amelia shouted triumphantly. 'The Slow One has got it at last ...... hold on ... you Bitch,' Amelia harangued the looking glass, 'I know your game, you just want me to make a fool of myself; people to laugh at me rather than think I'm wonderful.' Undeterred, with insult pronounced, she felt free to enlarge. 'I know, what better than a *look* on the face. A way of knowing instantly that person has found God. An, I walk with God kind of saintly look. A, God loves me look, A…'

'*I get it, I get it,*' Lemon butted in, her lips curling into a grimace.

'Well that's certainly not it,' Amelia answered her. 'That look would frighten the horses let alone anyone trying to find God.'

Meanwhile, Reg had performed an ecstatic Hey Up. '*Hey up, how awe-inspiring*' he said, his squidgy nose rising to unsafe heights, threatening a nosebleed. '*To be acknowledged everywhere as a Superior Being, as someone conversant with God, unlike the masses.*' Reg promulgated the word masses as if the hungriest of dogs would be too revolted to allow his starving mouth to feed from it, or the driest of thirsty tongues to drink from it.

Lemon ignored Reg's moment of glory by feigning interest in Amelia's unpromising concoction. '*So what sort of look are you going to use as your silent code?*' She asked sarcastically.

'This.' The word came out with a twist, as she attempted her silent code look at the same time.

'*What on earth are you doing?*' Lemon said the words, but Sugarplum and Reg also turned to Amelia, their concern worryingly genuine. Sunshine felt her skin prickling uncomfortably.

'I'm doing it,' Amelia said to her counterpart - again rather freakish. 'I'm doing my silent code now. It's a smile, a beautiful Godly smile. Look, I'm doing it. How Godly do I look? Can you tell that I'm a person who has found God and therefore can also help you find God?' She waited patiently until Lemon had recovered herself from the hysteria that had suddenly erupted and which she was clearly making no effort whatsoever to hide.

117

'When you've reassembled yourself and immerged from the cushion you're burying your head in, I'd be glad of your attention please.' Amelia smouldered huffily, 'I can feel you shaking you know, I know you're laughing at me.'

'*What exactly do you expect, you ridiculous fool?*' Lemon roared her laughter with uncontrollable glee and relentless malice.

After an age of scorn swirling around her, Reg, up in arms at Amelia degrading herself, scolded her. '*Hey up now, for God's sake, get a hold of yourself. I cannot bear to be humiliated. Thank God there is nobody here to see this spectacle,*' he squidged in umbrage.

Reg's egoistic mix of backchat and blasphemy forced Lemon's laugh to colour with frenzy.

As these words and the abetting laughter cut through her delicate soul, Amelia stood, instantly frozen in a hurtful memory at the cutting remarks that Lemon's mockery had suddenly pushed into her mind; constant niggling 'put downs' she had surrendered to at the hands of a man with whom she had once thought herself to be in love. The man she thought had rescued her from the chains of Tristan and the world of pain she experienced when her engagement to Tristan was broken off - his hasty marriage to Bella still an unforeseen future. But the reality with this new man, this Knight in shining Armour, had been very different – his armour tarnishing to reveal an insecure brute hidden behind the charm.

This relationship had sent her into a yearning for Tristan whilst still resenting him for the imprisonment of her heart. 'I wanted to be free of Tristan. My rebound-man was supposed to prove to the world I didn't need Tris and yet, I ended up with an overbearing oppressor … and loving Tristan all the more.'

Inert with the recollection of darker times, all thoughts of her showing to the world how much she had changed abandoned as she remembered him: that man who had invaded her life masquerading as her partner; her confidant; her best friend, only to insult and hurt her with words such as "You ridiculous fool," repeated so many times she had come to believe them of herself. 'I remember you,' she thought. 'I remember how you pushed yourself up the stinking pile of human neurosis by pushing me *down*, drowning me. I was the idiot, you were always right.'

Unwelcome thoughts painfully pushed their way to the surface, ripping her heart back open as they did so, into the raw sorrow that was once so familiar.

Maybe it was just the way she had chosen to interpret it. Maybe he knew, felt, she was still in love with Tristan and would never love anyone else the same way. Maybe the only way he could deal with his own emotional wounds was to ridicule her.

She turned her back on her perfidious world of maybe and faced the comparative safety of the present by staring at her reflection. Once memories of rebound-man were adequately suffocated, allowing Amelia to focus on the here and now, she returned to the job in hand, that being, verbal fisticuffs with Lemon. 'You called me a ridiculous fool because I had my Godlike smile on. The Bible says we will be mocked and laughed at by ignorant people who don't know any better and we have to forgive them. What do you say to that?'

'*You're an idiot, that's what I say to that. Your Godlike smile, as you like to call it, has more resemblance to a cat's bum. No, that's wrong. I can't quite place it. Oh yes I have it, It's a GRIN.*' Lemon responded, typically blunt.

'What's wrong with a grin?' Amelia asked, suspiciously expecting a far worse insult than a mere grin.

'It's a grin. A cretin-like, mindless grin. You look like a debauched dipstick. You look as if you've been holding in an enema ... for the last three days! You look as if you need to be........'

'Alright, alright don't start again. You've already triggered one near panic attack thinking about a past loser I was ill-fated enough to have crossed paths with.' Amelia interrupted swiftly, 'I don't want to have another one, thinking about how useless I am and how unproductive is my fragile, empty life. Anyway, it is *not* a GRIN.' she retorted inexorably. 'It's a pure reflection of the genuine love I now feel for all mankind since I found God.'

Amelia announced this with great Reg-like pomposity, ignoring Lemon's indistinct response of, *'all of mankind except yourself.'* Amelia did not include herself when thinking about love and forgiveness for all humanity.

'You know Amelia dear, most of your problems are because you think we don't count.' Sugarplum stated calmly.

'Hey where did that come from, don't start getting all wise on me now,' Amelia shouted, 'and stop reading my thoughts, that's not fair.'

Sugarplum chuckled kindly, *'we are your thoughts you silly girl, like it or not.'*

'Don't bloody well start that, "of course we live in your head," stuff again. We know all that. Come on, to basics.' said Lemon returning to the conversation, backed by Reg, not wanting to be left out. *'It is a grin and you look preposterous and people will ridicule you. Personally to me, it matters not, but Reg becomes impossible to live with when under provocative traduce, so I'd advise you to see sense and get over yourself. In short: Get a Grip!'*

'What did Lemon just call me? I'm not a tractor. Stop talking about me – in front of me. I am here you know. I am most

definitely not an under-productive tractor,' Reg whorled to a stamp of his infantile foot.

'Under productive is a pretty good way of describing you as it happens Reg, however you are correct, I could find a better way of saying it. Protozoan is a closer characterisation I believe, yes that's it, Protozoan..... A 'Protuberant-Protozoan' what-is-more.' Lemon squirted venomous juice in the eye of persecuted Reg.

'Ah, yes, that sounds a nice description, what does it mean I wonder? Hey Up, It's not some sort of religion is it, and I'm high up in it – that's what pro..protuberant means doesn't it Sugarplum? Sugarplum, are you listening? Is it a nice religion? Will I like being a 'High-up Protozoan?' Oh no, I won't have to become all humble will I? Can't do humble. That's sooo not going to happen.' Reg's initial satisfaction at Lemon's description of him had quickly dissipated, not without some intelligence on his part, causing him to swiftly turn to his friend and ally for support and reassurance.

'Smartarse,' Amelia snapped childishly at Lemon, ignoring poor Reg and unable to think of anything worthwhile to say in return, satisfied an insult would fit the bill.

'Watch it,' Lemon rejoined gleefully, *'Your halo's slipping.'*

Amelia was confused by her own feelings. Was it weakness to love, or strength? Was it weakness to believe, or strength? Was it weakness to want to show the world she was a good person, or mind-bogglingly pathetic?

Unable to control her rampaging doubts and worries, unable to stop the tumult, she was floundering but still on course, gathering speed, for her head-spinning fall.

Chapter 12

Reflection

(A true friend is someone who is there for you when he'd rather be anywhere else – Len Wein)

Looking back, Amelia could see her days were numbered. That is, her days holding a modicum of sanity. Locking herself in at home gave no respite anymore than had her brief secret holiday, supposedly to get away from it all, a few weeks previously. Missing work for a further two weeks without answering any of her friends' increasingly concerned phone messages had left her stress levels untouched, remaining impossibly high. She began feverishly writing, meditating and talking, indefatigably calling upon God.

Meditation and frenetic discussions, whilst closed to the rest of the world, she found to be at such odds with each other, the juxtaposition left her imagining her fevered brain developing into a discontented lump of useless lather. When she attempted to meditate she could not stop her monkey mind from darting here, there, and everywhere. When she tried to write, she would stare at the blank piece of paper for hours, willing her hand to write something that made some kind of sense, to record God's words as she had heard them.

She took to striding around the room, a small circuit representing life or death. She had no clue why, other than it brought some sort of normality to her life. If she stopped, she would slide into insanity. Afterwards, she remembered the pacing as commonplace, the one natural run-of-the-mill thing to do in her crazy mad world - walk.

As her faith grew, so did her voices – the volume of recusant heresy roaring through her head relentlessly like an unstoppable comet. Her inner turmoil was unforgiving; she knew no respite from the turbulence that was now raging at dangerously high speed through her essence.

She rallied, emerging back into her circle of friends and the people around her. Long ago, Amelia had learned to contrive a halcyon stillness, a mask of calmness. This she now used to good effect. With great waves of righteous energy, she set about organising a plan. A plan to save the world and which, coincidently, would also save her.

She lobbied for support, arranging meetings, or 'Circle-Sessions' as she reverted to calling them in the realisation she would not fill the large assembly room she was planning to book.

"How come no one's interested in saving the world? How come, nobody wants to find God?" she demanded, when discussing with her pressure group of one, Chris, as they sat in her sitting room waiting for the doorbell to ring on the evening of her first meeting.

"Amelia, don't give up."

"Where's Tris and Lulu? Even Greg said he'd try and make it. Where are they? The infidels. You wait, I'm not letting them into my Arc – not now – they can drown with the rest of them, and I'll watch them!" Amelia's right leg adopted a volatile tic.

"Amelia, have patience, learn more about yourself first, rather than worrying about others. I don't think God particularly wants or expects you to save their souls by threatening extinction." Chris smiled.

"You're laughing at me now. Not much of a campaign is it? Why am I such an idiot?"

"I'm not laughing at you." Chris's patience was infinite, "You are not an idiot, this is new to you and this is your journey. Allow them theirs. Amelia, why don't we start? What's the itinerary?"

"What?"

"What have you planned for the evening?"

"Erm, well, a prayer. Then I was going to hand over to you. You can talk about God till the cows come home, can't you. Then I was going to sign them up – to my campaigns, get them all out there preaching, telling the population the end of the world is nigh and all that, unless they change – Greg'll look good in a sandwich board, and the ones that Tris doesn't persuade by his clever talk, Lucinda can seduce with her sexy, come-hither good looks."

"Really? Interesting stratagem for them all."

Amelia continued to fidget. "Did I pitch it wrong? Maybe a bit passé, people want something new and exciting these days. Maybe I should have told them God doesn't do thunderbolts - but He might be deaf. Not sure I've ascertained deafness yet you see and I didn't say anything about 'The Bolts' because I thought it would be too soon. You mustn't tell people too much at first you know, they can't cope with it - start jumping off tall buildings and all that nonsense, in fear of what's to become of them. Idiots."

Amelia fell silent, then asked earnestly. "What about the titles Chris, the titles of my campaigns? Are they good? I liked them, thought they were catchy, but maybe people didn't get it, too subtle for the general public." she reflected as her eyes perused her stack of soon-to-be discarded fliers.

"Not at all Amelia, I think a general discussion about God and asking people to talk about their beliefs is a good way to start ..... and your titles are great – yes, very catchy."

Chris, deciding that the occasional white-lie was in a good cause and definitely for the best as far as Amelia was concerned, drove thankfully home to the love and sanity of his wife.

Following her brief foray into inaugurating two campaigns, titled, *'It's Great to Grin'* and *'Grin if you've found God,'* she found to her bitter disappointment that neither went down too well with her friends - other than to provide a certain amount of jocularity on their part that is. Amelia had to admit defeat, her plan dead and buried before it hardly raised its idealistic head.

She studied her reflection in the large, gilt framed mirror. Normal-face stared back, glumly. She shifted her features into a stretch, causing her satanic side Lemon to grin manically in response. She positioned her stare on her demon-disciple Lemon, distancing other parts of her once more. As oft the case, Lemon appeared to be taking up too much space in the world. 'Curious thing' Amelia ruminated, 'no matter how much I starve myself in an effort to shrink Lemon, she still looks like a fat cow-plop to me. There she is, everywhere I go, looming in the shadows, threatening to take over, an ever-present menace. Fat cow - with a Reg.'

'*Idiot,*' Lemon retorted, stung by the analogy. '*How can grinning insanely everywhere you go and at everyone who is unlucky enough to cross your path, possibly reflect your newfound spiritual status? What if everyone did this, half of the population would be walking around looking like, well, quite frankly, looking like you – a brainless dollop - and the other half would go around looking like me - scared out their wits because of all the loonies inhabiting the planet. Thankfully, it just doesn't work like that – Gimp!'*

'*Language dear,*' tutted Sugarplum sweetly.

'Okay, okay, I get the message.' Amelia grouched. 'I'm not sure whether to be almost fatally wounded by your denunciation, Lemon, or relieved at the sense of it - enabling me to give up. Gosh, I'm quite worn out. Have you got any idea how tiring it is, smiling all the time? I'm exhausted.' She ended with an exaggerated flop into Old Faithful.

'*Not surprising really is it?*' Lemon said haughtily. '*It's FAKE, it's completely fake: A façade of eternal paradise; a cover up. Further, not to put too finer point on it, but just so we're clear – there is no such thing as almost fatal. It's either fatal or it isn't – you bonsai-brain.*'

'You're enjoying this aren't you,' Amelia snarled, 'What should I do then?' she dribbled as she rescued her desiccating top lip, fastened limpet-like, from her upper teeth.

'*What is it you want people to see when they look at you?*' Lemon's atypically polite underscoring took Amelia by surprise.

'You just called me a bonsai-brain – now you're asking me what I want. Why do you persist in messing with my head? What I want them to see is peace; contentment, unconditional love.'

'*Hah, haha, hah, haha. You want what?*' Lemon and Reg shared the joke. Lemon's return to sharp and bitter after her warm and snug moment was swift. Sugarplum overrode them.

'*Do you see it in yourself Amelia?*'

Now feeling distinctly uncomfortable, knowing that when her Sugarplum became serious it invariably signposted a lecture on the way, Amelia sulked her mutinous response.

'No.'

'You know Amelia, once you see it in yourself and start believing what is inside, others will see it also, without you having to contract face-ache with mindless grinning. You don't have to be perfect. You don't have to save the world; you don't even have to believe in God. Believe in yourself. You just merely need to feel love. You just have to BE.'

'So, the Grinning has got to stop then has it?' Amelia demanded.

'Yes, the Grinning has GOT to stop. A smile will suffice. A smile is all that's needed. It says it all. Smile and the world smiles with you.'

'Who said that first?' That, "Smile and the world smiles with you" thingy quote.'

'I don't know - but it wasn't me,' said Sugarplum.

'No, it wasn't me either,' said Lemon.

'Nor me,' piped up Reg.

'No, of course it wasn't. Good though, all the same.'

Back in the real world, or real as she could make it these days, Amelia had anticipated correctly, once again the truce in her head wasn't to last...............

Chapter 13

The Procrastinator

(It is one of the blessings of old friends; you can afford to be stupid with them – *Ralph Waldo Emerson*).

'*What is it, what is it dear?*' squeaked Sugarplum with concern.

'*Hey up, what is it, what is it?*' shouted Reg.

'*What's going on you coagulated cockerel?*' thundered Lemon.

'*It's not me,*' whined Reg, '*I'm not causing a fuss.*'

'*For a change; so who is then? I'm getting a headache.*'

'*It's Sunshine; she's suddenly started shaking. She's in a state, really frightened. Lemon do something.*'

'*Stand back, stand back, let a professional through. Now then Sunshine, what's all this? You know there's nothing to be frightened of don't you?*' Being so alien to her, Lemon's rare efforts at sympathy were precursory to a major migraine attack for Amelia.

Sunshine indicated towards the door.

'*Oh I know what it is, it's the Postman.*' Sugarplum breathed the word in a small voice as if he was the latest pathological mass murderer to inhabit the neighbourhood.

'*She's not still frightened of the postman is she? Thought we'd managed to coax her out of that one.*'

'*Yes but he brought a letter. A letter in a brown envelope.*'

'*The swine!*' Reg was outraged. '*The scoundrel!*' he barked again, '*how dare he?*'

'*It's his job you clodhopper,*' snarled Lemon. '*What do you expect him to do, whip out his guitar and serenade her? Bake her a cake? Fix the broken gutter? No, no, I'm sorry Sunshine,*

I'm not annoyed with you. Now, there is nothing to worry about, you know that don't you.'
          'She says there is. It might be someone being mean to Amelia. Someone demanding money or even worse, it could be one of those nasty forms that leave Amelia in tears.' Sugarplum was often Sunshine's self-appointed voice.
          'What nasty forms, what are you talking about? I think your brain's dissolved into sugar crystals.'
          'You know. Forms. Forms. Forms. The kind of forms that ask Amelia questions; she hates them, she goes all funny and stressy.'
          'Like what? What sort of forms? I don't know what you're talking about?' Lemon's fury detonated, incapable of understanding how on earth a stupid bit of paper could have Sunshine quaking in the corner (again) and Amelia cry-babying her eyes out (another again). Her blood pressure was in danger of boiling over at the sheer lunacy of it all.
          'Like the one she had to fill out for her bank,' was Sugarplum's nervous reply. *'It's all right for you Lemon dear, but Amelia gets a mental block and becomes very upset. She has to deal with these things by herself and she hates it.'* Sugarplum supported Amelia despite Lemon's rising temper.
          'I'll give you lot a mental block in a minute, right up your jacksie. It was to update her details - easy!' Lemon exploded, in danger of losing her pips, her words ricocheted around Amelia's brain cells, increasing the activated familiar aching throb, as often triggered by a visit from Mr Postman.
          'Now look here, it wasn't her employer telling her not to bother going back to work because they're better off without her. It wasn't a fine for parking on the pavement. It wasn't a date for a court appearance under the Public Order Act for exposing herself in public - you remember that time she was caught peeing behind

the bush near the motorway, not realising, until she turned her head at a 180 degree angle that is, that she could be seen for miles.' Lemon couldn't resist pausing for a little smirk at the memory of Amelia's acute embarrassment when she had realised her gaffe.

Relishing her stricture, Lemon continued, *'it wasn't a death warrant informing of her pending execution. It was an info update form. Pure and simple. Took her five minutes once she put her mind to it, the dorky-frigging-dork.'*

'Oh Lemon, wash out your mouth,' breathed Reg with hurt pride. *'This is Amelia you're talking about. She is not a dorky-frigging-dork.'*

'Yes she is, if she's frightened by an itsy-bitsy little old form, she most definitely is. Wash out my mouth? I've only just started you diaphretic anus. She's a kamikaze fuckuoso – everything she touches turns to a fucking shambolic pile of shit! And you're an armadillo's armpit. A malodorous armadillo's armpit!'

Having exhausted his stash of stolen property from Lemon's word pantry, Reg had no idea of the measure of the insults being thrown his way, but he knew, Lemon being Lemon, it would be nasty; he began to quiver uncontrollably.

'It's not fair, it's not fair, you're so nasty to me, I haven't done anything to deserve your horrible foul-mouth. You call me names all the time, stop it, stop it. Now look what you've made me do,' he ended with a whine as his fart echoed far and wide causing Sunshine to gag.

Lemon, now catatonic with fury, fixed her choice, beady, 'I'm a happy-in-my-skin psychopath' look on the shivering Reg.

'If you don't stop turdifying my chambers you will be transmogrified - into my new sink plunger – do you understand?'

'*Children,   children,*'   Sugarplum   sang apprehensively, '*don't start now, be nice, be nice, be nice.*'

'*Oh Fuck,*' spat Lemon vulgarly.

Sugarplum cleverly managed to deftly intercept the word and transpose it before reaching Amelia's lips.

"Oh blast," Amelia articulated her discomposure to a patient Lucinda who had been left waiting for her friend to open the door wide enough to walk in.

"This headache is reaching epic proportions, I'm in for a bad one; I don't know what sets them off. Sorry I kept you waiting, come on in, Let me just take a couple of pills before we go. Look what the postman's kindly brought me, a brown envelope. Is that a bill do you think?" Amelia waved the letter under her nose, trying to appear offhand without letting on that what she really wanted to do was wildly search out the nearest bucket of sand in which to bury her head.

"That's okay honey; it was only my *third* ring of your doorbell. Want me to open the letter for you Millie while you get your pills?"

"NO. I'm mean, no. No thanks. Well, maybe, I don't know. I don't like brown envelopes, always bad news."

"Deal with it now before we go, then you can relax. Oh and by the way, is it okay if we run a couple of errands first, or I could pop off now, get them done and then meet you there, only take me about half an hour, maybe a little more. …. Millie? Which would you prefer? Amelia?"

The shivering and quivering from Sunshine, Reg and Sugarplum; Lemon's miscellaneous rampage of rancour, alongside Lucinda's querying air was causing

Amelia's headache to reach a monumental high. Her legs were weakening.

"Don't worry, I'm OK, I'll take my pills first, feeling a bit sick. No … " Amelia suddenly reached out and grabbed Lucinda's arm. "Please don't go, have you got time to wait for me, then I can come with you in the car, you don't mind do you?"

"Of course I don't mind honey. Don't you want to drive? Is your head that bad?"

'Is her head that bad?' Lemon growled, *'You don't know the half of it Lady.'*

"Afraid so, but I don't want to cancel lunch, in fact I think it will do me good to get out. I just need a few minutes if you're sure that's OK."

'Do you good to get out? Run away more like. Go on then little Amelia, don't face your responsibilities, don't open your silly letter that, for some unfathomable reason known only to a madwoman, is frightening you into a pathetic quivering wreck.' Lemon was enjoying her rant in full knowledge it was adding to the angst Amelia was currently experiencing. *'You'll be throwing up soon with any luck,'* Lemon grinned cruelly.

Amelia sidled off towards the kitchen, knowing that Lucinda was right but still quailing at the thought of reading the contents of the brown envelope. 'I will open it. So naff off!' She replied stoutly to her internal tormentor.

"Sorry sweetie, what was that, I missed it?" Lucinda had followed her into the kitchen.

Amelia jumped. 'Damn it, talking out loud to myself again.'

She faced Lucinda. "Nothing. I wasn't talking to… I mean, I didn't say anything, just humming under my breath. You know. It takes my mind off the pain." She trailed off lamely. "You go and sit down for a minute, I'll make a pot of coffee, pop a pill and then we can be out of here in a jiffy. How's that?"

"Sure, whatever you say. I've got the whole morning free so there's no need to rush about."

A disturbed Lucinda turned back towards the sitting room to await her cup of coffee, with awareness of the clear signal by Amelia that she didn't want her standing over her in the kitchen. Amelia had not returned her calls for about two weeks and Lucinda, feeling guilty about missing her opening meeting, had put a note through the door the previous day saying she would be coming round the following day to take Amelia out for lunch, no matter what. She heard on the grapevine Amelia had not been to work either. "Something's up, that I do know." She reported to Greg when she phoned him to ask if he had spoken to Amelia recently.

Having checked Lucinda had done as she was told, Amelia took a deep breath:

Number one: Take some headache pills.

Number two: Make the coffee.

Number three: Open the letter.

Number four: Don't panic, no matter what it is.

Number five: Get out of here.

'OK, I can do this, I can do this: stop procrastinating, it always makes things worse. Lulu's here, you don't want her to see what a dorky-dork you are. Fancy that, a grown adult scared to open a letter. Yes, but I am though – prize ninny that's me.' She hastily swallowed the pills, two more than prescribed, and set about making the coffee. This, at least, accomplished, she glanced along the hallway for any sign of Lucinda. She didn't want to be caught out talking to herself again, or for Lucinda to spot her hands shaking violently as she clumsily opened the dreaded instrument of torture. 'NO. Oh my God, it's gone quiet, where's Luce gone? I can't risk her seeing me like this, she'll take me off for counselling.'

'Probably a good idea,' whispered Lemon, *'best thing for you - before they come and lock you away for good.'*

"LUCE?"

"I'm in the sitting room where you told me to go, you sure you don't want to meet me there – at the restaurant?"

Lucinda was fishing. Amelia knew her behaviour wouldn't go unnoticed. How could it? 'Who on God's earth becomes upset, to the point of agony, by their own mail?' She was definitely wrong footed by Lucinda's presence when the letter arrived and the subsequent battle to smother her irrational fear.

"I'm sorry Lulu, coffee's brewing, I'll be through in a tick then we can go and do your chores. I'm really looking forward to lunch; I hope we get our table."

"No problem there, I don't think, the place has gone down a bit since the new guy took over. I'm not hearing good things about it. We may have to find a new lunchtime watering hole."

Amelia scrunched up her eyes:

Number one: Done.

Number two: Done.

Number three: ....

"What is it honey?"

"What?"

"The letter. What is it?"

"Oh. It's a... it's a..." From out of sight, Amelia scanned it with one eye closed tightly.

"Oh."

"Oh what? What is it, not bad news is it? You're worrying me now." Lucinda moved swiftly and popped a concerned head around the kitchen door. Amelia was being evasive and it was becoming a habit.

"It's a reminder, to tax my car."

"Oh that's alright then isn't it? You hadn't forgotten it was due had you?"

"No."

"And you've got the money?" Lucinda turned to walk back towards the sitting room, taking with her the tray holding all the coffee paraphernalia, leaving Amelia in the kitchen where, as if rooted to the spot, she was still spending an unnecessary length of time. Lucinda had patted her pocket before picking up the tray, indicating she would lend Amelia the money if she did not have enough - worried that this may be the cause of the peculiar behaviour of her friend and yet puzzled, knowing money should not be a problem for Amelia.

"Oh yes. Thanks hun, yes I've got the money."

"Well everything's alright then isn't it."

"Yes my gorgeous friend. Everything IS alright."

Number three: Done.

Number four: Don't panic. Keep breathing; slowly, breathe slowly and deeply. It's alright, of course it's alright. I can renew my car tax; easy. Keep breathing deeply. It's easy. The letter helps me do it, she reasoned, gives me a reference number and everything. Easy.

Number five: Discarding the letter, her two still-shaking hands, managed a careless throw in the general direction of the scrubbed pine table, not noticing as it slipped effortlessly onto the floor and fluttered under the fridge, she walked away from the scene of her latest humiliation. Done.

After their quick cup of coffee, headache receding, Amelia felt her muscles relax a little as they walked towards Lucinda's car. "Glad we're car sharing, my head's left me a bit muzzy."

"Ok poppet, I'll try not to be too long. Just got to buy a couple of things for Coten."

"How's she settling in now at Uni?"

"Loving it; misses her family though, I've promised her a visit from us all, as soon as we can."

"Of course, bless her. I'd love that." Amelia fell quiet.

"I can't tell you how sorry I was to have missed your meeting Millie. Coten was having a problem with her Landlord and I drove up there to help her; it's all sorted now. Didn't you get my phone message – and my text? I did try to get hold of you, so did Greg, he came with me – in case the Landlord turned out to be a bit of a Silver-Back ...... Fancy a spot of window shopping?"

What the hell was all that about with the letter nonsense and pill popping – I saw her, Lucinda speculated as she headed out towards the main shopping centre. Daresay I'll find out in due course, but I'm feeling very uneasy about this. She usually gobbles up information about Coten and plans all number of treats and presents for her. But her behaviour has become distinctly out of character of late.

Amelia sat beside her in subdued thoughtfulness. "I'd rather not talk about the meeting to be honest, not one of my better ideas. I don't feel like shopping today thanks Luce," she smiled, "I'm not up to it, but don't let me stop you, I can wait for you in the car, no problem." She took three slow, deep breaths. She had withdrawn from her friends, even giving up on trying to contact Tristan, who had been annoyingly preoccupied recently.

She remained silently impassive next to Lucinda, until she again asked her if she was OK. She repeated her smile in an effort to reassure her friend she was fine. She was good old Amelia: helpful, funny, unpredictable and chaotic. She knew she was drowning in her own fear.

As Lucinda drove, she decided to tell her about problems at work. They had been ongoing for some time and whilst not being the mainspring, had certainly added to her strife. She knew Lucinda would take it that this was the reason for her inexplicable behaviour this morning, having witnessed her so distracted and troubled. 'This will head her off at the pass; she will think this is why I'm not coping with the mundane stuff, rather than the real reason.'

The real reason that this particular morning witnessed, an already seriously troubled Amelia throwing herself, lemming-like, off the emotional cliff, was an email she had received from an old friend. A friend she had lost contact with and believed was still in the religion. Not so. Her friend had managed to locate her and send an email informing her, she too had left the cult not without great concern as to certain things happening within. Had Amelia heard anything? How were her parents? Amelia's head was in a spin. Having resolved to make attempts to establish contact with her family, she now read of things so disturbing, she was flummoxed as to her next course of action.

Amelia's old, long ago established, maladaptive coping mechanisms were rising to the fore and turning her into a phobia addict: an eating disorder; alcohol dependency; sequestering herself; fear of being lost and abandoned; fear of the mail; "fear of the mail for goodness sake," she repeated, silently snorting, reviled by her own behaviour. She knew what it was about: Frightened of the outside world; frightened of people. Frightened to discover what was going on inside the secret confines of her ex-cult, and if her mother and father knew the real truth, and

137

importantly, how are they? 'What the Hell am I going to say to them? How do I broach the subject?'

In the face of this latest onslaught, her mental state reached new depths as she plummeted back and forth in a melting pot of negative emotion. Therefore, daily, everyday letters, plopping through her door, represented contact with others, represented responsibility she felt unable to meet. In her present state of mind, it scared her senseless. She invented a reason to give to her old friend so that she was not so worried, 'That'll keep the gossips at bay, give me time to think.' She also knew Lucinda would have some very sound advice for her.

This thought heartened her and she felt her mood shift. Yes, problems at work, that'll do it, give us something to talk about – it was true anyway so she wasn't lying to her, and in her heart, Amelia knew that the stress it was causing her played an important part in her current lack of coping skills. She tried to suppress the mounting giggle as she sat next to Lucinda in the car; 'my brain has been pummelled into a soggy mass of pulp; a pulpy paste of mush.' She sang to herself. 'Mush, mush, mashy mush; pulpy sticky mash mash....'

"What did you say Amelia?"

"Oh nothing, just humming to myself again. Gosh I'm starving."

"Yes, I must say, you look as if you are too."

"All good then, seeing as we're going for lunch. Not sure about the restaurant though. The place has gone down a bit since the new guy took over. I'm not hearing good things about it. We may have to find a new lunchtime watering hole. What? What are you looking at me like that for? Keep your eyes on the road for goodness sake."

Amelia was unaware she had just repeated verbatim Lucinda's commentary on the restaurant, so could not possibly comprehend the look of concern flashing across her friend's face as she drove.

During lunch Amelia discussed work issues with Lucinda. She related how she had missed a deadline on a report and felt sometimes as if she was drowning under the workload and being choked by her pending tray. She mentioned the colleague currently making something of a misery of her work-life, stretching Amelia's patience to breaking point. "She constantly undermines her colleagues, one way or another. No one trusts her."

"Have a word with your manager, honey," Lucinda urged. "If you've tried talking to her like a rational human being and she's not responding appropriately, then you have every right to take it one step further and go to your Line Manager."

"Yes, you're right, I know you're right and I will. Thanks for the chat, I feel so much better now. Tell me about you, I haven't seen you for ages, what's been going on for you? Then fill me in on Coten's news; how's the course going, has she made friends yet, when can we go and see her?" Amelia managed to make it sound as if it was Lucinda's fault they had not been in touch for a while, knowing full well it was she who had been the mistress of avoidance and not the other way around.

Lucinda let it go – noted it, but let it go. She searched Amelia's face but could not penetrate. 'I feel as if she's holding something back, something important but she's certainly not telling. She's not unduly upset about us missing her meeting; in fact I think she's relieved it came to nothing – too much like hard work she'd told Chris apparently. Plus she's usually the first one to consider Coten's needs and knows our absence was genuine.' Lucinda had no option but to relax and change the subject.

Heaven is a Donut

They continued to chat for a while over a very unimpressive lunch, vowing they would never return and then changed their minds when the waitress said new staff was arriving next week, one of them being a hot looking young waiter that all the girls were drooling over.

"Well, I guess we could give it one more try Lulu," said Amelia guilefully, "the boss is new and still finding his feet. Old customers like us have got to give the new guy a chance haven't we?"

"Don't give me that, I know your game, you want to check out the new waiter next week, don't you? Actually, I'm glad to see you back to your old self."

"My old self? You make it sound as if my old self is a scheming licentious old lecher."

"If the cap fits my dear," said Lucinda happily.

As she drove Amelia back to her house, Lucinda felt a little more comfortable. Something about Amelia's demeanour was still niggling her, but she thought it must be work-related stress. 'She's in a terrible hurry to get home,' Lucinda thought as she cast a sidelong glance at her friend, 'none of the usual, let's shop for shoes type conversation. Maybe just tired, she had a stonker of a headache this morning.'

"Well then old matey, same time next week?"

"That would be perfectly lovely. Thanks for today Luce, I needed taking out of myself a bit and thanks for the advice too. I'll keep you posted." She blanched inwardly as she said the word *posted*. After her performance earlier she was not happy that she had just reminded herself of what was waiting for her in the kitchen. 'Well don't go in the kitchen then.' She reasoned, jumping straight into the pool of procrastination she preferred to swim in much of her life. 'Go straight upstairs and get out your cards, do a reading; do some meditating. Talk to God, ask Him for advice on what to do.' Oh yes, she could not wait to get inside, shut the world out and talk to God.

Lucinda pulled up, parking the car in Amelia's driveway: as she did so, Amelia silently re-played instructions to herself for their parting. 'Don't slam the car door, I'll look too anxious to leave; make some excuse for not inviting her in for coffee. This is important - don't forget to thank her for driving me there and back, before I get out the car; it's polite to acknowledge she's come out of her way for my benefit and it'll only raise her suspicions if I don't. Do it now. Get ready, Go ..... Speak.'

Amelia flung the car door open wide, springing out with a hurried step and not a backward glance to record Lucinda's waving salute goodbye.

"Bye Lulu." Slam.

Chapter 14

The Dream

(It is wonderful how much time good people spend fighting the Devil. If they would only expend the same amount of energy loving their fellow men, the Devil would die in his own tracks of ennui. – *Helen Keller*)

Amelia could not contact God. There was no voice in her head. She did not receive satisfying messages from her cards. 'Telling me to be patient' she snorted. 'Patient! How long does a person have to wait to get noticed by God? How long have I waited? How long does it take for good things to start to happen?'

Lucinda's comments over lunch earlier that day, "eat up, you've the appetite of a sparrow," had irritated her intensely.

'What do I care? Does it matter?'

She went downstairs for a bottle of wine, opening it, grabbing a glass, she ran back upstairs, expertly saving the wine from spilling. 'Help me sleep' she said, 'seeing as God clearly isn't going to.'

She managed to stop at three quarters of a bottle, 'Not bad for me,' she thought. She tried to sleep, went downstairs again to pop a sleeping pill, having instructed that under no circumstance was she to take the medication if she'd been drinking alcohol. 'Don't care, God doesn't, why should I?'

The extraordinary dream followed…..

"Dear God?"

"Yes Amelia?"

"I had a dream."

Amelia waited……….

"Is that it? Aren't you going to ask me about it? Aren't you just the slightest bit interested?"

"Amelia, please tell me about your dream - if you want to, that is."

"Thank you for taking an interest – I would like to discuss my dream as it happens - but only if You want to... that is." Amelia puffed out her words, waiting to launch.

"Please continue."

Amelia launched - enthusiastically. "It was surreal, felt as if I was visiting a previous life, or even a future life. I'm not quite sure which."

"Perhaps you did." God suggested helpfully.

"Can you do that? Can people visit past or future lives?"

"It happens all the time Amelia, to describe it in a way you would understand."

"WOW."

Once again Amelia faced silence.......

"God, where are you?"

"Have you not finished what you were saying Amelia?"

"What!" Amelia's outrage was clear and genuine. "How can this conversation be finished? Not only have you not heard my dream, you also just said people visit past and future lives all the time and expect that to be an end of the confab. Are you completely bonkers God? And what do you mean, "describe it in a way I can understand," I think it's you not making much sense here."

"What else would you like to know Amelia?"

"What else?" Amelia was incredulous at God's apparent lack of awareness. "Why not put the proverbial huge elephant on the table and ignore it. While you're at it, paint a few yellow spots on it too, just in case someone doesn't get the message."

"But you already know."

"Know what? What can I possibly know about whether we can visit the past or the future? You'll be telling me there's such a thing as aliens next."

"That depends on what you call an alien Amelia. They think of you as alien."

"ME?" said with a large degree of Amelia-style outrage.

"The human race that is, not you personally. You just happen to belong to one of the life forms inhabiting the universe just now."

"I'm speechless."

"That truly makes a change Amelia."

Amelia threw her hands in the air wildly to demonstrate her frustration. "That's not funny God. It's not big and it's not clever. I don't know what to ask you first. Is there such a thing as alien life? Is there more than one planet of them? Are they hostile to us? Can we visit past lives? Can we see the future? Oh my God, do we visit alien planets? Do they come here?" She faltered, breathless.

"That is very good for someone rendered speechless Amelia, remarkable in fact."

"God, You are so annoying and don't laugh at me, I can't help the way I am. Do you promise to tell me everything?"

"My undertaking is to tell you anything that is helpful for you to know Amelia."

"Really? Well, You're not very good at this undertaking of yours then are you - considering I don't know anything."

"I thought you wanted the jokes to stop Amelia?"

"What makes you think I'm joking?" Amelia smouldered. She drew in a long breath to control her irritation and re-inflate her lungs; when she felt she had sufficiently curbed her emotions, she voiced her latest uncertainties.

"You said you'd tell me everything, but there's a lot to talk about." Amelia realised that any other time, she would have been pleased God was prepared to hear her dream, but she felt robbed of the moment due to the enormity of His disclosures. 'Confessions of a Mad God, if ever there's a book needs writing - it's that one.'

"Firstly, are you feeling well God?"

"I am touched by your concern Amelia. And, yes thank you, I feel very well. I look forward to hearing about your dream." He prompted.

"I think I'm more concerned about the future of the human race in your hands, rather than you to be honest. You're saying some weird stuff."

"Your dream?"

"OK. If you're sure you're ready - then I'll begin. It all started with me flying. Not all flippy-flappy like bird's wings." Amelia was heedlessly flapping her arms in an attempt to imitate a flying bird motion, and blind to how she looked as a result.

"I was flying straight and fast, very fast; like a bullet. But then I was able to swerve back and forth; back and forth, changing direction at the very last second. I can't remember ever feeling such exhilaration and power before. It was incredible and I'll never forget it. I covered an amazing amount of miles and time, not just flying but looking, searching."

"Looking and searching?" God enquired. "For what?"

"I was looking for people; people who needed my help. I was an Angel; a blue Angel."

"Blue?"

"As in 'dressed in blue.' Not literally blue, like my skin was blue - that would be wacky. I had long fair hair and a beautiful blue dress on." (Reg squidged a little trump of pride.)

"I am sure you looked very beautiful, as well as wearing a lovely dress."

"I asked you not to laugh at me God; I know you're doing it you know. I'm not stupid. Anyway, as it happens, yes of course I was beautiful....God, you're such hard work at times," she groused, as an afterthought under her breath. (Reg joyfully broke another two trumps of wind at the thought of God acknowledging the beauty of Amelia, even if the beauty was only in her dream.)

"Anyway, I was flying all over the world searching for people needing help, vigilant for their call as I travelled around the globe. I found an injured soldier from the First World War; he was partially buried in one of the trenches, lying there in agony. One lung was damaged and he had a severe leg injury; he'd been there for a long time, he wouldn't have lasted much longer, the loss of blood had weakened him considerably. He was freezing in the cold, and his boots were filled with icy water, his blood mingling with the blood of his friends who had fallen close by, congealing around his frostbitten feet."

Amelia's pause for breath was rapid - and noisy.

"As I stemmed his blood, I talked to him gently, telling him quietly that he wasn't going to die, that it wasn't his time. I told him to trust me; I knew it for sure. He would live to tell his grandchildren. He held on to me for so long, begging me not to leave him. I reassured him I would never leave him, I'd be with him for the rest of his time on earth and until he left this world for another, but that wouldn't happen for a very long time. I was summoned for help and when I knew he was in safe hands I was able to continue on my mission.

I left him there, but I never left him. I was there for him for the rest of his long life - you can do stuff like that in a dream, anything is possible. As I left I heard him thank me - and also thank You. He had prayed and I had been sent. He never forgot it."

Another swift intake of breath.

"I resumed my task. I knew that's what it was. My quest: that was my undertaking in life, to help people, to answer their call and help them through the depths of their despair. To save lives. Not like Superman or anything," Amelia added, attempting to be self-effacing but missing the fact that Reg, undeniably ever-present, was quivering with importance and giving her what could only be described as a nobly pious edge to her voice.

"No one else could see me. I was just a working Angel." (Reg deflated with a wheeze at this, '*doesn't sound very important does it – working Angel indeed*,' he sniffed.)

"I flew like a ducking, weaving missile. I then heard the call of someone on an operating table in hospital. He was lost. He'd come out of his body and wanted to return, but couldn't find a way back. He was clawing at the ceiling frantically, and blood was oozing from his desperate fingernails. When he saw me, he became terrified. There was so much fear in him, fear of leaving the only thing he knew; fear of death. He asked me if it was his time. Had I come to take him? I told him no. That wasn't my purpose. I told him he wasn't to fear his death when it came. It wasn't death as humans think of it, but a rebirth; his rebirth into another life; his chosen placing. That is what death truly is."

Amelia became impatient at the frequent breaks in her narrative, necessitated by all-important oxygen. '*You're not in the afterlife yet, you sponge-brained dunce,'* spat Lemon, *'you still need to breath! Hurry up, I'm feeling giddy'.*

"But it wasn't his time for that yet. I had been summoned to help him back to his present-day body. I motioned down, and he turned to see himself stretched out on the table with the surgeon and his colleagues working to bring life back into his motionless body. He smiled as I gently guided him down towards the already corpse-like figure lying there. As he gently re-entered, he turned to wave, and thanked me. He also thanked you. Many people turn to you when they are in trouble God. He did at that moment and he had never believed in you before. This experience changed his life. The machine hooking into him kicked back into life, heralding his triumphant return to his body, as I knew it would. I resumed my eternal journey."

Lemon's attempts to quell the flames of her enthusiasm foiled, Amelia continued, undiminished.

"Then a disturbing thing happened. I saw my Husband. My partner from my earthly life, the life I had before I passed on and became a Blue Angel. We had loved each other and he had mourned my passing - not understanding how happy I was; knowing only his own loss. He was with a woman; I knew instinctively it was his wife; his new wife - my replacement. I felt sad. At that moment, for a moment, I too mourned for the loss of him, of our love. They parted and he walked, waving at her as he did so, towards a shop on the corner of the street. She crossed the road. She was lovely and almost skipping her happiness as she went. I inhaled her love for him. As she turned to wave back she didn't notice the car speeding towards her. Too late....."

Amelia gulped volubly for air, spell-bound by her own story.

"She was flung awkwardly into the air, her beautiful face contorting in surprise and helplessness. The sound of the car crashing into the shop window after hitting its quarry split the air waves, vying for attention in competition with the crowd's screams, non louder than my Husband's; her Husband. She fell lifelessly in the road. Horrified onlookers stood gaping in those first blood-spilling seconds, not knowing what to do.

Amelia's tone dropped from excited babble, to that of the bereaved. "My dear, sweet man looked at her, now silenced. The look on his face I recognised well. I had seen that same look when I had left him; when I died. My passing, for him had been the beginning of a nightmare purgatory, which only ended when he started to feel alive again by meeting this once dazzling creature, now mangled and inert before him. She had brought love back into his life, and as I looked down upon her, I knew instinctively she was an exceptional human being and he had found the perfect mate. He would not outlive yet another loss of this magnitude."

Her serious words carried the weight of grief as she spoke.

"I flew to her side. She looked at me with closed eyes. "I really don't want to leave him." She whispered to me, "Do I have to go?" "No, sweet Lady" I reassured her, "I'm here to make sure you don't." I held her cold hand and willed the life back inside her dying, mutilated body. Restoring her life, as good as it had been; her mind and body as beautiful as they had always been. As I reinstated her life, I realised that my stricken man was beside her, beside me, holding her other hand. "No, not again, please don't die," he moaned. I breathed him in, and he turned in my direction. He looked straight at me but couldn't see me. She could; beautiful Lady could see me. She murmured temperately to him, "Don't worry, I'm not going to die, she just told me so."

Amelia raised her head sharply as she relived her dream. "He scanned the crowd. "Who told you so?" "Blue Angel," she said, "my Blue Angel". He began to cry softly with relief. He believed her. He knew it would be true. He trusted her Blue Angel. As I left them, they turned and thanked me. They also thanked You.

An approaching Golden Angel cut short my journey; she was stunning in her exquisite glory. She hovered over me, being much bigger and grander. I knew she was superior to me in every way. She told me not to be sad. That she had felt my sadness like an arrow piercing her heart. She spoke quietly in her beautiful voice, telling me that if I felt the human emotion of sadness, she was failing me. I reached out to her but stopped short of touching her, feeling unworthy. I reassured her that it was a fleeting memory trace of a life I had experienced on earth, and had served only to remind me of the frailty of humans and their need for our help. She smiled at me and said to remember this well, to take to my heart that this wisdom is only what such memories serve; they were not there to hanker for earthly emotion...."

Amelia paused this time to consider her words. Her accurate recounting of the dream was of vital importance to her. "She said the man I had loved when on earth was still living his life as it is for him now; as it is destined for him now; a life of which I was once a part, but am no longer. She reminded me he was entitled to live his life as he chose. She praised me for feeling compassion and for the joy I had just brought into their lives instead of the tragedy that could have been.

As I started to fly again, God, I woke up. I awoke and began crying because I'd woken up. It was so beautiful

I didn't want to leave it. It took me a second to realise it was just a dream and I really wasn't a Blue Angel. What does it mean God? It was so real, what is the meaning?"

"That you dream in colour?"

"Oh God, that's too much. You don't always have to try and outdo me in the witticisms you know. I'm being serious now."

"Amelia, not everybody can or does dream in colour. It struck me that the dream must have been very vivid and real to you."

"Hmm. So what do you really think?"

"What is the purpose of such a glimpse into other worlds Amelia?"

"You mean it wasn't just a dream?" Amelia practically breathed the words in her heady anticipation at the thought.

"What do you think Amelia?"

"God, I'm too excited to get annoyed by you turning everything into a question, that's what I think. I also think it was true; my dream was true. I think I did experience another time or life - or both. Do you know what else - something I forgot to tell you?"

"What is that Amelia, it sounds important to you?"

"I believe it is God. Do you remember the Golden Angel I told you about? I knew the Golden Angel - I mean in this life... I mean the life of the 'me' in the dream. Well..." Amelia was feeling tongue-tied. "Well..."

"May I clarify for you? In the dream, you recognised the Golden Angel as someone you had known before you became a Blue Angel?"

"That's it. Yes, this is the strangest thing. Before I had passed over to become a Blue Angel, she had been my daughter."

"So in your dream did your daughter pass over with you, Amelia, or sometime shortly before or after?"

"No that's the thing, she didn't. I only know this because I know this; dreams are like that, you just automatically know things. And I knew that my daughter had been raised by her father and his next wife and had lived a long and happy life."

"What is your conclusion?"

Amelia gave thought to this, "my conclusion is... I think... that I saw two periods of time at the same time, more than two actually. Also I was part of all of them."

"Very interesting Amelia. Tell me more."

"Well, the date of the man's surgery is unclear to me, but I was present as a Blue Angel during the First World War. I was present when the car crash happened a hundred or so years later - not forgetting that when the accident happened, my daughter was still a little girl. But I was also part of her future. She had become a Golden Angel many years after the crash, having passed over when she was an old woman. Hey, that's a thought. How come she got to be a Golden Angel before me? That's so not fair. She was my Boss. My daughter was my Boss."

"What might that say about your experiences Amelia?"

"Oh great. So it takes me longer than anyone else to learn my lessons does it? That's what you're saying my learning is. Yes let's be honest here – slow! Well that figures, my friends wouldn't be surprised to hear that one."

"Perhaps the soul who was your daughter in the life, experienced in your dream, was not at the same level of awareness and therefore had different perceptions than you; this may appear to you that she was an old-soul, as it is often described. It merely highlights that we are all at different times whilst at the same time. We all gain understanding in different ways and at a different pace to each other. Everyone is different and should be treated accordingly. And the same."

"You said different five times then God. Not very imaginative."

"Do I need to be? As long as you understand me."

"I guess so. So... we're all different then."

"Now who's being flippant?"

"Yes, I was waiting for my chance." Amelia said meekly. "But you said we are all the same also? We are different and the same? That's what you just said."

"Indeed."

"I think I get it. We are all one. In that sense we are all the same. If we acknowledge each other's differences, it's easier to treat each other the same?"

"I like your thinking Amelia."

"One other thing though God, I haven't got a daughter, or been married. Why did I in the dream? It was definitely me, but in real life I haven't got a daughter."

God corrected her. "In *this* life you have no daughter Amelia. All your lives are real."

"You mean, I will have a daughter, either in this life or in a different one?"

"You have had many lives Amelia, but not as many as the Golden Angel of whom you dreamt - the soul who was your daughter in your dream. You are correct, that soul was once your daughter in a life on earth. She has also been your Mother in another life. In one life, you were the closest of friends. Souls will gravitate towards each other in their earthly lives; they often have a pact to meet each other and help in some way in each individual's - as you think of it - lesson. Every soul will have physical experience on earth in order to remember. Amelia, souls go to earth to experience. They all have choices as to whether they go to earth or stay as spirit. They go to earth only to remember who they are and all they have forgotten."

"What do they, sorry, we - need to learn? God, wait. May I try and answer that myself?"

Silence.

Amelia carried on, "I think we come to earth to learn love: to learn how to love and how to treat each other with love, dignity and compassion. Bloody hell, bit of task, isn't it. Slow learners aren't we, how long have you been at it God, this overseeing of the primitive earthling? I think I'd have lost interest by now, walked off and started again. I bet I've had hundreds of lives and have to keep coming back because I keep treating people like shi... I mean, treating people badly. No wonder some things seem familiar – touch of the old déjà vu and all that."

"Amelia, it is akin to learning; that is why I used the word lesson. In that sense, you do learn things as you go through your earthly life. All life is an experience if you remember the things you speak of: love, dignity, compassion, you will truly benefit from the experience and from remembering who you are and finding joy. You can only know who you are if your starting point is who you are not. That is the meaning of life. You can choose to use many lives to experience this. And no, I would never lose interest Amelia, nor have you ever lost your interest in experience. We are experiencing the experience. All is correct and as it should be."

"Does that mean I keep coming back because I want to, not because I really have missed the crux of it all and so *have* to?"

"A hypothesis to think about Amelia. Any other?"

"Yes God. I think we have the wrong idea about time. It seems to me there is no past or future. Only the present as we know it and experience it. But..." She waited,

154

checking unnecessarily He was paying heed. She felt she was making important links, and Reg craved praise. "We are learning in the experience. For instance, I learned a very great lesson when I felt a human emotion as an Angel. I learned that I could use it to the good and not respond to it in the same way I would have done on earth."

"How do you think you would have responded as a human Amelia?"

"I would have been jealous. It's possible the emotion would have been so strong it would have compromised my task. I had been called there to save this woman. Had I acted on my jealousy I may not have wanted to save her."

"As you have had a glimpse of this now Amelia, how can you use this experience for the present you are currently in, rather than waiting until your present as a Blue Angel?"

"That's the amazing thing isn't it God. It's like seeing the bigger picture. Instead of concentrating on my own feelings, I gave help and support to someone needing it rather than turning away uninterested. I saw the beauty and love in a person who, in a real life situation, I would have seen as a rival. I understood their wants and needs and with all my heart wanted them to achieve them. In helping them, it made me feel good. To bring about joy, hope and love for others is to feel all those things for oneself. I like this. What a great dream I've had... or been given. I feel really positive now I've had this experience sent to me. I might just start to run about the countryside singing, *The Hills are Alive*."

"Have you considered why?"

"Why I might run about the countryside singing, *The Hills are Alive*?"

"No Amelia. Why, as you say, this experience has been sent to you. Why you were given this dream?"

"Oh.... no I haven't. Yes. Oh no. Are you telling me I'm a jealous bitch? Are you telling me I'm a selfish cow in real life, I mean this life? That I'd have taken the woman by her throat and dragged her further into the street, to be flattened by a passing steamroller? That's not very nice of you God, I may think about it, but I wouldn't really do it – and it's not that easy to get your hands on steamrollers these days."

"Amelia?"

"Yes God?"

"What are you going to do with this experience now you have it?"

"What?"

"If it helps to use your language, what are you going to do with this learning?" God repeated patiently.

"I'm going to try and remember it. I may not always live up to it - I'm only human you know."

"So you keep reminding me Amelia. Don't worry, I won't forget."

"Thank you God. I will try and remember it, the learning that is, not that I'm only human; It's you who forgets that, not me. But there's something else as well that I've noticed - it's not just that it made me feel good, or even that I made someone else feel good. It's also that if we all did it, how much better the world would be to live in. Yes, I've felt jealousy and acted on it. Yes, I've been selfish and uncaring towards others, and reacted to it by ignoring the hurt or pain I may have caused. Yes, I've been self-pitying or negative or..."

"Steady on Amelia, do not be so hard on yourself - even though it is possible to see some truth there."

"Ha Ha, very funny."

156

"Amelia, I have...."

"I know what you're going to say. You're going to say, I've told you all this before. You're going to say, what took you so long to get it? Why did I have to send the dream?"

"Am I going to say all that Amelia? You must have extraordinary powers to be so assured you have read my mind with such accuracy."

"Well it stands to reason. All I can say in my defence is that it's different when you live it, rather than just being told it. When I had my dream, it was so real, I felt I was living it. I felt it. I felt the difference between loving and hating. It was so pure, if we all felt it, the world would be remarkable."

"It is not just you I have been telling of this magnificent truth Amelia. I have been telling the whole human race for many centuries."

"You mean it isn't just me who's thick then?"

"That is not what I am saying at all Amelia and you know it."

"Ooh, where's your sense of humour gone?"

"Touché."

"Thank you God. And thank you for my dream. I know it was You."

"You are welcome Amelia."

"God, hold on, don't go yet. What about the aliens?"

"What about them?"

"Why didn't you tell us about them?"

"Why should I?"

Amelia couldn't think of an answer to that. "Well, it's only polite." was all she could come up with.

"God? Do they know about us?"

"Yes."

"Will they harm us?"

"No."

"Are they interested in us?"

"Very."

"Why, what do they want from us?"

"Nothing. It is merely that Higher Evolved Beings care about all primitive cultures and realise you have the ability to destroy your own planet. They do not want that outcome for you."

"Bloody Hell, God. You don't beat around the bush do you?"

"I have only ever given information you have needed, or with which you can cope. Intelligent species, holding primitive views and emotion, risk losing their planet. They are capable of destroying everything. So the process will start again. Destroyed, but not gone; never gone. There are different outcomes of course; the human race just has to choose."

"What should we do God, please tell me, what should we do?" Amelia felt herself pleading with Him.

"You know this. Think of your dream Amelia. Think of the bigger picture. What worked and why? What is it I have told you and all humanity over and over again?"

"Have love for everyone. Love each other, as we love ourselves and our families, treat each other with the consideration we would want to receive for ourselves?"

"Amelia, you were born knowing this; as was every other human being on earth; since the very first human beings came to be; remember now what you have forgotten. Why do you carve the world up into little pieces of land that you call countries and then fight over them? Why do you fight over your religions? Why do you wage pointless war on each other?"

"God I don't know where to start. I feel like starting with that religion, you know the one – it's a cult isn't it? Cults are wrong aren't they God?" Amelia felt like sobbing now, her previous high spirits dashed to pieces.

"You have started Amelia, by listening to your soul. Think love; act love; be love. Many of your fellow humans do this; many have done it before you. Do not judge harshly the millions of people following set beliefs. Set an example, with love, when enough of you are doing this, you will reach tipping point and truly save your planet as it stands. Then you will begin to advance into Higher Evolved Beings where there is only love. Hatred is merely a reverberation of dearth - a dearth of love."

"Dearth?"

"Scarcity, no love, or at least, not enough to make a difference. Amelia, love and be loved. That is the answer for humankind."

"Thank you God. What should I do though – or should I do anything?"

"You are welcome Amelia, you are very welcome. We all look forward to your survival, the survival of the human race. The message of love for all, is working and you have to think for yourself."

Chapter 15

Impatient Confusion

(Before I came here I was confused about this subject. Having listened to your lecture, I am still confused, but on a higher level – *Enrico Fermi*)

Amelia awoke suddenly. Disoriented, she glanced around frantically. Unable to assemble coherent thoughts, memories of the night began crowding her. 'I was flying. No, I was dreaming I was flying. Different thing. Is it though? My dream seemed real and I remember it vividly, so it must have happened. It was amazing. God was talking to me and sent a dream to me. To me? Oh, how it felt, almost… almost ecstatic. It happened; it must have done, to feel like this. No, it couldn't have done.' She tried to shake herself awake. 'Just calm yourself.' She looked down and saw she was dripping with sweat. 'After my dream, I had a long discussion with God about it….Or was I dreaming that too?'

The pain in Amelia's throbbing temples deepened miserably. She could not fathom why she felt heady with excitement one moment, only to plummet to a deep recondite depression the next. Why did she feel so agitated? 'It was an amazing dream. Supposing it was real though, supposing that's my afterlife? Perhaps it means I will die soon. Is that what it was, a signal to my death? 'But it doesn't matter,' she thought, 'it was amazing, I felt amazing.'

Therein lay Lemon's problem. *'You have no right feeling happiness, or joy or any other of that bland stuff you keep banging on about these days,'* she taunted. *'Don't get cocky now, you're just silly stupid Amelia, you have no right to move on to anything amazing and you certainly won't be a blue angel.*

You'll be a shrivelled up old slug. Shrivelled up old slug that's not going to die anytime soon, not if I can help it.'

'Happy, happy - we are happy,' chanted Sugarplum. *'Come on Lemon, you've got to face the truth; it was an amazing dream.'*

'Can anybody think of another adjective other than amazing, or have you all lost your senses? Hello, anyone out there with more than one brain cell?'

Lemon's vinegar lips shouted into the space above her head. Her world was being threatened and she was staunchly keeping up the fight. She knew that she could withstand a world of peace and harmony with the others, and that would be good for Amelia. But she had reigned almost supreme in her world for so long, albeit oft diluted by Sugarplum. Thus far, she had carte blanche to throw around her dominating weight, orbiting her domain like an avenging Angel of Satan.

Lemon remembered a life of subservience when Amelia was biddable and submissive and Reg was a little swamp, *'too timid to squidge anywhere that's for sure,'* thought Lemon. *'Why should I go back to that?'*

Amelia always knew this would happen. She knew she couldn't happily find God and be left in peace. 'Too much to ask isn't it?' She stumbled out of bed, steadying herself on the nearest post of her beautiful, beloved four-poster. 'Gosh, I do feel a little odd.'

'Little? A little odd?' scowled Lemon, giving up the shouting in favour of a more subtle approach. *'You're as odd as a paper fireguard. As odd as a green squirrel. As odd as a chocolate motorbike. You're as odd as a....'*

'Thought you were going to try the subtle approach,' said Reg. *'Look, you're frightening Sunshine, leave her out of it.'*

'Sorry Sunshine, matter of survival you see. Got to be done. Amelia, you know you've lost all reason, don't you?'

Heaven is a Donut

Lemon felt the urge to return to her natural self so with the delicacy of a battering ram, began an onslaught of bulldozing tyranny. Always to be relied upon for successfully bringing on one of her *heads*, especially when Sunshine begins quaking in her boots.

'Lemon, stop it, you're behaving like a thug; a prize thug who needs locking up.' Sugarplum was now really worried about Sunshine; she truly was quaking in her boots, as Lemon's prediction.

Lemon burst into manic laughter. *'Locking up, where do you think we are?'* she asked spitefully. *'Is this freedom? If I was free I'd be running the world by now, but no, I'm chained to you imbeciles.'*

Enticed away from little Sunshine by majestic dreams of world domination, Reg squidged to know more. *'Running the world? You mean - we could run the world?'*

'No, you Crapulent Entozoon, not we, me! I could run the world if I didn't have to stay here with you … and them.' Lemon gestured angrily at the shaking Sunshine and quietly strong and brave Sugarplum. *'Not to mention the brain challenged dipsomaniac we have to live in,'* she executed her tirade with a stab at Amelia.

'Oh, hush your mouth. Don't talk about Amelia like that. You wouldn't even be here if it weren't for her.' Sugarplum, as ever, stood stoically between Lemon and the petrified Sunshine and the smarting Reg - still puzzling over the word Entozoon. He knew it must be harsh. As for the meaning of crapulent he could hazard a guess, but he would be wrong.

'Have I misunderstood again,' he wondered? *'Sugarplum, what's a crappable entry-zone…..?'*

'Not now Reg dear,' she refereed sweetly, *'you really don't need to know.'*

'*Don't I? Are you sure? Is it a toilet? Is Lemon calling me a toilet? She's a bastard.*'

'*No dear, she's not calling you a toilet and yes dear, I'm very sure you don't need to know .... and mind your language please dear. What we have to focus on now, is calming Lemon down.*'

'*I'm never very good at that. Sorry. Sorry Sugarplum – I'll mind my language – even though Lemon doesn't.*'

Amelia splashed her face with cold water, her head throbbing to exploding point. 'Can I face work? Why do I feel so tired when I've only just woken up?' Her malaise remained; she felt ill but couldn't identify the cause. 'What's wrong with me?' She staggered across the room, grasping her pounding head as she sat down on her small bedroom chair. Opening her cards, they fell despondently to the floor. She was unsure of God's meaning when He said, 'do not judge harshly,' did that mean she should mind her own business? 'I'll only find peace when I'm dead,' she supposed with foreboding, 'when I'm in my Blue Angel phase. Only then.' Amelia persuaded herself to stop obsessing about the religion in which she was raised, 'it's not up to me is it and it's only making me ill thinking about it. I'll lead by example – yes.'

She scratched at the fallen cards in half-hearted attempt to gather them up, but she could not quell the rising sickness.

"God? It's not supposed to be like this. I should be feeling good - I feel crap. I read the newspapers yesterday, have you got any idea how depressing the news is?"

"Why don't you just stop all the misery?" she pleaded. Then an afterthought, 'how can I not do something – children are being abused and until someone does something, it will continue.'

Silence.

Heaven is a Donut

"God......... ?"

Chapter 16

A Serious Question

(Children in famine, victims tortured by oppressors, helpless old people a hated burden to their sons, and the whole world of loneliness, poverty, and pain make a mockery of what human life should be. I long to alleviate the evil, but I cannot, and I too suffer. What have I lived for? - *Bertrand Russell*)

"Dear God?"

"Yes Amelia?"

"Why are we all so miserable? Why don't you stop people being so malicious and nasty to each other all the time? Why do so many people want to have power and control over others?" She waited, knowing she sounded like a child. 'I think I've thrown God a biggie, he's gone very quiet.'

"Are you still talking to me?" she asked cautiously. "If you are who you say you are - you could do it couldn't you? You could stop it all in a second. So why don't you?"

She knew she had asked God questions she wasn't supposed to ask, and He would expect her to accept the age-old explanation of, *God moves in mysterious ways.* "Well I don't accept it; never have," she stood defiantly. "What's the point of being mysterious?" she had thrown at Him. "Why don't you just get on with it and save the rotting masses?" She waited, her quiet pose not projecting the rising panic and the inevitable reasons to justify her heinous scepticism that was creeping in.

'*Surely you are entitled to ask?*' Lemon broke in sharply with equal insolence.

"Thank you, Lemon." Amelia stated, maintaining her precarious insubordination to God.

"Amelia?"

Oh God, here it comes (must stop the blasphemy, even if it is only in my head). "Yes God?"

"If a small boy runs towards danger, his hands outstretched, feeling pure enjoyment at the excitement, and each time he did this, his Mother pulled him gently away so he did not harm himself, what would that mean?"

"It would mean she was a very loving and vigilant Mother and he was lucky to have her to protect him."

God continued, "What if every time the little boy did this, his Mother just gently pulled him away without saying a word, perhaps attempting to distract him with other pursuits and this was the way of it throughout all of his life. Not saying a word to him, just taking him away from the danger each time?"

"Well, he would be safe, that's true. But... he would also be dependent upon her, never understanding the meaning of danger." Amelia answered confidently.

"Yes and he would have never been exposed to it or had it explained to him."

"God, are you saying he has to hurt himself first so he learns how to avoid it?"

"You are not listening to my Truth. I am saying he needs to understand and believe the explanation. He needs to believe the Truth to not be hurt. If he does not believe, he may injure himself first and then believe his Mother. Humankind can either have Faith, and not be harmed or be harmed before they believe."

"Umh, right then. I think I know where you're going with this." She nodded sagely as if it was all her idea. "What you're saying is we can have faith, or we find out for ourselves, which is usually the hard way." She digressed, "I think I've heard that story before God, or read it somewhere," irked that this wasn't an original piece of God wisdom.

"Do you think you are the first person to ask me this Amelia?"

"OK God, You've got a point there." (She hoped God wasn't always going to be right. It reminded her of rebound-man, and had found it to be not only extremely irritating, but impossible to live with).

"Amelia?"

"Yes God?"

"I have given mankind everything necessary to create a joyful and fulfilling life. What more could you all want from me? What more could I give the human race they do not already possess? What would be the purpose of me protecting humankind from life itself, from life as it really is? From freedom of choice? What would you learn?"

"Nothing God. Absolutely nothing. Sometimes though God, it really hurts. To be honest, sometimes life sucks, it just plain sucks. I don't know how to find happiness. Surely that's not too much to ask? Why can't I be happy? That's all I want. Not mega riches. I'm not power crazy. I don't have any master plan to take over the world or usurp You by starting an eccentric cult - interesting thought though, I'll save that one for another time, perhaps when I've had a glass of wine or so, I'd probably make quite a good Despot. But mainly, I just want to be happy. Just good old happy. How do I find happiness? It's certainly been eluding me all my life!" Amelia was aware of the hysteria sneaking in, raising her voice harshly to exclamation.

"Amelia?"

"Yes God?"

"What is happiness?"

'*Silly question,*' whispered Lemon.

'*Hey up, I know, I know, I know what happiness is.*' squidged Reg. '*it's not silly at all, you're just stupid Lemon. Happiness is when I'm being noticed and respected.*' Reg breathed in his delight and began stroking himself as he spoke.

Ignoring Reg's self-importance, she answered, "It's a feeling isn't it, an internal feeling. From inside oneself," she added in case God wasn't sure what internal meant.

"So why are you looking for happiness outside yourself?" God challenged her this time.

Amelia could understand his line of reasoning. Even her Lemon popped up looking impressed. Reg squidged in bewilderment. 'Happiness wasn't a place in the middle of nowhere. A hard to find out of the way place in the back of beyond: end of line, hidden terminus. Or a mirage; always in sight but forever out of reach.' She organised her unsettled thoughts knowing this would entail a good deal of effort on her part, 'I've got to start thinking *happy* haven't I. If I think it - I am it. If I feel it - I'll live it. My thoughts become my reality.'

'Is this a light-bulb moment?' Amelia asked Lemon and Reg, but they had gone suspiciously quiet.

'*Yes, yes*' squeaked Sugarplum joyously looking forward to '*happy, happy, happy.*'

Amelia suffered an immediate setback, clearly not ready to accept that responsibility for her happiness lay totally at her own door. 'With any luck my light-bulb moment has electrocuted them,' Amelia thought nastily about her two troublemakers Lemon and Reg, 'that would be true happiness, and you needn't start either, you crotchety candy bar,' she frowned at Sugarplum.

Lemon spoke with seriousness. '*Well then, stay in your pathetic self-pitying misery.*' She felt the hidden pain clawing to Amelia's fore, piercing through her heart and tearing her flesh. *'But you don't want to stay in misery,'* Lemon mitigated. *'Amelia, listen to me - you don't have to ignore the bad in you to see the good in you. You don't have to pretend there's no bad in you, and that it's something or someone else who is evil. That is not so - not even Reg, he's not evil. That also includes me by the way. We are the sum of all parts; we are one. You separate us because you cannot face these parts of you. Solely, we are selfish and destructive. United, we can reach Higher Self.'*

'I know. But that's scary, that means it's down to me - I have to take responsibility.'

Incredibly, it was Lemon who made progress towards the merging and healing of a split personality, despite her more than slight reservations in the knowledge that she was talking herself out of a job. She also knew, with underlying certainty, that for Amelia's survival it had to be. Lemon, somewhere somehow, in a more enlightened guise, was extant within Amelia and therefore, really didn't have anything to worry about.

Lemon burst into song, *'I will survive. I will survive.....'*

"God, is this really a light-bulb moment? A moment of clarity?" said Amelia, whilst vaguely wondering why music had suddenly filtered into her mentality, skipping jubilantly through her brain cells like dancers around a maypole.

"That is up to you Amelia."

"Smartipants", she replied to God, adding a little prayer of hope that he really did have a sense of humour.

"Thank you Amelia," he smiled.

"I will survive, I will survive ..... I don't know why I'm singing that, just popped into my head..... I am a bit of a Prissy Miss aren't I?"

"You have come a long way Amelia in such a short time. You should stop disliking yourself. Be proud of yourself."

Amelia blanched. "Proud of myself? What have I ever done to be proud of?"

"You have just challenged yourself, looked at yourself in the mirror..."

"The fat side."

"Yes, the fat side of the mirror, the magnified you. You have studied yourself, your whole self not just the parts you like or don't like, and have begun to piece them together where they belong. Think of the little boy. What will he learn if his Mother does not allow him to discover how to keep himself safe, how to live in the world?"

"He'll always be looking to her or someone else to do it for him."

"For what? What will he expect from her and all others?"

"Everything I guess. He is devoid of all responsibility isn't he, including his own happiness as well as his own welfare. He'll not only be looking to others to make him happy, he'll also be blaming them if he's not. Like me - I hear you say?"

"Excellent comprehension. This is the coming together of a complicated puzzle. You have realised you can manage this life with dignity, strength and wisdom. You have realised your own responsibility. You have realised there is nothing you need from me, you can do it all by yourself."

"Gosh, have I really? Who'd have thought."

"I have always thought. I have always known. You are no different to anyone else. Every living person on earth, no matter what their beginnings, can do the same.

You are the same. You are all one, as you know, this you have said."

"It was Lemon who said it."

"YOU said it. You make your own life Amelia, that is as good as it gets."

"Gosh." Amelia repeated feebly, with the hint of a grin.

Heaven is a Donut

Chapter 17

The Rollercoaster

(A friend is someone who gives you total freedom to be yourself – Jim Morrison)

Amelia was feeling flowery: Flowery and spiritual again, bursting to tell everybody else what to do so they felt the same. How they absolutely must start praying and grinning because grinning showed the world how happy you are. And being happy meant you felt flowery and spiritual. 'How to change what people think?' she queried to herself. 'My, "It's Great to Grin" and "Grin if you've found God" campaigns were an abysmal failure, no idea why.'

'It all makes sense to me, so if it makes sense to me then everybody else must surely understand; I'm always the last one to *get* anything.' However, she appeared to hit stonewall with her next sortie, "Feel Flowery and Convert Mankind" crusade, hitting the decks even quicker than her previous two ingenious attempts, and it happened very close to home. Lucinda said she didn't need to pray to God to feel flowery, she felt like that every time she went out for a drink and funnily enough, she started grinning pretty soon after. Greg said he felt flowery every time he went shopping for clothes and started grinning when he looked at himself in the mirror because he was so fit.

'I don't know what would make Tris feel flowery,' she thought desolately, 'he's occupied elsewhere these days, but it would probably be watching a rugby game, or pulling on his cricket whites ready for a match, or choir practice. Yes, that would do it for him - and he grins whilst singing, that's why he looks so stupid' she judged, in a spiteful but futile attempt to smother her love for him.

172

A shadow quickly cast, she spiralled to earth with a very painful bump. 'It's not supposed to be like this. What God said at the time made perfect sense. Now I'm feeling glum again. Fed up. Sad. Ill. He said if I say I'm happy, I'd be happy. Did He say that? I can't remember now.' Worry set in. Worry and fear, fear for the human race, fear for self. 'What sort of crazy rollercoaster pendulum is this? It's no fun to be up in the heady heights of spiritual joy one minute and then down into suicidal depths of despair the next. God – I'm exhausted.'

Amelia was no longer feeling flowery, when later that week she carried her coffee to one of the tables outside the café and squashed herself in a chair up against the wall, in an attempt to be invisible. She returned once again to her intemperate conjectures. 'Can you have a rollercoastering pendulum – what would it look like? I'm supposed to be feeling happy and flowery not like I won the lottery but lost my ticket. But I am though aren't I? That's exactly how I feel. Even Lemon was pleasant for a while. Lemon suggested if we work together we'd be like Higher Self. Now I think she was just winding me up again. Lemon? Oh so we've gone quiet now have we?'

Her thoughts chugging like an old engine past its prime, she suddenly recognised Greg striding, or was that strutting, towards her from across the square. 'Gosh, he's got a fab walk' she deliberated as she admired his progress.

"Hey Grip, you know you've got it all going on don't you?"

"Sure have honey child. What are you doing sitting out here talking animatedly to your invisible friend?"

"I wasn't. Just wanted a quiet cup of coffee outside and watch the world go by, do a bit of people watching, you know the sort of thing. "

"It looked to me like a protracted chinwag and no one has got up and walked away, therefore, I can only conclude, you were talking to yourself. Anyway, aren't you supposed to be at work?"

"Aren't you?"

"On my way, honey child. But I'll stay with you if you need someone to talk to – other than yourself of course?"

"Bless your beautiful heart my love. No, off you go, you can fill me in later on how the play is going."

Greg was not ready to tell his friend his sorry tale of multiple job losses just yet and was terribly late - again. He turned to walk away as he squeezed her gently on the shoulder; suddenly he spun back round to face her, "How's the ... the... you know, flowery grinning and finding God stuff going on?"

"Think I've lost Him again."

"Don't worry Millie-Moo; I'm sure He won't have gone far. And, in the meantime, you've still got me. Catch up with you later. Get back to work you lazy girl."

She smiled at his comment as she watched his sickeningly attractive back disappear, carried by *that* walk and she found herself wishing for the hundredth time he wasn't gay, 'we'd make such a hot couple' - she ejected Tristan temporarily from her Ideal-Home vision. 'Life is so unfair. Oh God,' she groaned, 'I wish he hadn't caught me talking to Lemon, he'll tell everyone now.'

'Can I remind you: me – that would be Lemon - is you. Therefore, he was correct in his assumption that you were sitting in deep and audible conversation with yourself, causing great concern to all those near and dear to you.' Lemon coolly asserted herself.

"I'm going to kill you." Amelia spoke in monotone to Lemon.

"What me?" said a startled man who, until then, had been sitting quietly reading his newspaper at a nearby table. So quietly, she hadn't noticed him.

"You plan to kill me?" His words jarred the air.

"Oh no, not you."

"You're going to kill the man who just walked away?"

"Oh no, not him. Her."

The man moved edgily, trying to look furtively around for the 'her' to whom the crazy woman referred, whilst trying to stay ahead of the situation; keep calm, no sudden movements to unhinge her; be alert to any move in his direction, however slight. There was no one there, he estimated, and had never been - not a female anyway. Had he got time to run? Would she catch up and thrust a knife into his back. He should have moved the moment he'd heard her talking to herself, he chastised himself for his tardiness; it could now mean the difference between life and death – his.

"Do you believe in God?" Amelia quizzed him with piercing blue eyes above a fiendishly beatific grin.

He ran, knocking over his chair as he went. 'Not as elegant as Greg' she pondered. 'What's his problem?'

"He didn't pay for his coffee," she informed the waitress emerging from the café to see the cause of the rumpus. "Tell you what," Amelia wanted her flowery feeling back, "I'll pay for his coffee, no need for you to suffer by having it taken out of your wages just because of some thoughtless little waster."

She felt agitated. The man's actions had prompted her to want to ask God why some people behaved so oddly towards others. And what about Greg? She desperately wanted to talk to God about Greg,

She scuttled home, ignoring her phone jangling noisily.

She knew what the Bible said about homosexuality, or thought she did, but hoped God would have something different to say. 'Why would He say something different to the Bible? Why wouldn't He? Things change, society changes, notions change, and people interpret it differently.' She sweated with worry over her beloved friend. 'How could God censure such a good man?'

What would God's answer be?

Chapter 18

Money and Saving the World

(What are you committed to? Have you started, or are you still thinking about it and making excuses? Do you work toward your goal each day? – *Jonathan Lockwood Huie*)

"Dear God?"

"Yes Amelia?"

"I've been thinking."

"Really?"

Not a very positive response from God, judging by the wearied tone she sensed. "Why are you being sceptical God? What have I done to deserve that? Are you implying there's something wrong with my thought processes?" she demanded to know.

"Nothing at all Amelia. Remember the last time you made this statement? The last time you said, 'God I've been thinking', you wanted to storm the Vatican; protest outside, chain yourself to the railings without knowing if there are any railings with which to chain yourself, until granted an audience with the Pope so as to impart your wisdom. In other words, deliver an almighty verbal grilling, apropos to changing some of his Church's policies."

Amelia wanted to convey that it was a perfectly acceptable plan, and, 'let's face it in the 21st century, someone has to do it.' However, God wasn't going to allow a hijacking of discussion. With brooding silence, she smouldered inwardly at his shabby listening skills.

"Previously, you were planning to stalk a major celebrity, coercing him into capitulation of your demands, handing over millions of his own money so you could set up a centre to help stop domestic violence; working with the perpetrators, victims and their families."

"Yes, yes, yes." She could hold her silence no longer. "Can you think of many better causes than that? We're talking about rebuilding families here, you know." she challenged Him.

"It is truly a worthy enterprise Amelia."

"So?"

"Who was it, your victim … I refer to your chosen celebrity?" God posed an unexpected question.

"What?" her reply a cautious slingshot.

"Whom did you intend to stalk and extract millions from?"

"Kerry McKenzie."

"Whom?" God enquired inscrutably.

'Doesn't He know who Kerry McKenzie is? Yes of course he does, God knows everybody – He even knows me, and I'm nobody.'

"Kerry McKenzie – the pop star."

"Why Kerry McKenzie?" God wanted to know.

"Stands to reason for goodness sake," she injected enthusiasm into her argument, now feeling on safer territory. "He can spare it. Why does anyone need all that money? We can only be in one room at any given time, yet some people have hundreds; and big toys, like cars and boats. I don't know about Kezza - that's Kerry McKenzie by the way, (she helpfully informed God, as if on pet-name terms with a man she had never met), but from what I've read about him, he's ready to help those who haven't had his success in life and is happy to spread it around a bit. He likes to have a finger or two in a 'Charity-Pie' here and there – as long as it's a veggie of course - hah. Veggie Pie." Amelia beamed as she congratulated herself on her spontaneous wit. "Anyway, what's wrong with my ideas? It's just as easy to think big as it is to think small you know!" She discharged her rant with a flourish and she was particularly fond of that quote - having no idea from whence it came.

"Nothing. In fact, I commend your honourable motive, as I do Mr McKenzie and anyone else who supports their environment and fellow mankind."

"Thank you. So why do I feel a 'But' coming on then?" she enquired.

"Because there is one. Actually there are three."

"THREE?" Go for it then," she challenged, "I'm up for it. Hit me with it, I'm ready."

"The first 'But' being, have you considered the implications of your actions? Have you considered the affect on someone of being stalked? Does he know you? No, he does not."

'Typical,' she thought huffily, 'God answering his own question; I would never do such a thing.'

"How would you feel Amelia? A stranger pursuing you, someone knowing where you are, what you are doing, possibly aware that this stranger also knows who and where your family are?"

"Alright. I see your point. OK, I haven't thought that one through exactly. Possibly, just possibly, tracking down my intended target like a big game hunter isn't going to be conducive to him handing over lots of his cash. But it's still a good idea, right?" Amelia attempted to claw her way back to her rightful place - the brainwave section of God's head.

"Enlisting support to help families live together without abuse is a very worthwhile undertaking Amelia." God soothed her.

She felt soothed.

"Thank you," she said nobly.

"But not by using intimidation Amelia."

Her noblesse oblige squashed with a reprimand, the situation worsened, He identified *three* 'Buts', she remembered with a groan: three possible fatal flaws in her plans. No she couldn't believe it. "OK, so that's the first one dealt with." 'No biggy really, after all, risking possible arrest and a jail term for stalking and extorting funds by coercion is easily sorted. Just don't do it.'

"What's next then?"

"Well Amelia, the second 'But' is why is it you feel the need to change the policies of a religion that has been in existence far longer than you have?"

"They're wrong."

"On whose authority?"

"Mine."

"Anyone else?"

"No. Well, actually there are possibly a few others who agree with me. They think that certain things are wrong and need amending to come into line with society today."

"But you do not know for sure? Basically what you are saying is, you know how you feel about it but you cannot speak for others. Is that what you are saying Amelia?"

"Yes" she whispered.

"I did not quite hear that Amelia, and no it is not because I am deaf." Had God seen her head rise slightly at this and anticipated her cheeky reminder that he needed to get his ears checked?

"YES,"

"There is no need to shout Amelia."

"Sorry."

"This leads me to my last 'But'." God relentlessly persisted with his central theme, namely, have-a-go-at-Amelia day. He umpired her best-loved negative reaction of Poor-Me with, "You have not actually *done* anything."

"What?"

"You have done nothing. Have you booked your plane ticket to Rome?"

"No."

"Have you put together a business plan for Mr McKenzie?"

"No."

"Do you know how to contact him?"

"No."

"Do you............"

"Alright, alright. Jesus Christ, God, you're turning into me - so repetitive. I get the message you know. What can I say," Amelia defended herself, "I'm an *ideas* person, not an Action Man, I can't do it all myself can I?"

"But Amelia, you are not doing *anything* yourself are you, except sitting on the fence pontificating."

"God that's harsh."

"Amelia, it is a very safe place to be and many fine ideas can come about whilst neutrally fence sitting. Tell me, what do ideas achieve without action? Does it feed the hungry? Does it clothe the poor? Does it give the victimised and the abused somewhere to go to heal their emotional and physical wounds? Does it help challenge and stop injustice?"

"That's rich, coming from you God. You know how to twist the knife don't you. You're the biggest fence sitter there is. I don't see you doing anything much. Do You? Well, do You? Oh I see, you expect me to do it all? Me to do your job for you, as quite clearly you're not doing it yourself." Having decided attack was the best means of defence - she became a little taken aback by her own outburst.

"Do not look so worried Amelia; I will let that one go."

"Well, you would wouldn't you? Mr Fence-sitter, I rest my case."

"I let it go Amelia because we've discussed this before." Patience surely, only God could find.

Amelia had a vision - God was wearing spectacles and looking over the top of them right now all school-teacherish, having an air about him of 'I'm trying to get you to understand but you're making it bloody hard work.'

God persevered, "Amelia?"

"Yes God?" She was suddenly cheered at the thought she had managed to exasperate Him - no mean feat surely.

"Amelia, I have given all humankind everything they need to make a difference, to make changes where change is necessary. I want nothing from you other than you *know* yourself and you *Be* yourself. Through that, you can change the world. Through that, humankind can change anything. Anything. When people start being selfish and thinking about themselves they'll start thinking as one. That is when changes for the better will be possible."

"Hey, hey, now hold your horses Mr God! Selfish? Selfish?" Amelia's voice rose. "You're the One always telling us mere mortals *not* to be selfish. Have you been drinking? Are you drunk? You sound it. What would happen to us all if you got drunk? That's an interesting thought isn't it God? I know what happens to me in my world when I get drunk." Having invoked a rather lurid fascination, Amelia was undecided whether to be worried, or to imperviously await the havoc an intoxicated God could wreak upon the earth.

"Amelia, if your child was starving. What would you do?" God startled her with what appeared to be a change of subject, or was it?

"Anything it took, God. Work harder, beg, steal, and borrow. Anything of course."

"If your home was washed away by floods, what would you do?"

"I'd find a new home, or I'd rebuild that one. Brick by brick if necessary, I'd be that determined. I don't like being cold and wet."

God had another question for her, "If your loved one was dying for want of a transplant, what would you do?"

"I'd make a nuisance of myself - not difficult - I'd lobby for changes in the system. I'd contact a hundred or more celebrities - not just one, if money helped. I'd use TV and the media to raise awareness. I'd appeal - Oh God I don't know, I'd do anything it took rather than stand by and watch someone I love die. Anyone would do the same in that situation."

"Of course, Amelia, already so much activity. So much *doing*: all because you are thinking about your*self* and your loved ones, the people *you* love. You do not want to live in a world without them. You do not want to see them suffer or have some injustice befall them, so you do something about it. Can you see how powerful it is to think about one*self*? When everyone begins *doing* that, what changes can be brought about in this world?"

"OMG, God. The earth will be transformed. By thinking about ourselves, being *self*ish as you call it, what we are actually doing is thinking of everyone as if oneself: the homeless; the starving; the dying. If they are *my* loved ones, I'll do something about it instead of just fence sitting. By thinking of everyone, we are changing the world just as if it was happening in our own personal life, to our own family and friends; can't push it under the carpet so you don't have to look at it, when you say it like that. Now I truly understand the expression, "turn a blind eye." That's what we do. How cruel and unfeeling we are, to just ignore it. God what shall we do? Come on, you're the one with all the answers."

"Only humankind has the answers Amelia. I have not created this world - you have. Look to yourselves to make the changes necessary. Stop turning a blind eye."

"But God, it needs to be a collective you – I can't do it all by myself."

"That is understood Amelia."

"I agree with everything you said, but it's my turn for 'buts' - I struggle to keep it up, keep the momentum going. I get carried away with other things in life; work, or going out and enjoying myself, or saving up for that new designer handbag I've had my eye on for ages. How trivial it all sounds when you think about starvation and inequality. But it's life. That's how it is and that's how it has always been. How do we change it?"

"You know the answer to that. You change it. You change you. When enough of you change, you change the world."

"Wow………..God?"

"Yes Amelia?"

"I've just remembered something. I forgot to say what it was I'd been thinking about."

"You became sidetracked."

"ME! It was you not me, you went off on one of your rants. It's important, what's just been said is important I know that, but so is this."

"What is it you would like to say Amelia?"

"I'm worried about Greg. He is the nicest person you could ever meet. Kind and generous with a good heart."

"What is troubling you Amelia?"

"He's gay. That means homosexual in your old-fashioned language God."

"What troubles you so, Amelia?"

Ignoring God, Amelia continued. "At least, I've wondered if he may be bi. I happen to know something he doesn't remember telling me: he had a huge crush on a student at university, don't know who - but it...well, I know this, it was... it was a woman!"

Amelia hoped God was still listening. "I'm not saying he's secretly heterosexual, because I've known him fall madly in love with a man. You see, when he falls in love, it's about the person - not whether they are male or female. This suggests to me that it's not just about sex, as he'd have us all believe, but he feels much more deeply than he wants to let on – and there's lots of people just like that, but Greg won't talk about it. It upsets me because I see conflict in his eyes, but the main thing I want to ask you is...is..."

"I am listening to you Amelia."

"According to most religions, homosexuality is a sin. That makes him a sinner and therefore, bad. But he's not bad; he's good, mainly. He's had trouble being sexually faithful, but he tries to be honest in relationships and he never takes risks. I believe deep down he's a good and honourable man and it troubles me the way you judge him."

"Amelia, how have I judged him? Greg is as you describe. That is what I too see. I make no judgements on his or anyone else's lifestyle."

"You mean, it doesn't matter to you that he's gay?"

"I make no judgement on humankind. Humankind has free will."

"Gosh. So many though God, so many people have suffered over this, when they didn't need to? Is that what you're saying? If Greg knew this, he may not be lampooning his way through life to cover up his own tangled emotions. Oh God - and don't say pot & kettle – I get it."

"Amelia I wish only for people to find happiness and joy. Causing physical, spiritual, mental or emotional pain to others holds the human race to account. Selfish ego will bring about destruction - by your own hand, not by the hand of God."

Amelia tortured herself, 'How will the world understand these judgements are bigoted and unnecessary. What shall I do, what shall I do......how will we learn to stop fighting each other; to love each other; to treat all with equality and to stop standing by, watching others starve or suffer.' Her painful musings returned to the topic burning into her since she received the email, 'God is saying I should take more action, but what can I do......what can I do about a cult that thinks it's doing God's will, thus, out of ignorance, allowing innocents to suffer. "Suffer the little children" the Bible says. Doesn't it also say children are sacred? Any religion, or cult, or society that does not protect its children, is not treating them as sacred.'

She buckled under the weight of responsibility. It was a heavy burden – that of the ills and unfairness – of the WHOLE WORLD. Wake up Amelia, taking it on alone is an act of ego, God would tell her. Think through what it is realistic and useful to undertake, God would tell her.

But she had stopped listening.

Heaven is a Donut

Chapter 19

Work

(But mark my words; someday she'll get what is coming to her. Karma's a bigger bitch than she is – *Kathleen Brooks*).

After two weeks away, Amelia trudged the well-known corridors of her office with a heavy heart dreading the moment when she would have to paint on the smile and pretend to all how well she is and everything is fine. 'Well I'm not and it isn't.' Even Amelia was prepared to admit that now.

She responded gallantly to the many genuine echoes of, "Hope you're feeling better." She felt unreal. Her existence held no logic, no anchor. As she floated in and out of the computer screen, having taken all morning to renew her passwords so she could actually access her emails, she was aware only of rising panic-stricken regret. Deploring the new passwords telling tales of her failure, she could now actually see the hundreds of unread emails staring at her with recrimination. Self-reproaching for telling her doctor she was fine and ready to return to work. Regret. Regret rising from bed that morning. She was tired; so dog-tired.

"My bones are tired, do you hear me?" she catechised the unfeeling computer eye before her. No response. "Unsympathetic conceited Cyclops. All you do is moan at me, boss me around, telling me what I should do, shouldn't do. Give me work I don't want. You're like all the rest of them. I'm going to throw you out the window."

Her tormentor walked past at a well-chosen moment. Amelia's head ducked, endeavouring to be inconspicuous, feeling sure the woman had heard and

187

pretended to stifle a snicker. "Bitch," Amelia mouthed to the overweening head, "hope your hair-bun gets trapped in the lift doors," she added as she watched the immaculately neat hair-do disappear through the doorway.

In her back-to-work interview with her Line Manager, Amelia had not managed to enunciate how she was feeling and why she was withdrawn. It was hard to explain that she was not so weak and useless that one person's malice was enough to drive her to tears and helpless inactivity. She had tried to elucidate, she wasn't blaming someone else because she missed her deadlines. Nor did she have proof of anything untoward, other than a new staff member informing her that the woman had said, "The job must be easy. If Amelia can do it - anyone can do it." However, lucidity was a faraway dream, her Line Manager suggesting this could possibly be a way her colleague was helping a new member of staff feel at ease, "especially as everyone acknowledges how good you are at your job Amelia?" "Yes, possibly," Amelia deferred.

'Helping? Dripping with superiority complex more like.' Lemon snarled in Amelia's head. *'Couldn't have gone better.'* Lemon continued to sneer at Amelia as she withdrew to her desk.

'Ever heard of lemon curd?' was Amelia's tart response.

Amelia ruminated throughout the day. The persistent, unblinking computer screen failing in its duty to be of any use to her whatsoever: not one email was read, not one reply sent. 'I can't do this, why am I here?' She waited for an answer. None was forthcoming.

"Look here," she reproved the computer sternly, "I'm trying to save the world, how am I ever going to manage to do that if I can't even control the voices in my own head – let alone the rest of the galaxy?"

'*Now, now dear,*' said Sugarplum sweetly, '*that isn't what God said. He said change you. You change you - lead by example.*' Sugarplum's face (if she had one) infiltrated the screen as Amelia heard the disembodied words resonate around her head.

What could Amelia see? She never visualised her voices but could describe them perfectly, so strong were their characters. She leaned closer to the screen in an effort to see something. An image to which she could say, "There you are Sugarplum, so that's what you look like." Swirling coloured lights overpowered her eyes, enticing her to dizzy disorientation.

'*That's what Amelia's trying to say, you half-baked sugar loaf,*' Lemon scorned. '*She couldn't even change a light bulb, the state she's in at the moment, let alone turn the whole crazy world into a spectre of delight; a place of invigorating joyfulness in which we all reside in bliss – what bollocks.*'

Darkness had taken over the screen, beautiful lights ebbing. 'Oh that's evil. Lemon, you're evil. It's coming back, taking over,' Amelia breathed. 'How can I change me?' Tears threatened. She heard far away voices, not phantom sounds from inside but from the outside world. One or two of her colleagues had started gathering.

'*Oh look at them moving in for the kill,*' whispered Lemon perniciously.

"Amelia, whatever is the matter?" Katrina asked, bending protectively over Amelia, genuinely worried for her friend and colleague. "You have been coughing today, are you feeling unwell? Look if you do, just go home honey."

"Katrina you are sweet, thank you for your concern. I don't feel too well to be honest."

"Nothing is worth not looking after yourself for, especially not this job; you won't be thanked for it. I'll let the Manager know you have to go home, don't worry. Would you like me to take you?"

Anchored by Lemon's darkness, Amelia stared at the screen facing her, on which it felt her life depended. Unable to focus on Katrina and steeling herself not to be a fool at work, she directed her reply to the computer, "No I'll be alright, but thanks again, you are lovely and I do apprec...." The words tailed off incoherently.

"She's been like that all day." Said Tightbunhead as she glided past the small crowd. "Hasn't done a scrap of work. She's not ill; she's always been a bit oversensitive, weak to be honest, obviously just not ready – still a bit .... *fragile.*"

With that, Amelia arose, leaving the building without a backward glance at the now deeply disturbed Katrina.

Chapter 20

Sometimes

(If you can't get rid of the skeleton in your closet, you'd
best teach it to dance - *George Bernard Shaw*)

An exhausted, fretful Amelia struggled with sleep. She
noticed the redness in her eyes and the dark circles under
them. She sat up in bed, clasping her hands tightly,
desperation seeping through her veins.
"Dear God?"
"Yes Amelia?"
"Am I fragile?"
"Sometimes."
"Am I weak?"
"Sometimes, Amelia, yes you are."
"Oh." Amelia was aware that her shoulders were
hunching to the deflation creeping upon her, with a
familiar floating stealth, haunting her body. She reminded
herself of a balloon once bursting with the pride of some
wonderfully exotic thing, reaching its full potential only for
the air to slowly escape, inch by expelling inch, blackballing
into a shrivelled has-been, or has-balloon in this case,
impatiently whinnying its way to a chaotic undignified
landing.
"God?"
"Yes Amelia?"
"Am I lazy?"
"Sometimes, Amelia, yes you are."
"Great, well thanks. No I mean it ... thank you,
thank you so much." Amelia's ego otherwise known as
Hey-up Reg, sprang, squidging quickly into the favoured

locale - up front and larger than life. *'Hey up, who dares to criticise the great and magnificent Reg?'*

"Why do you ask Amelia?" 'God sounds unfeelingly cheerful,' thought Amelia.

"Oh you know. Work stuff. I have a feeling that someone at work doesn't like me very much. It shocked me a bit. I mean, why wouldn't anyone like me... Me?" Despite Lemon whispering in her ear that it was infinitely possible if not probable, that someone could take a dislike to her – instantly in some cases, Amelia waited for God to adjudicate with an appeasing comment along the lines of, "How could that possibly be? You are infinitely loveable and everybody who knows you, adores you... anyone worth knowing that is...." type of comment. Unfortunately she waited in vain. No verbal stroking forthcoming.

"Well that confirms it then. I'm obviously a horrible person ... and you agree."

"How have I done that Amelia?"

"You said I'm all those horrible things, lazy, weak (ugh), fragile. I'm horrible." Amelia was temporarily stuck for any adjective other than horrible to describe this terrible predicament of unlikeability in which she had just discovered herself.

"Anything else you want to tell me about while we're here God? Any other nasty little trait you know of, that I should be made aware?"

"How about self-pity?"

"Oh shut up." Amelia stuck her fingers in her ears and crumpled her face as she squeezed her eyes tightly closed. *'Like that'll shut God out,'* Lemon smirked, beginning to have fun. Amelia ventured on, realising that as painful as the truth is at times, it couldn't be left like this. She had to know what God really thought of her. After all she did ask.

"I'm sorry I told you to shut up God, it's just that it's hard to hear. That's all really; I don't like it. I want to be loved and popular, not hated." Her posture straightening as she spoke.

"Apology accepted Amelia, but you're missing the mark."

"It's all extremely obvious to me." Amelia was overconfident she had not missed the mark, the painful truth glaring her in the face.

"No Amelia, I said *sometimes*, as I have said before, not the sum of all parts. *Sometimes* you are any one of those things. But you are not all of those things all of the time. There are many facets to you, as is the case with all."

"I didn't hear you saying anything NICE about me." Amelia mooched, blissfully unaware she was practicing her, suggested-by-God, trait of self-pity with great enthusiasm.

Amelia continued, "This is serious, how would you like it God if people see only the negative in you and never see or acknowledge good?" Amelia grappled with a gross sense of injustice welling, as if the venom of the whole world weighed upon her shoulders.

"This I experience." God answered quietly. "It poses interesting questions Amelia. Turn it around. How would I feel if I saw people of the world as having only negative in them and no good? How would I *react* if I thought there was only negative and no good in the world? What would I not be seeing?"

"The good in people? Those who love you? Not to mention reasons why the world is worth saving."

"Yes, and what else would I not be seeing - about myself?"

"The other stuff do you mean? When you *do* help people? And let's face it, while we're on the subject of peoples' shortcomings, you've got a few yourself you know - you don't always help do you."

"Are you calling me lazy Amelia?"

"Well God, you are - *sometimes*. Why is that? Why don't you always help out when you're needed?"

"Why do you not help when you're needed?"

"I don't know. I don't know. Sometimes I just don't want to. What's your excuse?"

"That is not an excuse Amelia; it is your honest answer. *Sometimes* you do not feel like it."

"But you're God. You've got to feel like it - all the time, for everyone, whether you like it or not. That's your job. You can't have a sometimes like the rest of us can."

"You are right. I do not have, nor do I need a sometimes. That is because I have already fulfilled all of my sometimes. I have fulfilled my purpose. The rest is up to you. I have given humankind all the skills ever needed to function in this world as positive, helpful, calm and happy individuals. So why do they not?"

"You're asking me? I don't know. That's like asking me the meaning of life."

"That is exactly what I'm asking you Amelia. Tell me this - what do you think I should do about it?"

Amelia, aware of excitement at the turn of discussion, impatient for knowledge, she felt on the brink of some great and worthwhile understanding.

God continued, "So, it is not easy is it, let us think now: If I were personal nursemaid to all; picking them up when they fall; reminding them when they forget; guiding them when they are lost: Are they being fragile? Are they being lazy? Are they being weak? Are they being self-pitying? Sorry Amelia, did you just sniff?"

"No."

"Ah. Where was I? Oh yes. I think we have already had this exchange Amelia. I have done my part."

"Didn't like to say of course, but yes, you are repeating Yourself."

"So, it would help to get back to discussing you Amelia."

"About time."

"Yes, I thought you would say that. So?"

"So what God?"

"So what else are you? If *sometimes* you are fragile and *sometimes* you are weak or lazy and *sometimes* you are self-pitying, *somet...*"

Amelia interrupted. "Do you have to rub it in? I get the picture."

God ignored Amelia's growing discomfiture by encouraging, "If you are all or any of those things *sometimes*, what else are you?"

"Well, I can be quite nice *sometimes*. I can be quite erm, pleasant, agreeable, even helpful - *sometimes*. I make people laugh - *sometimes*."

"Anything else?"

"I can be polite - *sometimes*. Quiet – *sometimes*. I can be friendly and approachable."

"*Sometime*s." God stated.

"Exactly, see, even you've noticed." Amelia said jubilantly.

"You like the word *sometimes* Amelia?"

"You started it."

"Yes I did and what is the purpose of *sometimes*?"

"Haven't got a clue God." Amelia said feeling a little more cheerful.

"You can do better than that." God reprimanded her gently.

"I know I can - *sometimes*! Hah."

"Amelia…"

"Alright, alright God, I'm being facetious, I just can't help myself *someti*…OK I'll be serious. You should be pleased I'm not feeling sorry for myself anymore, I feel quite enthused actually. I'm really quite bright aren't I?"

"Yes Amelia, your mood has changed quite noticeably. Why is that?"

"What?"

"Why?" God remained stoic in the face of adversity.

"You did it."

"Who did it?" God prompted.

"You did. Oh, that's not the right answer is it? I realise that I'm many things: I have many different traits, qualities, faults, attributes, quirks, you name it and whatever you want to call it - I've got it." Amelia beamed happily at the thought. "God, I've realised something else too."

"What is it you have realised?"

"That none of them have to be labelled. You know, like negative or positive. It's how I use them that's important."

"Say a bit more Amelia please."

"Oh God, thank goodness you've asked, I'm bursting to tell you."

"I can see that. Please do not burst."

"Ha, ha. What I'm trying to say, if You let me without keep interrupting…it's up to me how I use these characteristics. All the things that make me who I am: my genes; my core values; my life experiences and my attitudes. Whatever it is that makes me who I am, I can use either positively or negatively. I have a choice. Free will."

"Tell me Amelia, where did all that realisation come from?"

196

"You're being a bit of a smartipants aren't you God really." Amelia's concluded. "You've brought me very neatly around in a circle back to you saying, again I might add, that you don't need to do a thing. You want nothing from us at all; you've already given us what we need to live and live well, with joy and abundance. It's entirely up to us how we do it. We have free will; we have choices. All of this you have given us. Your job is done. I get all of that. But it doesn't explain everything. *Sometimes* I think you do help out, when we're in the depths of despair, you come forward or you send someone on your behalf."

Amelia fell into quietude before questioning, "God, there's so much I don't understand. Will you talk some more about stuff - without skulking off for a century or two just to avoid me?"

"I never skulk off Amelia."

"Try telling that to the world God."

"Not everyone listens."

"I like the word *sometimes*. It makes me feel better."

"Evidently."

"It takes the pressure off doesn't it? Like its saying it's okay to get it wrong *sometimes*. We can't be perfect all the time - only *sometimes*.

Amelia drifted off to sleep with the tenor of God's counsel floating through her subconscious. On every occasion that she heard God, His words were like balm, filled with the wisdom of life. Her predicament lay in the permanent struggle that had arisen between the sagacity of God and the humanness of her irascible spirit. If she could exorcise her voices and learn to live with herself and accept herself - she would then have hope of salvation. If only... but they would not die.

"No, no" she prayed, "not if, but when! I can do this, I can."

Her invocations were weak when up against the power of time; one flank of combat had the strength of habit on side; ingrained, deep-rooted coping strategies that had, it was felt self-righteously, served Amelia well. 'We are the way,' her voices forced her to listen, 'you cannot survive without us.'

Her nights were becoming haunted by dreams, some she remembered on waking, leaving her exhausted and nervous, but some remaining an esoteric question mark of fearful experience. The more she believed she was genuinely talking to, and with, God, the more detached from the reality of her life she became. Thoughts of God consumed her.

Contact with the outside world was becoming a chore and her nagging cough persisted.

Heaven is a Donut

Chapter 21

Lunch with Lucinda and Get-a-Grip Greg

('We'll be friends forever won't we Pooh?' asked Piglet. 'Even longer,' Pooh answered - *AA Milne*).

Amelia watched her friend shimmy through the unexpectedly crowded restaurant; hips seductively first to reach their destination, her body obediently displaying the elegance bequeathed at birth. Amelia smiled with pride. How does she do it she thought; she looks absolutely gorgeous, in her mid thirties, mother of an eighteen-year-old university student - a head-turner still. As Amelia's smile widened, Lucinda waved happily, unintentionally lighting up the restaurant with her glory, causing Amelia to glow with the pleasure she always felt on first sight of her friend.

All the parts of Amelia loved Lucinda. Lemon threw back her head with a guttural laugh on many an occasion, such was Lucinda's ability to "say it like it is" with forthright, intelligent humour, managing to retain a ladylike demeanour whilst the coarsest of comments were emitting from her alluring mouth. She could exercise self-deprecation without banal repetition; see the funny side to life, expressing it with clever wit.

Reg was never happier than when he could bathe in the glow of a physically beautiful woman, hoping some of her huge popularity would envelop him. Oh yes, Lucinda was Reg's kind of girl: she had it all: the beauty, the grace, the intelligence.

Sunshine loved how Lucinda, despite her wicked humour at times, could also be compassionate and empathic, and always, always, Amelia's champion.

Heaven is a Donut

Sugarplum loved everybody, but Lucinda would always hold a special place in Sugarplum's regard because of her warmth and sweetness, particularly towards her friend Amelia.

With gusto, Amelia rose to hug her friend as she approached the table, experiencing the usual outflow of love and affection. "Oh, it's been so long since we've had a proper chat. How are you? You look fab – as ever. I was a bit distracted by my headache when we went out last week, but I'm feeling great now."

"Look what you've done you clumsy Clora; you look fab too." Lucinda, turning an unbelieving blind eye at her friend's insistence of wellbeing, managed to make a reprimand sound a worthy compliment as she smiled at the spilled glass of water Amelia had knocked over when she stood to greet her. "Thank goodness it wasn't your wine," Lucinda fixed her beautiful silky green eyes on her friend, "or even worse, MY wine. It's so good to see you Millie. I'm great. And that's enough of me: how about you, how's your week been?"

As Lucinda's smile broadened to treat Amelia with a dazzle, she managed yet again to make her feel a zillion dollars of importance rather than the inept duffer she believed deep down she truly was. Oh how Amelia could have benefited from Lucinda's friendship as she was growing up, what a boost to an individual's confidence, to be part of such a golden girl's life. Sadly they had not met until Amelia was a young woman at university and already fighting her lemony demons (or was it demony lemons? Amelia was haunted by indecision), by that time in her life.

"I told you, I'm okay Luce, okay really."

"No you're not, I can tell that much immediately. I'm glad your headache hasn't returned, but there's more to this than meets the eye – if you forgive the pun. There's

200

something else as well. Something's bothering you, we've all noticed and we're all worried about you. Come on spill the beans, you've just spilled the water so keep spilling." Lucinda grinned warmly at her.

"Oh you know. Stuff."

"Stuff?"

"Stuff. You know, stuff that gets in the way of life-stuff. Stuff that stops you enjoying yourself; that kind of stuff-stuff."

"That kind of stuff-stuff eh? Sounds serious."

"No. Well, I suppose it is really. I've just broken up with Ben. Well, a few weeks ago really, or was it months? Anyway I forgot to tell you. You remember Ben?"

"No. Which one was he? The doctor or the musician? Obviously very important as you've only just mentioned it."

"Neither, and don't be funny. I'm not broken hearted or anything, just a bit depressed; oh and my date stood me up – outrageous; how dare he! And there's work stuff-stuff going on too as you know."

"Give me an update on the work stuff-stuff?"

"That awful woman at work, you know the one I told you about. I know I'm obsessing, but she's gruesome, she really is, it gets me down sometimes."

"But I thought your Manager had words with her, told her to back off with the bullying?"

"He did but, well, it's so subversive, difficult to prove. You know when someone does or says something and only you know the hidden meaning. Her work had been investigated and she thought I was part of it, so she was intent on revenge. Does that make any sense at all? It sounds so trivial when I repeat it. Or maybe I'm being paranoid? That's what I'm accused of." Amelia trailed off miserably voicing her afterthought, "Oh God, it sounds so bloody paranoid no one would believe me. *I* wouldn't believe me."

"It makes perfect sense Amelia. It's what bullies do; it's one of their tactics. You know all about passive-aggressive behaviour. The bully seeks to alienate the victim by manipulating situations that cause maximum negative impact, without other people realising, and without them actively doing anything that can be laid at their door, appearing perfectly normal to the rest of the world. But both the victim and the perpetrator know the truth. It's mental and/or emotional abuse and very difficult to prove, as you well know from your study books. So, what are you going to do about it my love?"

"My Manager spoke to her, but I think bitch-face was able to persuade him that I was just being over-sensitive and said that, in the future, she'll be mindful I'm a bit touchy and can't take a joke. She managed to turn a reprimand into a triviality, shrugging it off with one of her fake charming grins, leaving the boss to rethink who's at fault. Am I exaggerating?" Amelia briefly headlined the idea.

"She's completely narcissistic. She uses people and exploits her colleagues; in fact, she's the original arriviste, with all manner of grandiose ideas about her capabilities. The tragedy is, she's a liability and we're always mopping up after her; hence her latest charge on me.

"And, she's a pathological liar, so it's almost impossible to second-guess her; you never know what's coming next. The rest of us are ordinary people who all get along very well and therefore no match for her deviousness. She hates anyone good at the job, or anyone pretty, or anyone younger, or thinner – unless they're, by her standards, an ugly jabberjowl or a fat arsed fussock!

"Most people at work know what she's like; but she either draws them in because she's so believable or they keep their head down so they're not on her radar. She's put herself on such a high pedestal that I find myself wishing she falls off breaking her scrawny tight-arsed neck. I've started indulging in evil little fantasies of my own that invariably entail her ego meeting with a grisly end of some sort. My current favourite is, having been told to clear her desk, she is escorted off the premises, to the accompaniment of a slow handclap and an obvious stumble as she slopes in shame out of the building, never to be seen or heard of in intelligent company again. How nasty am I then?"

Refilling her lungs following her long tirade, Amelia fell silent, concentrating on gasping for much required breath. She had felt her eyes smarting through her piteous narrative; but having caught Lucinda's sympathetic expression, full of support but yet somehow managing to convey a humorous side to Amelia's quandary, Amelia felt herself calming. As she studied her friend, Amelia knew from past experience that despite the seriousness, her dear Lulu would cast an amusing remark, bringing her to tears of laughter rather than the tears of despair that were currently threatening. Amelia swam towards those glowing green gems that were looking at her compassionately, drawing her in by the amused warmth gathering around them.

Even before Lucinda had uttered a word, Amelia felt her mood lift and the funny side of her predicament overtook her world.

"It's not funny Lulu!" she boomed, attempting to stand her ground.

"I haven't spoken a word yet." protested Lucinda, "I'm giving my response great consideration.......as you deserve." Lucinda paused, causing Amelia's rising giggle to wait in suspended anticipation. Lucinda, deciding she had withheld long enough, proceeded - with much animation.

"Fussock! What the hell is that? Don't get me wrong it's a great word, but what does it mean? Do you even know? And when you've explained that one, run jabberjowl by me please. Are they her words? No, can't be, they sound far too clever for that gowk – and that's my word, it means, stupid. What are you having for lunch?" Lucinda, changing the subject abruptly as she often did, lightly placed her designer spectacles on her refined nose, lifted her menu and peeked over the top at Amelia, whose giggle, having reached the end of the road, burst forth with throaty appeal at the ludicrous tale she had just spat out with such feeling. Lucinda joined her. As expected, before long they were both shaking with tears of laughter.

"I think I'll have a jabberjowl for lunch," gurgled Amelia.

"Really? You should try the fussock, particularly good at this time of year, they're in season don't you know. By the way, whatever is a tight-arsed neck? I do so hope it isn't on the menu, it sounds like a form of perverted torture. What sort of restaurant is this anyway? Do you think they serve rack of tight-arsed neck, or slow-roasted breast of scrawny bird maybe?"

"Tight-arsed neck of scrawny Gowk, I should think," babbled Amelia, heady with the pleasure that squashing the bully's ego gave her. "I'm definitely going to give that a try."

Mascara had bolted; snot had snotted and two blonde heads bowed in shameful hilarity. "My mascara's gone south," Amelia hiccupped into her napkin, "I daren't look up." As the immaculately manicured fingernails of Lucinda and the bitten-down nails of Amelia clung to the tabletop to avoid what would amount to an immense loss of dignity if one or both of the connected bodies were to tumble to the floor - a voice looming above them spoke with discernible disapproving tone.

"I thought it was you two - making a scene as usual. Why don't you get a...."

The two dishevelled heads shot up in unparalleled joy, both exclaiming the word they knew was about to be uttered as their eyes locked into those of their friend.

"GRIP."

Screeches of laughter cackled around the room, causing some diners concern, causing others, the more discerning, to smile at the merriment on show in the corner.

"Greg," Amelia managed to finally splutter her friend's name. "What are you doing here?"

"Yes, Grip, what are you doing here?" Lucinda repeated unnecessarily.

"I work here. Of more interest, what's the pointy-hat brigade doing here? Why aren't you at work, you pair of witches?" Fake disapproval was quickly overtaken by pleasure at bumping into his two all-time favourite females.

Again in unison, "What?"

Lucinda took over. "You work here?" zooming in on Greg's predicament of working in a diner rather than the witch insult to them both, which she felt was a fair assessment, she spoke with a little too much incredulity in her voice to be polite.

'Ah,' Amelia thought, 'that's what he was doing the other day when I was having coffee, on his way to work – here.' She had remained quiet about her chance meeting with Greg for both their sakes. She hadn't yet told Lucinda she walked out of work and was signed off through stress again. Hence her presence outside a café supping on a latte without a care in the world, whilst sending crazy with fear anyone within a metre radius with threats to kill, when she should have been in the comparative safety of the office.

"Yes. What's wrong with it?" Greg accented his reply with a hasty look around, firstly to note if anyone had detected an insult to his newly established place of work, and, secondly to try and reaffirm that it really wasn't that bad. "You're lunching here so it can't be that awful, even with your suspect taste," he sniffed.

"Oh Grip, you sweetie, nothing wrong with the place at all - for lunching that is," she added tellingly. "It's just that, you're a psychologist, but after having thrown away the fab job of trying to straighten out people's idiosyncrasies, we thought you were heading for glory treading the boards. Aren't you supposed to be rehearsing for a hit musical somewhere?"

"My boyfriend threw me out, changed his mind about an open relationship."

"But..." began Amelia.

"He's the producer."

"Oh." concluded Amelia, feeling loyally saddened on her friend's behalf whilst secretly deflated by what she knew of old to be Greg's inability to stay faithful. How she wished he would talk about it with her; 'he's just confused.' That she knew, without a word, the root of his problems, would have alarmed him considerably had he but known.

"Oh darling boy. When do you have a break? Come and join us, or we'll go somewhere else when you've finished your shift and commiserate by dancing and laughing the night away. In other words, we'll get pissed and forget all our woes." Lucinda made it sound as if this was a huge sacrifice she was prepared to undergo for the sake of her friend.

"Oh how such vulgar terminology sounds so cultured coming from your lusciously sculptured lips my dear. Actually," Greg eventually turned his attention to Lucinda's suggestion, "It's really not that bad here and I've got an audition next week."

"Hey well done." said Amelia wanting to boost his spirits. "You don't let the grass grow do you."

"Well darlings, I just thought to myself, 'It's no good crying over spilt milk. Get a grip and move on.'" Greg flopped himself down in a chair, wedging himself between his two best friends, instantly forgetting that he was a member of staff and not a customer.

Amelia and Lucinda stared at each other, knowing they shared the same thought, not needing it to be voiced. 'Spilt milk? Only Greg could describe blatant serial unfaithfulness to his longsuffering boyfriend as, spilt milk. It was only a matter of time before he'd had enough,' their eyeballing body language communicated to each other - with a wise after the event sort of nod.

Greg, picking up on the non-verbal and feeling decidedly left out, retaliated with, "Look at the state of you both, your make up's gone walkabout and your eyes are puffing up, in a very unattractive way I might add. Are you going to share the joke?"

"We certainly will," said Lucinda, knowing Amelia's problem was just the thing to cheer up Greg. He was an expert in bringing the uppity down a peg or two. Let him loose on Miss Virago.

Lucinda sallied forth with Amelia's trials. Not only being word perfect in the repeating of her story, but able to embellish with such expert tale-telling skill, Greg was open mouthed by the end of it and vowed to be Amelia's nemesis. "I'll be your Avenging Angel, dear-heart, to the foul-mouth swaggerlagger. I'll teach Missy Self-Important a thing or two. I've crossed swords with that one before you know, I thought being on the end of Grip-the-Quip's tongue lashing would have taught her to take a look at herself – the advice I left her with, if I recall."

Seizing his proffered hand, Amelia thanked him, "Grip, I really appreciate your support, and you Luce," she said turning to look at her friend, anxious she too felt recognised, "but neither of you work with her anymore. I'm the one left to deal with it when she starts. She picks people up like pawns and puts them down where it suits. It's a sad game she plays."

"Well, she'll never be happy then, will she?" stated Lucinda drily with a liberal shake of her head and generous attempt at compassion.

"No she won't. That's why when I'm not at work I can see it from a different viewpoint. You both know I'm trying hard to be a …..a ….. *good* person……What? What?" Amelia turned her confessional into an interrogation as she picked up on Greg's snorts of dissent, catching him mouth, "boring" in Lucinda's direction.

Lucinda, managing to keep a straight face by avoiding any further eye contact with Greg and furiously concentrating on the splodge of mascara resettled on Amelia's right cheek, answered, "But it doesn't mean you have to be a martyr my love, does it?"

"I know that, but I like it. Not the martyr bit, urgh no; I'm not cut out to be a martyr. But the "good" bit is good. I like being good. It's working, I feel different, a sort of peace. I'm struggling with this because I sometimes feel hatred. I hate being in the same room as the woman; I hate the sound of her voice; I hate the nasty games she plays and the damage she's done to other people; I keep wanting to get my own back which is *not* good - and I definitely hate that. Which means………" Amelia stopped to search both faces to see if she still had their interest. She had - just - but Greg was on the edge of his seat itching to tell her to get a grip again and change the subject to his fabulous new shirt, and would have done so by now had it not been for Lucinda pinning him down with a firm reign on his arm.

"Which means," Amelia spoke slowly, "I hate to hate, but I'm feeling hatred for someone. So either way you look at it, I'm stuffed. And what's wrong with your eyes Lulu? They've gone all crossed."

Lucinda experienced a flush of vertigo as she tussled to refocus her eyes whilst blinking with furious attempts to rid herself of the image of Amelia's mascara blob that held steadfast, even when she scrunched them closed. Greg looked up in sudden fascination of the ceiling, which held delightful nymphs and chubby baby angels frolicking mischievously across the room in painted re-creation of an Italian masterpiece. He breathed the words, "'tis pitiful weakness - wanting to be liked."

"You read that somewhere." Amelia's tone held an accusation.

"Yes." he confessed tightly, eyes still fixed in great earnest on above, as he pondered the dubious virtue of ceiling murals.

Lucinda's face cradled confusion, "You hate to hate?"

"Of course. Hate is bad. Love is good. But by God is she hard to love. I don't want this feeling of hate inside me. Up until her shenanigans, I was doing quite well at it. It's all her fault."

Amelia found reverting to blaming extremely comforting.

Having resolved once and for all that oversized babies with wings romping above one's head amidst dated 1990's décor was extremely poor taste, Greg's eyes returned from the ceiling to study his fingernails.

"Ah, well, there you go. There you have it." he divulged wisely. "This is a test. You're being tested. She's been sent your way to see how you deal with it."

Two pairs of beautiful but makeup-smudged eyes turned to stare harshly.

Reeling under their glare, Greg arched his scrutiny away from his pampered fingernails to square up to them, "Don't look at me like that both of you. It stands to reason."

"No no, I don't believe anymore that God does tests," said the blazing blue eyes of Amelia.

"Neither do I." the beguiling green eyes of Lucinda corroborated hastily. "No definitely not. Miss Swollen-Features has not been sent by God to persecute Millie; don't give her undue importance."

"You don't know that. You don't know what God might do or not do. He might want some proof that Amelia has really changed and uses Ego-Head to find out." said Greg adamantly. "Anyway, even if you're not sure, it wouldn't hurt to do a bit of assuaging; a bit of praying. You know the sort of thing; invest in a bit of goodliness to help her change her ways. Give her some emotional massaging. Maybe God sent Amelia to save her soul, what about that then, you didn't think of that did you? Maybe Millie-Moo should be chanting a bit of Godly light in her direction. By the way, whilst you're at it, take a look in the mirror before you call someone swollen-features."

Lucinda stared in horror, "Have you lost all reason? Are you well? I think you need an aspirin or something. Do you think for one minute you can change this woman? That you can help her transmute into a decent human being? It's not going to happen, honestly. Anyway, have you seen her recently?" she shrieked, jokily matching his indignation, knowing he wouldn't be able to resist her pitch. "She can't take anymore light that's for sure – Godly or otherwise, silly cow's so fake tanned she already resembles a tangerine, anymore glowing and she'll turn into a nuclear warhead. Come to think of it, she IS a nuclear warhead. Point taken about the slightly bloated look I'm currently sporting though – but at least it will wear off presently, unlike some distended ego-heads of whom we know."

As predicted, Greg, fascinated by the thought of a luminous orange ball on legs, was on the bandwagon with relish, expropriating Lucinda's phrase, "Yes come to think of it, come to think of it we shall, and you're so right. Last time I saw her she was strutting down the high street and I swear to God I thought it was a fat-thighed gingerbread man, such was the false tan, gave me a fright at first I can tell you. Thought I'd woken up in a B movie horror film. The Walking Gingerbread Man." Greg ended with a dramatic twist, moving his arms zombie-like for effect.

Not wanting to miss out on the fun, Amelia and Lucinda darted in with their contribution.

"The Stalking Sticky Cake." suggested Lucinda.

"The Night of the Waking Sponge," volunteered Amelia as her libertine Lemon rose to the occasion, helping her to forget her pledge to be good. "Anymore tanning and she'll look like my old teak table."

"What old teak table?"

"The tatty old thing I'm trying to sell, but nobody wants. She'll end up looking like that."

"What, you mean thick as a plank and twice as gnarled?" Lucinda spat the words out in laughter.

"No she means her *antique* table. Well used, cracked and full of woodworm, featuring slightly bowed legs." quipped Grip-the-Quip, "For sale, antique table with matching sideboard thrown in. Sold as seen. Buyer collects. No refund. Termites free to a good home."

'*Now, now, that's enough.*' Sugarplum rose Boudicca-like to the defence of the, unlikeable but not present so unable to defend herself, object of their conversation, causing Amelia to make a bold attempt at bringing a halt to the proceedings, despite the guffaws of laughter going on around her.

"Look, she's probably been deeply traumatised by some childhood incident..."

More guffaws.

"...which has troubled her ever since." Amelia ended lamely.

"Yes, to major dysfunction. I'm sorry Millie-Merecat, my little smorgasbord, but I've changed my mind about you doing God's work on this one. I don't think you should even try to be nice to this pseudo. She's fake nice when it suits, to get her own way, then doesn't hesitate to plant a knife firmly between shoulder blades with which to jiggle vigorously, for as long as it gives her pleasure - when one becomes surplus to requirements. Get a Grip. Get rid! That's my advice sweetface."

"Go Grip Go," chanted Lucinda. "I can't help but agree with Greg about this Amelia. I know you've tried different tactics, but she won't change, she can't change. Tell it like it is. When she starts on you again - go public; tell her you're not putting up with it. She's a nonentity and you should treat her as such. Don't bother even trying to be kind to her. You always do this, why can't you accept that she's a Fake-Tan-Fanny-arse of a woman and be done with it?"

"I can't help it. Something in me always rises to the defence of ...of...anyone really. Ok, well, I'll try not to care so much, to be affected by it so much. But I will pray for some Love & Light for her. After all, we've all been there, just not to the extremes to which she goes."

Amelia made an impressive attempt at humility. Lucinda and Greg nodded as much to each other in quiet recognition of the effort it must have taken, notwithstanding their silent hilarity at the prospect of, Saint Amelia.

"Well, if you insist on putting her at risk of instantaneous combustion when your Love & Light meets her magnetic rays of orange tan - so be it, as they say. But I think you should be sending yourself some Love & Light, not to mention your adoring friends." Get-a-Grip Greg rendered with a showy wave as he gesticulated at himself and Lucinda before adding, "I've just thought of something. What happens when like meets like?"

"Could be nothing. Could be fireworks," suggested Lucinda, not very helpfully, but with a grain of truth.

"What's going on in your devious mind Grip?" Amelia couldn't help smiling, knowing he was off on a trail of an evil endeavour that she would think necessary to voice disapproval – even if she liked the idea.

"When like meets like. We all know she's a textbook narcissist and generally the advice given is that they won't change so they're best avoided. However," Greg paused to check - yes he had intrigued them. Pleased with this finding, he continued, "What would happen if two of them worked together? When Narcissist meets Narcissist?"

"Oh my goodness, the Clash of the Narcissists?" breathed Amelia in fascination at the prospect.

"Can you imagine the havoc? Hang on though, a thought occurs. Are you suggesting Amelia is, or is capable of being, a narcissist?" Lucinda's original pleasure turned into a cool stare of accusation towards Greg.

"Yes come on Greg. It's not easy to fake stuff like that. I couldn't do it."

"Don't be silly. Anyone could do it. It's in all of us really. It's how we normally think and feel but just a bit exaggerated, that's all."

"No, that isn't just all. It's behaviour way beyond exaggerated normal. I do exaggerated normal all the time, but I'm not narcissistic." Amelia responded huffily at the very idea.

"Bet you could try, we all could. Ready? How to be a narcissist:-

Step 1: It's all about you.

Step 2: You are better, grander, more talented, skilled, beautiful, thinner, younger looking etc, etc, than all others.

Step 3: All others must be made to realise this.

Step 4: All others are there to be used in any way in order for all others to agree with step 2 & therefore (paused again for his captivated audience to keep up) ….. fulfil step 3.

Step 5: All other's feelings are inconsequential.

Step 6: If they're not for you, they're against you and therefore your deadly enemy.

Step 7: All deadly enemies are to be annihilated.

Step 8: All others are to be used in any way necessary in order to annihilate your deadly enemies.

Step 9: Give yourself excessive praise and admiration for your success.

And finally,

Step 10: It's all about you! "

"Wow, that's impressive." Lucinda clapped her hands enthusiastically.

"Not bad for off the top of my head." said Greg pompously, in a slightly narcissistic kind of way.

"Worryingly good. A subject you appear to be very familiar with." Amelia's tone indicated she was still smarting at the suggestion that she too held a narcissist lurking within – Outrageous.

On cue, Lemon, who had been slumbering with a small but vicious grin on her face, deep in a fantasy plethora involving an exploding Satsuma blob that experienced a second of awareness as to who was responsible for its demise as it slowly melted into a fuscous insipid puddle, awoke with a yawn on hearing her favourite word currently blowing around Amelia's brain.

'Outrageous?' she turned to Sugarplum.

Sugarplum, having incited a riotous chant in Amelia's head, *'sugar and spice, sugar and spice, everyone's nice, everyone's nice'…* was now standing nervously by Lemon's side wondering what was coming next, knowing whatever it was, it wouldn't be good. She didn't have long to wait.

'Outrageous?' Now fully awake and deadly, Lemon repeated, her inner rage bursting towards crescendo. *'Of course Amelia is capable of being a narcissist,'* she bellowed, *'I live in her head don't I? It's my only ambition. I've just been dreaming that I've disposed of a piece of mouldy fruit, which of course represented a certain person I hate, and Amelia is trying to pretend that she doesn't, and in true egotistical manner, said aforementioned unnamed but we all know who we're talking about person, knew in her final moments who the culprit was. All true narcissists want to take the credit for their dastardly deeds and to look their victims in the eye as they wield the fatal blow.'* Lemon added, feeling it important to educate the chaste Sugarplum on all matters despicable.

'For crying out loud,' Lemon's bawl galloped swiftly into a Reg-like lament, *'of course I'm a bloody narcissist.'*

'*Hey up, me too,*' rumbled Reg. Feeling rather miffed at being left out of all the ego-talk for so long, he squidged his slimy meatball of a head to fill the vacuum created by Sugarplum and Sunshine, who had decided it better part of valour to decamp to a quiet corner until Lemon's manic storm had passed.

'*I'm more of a narcotic than you are,*' Reg informed Lemon proudly.

Lemon leisurely fixed a satanic eye on Reg, causing him to shudder uncontrollably. '*You bumbling amoeba. Narcotic? More like permanent narcosis, you Twerthead!*'

'*Stop it, stop it,*' Reg retorted with hurt pride, '*so I got the word wrong again, you know what I mean. I'm the nasturtium around here, not you. What makes you think you're so special?*'

'*Oh believe me, you're the special one. Special needs that is,*' said Lemon sharply. '*I do believe you are a nasturtium, you certainly display all the intelligence of a watercress sandwich.*'

Reg, not understanding the link between a narcissist and a watercress sandwich but realising there must be one otherwise Lemon would not have used it to taunt him, shuffled off, joining his girls to provoke them with tales of superiority without having his head bitten off, being, he whispered to himself, '*very devoted to my head. Watercress sandwich indeed - at least I'm not a bitter, citric tree-hanger.*'

Reg ducked his head as if to prevent the thundering, '*I heard that you fat Malaprop,*' coming at full pelt from Lemon's direction.

'*Never mind Reg dear,*' said soothing Sugarplum sweetly, '*we like watercress sandwiches don't we Sunshine.*'

Reg farted in anguish. '*Sugarplum?*'

'Yes dear?'

'What has watercress sandwiches got to do with nas.. narcitwits....?'

'Nothing dear. And it's pronounced narcissist.'

'Didn't I say that? I did say that. That's what I said.' Reg was becoming greatly perturbed.

'No dear, you didn't say that. It's what you meant, but not what you said. You said something else by mistake.'

'And I suppose that the something else I said by mistake has got something to do with watercress sandwiches?'

'Loosely, yes dear, you've got it. Well done dear.'

'Sugarplum? I know I stole her words and she's still mad at me even though she can't prove it was me, I'm all out now, I haven't got any good words left. So I'm back to getting them all mixed up and saying them wrong again, or I use the wrong word at the wrong time. Lemon doesn't help me, she just laughs at me and the more upset I get, the more she does it and laughs louder. It makes me very angry. The more upset I am, the funnier she finds it. Why is that? '

'She can't help herself dear, it's her way. The best thing to do is to forgive her.'

'Forgive her? Well you would say that. She needs a hobnailed boot up her smelly-bottom, that's what she needs, and all her pips shoved up her nose – sideways,' defiant self-righteousness coming to Reg's rescue.

'No dear, forgiveness is the answer. If you forgive, she's got nothing else to laugh at you for has she? She'll be the one looking silly, mark my words.'

Reg, not entirely convinced, decided Lemon looked silly enough already without any of his help, so returned to the word that had been causing him much ear scratching.

'Sugarplum?'

'Yes dear?'

'*What's a mapalop?*'

"HELLO. Earth to Amelia. Where have you been for the last 5 minutes? I've been talking to you." Greg was theatrically injured by her apparent indifference to his cleverness.

"Urm, I'll have a watercress sandwich please."

Greg's assumed hurt turned into surprise as he linked eye contact with Lucinda at Amelia's off-the-wall response.

"Pardon?"

"Sorry, didn't you just ask me what I'd like to have for lunch?"

"No I did not. Although I do accept that is what I'm here for and of course I had momentarily forgotten that. But it is definitely not what I just said, and we definitely do not serve bloody watercress sandwiches. Where do you think you bloody well are Millie-Moo, the Queen's bloody garden party?"

"Well bearing in mind that *is* what you are here for, perhaps you would like to pass the young ladies our Lunchtime Specials menu – without the name calling and the language that is."

All three jumped guiltily at the voice of the newcomer, unidentifiable to Amelia and Lucinda. However, Greg knew only too well to whom the disapproving tones belonged, 'my buffoon of a boss. Oh God, bloody well sussed again,' he groaned to himself as he turned to face his tormentor. "Mr Porter, you startled me."

"Clearly."

"I was just about to offer the young ladies our Lunchtime Specials menu."

"Yes, yes he was," said Lucinda and Amelia nodding together and speaking far too energetically to be believable.

"I was, er, I was inquiring about sandwiches, I'm afraid I've kept your staff far too long with my indecision. I wanted to know if you have fus..." Under the table Lucinda's foot reached out and delivered a small but sharp kick on Amelia's shin, indicating that mentioning fussocks may not help matters.

"We've decided now." Lucinda's tone was to the point. "Two cheese salads please. Oh and Mr Porter?"

"Yes Madam?" replied an emasculated Mr Porter, currently experiencing a surge of confusing pleasure coursing his veins as his name was remembered by a beautiful, but way out of his league, young woman.

"Do you have any watercress?"

Later, in consolation for the mediocre lunch, a shopping spree was deemed the only way forward. Having been joined by Greg when his shift was over, (or more accurately nearly over, sneaking out 15 minutes early on the assumption the manager wasn't bright enough to notice - wrongly as it turned out), their shopping expedition turned happily into a delightful cocktail hour, which then progressed naturally into a liquid supper at their favourite pub.

'Oh look everyone,' cried Sugarplum in euphoric seventh heaven, *'Sunshine's dancing.'*

'What? I didn't know she could dance' said Lemon, unsure whether to be pleased. If it had been anyone other than Sunshine she would have ruptured into mockery.

Reg, with haughty pride retorted, *'Of course she can dance, Sunshine can do anything.'* He wheezed pompously, *'when Sunshine's in good form, Amelia is a fantastic athlete; when Sunshine helps her play the piano, it has such feeling it brings tears to the eyes.'*

'I'll bring tears to your eyes in a minute, with my fist, if you don't stop your blathering,' thundered Lemon, *'For goodness sake you Buggerlugs, so what? It's nothing special.'*

'Oh yes it is,' they chorused back. *'She can only do it when Amelia's drunk and our Millie is tying one on right now, she's really going for broke.'*

'Oh God, you know what that means.' Lemon squeezed her words between clamped teeth.

'Yes of course we do dear,' replied Sugarplum merrily, *'that's why we're making the most of it. We know we'll all feel sick shortly and have a headache. Reg has been practicing a new technique of how to talk and burp at the same time. I'm spinning sugar into great cotton balls of silver loveliness – in a happy carefree sort of way. What are you going to do Lemon?'* Sugarplum's voice rose to a fever pitch of rhapsody beyond all reason.

'I'm already doing it,' she snarled...*'it's called disgorging the contents of one's stomach over the shoes of the person standing next to ONE – an agreeable pastime to which I subscribe from time to time.'*

Sunshine did undeniably have many talents, as often found in sensitive and insightful people; what an actress she would have made, glorying in the admiration of her public. As it was, with little or no parental encouragement to nurture this budding talent, Sunshine's abilities had withered over the years to an occasional showing off exhibitionism, which Lemon would then hijack, degenerating into a scene of carnage.

Therefore, in the main, Amelia's only audience these days was a handful of her equally drunk friends in the pub with little memory the next day of her antics – much to her relief.

Chapter 22

All about Greg

(Who, being loved, is poor? - *Oscar Wilde*)

"Oh Greg, whatever is wrong? I've never seen you like this."

Greg was in trouble; demands, bills, threats - coming in fast and furious. He stared disbelievingly at the offensive pile, forlornly fanning them out on the table as they dispassionately returned his repugnance.

"I lost my job at the restaurant. I've got nothing coming in now. I don't know where to turn. I can't sleep and I nearly had a full-blown panic attack yesterday just thinking about how to pay these.

"Have you been to your GP?"

"What for Millie, pump me full of anti-depressants? I'm not depressed. I'm frightened and worried - for good reason. The medical profession still cannot distinguish between depression and an old-fashioned nervous breakdown. This…" Greg pointed both hands at his body and waved them savagely up and down, "is high level anxiety, in other words – a nervous breakdown!"

Amelia was smitten with guilt. The episode he'd encountered with herself and Lucinda had not exactly helped his status with his new employer.

"I'm so sorry, it's all our fault. We did rather laugh at the poor man; but he was so mean to you, we couldn't help ourselves. We watched him, he stood over you as if you couldn't be trusted in the simplest of tasks and when your back was turned we saw him mimic your walk, but he really camped it up. You're not camp by the way, not at all, you've got a fabulous walk; he was just plain mean - jealous probably. He poked fun at you and we couldn't stand it, but we're so sorry it got you fired."

"No, honeybiscuit, you didn't get me fired, don't take that one on board. He saw me leaving early apparently and rather than challenge me there and then like any reasonable boss, he let me do it then sacked me the next day – loser! Anyway, he's an idiot so it was worth it. Did you see his face when he returned with little more than a pathetic looking lump of dried out cheese and two lettuce leaves on the plate? Lulu took one look at it and realised she'd been wrong to kick you into silence, so retaliated with, "Oh and may we have one portion of fussock dressing, and a light portion of jabberjowl, both on the side please?" Yes Millie-Moo, it was *so* worth getting fired for *that* look alone. Anyway, I didn't like the ghastly decor, already decided I couldn't live with it a moment longer. Thanks by the way, for not saying anything to Lulu when you saw me on the way there the other day."

"Well, I didn't put two and two together until we saw you working at the restaurant; it explained why I'd seen you in the café quarter. Thanks to you also, Greg, you know, for not saying. I hadn't told Luce I walked out of work after on and off skiving, only this time I went back to my GP and made it official."

"Oh my Amsy, I know you're not malingering. You're not well and you need space and time to get better. I haven't noticed that cough so much today, how are you now? God you look rough, what's going on?"

She considered lying, but thought better of it by this stage. "Not good Greg. Can't describe it; I don't know what's happening to me, I just know I'm not good and I'm not sure what the answer is." She wanted to change the subject quickly back to Greg. He was being so charitable, worrying about her even when facing major problems of his own. "All the same Greg, we both feel terrible about your job. How did your audition go?"

Greg puffed with gratitude in the recognition that he was in one hell of a predicament and his friends were responding in a way that demonstrated their concern for him. "No, Millie, not at all, you must stop thinking you were in anyway responsible. All my own doing."

"You're very generous about it all Greg. However, no amount of staring at those pieces of paper will help pay them." Amelia said flatly.

"Oh thanks, your critique does much to ease the panic rising in my GUT! Not to mention the smell of hypocrisy coming from your direction young Lady. At least I open my mail."

"Oh come on, I'm trying to help here honestly I am. Yes, I hear what you say, I'm as bad, no OK, worse," she added hastily, watching elegant eyebrow arch sharply on his face. "But that's why I feel entitled to speak my mind. After all, you do - don't you? When it's me in trouble." Amelia, having thrown up her hands in acknowledgement of Greg's criticism, relaxed knowing she'd won her argument.

"Why won't you take my offer of a loan? A loan." she stressed emphatically. "Don't be so proud, it's not charity, you can pay it back when you're better placed and you'd do the same for me." Greg remained impassive. Amelia tried her second and preferred option. She had wanted to run the loan idea past him first, knowing his pride would find it hard to take, but hopefully meant he'd think more sensibly about the second one. "I know it's the last thing you want to happen, but why don't you come back? Work with us, we need staff. They're going to advertise - that's how short-staffed we are just now, even more now I'm off. They haven't advertised externally for at least two years ..... and you..."

She tapped his chest lightly as if to ensure he knew of whom she was referring, "you're a brilliant psychologist and you know you are. Instead of using your skills having failed in your thespian attempts, no sorry I take that back whilst *resting* - and I take it you didn't get the part, judging by your silence when I asked - you choose to wipe down tables in a restaurant with dodgy décor. Of which must upset your equilibrium hugely, not to mention a boss at said dodgy restaurant whom you hate above all beings, and having to serve people you secretly despise."

"Oh that's a bit strong, that man is a jack-ass that's all. I don't waste my energy hating him, he's an ignoramus; a homophobic idiot, and I'm used to dealing with the likes of him. As for the customers, I don't despise them – just mock them a little, that's all. They never twig, they're not bright enough."

"Patronising git," murmured Amelia.

"I know I'm sorry, I can't help myself sometimes. People can be so rude to staff waiting tables you know, as if they, we," he corrected, "are a different species, lower than them. I know, I know," Greg shot up his hands as he spoke, "I should know better. I understand the human psyche and so therefore, should forgive them their little idiosyncrasies."

Greg's shaking of his head from side to side as he spoke suggested more than a little superciliousness, giving substantial weight to Amelia's appraisal of his air of superiority. However, having just mounted the dais of the partisan, he persisted. "Well I don't so there - know better that is. Well, that is to say, I do, but choose not to act upon it. Everyone knows basic good manners, everyone knows right from wrong; they come in lording it over the staff and showing off. The little pricks can go away and grow up - before I feel the urge to spit in their food." Greg pouted.

"Anyway," he sensed a well-timed soapbox as he took pleasure in the anticipatory nature of the word anyway, "I'm not that good a psychologist, never been good with the empathy bit. Sometimes I just think, for goodness sake get-a-grip."

Knowing what had been coming, Amelia, a smile hovering, spoke the words with him. "Get a grip."

"Well seriously." He continued, "Some people think they've suffered, think they've had it bad. They should try growing up in a household where sex is a dirty never-to-be-mentioned subject and all homosexuals should be stoned to death. Can you imagine how I felt? I loved my parents so much, before I knew them better, and tried so hard to please them: but I have failed them – on all counts. Well, one count actually and that's the count that... counts."

Greg looked a little baffled by his own argument - but knew it made sense, at least to him. "I am gay. Did I choose to be? No. Did I want to be when I was growing up? No. Why not? Because I was told it was a sin. One of the worst sins that could ever be...well, urm, be..." Greg stuttered for the appropriate word. Not finding it he settled for, "sinned. That's it, the worse sin that could ever be sinned."

Without speaking, Amelia reached out and touched his arm, understanding only too well the friction of Greg's childhood. Eventually she said, "Isn't that why you became a psychologist? Why you're so good at it? You understand these things. You, more than many, know isolation; not fitting in; not being the same as others and your family's attitude was, and is, very out of date. My family are exactly the same."

"But you're not gay." Greg was pouting again.

"I don't have to be, to be in contention with my family's religious beliefs. I tried but couldn't live the way they live - and that's hard for them to deal with. I'm just as much an outcast as you really. Until now, I've lived quietly, not telling them too much, so I haven't been on their moral radar. If they knew half of what my life is about, I'd have been struck down years ago - I believe in guardian angels and tarot cards for goodness sake, they'll never forgive that one alone."

"Well, Millie darling, many people would think you're a crackpot on that account, not just your Ma and Pa. Anyway, at least your family have principles, mine don't. They are just mindless homophobic cretins who hate for hate's sake and use the word sin to force their views down my throat rather than from any religious belief, which is far worse."

"Oh Greg. For what it's worth, I wish you weren't gay as well. You're my perfect man – or would be if it wasn't for that one little fact." Amelia tried to lighten Greg's emerging self-pity into banter.

Ignoring the bait, Greg reached out to stroke Amelia's cheek, "what is it Mille-Moo, you're so unhappy, what's wrong, and what did you mean by, 'until now?' Something's happened hasn't it, tell your BF Greg."

Recent dark events, so fresh in Amelia's memory, meant she could hold out no longer. She flung her arms around him, sobbing into his chest. She held on tightly to catch his love for her and feel the strength of it revive her beaten soul. Through tears and hiccups, she told him of the impromptu visit to her parents that morning, of what she had to say to them and why. She told him of their inexplicable response and how she was asked to leave the home where she had spent her early childhood, never to return.

Greg held her, gently rocking her, knowing she needed time-out without comment, without him voicing his opinion – she needed his silence. He gave her that time, waiting patiently for her to calm.

Finally, "All I'll say at this point Ams, is that you are not alone in this. Whatever you decide to do, and I must say, I agree something must and will be done; we will back you all the way. The first thing I'm going to do is tell Tris, we need a legal head for this and he's your man. Now, I'm going to change the subject, because we've done all we can do with this, right now, Ok?"

Amelia nodded silently at his shirt collar.

"So," Greg paused, deciding it was time to bring her back by catching onto her humour, "there's something that's been bothering me, something you said. What do you mean by "that one *little* fact," hey, come on now, not so much of the little! Anyway…" How he loved that word he realised. Using the word, anyway, always aroused curiosity, allowing him to keep his audience, and he realised he needed all his skills to keep this particular audience. He decided to bring the subject back to the safety of work issues. "Anyway, I've got principles you know. I abhor…" Greg waved his arms elaborately, "the whole set up. You know I do,"

Now returning Amelia's earlier gesture in overstated form, pulling her away, he waved an excited finger under her nose, "and you've succumbed, you've given in and become one of them, you turncoat. You and Lulu have both joined the stinking ranks of the beaten and downtrodden."

Amelia, feeling comfort and secure by her friend's show of love for her, allowed herself to drift easily into the space where Greg was leading her, loving him all the more for it. She glazed her eyes, drifting them upwards. "Oh Greg, here we go again. Am I going to get the "government targets are the blight of all humanity" lecture – again?"

"No," (unconvincing tone). "No," (stubborn tone doing little to persuade Amelia).

Amelia was conscious of a Greg style verbal explosion heading her way.

Greg, with relief that the change in subject appeared to be working, capitulated to the Bolshevik living inside and gave in to the irresistible urge to make a speech. "Well, you know I'm right, and you Madam, you cow-tail to it. If enough of us held out and were prepared to take a stand – like I do – this sickening target-driven society would end, immediately! Payment by results!"

He spat the words, punctuating them with exclamation marks, as if fearing they would poison him. "Who suffers from Payment by Results? And I quote: The most needy – funny that! The susceptible; the poor; the sick; the uneducated! Targets reward pro-social looking statistics. They cause people to lie! Teachers select pupils most likely to pass exams; employment agencies, those more likely to get a job; hospital trolleys re-classified as beds, and people abandoned in ambulances until they can be seen! But that's okay because they've hit their target. Targets instigate a vile disruption to humanity." He ended his verbatim quote grandly.

"Who are you quoting? You know all this for a fact do you?" Amelia had heard Greg's rant many times, usually after a few bevies, she thought. On this occasion, it appeared to be the stress of faceless people browbeating him into parting with his increasingly dwindling funds that had set him off. At every turn, people clamouring for payment of taxes, utilities, food, rent, and the privilege of being alive. It struck a familiar and sickening cord for Amelia. 'Living' was clearly an expensive luxury she reckoned grimly; little wonder the world's masses are suffering depression and we're all losing the plot. She returned swiftly to the breakdown currently playing out in front of her, searching Greg's face. 'What a pair we are,' she smiled grimly to herself, 'first him, then me, then him again.'

"Yes I do." He answered emphatically. "Read it on the Internet, can't remember where or who wrote it - but I don't doubt the truth of it, not for one second. 'What can be done to reach our targets - by crafty practice?' It's disgraceful! Anyway, you know I've seen it at work. And, let me tell you, when priorities are budgets, targets and audit passing, we cannot deliver best practice. It's 21st century madness."

As Greg lapsed into further, well rehearsed, quotes from unremembered sources, Amelia waited patiently for him to draw breath. She seized her moment and began to wave a piece of paper under his nose, on which she'd written a phone number.

"So you'll call them to arrange some peripatetic work?"

"YES – but you know they're all egotistical bullies don't you, those so called *managers*?" Greg grabbed the paper and flounced into the kitchen with the satisfaction he had dispensed an insult within his capitulation.

"Fancy a brew then Millie-Merecat?"

"Thought you'd never ask," she grinned with relief at the passing of the diatribe.

Greg was soon walking over to Amelia carrying a tray holding a teapot; two cups, saucers and spoons; a small jug of milk; sugar, tongs and plate of biscuits. Appearing much calmer and his old self, he queried, "Here we are my cherub; how was your head by the way?"

"My head?"

"Yes, your head. After our gargantuan, "Let's put the world to rights," drinking session."

"Oh. Awful. I felt awful. Lost a day - a whole day. How ridiculous is that. I'm not doing that again, foolish waste of time. Why are you laughing? I mean it – this time."

"Can you remember anything?" He peered closely down at her as he grilled her. "Dancing on the table? Stealing someone's cigarettes and smoking four at a time? Reciting word perfect Wordsworth's, 'I wandered lonely as a cloud'? Standing on a chair and singing, 'Bridge over Troubled Water'? Declaring you were going to marry Leonard Cohen? Throwing up in the gutter outside? Demanding I make mad passionate love to you?"

As Greg ticked off her plaintive list of transgressions, most of which she had scant memory, Amelia's face dropped to an all-time guilt-ridden mask of shame.

"No, oh no. Don't tell me anymore. I do remember throwing up though. God, I felt ill. It was the cigarettes that did it, you know I don't smoke."

"Of course my petal and nothing to do with the serious intent of performing and perfecting your magic trick of turning blood into alcohol – whilst still in your veins. Never mind sweetface, we shared a taxi and saw you home, trundling you through your door. But don't make a habit of it lovely, it's not good for you."

"I know. I'm too ashamed of myself to even try and argue with you. Thanks again for looking after me," she smiled genuinely.

Her face then fell to a serious task, one that had been making her anxious. "Greg? Have you seen Tris lately?"

"Well you'd know the answer to that one if you were more reliable and answered your phone a little more frequently, that's why our little sojourn the other day was so nice – until it turned into a flagrant breach of common sense, that is. Yes," he quickly returned to the topic of Tristan, "I see him every week."

"Well? Don't make me beg, you know why I'm asking. How's he doing?"

"He's fine. Been rather immersed entertaining a certain well-endowed young woman who's been keeping him very busy over the last month or two. Would you like me to pass on your regards to him?"

"Don't you dare, I just wanted to know that's all. Thought it would be something like that. He hasn't called me like he usually does; you know, just to check with me, see how things are going. As long as he's OK?"

"He's fine."

Amelia scuttled home. She couldn't wait to get in and close the door on the world. She couldn't understand why, when in the presence of her friends, her mood lifted and she felt a fragile modicum of peace with the world, but the moment she turned and made her way home, she plummeted into the depths of despair and self-loathing. 'And what was going on with Tristan?' she fretted.

She had mixed feelings. 'How could he desert me this way? But at least I now know he's OK, and as the situation between us is entirely down to me, I can't really complain now can I?' She scolded herself, 'I've brought this on myself. He hasn't deserted me; he's getting on with his own life. Oh, I don't want to lose him though,' she brooded. 'I recovered from his short marriage - the Bella-business, how would I survive something like that again. I've got to tell him how I feel about him or one day I'll lose him forever.'

Amelia realised with a heart-lurching certainty that she would not be able to bear it, bear life, if she were to lose Tristan. But knew she was not coping with anything in life at present, so what could she offer Tristan other than her own brand of nervous breakdowns, self-pity and a war of words permanently raging in her head. Why would he want to get involved with her again? She felt herself retiring tortoise-like into a bleak shell as she reminded herself how impossible she was.

She did, however, garner some pleasure from her success in persuading Greg to take the phone number she'd given him. He had taken the bait and promised to call. "Hopefully that's him sorted out with some work to tide him over." She told Lucinda on the phone much later that evening.

"Well done Millie. So, what about you, how's work?"

Amelia didn't want to talk on the phone. She wanted hermetic sanctuary. She wanted to read her new cards. She wanted to hear God's voice again, her latest obsession, she turned the thought around in her head. She loved her friends, feeling more like her old self when with them and yet, wanted them to leave her alone. How long she could continue she had no idea, but she didn't want to deal with people. It had taken a lot of effort to go and see Greg, after the traumatic visit of the morning, but she cared for him so deeply, she couldn't bear to see him in trouble and not at least try and do something.

Magically, she had received a call from Tristan just before Lucinda phoned. She suspected it was Greg passing on to him that she'd been asking after him. 'Bloody Greg, not keeping his mouth shut, on this occasion anyway. Leave me alone Lulu, leave me alone, all of you leave me alone. If it takes Greg to remind you that I exist Tristan, then you can definitely leave me alone.'

"Oh Luce, thanks for asking, well, I have been signed off again, just wasn't ready, you know, they talk about burn out in this line of work don't they? I'd reached my boiling point and I'm taking some time out. I've heard from Tris by the way and he's coming round for supper a week on Friday, he's away on business until then."

She made it sound very matter of fact. She wasn't sure if Lucinda had fallen for it, so she added a little more, "I told Greg today I wasn't doing too well, but the Doc said the answer was to stay away from work, so that's what I'm doing, and, well, I saw my parents this morning, before I went to Greg's."

"Oh that's great news. How were they?"

"Ok, they're in good health."

"That's good then isn't it?"

Leave me alone. I cannot tell Luce what transpired between my parents, not yet, she'll find out in good time, I've already broken down in front of Greg – no doubt he'll tell all on my behalf.

"Yes, very good."

"Anything I can do?"

Leave me alone.

"No, sweetie, I'll be fine, honestly. Plenty of sleep is the best remedy. Rest and rehabilitation and all that jargon, you know."

"OK, well if you're sure."

Just go away. I love you but go away.

"No really I'm fine, but thanks for caring, love you honey, bye."

No one, other than Greg, could have known the turmoil Amelia was now facing and the real reason for her decision to see her parents. Having unexpectedly heard from an old friend who, being so intrinsically wrapped up in her religious beliefs, Amelia thought she would never awaken to see the truth. But she had and Amelia knew both they're lives would change dramatically as a result.

Amelia was left reeling with news that cut her into pieces of pernicious distress, at a time when she was least equipped to deal with, what she knew would become, a major promise of undertaking.

An unaware and unsuspecting Tristan didn't stand a chance.

Chapter 23

All about Tristan

(The course of true love never did run smooth – *William Shakespeare*)

Tristan knocked on Amelia's front door with the trepidation always felt when he hadn't seen her for a while. 'Will she be curious as to why I've been so remote recently? Slightly worried maybe? In your dreams Tristan.' he said to himself wryly, shattering his tentative illusions. 'She's so sure of me she'd never fret about losing me to someone else, even when she did, to all intent and purpose, lose me to someone else. No, she knows the truth. She'll never lose me. Let's face it, every time I strayed from the Amelia path, (dragged along by your penis, Amelia once informed him) blindly tailing a pretty girl, even as far as marriage – Amelia knows it's her I love.'

Tristan continued to abstractedly pass the time. 'I have to give Amelia her due; she played the part well. She fostered her relationship with Arabella; bridesmaid at the wedding, Godmother to our son Julian. Shoulder to cry on (for me of course) when it all fell apart and Bella went home to Daddy, taking Jules with her.'

Amelia had not put a foot wrong, in fact she and Bella remained close and although Amelia had been scrupulously honest with Bella that Tristan was her friend and therein shall always lay her loyalties, she never posed a threat to Bella or their short-lived marriage. 'Amsy certainly remained detached' he observed, 'emotionally as well as sexually.' he added, knowing they had socialised the same as always, but with Bella as the new and welcome recruit.

Amelia's friendship with Bella had been very helpful to Tristan when wading through the mire of divorce and access to Jules; she had been an admirable go-between and they both thanked her profusely. But therein lay the dichotomy. He wanted marriage, children: the whole thing. But he was hopelessly in love with Amelia, who clearly didn't want any of those things, in fact, as she rather bluntly put it when she ended their engagement all those years ago, "I'd rather spend the rest of my days locked in a cupboard."

He skimmed over the anguish he had experienced at her words, not willing to linger too long, such was the agony he felt at the time.

"Tris, oh Tris, I didn't mean because it's you." Amelia, experiencing her time worn contrition when she knew her acid tongue had gone too far, laboured to ease the pain she could see etched on his face. She bit back the words "It's not you, it's me," at least realising that could be a death knell. She attempted to explain. "I mean marriage, I'd rather be locked up than married to someone. Anyone. It's the marriage thing, not you. I love you. I'd do anything for you, you know that."

"Except marry me and make me the happiest man on earth?"

"I can't do it. I just can't. I'd be a terrible wife... and Mother. I can hardly look after myself, let alone be responsible for anyone else. You would be the *un*happiest man on earth - I haven't worked out yet how to tie my own shoelaces.

Her weak attempts at humour succeeded in making Tristan feel all the more confused and frustrated by her lack of self-confidence.

That angry exchange had heralded the first of their break ups. There had been two more since then and they had both moved on to other relationships. But that first one was the worst, for Tristan at least: he had left her, standing there on her doorstep, this very doorstep he suddenly remembered as he looked about him, dear old Uncle Billy's house, and the home he'd offered to Amelia after her sister died. Tristan remembered seeing Uncle Billy shake his head with sorrow as he looked on helplessly watching them both in their own private hell and hearing Tristan firing the bitter words, "Don't be so bloody stupid, of course we can't be *just* friends. You're a child Amelia, why don't you grow up!"

Tristan locked that experience away and kept it hidden, managing to almost erase it. 'If I don't acknowledge it, it never happened.' It worked for him to a manageable degree and some months later the day came when their predicament reversed, after her pathetic attempts at finding new love had failed so spectacularly, she stood on his doorstep, her dishevelled torment at their parting visible. He welcomed her in, held her close and resumed his feelings of love for her as if the darkest age of his life had never existed. She was back. That's all he needed to know. The light flooded into his life once more.

For Amelia, her world had fallen apart. The new man in her life was not Tristan and life without Tristan was unbearable, unthinkable. Why hadn't he called? What was he doing? Had he found someone else? She heard different rumours of course and she fed greedily on the gossip. The pain - the physical pain, she had never experienced anything like it.

"Why don't you go and see him?" Lucinda had said. "Go and see him - cap in hand - apologise, tell him you panicked, that you really love him, only him, then GET MARRIED."

"I can't" cried the tortured Amelia. "It wouldn't work; I'd let him down and end up hurting him - and myself."

Lucinda's frustration levels were rising. "What do you think you're doing now then, if not hurting yourself - and him? If you love him and he's the only man for you… "

"He is, he is." Amelia resonated passionately.

"Then why not marry him?"

"I can't. I'm not good enough to marry him, or anyone for that matter."

Lucinda groaned and had been sorely tempted to echo Tristan's words of "grow up" to her agonised but cantankerous friend. She refrained of course, knowing it would only serve to make herself feel better by momentarily easing her annoyance, but would certainly not be helpful to Amelia, possibly shrinking her even further back into herself.

Returning his drifting thoughts to the present, Tristan stood waiting for Amelia to come to the door, uninformed of the many conversations their friends had in defence of his love for her, he decided that if anything she's probably secretly seething he'd missed her birthday. Birthdays are so important to her; she hates it if her loved ones, her true family as she calls all her closest friends, do not surround her on the occasion. Knowing this he had purposefully avoided her special day, achieving the conspicuous in absentia effect, he desired.

Sensing his hesitancy as she heard him at the door, as was often her way with Tristan, she shouted him to come in with more volume than really required. 'Why can't he just knock and walk in,' she thought peevishly, 'I'm desperate to see him; he's known me since we were teenagers and we were sleeping together for years, *until he spoiled it by getting all serious,*' whispered Lemon, for goodness sake, why does he pussyfoot around me all the time.' Fully aware that that last thing she should be doing right now, or was capable after the hard-hitting days she had recently experienced with her parents, was to attempt to pick up the pieces of her relationship with Tris. Not willing to concede that her flashes of vexation with her friend and lover were the very reason for his eggshell behaviour, she turned abruptly as he eventually sidled through the doorway. As ever though at sight of him, all recent trauma aside, she melted into a great rush of pleasure, misunderstood *displeasure* forgotten.

"Tris, you lovely man, thank you so much for coming. How are you? I haven't seen you in an age, where have you been? What have you been up to? Why didn't you reply to my earlier messages? How's your Mother? Did your sister get the job she was after?"

'*Of course the dunderhead didn't get the job. Daddy's influence couldn't reach that far, on this occasion.*' Lemon breathed as Amelia silently congratulated herself for not mentioning her birthday.

Amelia ran towards his familiar and ever welcoming arms as he groaned his time-honoured mantra silently into her precious golden hair, 'Oh why do I love this insufferable woman?' He folded her into his embrace, happy to stay locked together like this for the rest of his life. She gave him less than two minutes before squirming free as she sensed an old comfortable belonging that made her feel suddenly unsure of herself.

'Why does he make me feel uncertain of everything, with that *who am I*, feeling' she thought, unconsciously withdrawing, her love for him always incongruent. 'I miss him so much when I don't see him but yet, I lose who I am when with him' she concluded, and that was why she called time on their relationship as partners. Tristan had proposed to her and she had said yes – then run a mile, only to come tiptoeing back to him some months later, begging forgiveness for treating him so badly and to risk asking once more if they could be friends.

Tristan had also run his mile. A mile of hurt and indignation, but he couldn't shake free of her. He swallowed his pride; reprimanded his parents and friends for judging and berating her so harshly and committed to life on her terms, no matter which way she wanted it. He let her call the shots, and she did – big time. Tristan was there for her every time she fouled up. When she fell, he picked her up. When her pride was wounded, he gently massaged back her bruised ego and self-belief. When her heart was broken, he lovingly pieced it together again. When she was angry at the world, he listened. When she wanted to get physical, he obliged – only to be turned out in the morning with a cheery, 'It's so good we understand each other Tris.'

Then Arabella came into the picture and for a while, Amelia floundered, having been ousted. Since his divorce, they gravitated endlessly back and forth in the same treacherous pattern. 'Did she know?' He often speculated. 'Did she have any idea of the humiliation he felt at being used and yet not being able to resist her?'

She stood there looking up at him enquiringly, mesmerising him with what he'd always found to be an enchanting half smile on her face.

"Why do I love you so much?" He grinned at her.

"Because you're a mad man," she laughed back. "Well?" she added.

Knowing her of old, he knew she was referring to the barrage she had just fired at him.

"In good time my love, get the bottle open first."

Her smile widened as she grabbed the bottle of wine from him. "Ever the practical. OK, let me deal with this, you go and get comfortable on Old Faithful, I'll come and join you as quickly as you can say, Amelia you are more beautiful than ever and have clearly lost at least 10 pounds since I last saw you." Switching attention to the bottle, "Gosh, you're a good one," she then disappeared through to the kitchen. As Tristan settled comfortably, Old Faithful reminded him of some very happy intimate moments with Amelia, some of which he knew for sure, were never to be repeated – his proposal for a start, and her acceptance.

'Well old boy' he said patting the sofa's squashy burgundy cushions; 'if you could talk….' he stopped abruptly as the familiar mix of pain and love surfaced. 'Come on Tristan, for the thousandth time, this is what you agreed to accept so get on with it.' He reminisced as he waited, thinking about their first meeting…..

"Tristan? Tristan Treadwell? Well now, that's quite a name isn't it?"

Tristan smiled, sensing the young girl was laughing at him yet helpless to respond with anything other than a gormless grin on his face, so smitten was he.

"Yes" he eventually managed to stammer out a reply. "My Father insisted on the name, it's been in the family for a long time. Tradition and all that."

"Really?" smiled the fifteen-year-old Amelia enigmatically, unknowingly with all the charms of a beautiful woman. Unbeknown to Tristan, this fetching girl with the face of an angel had recently learned some rather colourful language and her young Lemon was impatient to discover amusing ways to utilise her knowledge.

He couldn't read her. Not then. 'Say something you idiot,' he said to himself, 'don't let her turn away, turn and walk away forever. Say something.'

Of course, this wasn't necessary. Fledgling bitter Lemon had begun to happily stir her wooden spoon of discontent and therefore, Amelia beat him to it.

"And what is your Father's name?"

"Gosh, oh well, its George, George Treadwell." A confused Tristan stumbled with the answer, unsure of her interest, but in all his eighteen years, he had never been quite so affected by someone, as this girl standing before him managed, with just one look. "In full... of course... it's Sir George Ian Treadwell." The thrill he felt surging up and down his spine at the thought that this gorgeous creature could possibly be interested in him, found him pronouncing his father's name with pride - hoping to impress.

"Of course." She mocked, repeating his words.

'She's not mocking me is she? Please don't let her be mocking me.' Despite his obvious good looks, Tristan had more than his fair share of scorn thrown his way in a culture where being upper class was no longer a privileged benefit to one hoping to make his own way in the world, but rather, something of a hindrance.

The girl standing before him began to smile broadly. "George Ian Treadwell. And did your Father share his middle name with you also?"

"No." Why did she want to know?

"Thank goodness for that. Your forebears were not very careful when handing out initials. Your Father is a GIT. Just as well they didn't name you Tristan Ian."

Tristan stared blankly at this vision of loveliness, not quite understanding the problem the name Tristan Ian Treadwell would have presented in his life.

Amelia could trace his thought patterns; '*Yes, go on, you're almost there*' said Lemon snidely, '*think initials. Ah I see a glimmer.*'

"Tit?" He queried artlessly.

"Tristan Ian Treadwell. TIT."

"Oh I see, yes very funny. No it's alright, you don't have to worry, I'm not a tit."

"I'm not," she laughed, "worried that is." Suddenly concerned that she was being incredibly rude and offhand to this rather gorgeous looking young man, she said, "I'm so sorry, I hope I haven't offended you, it's just my sense of humour. Of course you're not – a tit."

"Well I might be. You don't know me yet. I hope you do get to know me one day."

"In that case," she smiled, "I'll wait till then and let you know. So do you have a middle name?"

"William."

This allowed Lemon full rein to silently taunt her with the thought, *'Oh My God! Do you think they snuck an Arthur in there too? Tristan William Arthur Treadwell?'* Lemon, still absorbed with the childish pursuit of how to turn initials into a rude word was convulsed with laughter, having just struck gold.

Tristan reddened with embarrassment as Amelia's intense smile fastened, her eyes lacquered with the unknowable. "You don't like the name William?" aware of his lame gamble, he swallowed the nuisance butterflies currently threatening his credibility and awaited her response.

"I love the name William, and the name Tristan. It suits you." Her smile suddenly warmed with genuine liking for this shy young man, quite obviously older in years than her, but seemingly innocent in worldly ways.

Many years later, Amelia had told him the reason for her levity and how she had fought to control her rebellious laughter – and that it was at that precise moment when she fell in love with him.

Tristan sat grinning to himself as he allowed his memories of Amelia to dwell on happy times. At this, she walked in the room carefully carrying 2 glasses and the bottle of wine, now open.

"Tit." She said, reading his thoughts with a smile.

"Almost a twat even." he laughed with her, suddenly comfortable and at ease.

"Never that." She said fondly. "Nor a tit. You are perfect, my love."

"Perfect enough to marry one day?"

"No, too perfect. That's why I can never marry you. Couldn't possibly keep up the intensity of being worthy of you. Far too much like hard work."

Tristan's face clouded as he remembered the conversation with his father that had killed his relationship with Amelia in a heartbeat. He had answered his phone.

"Hello Tristan," his father's voice.

"Hi Dad, how you doing?"

"Hey not so bad. You decided yet on Ascot this year son, Royal Enclosure as per usual of course? I'm planning to book."

"Who's going?"

"Oh you know, usual crowd."

Tristan, mindful of Amelia's reluctance to spend any time with his family, shot a glance in her direction, where she sat engrossed in her book. "Oh I don't think so Pops, I, we, can't make it this year."

"Why's that, are you ashamed?"

Wrong-footed by the unexpected comment, he laughed edgily, "No, no Pops, we just can't make the dates you gave me." Tristan quickly stole another peep in Amelia's direction as he ended the call after the usual pleasantries and having politely asked after his Mother and sent his regards to all and sundry.

Amelia's body language gave no sign. He began to breathe a little easier. 'She's reading,' he thought, 'concentrating on her book, not listening to me.'

"That was Dad," he said breezily.

"I heard." Silence. Tristan's unease returned. 'Oh please don't tell me she heard him.'

Amelia had heard him. "Why would you be ashamed of me?" She eventually uttered starkly.

Tristan's worst nightmare sprang to life. She had heard. Amelia had heard the crass remark his father had made and he knew he hadn't handled it well.

"Oh Ams, it was just his little joke, don't be sensitive about it. You know what he's like." Making the situation much worse by trying to brush it off, Tristan attempted to appear uninterested and began to change the subject. "What shall we have for lunch, or would you rather go out. Let's go out. Do you fancy the bistr….." he tailed off as Amelia, ignoring him, launched her offensive.

"Let me get this straight. Your Father suggested, in joke, that you would be too ashamed of me to accompany you to Ascot with his chummy chums? And you just laughed it off. Did you say, Dad how dare you? Dad I don't like what you're suggesting. Dad, you're a pompous, supercilious, up your own arse twat. No, funnily enough, I don't think that's what I just heard. I think I heard, in fact I know I heard, your toadying little laugh that says, oh Pops - fawn, fawn, wag your tail - I understand why you feel like that, she's not as you say, *top drawer* but I love her so please try and move with the times. Please. Pretty please."

"Don't be ridiculous, of course I don't think like that; anyway, you are top drawer - top drawer without a title that's all. I want to marry you don't I?"

"Well, it's certainly not your Father's wishes." Amelia retired into a fog, remaining there, her hurt pride not relinquishing to empathy or forgiveness.

"Ams, there is no reason why my Father would not want us to marry. You are beautiful, intelligent and witty. Your manners are impeccable - most of the time and your dict..." Tristan managed a skilful duck, avoiding his mother's precious gift of Waterford crystal whizzing past his ear before finishing his sentence to the background sound of tinkling glass, "tion...diction, is...can be...perfect. I don't even mind the occasional appearance of *fishwife* lurking within; in fact, it's rather a turn on. Come on Ams, let's go back to bed?"

In true Tristan style, he was ignorant of the huge damage ignited by the phone call until it was too late; his thinking being that, after a quiet word with his father, he could smooth things over and make Amelia feel welcome and part of the family. That was not to be, the kindling hope for make-up sex – simmered and died, without trace. Tristan was soon to discover his life had changed forever by a brief conversation held over the phone, lasting no more than four minutes.

Amelia's memories of feeling livid with Tristan remained entrenched, with all her insecurities kicking her insides in a fury. 'How dare that little creep George look down on me?'

She remembered the day she arrived early to see Tristan, no one else was at the house except Sir George – 'Sir bloody George!' She still felt piqued at the memory. '*Sir* bloody George who made a pass at me - his son's girlfriend. Oh yes, I'm good enough for that, deemed good enough for a quick fumble when no one was about, and to top it all, to top it all,' she fumed privately, 'Gentleman George had quite openly registered shock when Tristan declared his undying love and intention to marry me. That repulsive man tried to get me into bed whilst shouting 'mésalliance' at his son.'

'*Hey up, he's a toad and Tristan Treadwell is the son of a toad,*' Reg harpooned – bearing remarkable likeness to said toad as he spoke.

Lemon's verbiage had opened with a rare display of applause for Reg. '*Well said, well said that man - quite eloquent for you Reggie my boy.*'

I've been practicing' replied Reg with false modesty.

Lemon had taken up the baton, '*The Sir George's of this world can't see further than the end of their over-privileged noses. You can't possibly have anything to do with that family Amelia; they'll bring you down. How dare he? Who does he think he is? His youngest son is a drug addict who has to be frisked every time he leaves the house; his daughter's a frumpy, thick as mince lollop who's happy just to live off her father rather than work for a living, and his eldest son – yes you Tristan, you numpty – you're so scared of him you'll do anything he tells you to do. Yes Sir, no Sir, three bags full Sir. What was that you said, Pater dear, jump? How high would you like me to jump? Over the cliff and far away, did you say? Outrageous.*'

As Lemon spoke, Reg had swollen to incredulous proportions, energetically jabbing his fat finger into the cavity of Amelia's head, initiating a wild throbbing ache, causing trouncing vomit.

Lemon had not, by any means, finished, '*True isn't it? I mean to say, you're not top drawer are you, even though Tristan thinks you are, and you try to be - saddo. You're simply not good enough and never will be. You didn't go to the right school long enough to smooth all your rough edges. Your Father's background didn't impress anybody and your Mother gave up her privileged lifestyle and everything that went with it when she met him and joined his religion. When you came under the elder's spotlight the pressure was on - that was it, your years at a public school were over. Well come on, what do you expect? You're not good enough Amelia, you're not good enough Amelia, you're not good enough for Tristan Amelia.'*

Lemon had sung the insults happily at Amelia as she sat there unmoving, hoping Tristan would come forward and support her. But nothing was forthcoming. *'He hasn't got a clue has he, fossil-features,'* Lemon spat contemptuously.

She couldn't tell Tristan, would never tell him, what his father had done and she could never explain to him the underlying feelings of inadequacy, into which, his father had inadvertently but carelessly locked.

Tristan had remained unaware of the full story, although Lucinda and Greg had urged her to tell him what his father had done. "Come on Millie," Greg had pleaded, "Tris thinks you've just got a big fat chip on your shoulder because your education was short-changed, and says you should get over it. But you know it's more than that." Greg pulled himself up to his full impressive height of 6ft 2ins, "One's prospective father-in-law," he began haughtily, "should not behave in such a way and Tristan has a right to know. He would understand your reluctance to marry into the family if you come clean and tell him his father is a thoroughly bad egg."

Amelia's response was to glare at Greg disdainfully. "Yes and talking like that doesn't make you one of them." She purposefully and cruelly touched a raw nerve. "It's you who's got the chip on the shoulder, not me."

"I'm leaving now." Greg looked hurt. "Think on Amelia. I'll forgive what you just said because you are distraught and your heart is broken," He paused to sniff prudishly, "but don't expect me to pick up the pieces when

Tristan moves on and finds happiness elsewhere, for he surely will. There's a queue of lovelies after him you know." Greg flounced off, draping his scarf around his neck with a flourish.

Lucinda turned on Amelia angrily at Greg's departure, "Poor Greg, he doesn't deserve that Amelia. He loves you and all you can do is lash out. Well, I have to go as well now, but please think about it. I agree with Greg, Tris has a right to know. It's selfish of you to keep him in the dark."

As the door shut behind Lucinda, not as censuring as Greg's slam but more than just a genteel close, Amelia stood raging with indignation.

'Rights, rights. Everyone's got rights....except me. Where are my rights? The distinguished Gentleman George - no sorry - Ungentleman George thinks he's got the right to take whatever he fancies whenever he fancies it, and a sense of entitlement so big he couldn't fit his stupid fat head through a hole the size of a crater; my fiancé thinks he's got the right to tell me I should get over it and not be upset by his family looking down on me, and my friends think they've got the right to bulldoze me into doing something I don't want to do. Well they can all go and stuff themselves. I have rights. I have the right to be thought of as equal – because I am.

I have the right to be treated with respect and not thought of merely as an object for sexual gratification. Good God, (Amelia couldn't let this go) people like that are still in the dark ages, good enough to shag but not good enough to marry... and Tris is part of it. How long before he turns into his father? It will happen I know it; they're all the same in the end; the apple never falls far from the tree... And, and I've got the right to be selfish. I have an immature prefrontal cortex – due to my stunted upbringing!' she shouted pointlessly at the door after the long-departed Greg and Lucinda.

Amelia returned her thoughts back to the present and realised at a glance Tristan was as lost in his memories as she had just been.

"This is Amelia; may I speak to Tristan William Treadwell please?"

"Sorry honey, past demons arise sometimes when I see you. I love you as a friend as well as wanting to marry you – yes still, nothing has changed." Tristan opened his palms towards her as he spoke tenderly, "Don't worry; I'm resigned to taking the friendship, even if I can't have the whole package. It hurts Ams, it hurts and I don't understand why you keep me at arm's length. That's why I keep my distance sometimes, but I'm always here for you, you know that, one word and I'll come running."

"Ah hem," Amelia cleared her throat excessively. "That's when you're not bedding Miss Big-Boobs-Betty, that's more the reason why I haven't seen you for a while and probably why you missed my birthday."

'Blast - wasn't going to mention my birthday, now he'll know how upset I was.'

"Oh, jealous are we? Fancy that. Yes, I had - *had* - been seeing someone and yes, I was rather taken with her. Being the sweet, thoughtful person she is, she had bought tickets for a concert merely because I'd mentioned I liked the look of it when we saw it advertised, and, yes it happened to coincide with your birthday. However..."

As he spoke Amelia felt her heart shrink into a small knot in her stomach. 'Sweet? Thoughtful? What a Bitch. Taken with her? Oh no, he's mine; I can't lose him, not again.' She centred on his words.

"However," he was saying, "realising we weren't ready to commit as yet, it's too soon after Bella so we agreed to cool it, just a little, for a while. Her name by the way, is *not* Big-Boobs-Betty, it's Clarissa. We remain friends, and it's not beyond the possibility of her turning up to a function or other as my guest or companion, and you, young Lady, are to be civil to her. The fact that you are aware of her body shape suggests to me that you've been making her the subject of petty gossip and discussing her, which, in turn, means you're interested to know what I'm doing and whom I'm seeing. But you have no right to quiz my friends or make pathetic attempts to sabotage her reputation or my feelings for her - or anyone else for that matter."

Amelia reeled in shock, unbalanced by Tristan's earnest telling off. She wasn't sure what angered her the most. Tristan indifferently placing Big-Boobs-Betty in the same category as her – that of friend and possibly much more; his superior tone of voice as he admonished her for name-calling; the fact that BBB was still on the scene; or that she had been caught out and Tristan had correctly come to the conclusion that she had being digging for information on him in a desperate attempt to find out what he'd been up to all these months.

She felt Lemon's venom rising to the bait. "You tell me you still love me and then launch into a tirade of abuse on your girlfriend's behalf. Clarissa eh, I should have known, another Arabella clone then, aren't you the lucky one – to find a sweet and thoughtful gal with bazookas to match. I'm sure *Daddy* would approve, especially if she went to the *right* schools and speaks as if she's just swallowed an angry wasp whose mission is to staccato her to death from the inside. Not to mention what he'll make of her huge gazongers! My God, he must have thrown himself on his knees and prayed thanks be to the Lord for this perfect creature being brought to his stable; he must have thought he'd died and gone to heaven when you walked through the door with that one." Amelia surprised even herself with the vitriolic edge to her voice as urgent jealousy began oozing from every pore.

"Amelia, whatever's wrong with you. That's just plain nasty. I'm a free man and I'll date whomever I choose. And what is it with you and my Dad? What is your problem? One faux par – for which he apologised when I told him you'd heard what he said over the phone - but you're never going to forgive him are you? I'd never realised you had it in you to be so vindictive and unforgiving."

Chapter 24

Storm Clouds Gathering

(What makes big boobs and perkiness so attractive to boys?
I mean, really. Two rounds of fat and a fake smile. Yeah,
winning attributes - *Gena Showalter*)

"That went well then," retorted Greg dryly when she
narrated her evening with Tristan to him, and Lucinda, the
following day.

"Oh dear," was Lucinda's response. "What
happened next?"

"I apologised."

"What! Good God, you really are not yourself are
you Ams." Greg stretched forward, smiling as he placed his
hand across Amelia's forehead to check her temperature.

"Greg stop it," Amelia brushed his hand away. "I
was wrong; I admit it. Unfortunately, Tris wasn't in a
forgiving mood and the evening wasn't quite the same after
that. He politely ate the food I put in front of him – lovingly
prepared that day...by me... for him I may add, not
realising how unappreciative he'd be otherwise I wouldn't
have bothered, I'd have opened a tin of beans for him – well
no actually, I wouldn't have even done that. All day I
slaved for him in my hot kitchen – all day."

Knowing Amelia of old, Greg's look suggested a
slightly cynical disbelief. "Well done for finding your way
around that old Aga at long last though." he ventured with
a veiled attempt at disguising his amusement.

Amelia ignored him. "He didn't even finish one
glass of wine, made sure he was alright to drive," she
added bitterly, "then got up to leave saying he had to run
because he had an early start and needed a good night's

sleep. Well that was the first I'd heard of an early start – early start my arse, I don't think it had been on his agenda until my little outburst, ok, correction, it was a rather large outburst I have to say."

"After all my careful planning and plotting on your behalf, you blow it."

"So it was you Greg. I knew it. Tris was very aware I'd been asking after him, not very discreet were you."

"Since when have you known Grip to be discreet Millie?" quizzed Lucinda, "you know how he is. No, it's all down to you not telling Tris what his Father did, and how it affected you. He probably just left thinking what a bitch you are – a jealous bitch."

'What a jealous bitch Amelia is.' Tristan kept reliving the scene, 'Why has she got it in for my Pa to this extent?' Tristan was beginning to feel sorry for his father. 'He's a bit of a dinosaur but he's not that bad,' he championed, 'he's merely a victim of his own upbringing that's all. For goodness sake, in her line of business she should be able to work that one out.'

He repeated this to Greg some days later when they sat having a drink together. Greg tried to explain that Amelia hadn't been herself lately and they had become quite worried about her.

"What do you mean, not herself? When is she ever herself? Does she even know what *herself* is?" Tristan was taking it badly.

"No, worse than that. She's found God, wants to be a good person and all that stuff. Lulu's concerned. She said Amelia told her she bought angel cards or something to try and communicate with God. She told me about them as well."

"What? Amelia, be a *good* person?"

"Yes."

"Crikes. Not doing too well at it then is she?"

"There's more. It's as if she's quarantining herself, it's not just you she hasn't been in touch with. And she split up with Dave, erm, no it was Ben – I think, can't remember, he's a nice enough fellow apart from being a bit of a bloke. He thought the world of her, but ..."

"But what?"

"Truth? Not you Tris. He's not you."

"Once upon a time I would have believed you, but not anymore. If she loved me she'd be with me. She wouldn't be chasing after this one or that one as if looking for someone or something that doesn't exist."

"Isn't that why? Not to mention she's eaten away with jealousy over B... I mean Clarissa. I don't know."

Greg pursued his thoughts. "All I know is, she loves you and always has, ever since I've known her anyway. But she's got problems Tris, believe me she's not right and splitting up from BenDave or DaveBen whatever his name is, has left her withdrawn and alone just when she needs support. She's had trouble at work with one of her colleagues, not to mention how stressful work is; not the easiest job in the world you know, and of course, don't forget to add her parents to the melting pot of stress. She rejected their religion and they believe anyone not in the religion is against them – against God - and so this logically includes Amelia. As much as they love her, their religion comes first."

Greg drew a deep breath and decided this was the moment to tell all. He knew Tristan would understand what Amelia had been dealing with over the last few weeks, and why it was truly pushing her over the edge.

Tristan had a fine legal brain and would know exactly where to start.

"Oh what the hell, I'm going to spill the beans. It's much worse than that Tris, much worse. Recently she visited them, and asked them if they were aware of the multi-million dollar damages awarded to a young woman in America, and the recent one in the UK, against the heads of the religion, for child sex abuse. In both cases, the now grown victims claimed the local elders knew of the abuse and, under spiritual instruction, did nothing to protect them. The abuse continued for years, so, later as adults, they sued the organisation – and won. It seems the congregation, the flock, know very little about this, or of all the other court cases of similar nature. It's shocking Tris, and this is so close to Amelia's heart, working with men who commit such offences, she knows how they think and operate, and covering up helps no one change their behaviour, and perpetuates victimisation. But when she tried to talk to her parents about it, they didn't believe her."

"What? Are you kidding me? Wow, that's brainwashing in the extreme. Poor Ams, she must be so distraught. Why didn't she tell me?"

"Because she hasn't recovered from the blow yet. Only recently, I found out enough to make me suspicious that something big was afoot, and forced her to tell me all she knew. Talk about snowballing, that's the thin end of the wedge. Listen to this: She heard of something known as, the 2 witness rule. The understanding is, if the victim cannot produce a witness to the abuse then it is not acted upon. More than that, it's dealt with spiritually rather than legally, so if the person, so far known only to be men, admits his guilt and shows repentance for the abuse, it is not taken any further than spiritual counselling. What seems to be emerging is that in some cases, the elders refuse to cooperate with the police. There is some dispute, naturally, as to whether they have acted under instruction, or from their own initiative."

"So nothing changes for the victim? These poor children have to return home, or to the same circumstance, as before? That means the abuser virtually receives permission to carry on - that's monstrous." Tristan's shock lived on his face as he grew to understand the significance of the grotesque information he was absorbing. "Let me get this straight; if a child is lucky enough to have had an audience, one who is willing to put their hand up and say, "Yes, s/he is telling the truth because I saw it happen," then and only then will it be taken seriously. But even in this unlikely, and frankly ridiculous, event, if the man repents, they would not report it to the police? I can hardly believe what you're telling me Greg."

"That's what she suspects, yes, and there's more. Amelia found out, by her parents' actions, that all the congregations are discouraged from discussing any of it; from visiting any websites that may be discussing this, or anything else considered anti. They intend to keep them in the dark. Anyone indulging in such Apostate thinking means they are 'mentally diseased.' Her parents went straight to the elders and told them what she was saying. Their response? She's lying, that in line with the law, there is a child protection policy in place and basically Amelia was to now be shunned as an Apostate. Her parents now believe they must have nothing more to do with her."

"I'm struggling to understand all this – this is big Greg, we all need to get involved with this one, and this shunning business - surely it contravenes the International Human Rights Act, I'll chase that up. "

"It's been driving her insane. Firstly, the organisation denies they shun, which as we all know is not the case – it's now happening to her. She doesn't want to hurt her parents, believing them to be brainwashed, but she's frustrated with their inability to see the bigger picture. The children need protecting, so regardless of her concern for them, this is her priority. What's also tearing her apart and why she's crazy with guilt is, why didn't she work it out years ago? She's tortured herself with this for weeks."

"No, she mustn't take this on her shoulders, they're generally thought of as harmless cranks, not a dangerous cult."

"As she says, the majority of them are completely unaware of what goes on at the top of the organisation, and are brainwashed into believing this is "the Truth" and trust what they're told implicitly. They're genuine, loving people."

"Mushrooms you mean, living in shit and kept in the dark."

"Exactly!"

Tristan continued, "She told me her parents felt that she'd become "worldly" as they call it, and they consider themselves not part of this world. I know she was very protected from the repercussions of that by Uncle Billy; we had many discussions about it, so no member of the organisation was ever aware that she had begun to live a very different life – you know, one that celebrates Christmas and birthdays etc. This meant that she was able to 'fade' from their eyes, which is why she wasn't disfellowshipped – I think it's called – when she was young. I'm guessing this shunning practice means just that; Amelia is now disfellowshipped. Worse probably because she's seen as someone against them, a false Prophet, and I'm pretty sure she will now speak out against them." Tris ended with a shake of his head, informed enough to understand the full implication of Amelia's situation.

"You got it in one."

"Wow, and all I was concerned about was her reaction to Clarissa, and, I didn't realise she's been ostracizing herself either. You're remarkably well informed Greg."

"We've seen changes in her and getting worried, even before knowing all this latest stuff, which is why I started probing. On top of all that, I don't think she's too well – she's had a cough on and off for a while and she's getting tired so quickly. She's been locking herself away and writing stuff – stuff about God, then saying God inspired her. She talks to herself."

"She's always done that, talk to herself I mean - the God stuff is quite new. What does Chris say about all this? How's he doing by the way? Have you seen him lately?"

"That's another thing; we were all worried about Chris's illness, not just Millie. But she, of course, was awfulising before she needed to, said she can't imagine a world without Chris in it and had him dead and buried poor man before the consultant had even completed his diagnosis."

"I spoke to him a few weeks ago, he told me then. How's it looking?"

"Thankfully Chris has been given the all clear. He's not going to die - even though Millie's worrying is enough to send him to his grave. He needs to take it easy though, bit of a wakeup call. He's been very positive and stoic about it. But Ams? Well, it was something else added to her stress pot. She's getting worse. She was ready to have me stalking the high street wearing a sandwich board with 'Grin if you've found God' stamped across it and handing out leaflets declaring 'It's Good to Grin' – can you imagine? Don't know about making people grin - she'd have me arrested more like, or beaten to a pulp! Then she asked me what made me feel flowery, I didn't have the heart to tell her the truth on that one."

"Good Lord!" Tristan hovered somewhere between faint disbelief and great relief that she hadn't asked him to wander the streets dressed in ridiculous garb, proclaiming religious nonsense with a desperate, rabid zeal.

"Honestly Tris, she's seriously cracking up. We're meeting up with her tomorrow, going round to her house for supper. Hopefully we can open up the conversation and see if we can glean anything else. Will you come?"

"No. Not tomorrow, I'm away, plus she's not very pleased with me at the moment, so my presence may close her down a little. Let me know how you get on, I'll go and see her afterwards. I may be able to help out with legal matters in some way; we need to gather some evidence of these allegations."

"Thanks Tris. We can't abandon her."

"Me, abandon Amelia? Are you kidding, knowing her like I do, I of all people have to tread carefully. But I can start making enquiries about all this. No, I'll start the ball rolling whilst you and Lulu look after her, you'll be far more successful with her right now than I could be, especially as she's throwing all manner of barbs and insults at me presently."

"That's because you enjoyed the delights of the luscious, curvy, Clarissa."

"Well alas; I am a mere mortal dear boy, a mere mortal. I made it quite clear to Amelia the other night that there would be no need of a Clarissa or anyone else if only she would give in to her feelings for me."

"Well I hope for your sake you didn't come across as an overbearing arse."

"Did I just now then?"

Heaven is a Donut

"Somewhat."

Chapter 25

The Confession

(When we talk to God, we are praying. When God talks to us, we're schizophrenic. – *Jane Wagner*)

"What did you just say? Can you just run all that by us again."

Amelia heard the crash. Something undoubtedly having slipped from Greg's startled hands as he was in the kitchen loading the dishwasher whilst simultaneously attempting to eavesdrop on the conversation in the dining room across the hall.

"Amelia, look at me." Lucinda peered anxiously at her friend's face. 'Temperature is higher than it should be I think - but no rash-like goings on, or has she? So covered up I can't tell. Pupils dilated? No can't tell that either.'

Amelia had been in the process of clearing the table as Lucinda spoke and was about to join Greg in the kitchen with the dirty plates, Lucinda intercepted and led her back towards a dining chair and guided her in gently, placing the crockery back down on the table.

"I'm not sick Luce," Amelia chided. "At least, I don't think so, possibly a bit of a cold coming on – my chest hurts. Anyway, stop looking at me like that and what have you done? I hope that's not my best china? And don't even think about putting it in the dishwasher." Her voice rising to a shout, Amelia leaned past Lucinda towards the kitchen where Greg was to be heard frantically sweeping up the shattered pieces of precious paper-thin Spode.

Greg stood, deciding to abort his feckless cleaning task, and walked through the hallway towards the dining room. His tall frame blocking the doorway, he stared at his friend with concern. His gaze turned with a hopeless air from one to the other of the two women before him; he was at a loss and eagerly looked to Lucinda for guidance.

"What do you mean Amelia, God talks to you?" he finally spoke.

"He does."

"What?" Lucinda couldn't think of anything to say, so she exchanged a worried frown with Greg - who decided the only thing to do was to lighten the atmosphere with his very own unique brand of helpful humour.

"It's like that movie. You know the one, the boy says, I hear voices." Greg changed from his pleasant baritone into a croaky whisper and repeated himself, "I hear voices."

"What?"

"I hear voices."

"Isn't it, I see people?" Distracted, Lucinda questioned Greg.

"What are you talking about?" Greg's control on the conversation started to unravel.

"I see people?"

"That can't be right. Everybody sees people. Nothing uncommon in that is there. Even I see people," retorted Greg.

"Dead people," stated Amelia flatly.

"What?"

"Lulu," began Greg tiredly, "Why do you keep saying 'what,' it's so ill-mannered."

Amelia's tone remained monotone, "the movie. I see dead people."

"Because I'm confused, and anyway, you just said it," replied Lucinda to Greg, ignoring Amelia.

"That's right," replied Greg to Amelia, ignoring Lucinda. "I see dead people."

"Do you?" A now even more confused-looking Lucinda, to Greg.

"No I don't. No, I do most definitely not." Despite the growing confusion, Greg's eccentricity drove him to return to the accusation of blurting out the word, 'what.' "And I didn't just say it, I said, "What are you talking about?" which is different from just saying 'what' all the time. I would never be so crude."

Satisfied he'd won that round, he returned to the worry of Amelia. "It's Amelia. Amelia sees dead people."

"No I don't…...I say 'What' all the time, but I didn't say I see dead people."

"Yes, but you always emphasise the last letter, and it sounds kinda cute and you did just say it; I see dead people, you said it."

"The movie. I said that's in the movie."

"Why are you talking about a movie for goodness sake," said Lucinda easing herself down into a chair next to Amelia with an internal niggle at her apparent lack of enunciation.

"I'm not. You are."

"Can we just start again please; this conversation is becoming ridiculously tiresome."

"Exactly!" Amelia felt justified in reminding her friends, "You two are worried about me, all because I said I talk to God, which you knew about anyway so why it's such a shock to you now I don't know. Now you're both acting as if I were ready for the funny farm, but you can't even engage in a sensible conversation without confusing yourselves into a whirlwind of total garbage."

Greg and Lucinda's caricatured body language hinted at vague insult, before acknowledging that Amelia was pretty accurate in her assessment.

"OK, OK," purred Greg, graciously assuming his *you've got a point* face, as he walked into the room and pulled up a chair next to Amelia, on the other side of Lucinda. Amelia was now ensconced between four solemn, well-meaning eyes, busily boring into her.

Amelia felt untimely giggles rising. She was trapped. Captive. Both her dearest friends were gaping at her very oddly, earnestly searching for a hand to hold.

'It's as if I've just dropped down from the planet Plob,' she laughed nervously to herself, thinking that a planet called Plob would be quite absurd and how silly the three of them must look, two people, one either side of a mad woman, both restraining her return to Plob with firm handholding, staring into her eyes to fruitlessly search for a sanity that had temporarily left home (or stayed in Plob). 'Come to think of it, if I had just dropped in from Plob they wouldn't be pinning me down in this way now would they? They'd be running out the door screaming.' Quenching her feral thinking and threatening hysteria, she braced herself, raised her hunched shoulders stoically and attempted to fight her corner.

"It's not that weird you know. It's called praying. People have been doing it for centuries."

"No, no Amelia, that's not quite how you said it. You said you talk to God and He talks to you. You said, He's told you aliens exist; that He says He doesn't help people even when they pray to Him - they've got to take responsibility for themselves – Hah there's a thought. You said He said there is no such thing as time. You said God doesn't mind about sin – as long as we're happy! You even sa...."

Patting Amelia's hand, Greg cut Lucinda off mid hesitation to take up the mantle, "Now now, Millie dear, that's not exactly the same as finding spirituality and getting your Faith back and saying your prayers every night before you go to sleep is it? You know what I mean; 'Now I lay me down to sleep...' what's the next bit, something about weep...peep? What rhymes with sleep? It's got to rhyme or it wouldn't be a prayer we all remember."

"Which you clearly don't," retorted Lucinda with her very best effort at joining her eyebrows together, still feeling rankled at the ill-timed traces of what she saw as Greg's obdurate nature.

Greg decorated his face with his much practiced *never been so insulted* look. "I think you'll find I'm trying to help here. The nub..." Liking the word, repeated it... "The nub as I think you'll agree is that our Millie's dialogues with God are not quite the same as a sweet childlike mantra before scrambling into bed and passing out into innocent slumber. Nor are they the same as Chris's experience who does, may I add, observe a religion, a relatively common one and does not.... Not... report to being God's right-hand man, discussing how to bring about world peace in personal interviews with Him."

"He's right Ams." Lucinda frantically nodded her agreement, shelving her irritation with Greg into abeyance. "He *is* right. It's not the same. You said God tells you to do things. You said you hear his voice."

Greg, feeling the urge for his obdurate nature to run wild and free, deemed it would be funny to repeat his squeaky ghost voice, "I hear voices."

"That's not funny Greg." Lucinda chided him, her impatience with him rattling inside the abeyance box. "Amelia, this is not right, this is not right at all."

"I knew no good would come of this being good malarkey," stated Greg with a wise after the event shake of his head, whilst still smarting from Lucinda's scolding.

Amelia had been looking from Greg to Lucinda and back. "I feel as if I'm watching a really boring game of tennis and I'm getting very fed up with it. It's nothing bad. God only tells me to do good things, tells me how to be good."

"Which comes back to my point....our point." Greg hastily corrected himself as he caught Lucinda's steely eye upon him. Having noted her approval, he continued, "No good comes of being good." A wallpaper of confusion adorning his face transcended his triumph at the cleverness of the pronouncement. However, Greg being Greg, chose to stick with his statement by repeating it, hoping this would clearly signal to them that it quite obviously makes sense, 'unless one is dealing with a fool of course' he silently weighed their intelligence haughtily. "No good comes of being good."

"What?" Lucinda, aware that the *what* word represented in Greg's eyes all that is stupid, felt her creeping embarrassment at its use once again, assuaged by the fact that Amelia had wholeheartedly joined in, both declaring in chorus with exactly the same amount of scepticism, and both with a well-defined, resounding T.

Greg, secretly pleased that within this conversation he had so far used more than one of his faces mainly hitherto practiced under the watchful eye of his lucky mirror, espoused his flamboyant, 'even when I'm wrong, I believe I'm right' look. He adjusted his posture accordingly.

"No good, I say. No good at all comes of trying to be good. You know, in the olden days, you would have been burned as a witch, or drowned." Greg warmed to his theme, "They used to hold them down in the water, if they drowned they were innocent; if they lived, choking their way to the surface, they were pronounced witches so they would drag them out; dry them off and then burn them."

"Oh how comforting." Lucinda envisaged helping Greg out of the door with her boot.

"Isn't it funny how it was only women?" Amelia quietly yielded.

"What?"

"Greg, stop saying What." Lucinda allowed herself a satisfied smile by settling the score of the too many, inarticulate *whats*. She returned to Amelia, "Witches were, are, only women. Wouldn't be a witch if it were a man. It would be a wizard."

"Did they burn wizards then?" queried Amelia, still inexplicably focused on her rights for women moment.

"No. I don't know. Anyway, can we get back to the subject please? Amelia, if you go around telling people you have intimate discussions with God and He gives you little tasks to do, like saving the world and such like, they are going to worry about you. What do you expect?"

"Urm," Greg shook his head once again, in a, I'm a very wise man, sort of way. "Can of worms, dear-heart, Can... Of...Worms. This must stop. Straight away – immediately even."

She averted her eyes as she felt tears prickle. "I know you're trying to help, but it's not, I mean, you're not. You don't know how hard it's been. No matter how hard I try. I fail time and time again. I want to be a HEB and keep failing at it. I can't do it, I just can't."

"What's a HEB?" Lucinda searched Amelia's tortured face but found she had retreated into her painful inner purgatory.

"What's a HEB Greg?" Lucinda turned to him.

"No idea. He Expects Beauty? erm,.... Hangover Encumbered Bloke?"

Lucinda felt her mouth tremor with amusement. 'Trust Greg, but he may be right. Customarily, oh what fun this would be. Maybe it would do Amelia a little good if we can coax her back into her happy self with some humour.'

"Hugely Exceptional Bottom?" she therefore suggested.

Sensing the game, Amelia's consciousness returned to the room, not to be outdone.

"Highly Elaborate Bouffant?" she even managed a small smile.

Greg patted his hair, in appreciation of her good hairdo riposte, kindly pretending it was much cleverer than it really was; he then proudly dished up his next word-feast course.

"Hernia Erupts Bizarrely?"

As Amelia laughed, her two friends grinned back at her with relief, thankful that true to form, she couldn't resist a joke.

"There you go; you're going to be fine." Lucinda felt it safe to return to the restoration and convalescence of her friend's mental health and so repeated her words to emphasise their truth.

"Now, you're going to be alright, you're just overworked, stressed out to the max and need some R & R."

Greg however, was now on a word-wave crest and enjoying the HEB game; so much so, he was more than able to forget its cause. Not knowing when to stop as usual he boomed his next and, he felt, cleverest quip so far.

"Hermaphrodite Equips Bisexuals," he announced, with some feeling.

Lucinda's warning shot of 'too far, too far,' across his boughs, fell on deaf ears and blind eyes and bounced out through the doorway.

"Handsome Ebullient Bush." Greg was not in the mood to be warned and began giggling idiotically at the visual imagery now being played out in his head.

Reaching the crescendo, "How about, Hereditary Evolution Bypass!"

Amelia raised her head sharply. "Actually, it's the opposite."

"What?"

Greg, with a, don't interrupt me so rudely, rebuke in readiness, received a swift jab from Lucinda, reminding him painfully why he was surfing his language skills so happily in the first place, and how quickly they had been reduced to a despised *what*.

"Sorry Millie-Moo, I forgot you were in a right old huggermugger." Greg raised his eyebrows in silent triumph at Lucinda for his rally from the *what* word into oration superiority. Over Amelia's head, he mouthed the word huggermugger in an impudent repetition that challenged Lucinda to know the meaning.

"Maybe Greg, as you're so clever with words, you can explain to me why Hereditary Evolution Bypass would be a philosophical polarity to a HEB?" Lucinda bestowed the sweetest of smiles upon Greg's features that were currently twisting from triumphant to hapless before her very eyes.

He stifled the only appropriate word, *what* from leaving his mouth, swallowing it down with a gulp of humble pie. He searched his brain dictionary, quickly scanning up and down his memory aisles.

Lucinda and Amelia, watched with interest, both keen to hear his rejoinder.

"Well, don't rush me; I've got to put it into a language you would both understand."

Lucinda was impressed with that comeback, but as she inclined her head towards him to communicate her endorsed waiting time, she noted the aggravated posture returning to Amelia, reflecting that her inner torment had taken over once more. 'Amelia's not ready to play games' she thought poignantly as she upped the level of comfort patting and stroking of her friend's hand.

"Don't worry, you'll be alright." It sounded so lame, even to her own ears, but she was out of her depth and knew little of how to help Amelia.

Without realising, Lucinda stopped the patting and began to clutch and squeeze Amelia's hand gently - at first. "Hearing God's voice in your head must be very scary Amelia, but we can help you, we can get you help."

"No no I don't have a problem with that. I love hearing from God and chatting with him. But it's hard being *good* all the time, or trying to be. I don't think I can manage it; if I can't be good, what's to become of me?"

Lucinda and Greg were not too sure how to react to this. Whatever they said in response could push her even further over the edge of insanity. They nodded to each other in noiseless accord, "Take it slowly," Greg mouthed quietly to Lucinda.

"Amsy, look at me my love." As one hand involuntarily tightened its grip, she gently pushed Amelia's head up with the other, to search her eyes once more.

"Amelia, being good is one thing, trying to be perfect is a very different matter. No one can be perfect, you mustn't expect so much of yourself; God wouldn't want that, He knows you're just creating more stress for yourself." Lucinda glanced at Greg for his sanction and permission to carry on - she noted she had won it.

"You've been splitting yourself in two and the strain of it is catching up with you. You are entitled to have

271

doubts and fears and any other human emotion, experience or condition, just like the rest of us."

"Yes," said Greg not able to keep quiet a moment longer. "Jealousy, greed, rage, sloth, avarice, lechery…"

"What Greg means," butted in Lucinda darting an evil look at Greg that said 'stop right there before you dig a deeper hole,' "what he means sweetie, is that perfection is impossible and trying to be, will only make you ill. Ease up on yourself. Let's think about what we can do to get you feeling better."

"How about bury the stick you've been beating yourself with?" suggested Greg sarcastically.

"Greg, this is no time for your quips." Lucinda secretly agreed with her ally but knew this was not the time to be flippant.

Amelia shattered her silence. "It's so confusing. It's much harder than I thought. I thought I could just forgive everyone everything they had ever done, including myself, (especially myself) and that would work. I would feel good and God would say well done and the world would be a happier place. But some people hate good people and turn on them; that's why they used to burn them in the lake and drown them on the stake."

Lucinda raised a hand quickly, palm facing Greg's nose without even glancing in his direction, realising it was imperative to hush his response to the absurdity conjured up with the, 'burning in the lake and drowning on the stake' misnomer, she sealed the gesture by pressing a firm finger to her lips. Greg, despite his desperate need for a quip, snapped his mouth shut, allowing Amelia to speak.

"But I still have bad thoughts about people; I still feel upset or outrage at people and wish they'd drop off the edge of the planet; I still get irritated at things I shouldn't be worried about. I still get jealous – of other people, other people's families and the success of others. I still... I don't know, feel the same I guess. I want to save the children. Stop the hunger and deprivation and yet I covet things I don't need. I still feel flawed and awkward and pathetic...and, and it's killing me."

Amelia unravelled. They sat together, the three friends bound by love for each other, heads bowed, as one troubled comrade spilled her heart into their laps. She told them her failure to be good was not God's fault. She assured them He had said the same thing to her as they had just said, "It is not healthy, nor required, to be so hard on oneself." That God had said, "Just be yourself Amelia, enjoy your life and live for the moment. Allow the helping of others to bring you joy." She told them God had said, "If you want changes in the world, then make them yourself for yourself, don't take on the responsibility of the whole human race." But she was struggling even to do just that – let alone change the world. Oh how she wanted to change the world.

Then she told them of all her voices, not just God's. She told them of the turmoil they create in her head causing her headaches and palpitations. How they argue with each other and make her say and do things she didn't want to say or do - like "swear or copulate." Or be too nice and people walk all over her, taking her for granted and using her. She was fodder to the bullies. How the voices wouldn't leave her alone; wouldn't leave her in peace, creating constant pain and persecution inside of her. And the children, oh, the children; she must do something; she must do something.

"Suffer the little children, that's what the Bible says doesn't it. Suffer the little children. Oh blast," trailed off Amelia miserably, "I'm in trouble aren't I." She began rocking gently back and forth. "Mea culpa. Mea culpa." she chanted soberly under her breath.

'*Oh fuck,*' exploded Lemon, '*I'm in trouble aren't I.*'

'*Hey up, who's in trouble, not ravishing me,*' retorted Reg confidently. '*It's certainly not my fault.*'

'*Yes you arsehole. You, me, and twinkle toes over there.*' Lemon gesticulated furiously at a worried looking Sugarplum, '*we're all fucked and it's entirely our own fault!*'

Chapter 26

Questions and Answers

(Rivers, ponds, lakes and streams – they all have different names, but they all contain water. Just as religions do, they all contain truths - Muhammad Ali)

Much later, when Lucinda thought Amelia was soundly sleeping off the sedative she had given her, (knowing she'd find a stash in Amelia's cupboard) and Greg and she were resting on Old Faithful, each nursing a much deserved cup of hot sweet tea as they huddled around the freshly lit fire crackling in the fireplace, they discussed all they had learned that day. Greg filled a horrified Lucinda in on the news that not only had Amelia discovered something she found so monumentally evil that she was contemplating what legal action could be taken, but also blaming herself for not realising years ago that this could be occurring.

"I'm exhausted Greg. Talk about David and Goliath, this is big stuff that she wants to take on, it won't be easy, and this is just the first round – it took ages to calm her. Not that I won't support her all the way in this, as shall we all. However, of primary concern right now is her state of health. So, hard as it seems, Tris is on it, so you and I can set aside the religion issues briefly, and think about how to get her better. She needs to be strong and healthy, let's discuss a plan of action. I need to pick your brains."

"Only if you fancy a treasure hunt dear-heart – I'm pooped, brain closing down shortly."

"Seriously, we can't walk out of here tomorrow morning as if nothing's happened. She needs us. Do you think anyone at her surgery will talk to us?"

"I think they'll have no choice but to talk to us. She's not capable of getting herself there and explaining what's been going on. I wonder how long it's been happening, poor little thing. I must say, God came out of it all quite well though," said Greg, dumbfounded by his own words. "I mean to say, as creepy as it was with the aliens and stuff, there was nothing about doom and gloom and God punishing the hedonistic lot of us, was there?"

"I agree," sighed a tired and doleful Lucinda. "I'm worried about the other lot though; the other voices, they are very damaging. Most of us can confess to praying during times of desperate need, even people who say they don't believe in God have resorted to the comfort of asking a Higher Being for help when in trouble. But all this other stuff going on in her head is seriously worrying."

"She's seriously screwed you mean. She said she's got fruit & vegetables living in her head and they talk to her. Fruit & vegetables if you please! She spent an hour going on about lemons, plums and veg."

"Veg? I thought she said Reg?"

"Reg? That's too preposterous – even for Amelia. She can't have a man called Reg stomping about in her head – can she? That would be too terrifying. No, she must have said veg; fruit and veg."

"Yes, that makes more sense doesn't it."

They looked at each other and through the worries they held for their friend and the exhaustion they felt, they found time to laugh at the ridiculous conclusions to which they had arrived.

"That makes more sense did you just say Luce?" spluttered Greg, "Oh I see, having a cabbage and cauliflower, alongside a banana or two, sharing a patch of Amelia's vegetable plot in her head-allotment, not forgetting a token carrot here and there, is far less scary than an axe-murdery maniac called Reg rampaging around her labyrinthine brain cells."

Some minutes later when they had managed to sober up from this macabre joke, Lucinda's mind wandered back to something Amelia had said earlier.

"Did she say…copulate?"

"She did."

"What's that about?"

"Well, it means…"

"I know what it means. *I* mean, it's a rare word to use these days, why think of it in that way? Nobody says, 'Hello dear, how are you? Come and meet Dick, he joined the company three months ago; we've been copulating since last Thursday.' Who says that? Who's she been seeing recently? Do you know of anyone? She split up with Ben at least four months ago and not mentioned anyone to me since, other than a blind date that didn't show."

"You mean, who's she been copulating with recently? I don't know. Don't like to think about it to be honest." said Greg with a delicate shudder.

"Well, it might be pertinent; some weirdo putting ideas into her head. Ask Chris, you know him better than I do, ask him. She tells him everything, even all her bad stuff."

"Yes, Chris is a good friend to Millie, as is Gail, they might know who she's been seeing - but I think they'll be very worried by this turn for the worse."

"Are we going to contact them then?"

"You bet your sweet derrière we are. I know Chris is recuperating at the moment but says he's feeling great, so he wouldn't thank us for keeping this quiet. And Tris, he must be told about the latest. I said I'd let him know how it went with her today. We need all the help we can get with this one – she may be in need of round the clock

277

observation. It's all hands on deck with this little hot potato my love."

"She's not suicidal you know."

"Yet. Think of the strain she's been under. And voices? They don't go away quickly let me tell you. Who's Dick anyway?" Greg grabbed at the flying cushion, usually living on Old Faithful, which Lucinda had swiftly dispatched in his direction in response to his change of subject.

"I'm serious about this copulation thing though." Lucinda ducked as Greg returned the missile.

"Glad to hear it" said Greg. "But as beautiful and wondrous as you are, and as much as I love you, do not think about copulation and me in the same breath. My days of fantasising about women are over," Greg relished making use of his superior and somewhat disdainful expression.

"Oh you fantasise about women eh? Perhaps you're more bi than gay – what do you think to that?"

"You're changing the subject that's what I think about that and it happened a long time ago, when I was eighteen. Let's get back to, what about Millie?" Greg's face changed from haughty to guarded.

Lucinda was well acquainted with the face pulling Greg liked to think of as honing his craft, so ignored the current caginess that had graced his handsome features when she'd prized open his 'Greg's Secret Feelings' box. Concerned she may have stumbled upon something he would rather remain private, she brought the subject back to Amelia as he requested.

"Well, I was thinking about her use of the word copulation – it's random. It's as if she's starting to feel guilty about having sex with someone, as if she's become pious and having gone *all religious* on us, it's now against

278

her moral principles. As if by using the word copulation, rather than make love, she's reducing it to a mere physical act and therefore to be frowned upon."

"That's a bit heavy for me honey. Personally I don't have a problem with a bit of good old-fashioned copulation, love doesn't necessarily have to come into it as far as I'm concerned, just oodles of lust." Greg was relieved at the opportunity to re-establish the, Greg is shallow, myth he had carefully nurtured over the years. "Is that what she was saying when she started rocking? God that was scary. What was it, my copulate or something, almost singing it she was, that's when I thought she'd lost all reason."

"'Mea culpa' she said, not my copulate. Mea culpa - my fault. She was blaming herself."

"I know that, I just misheard that's all." Despite the severity of the situation, Greg could not but help feel rankled that it had appeared to Lucinda she knew something he didn't - in Latin, his treasured language. He returned swiftly to the subject of blaming oneself. "Oh dear, well that belief doesn't get you anywhere – even when it's true. Mea culpa indeed."

"Bloody private schools. Have a lot to answer for - all this Greek or Latin or double Dutch, whatever. What do they ever teach you of any use, for goodness sake?" Lucinda felt indignant on her friend's behalf.

Greg snorted his agreement with Lucinda through hypocritical nostrils, his snobbery being no secret to all his friends. Glamorising his grammar school background with the addendum that it was a private school in all but name, with the best exam results in the country, known monotony.

"They teach you how to peel an orange in polite society," he said with envious admiration, "and how to pass the port without calling upon the Bishop of Norwich."

"Really?" Lucinda was baffled. Her self-esteem so steady, she had no need to reinvent herself or her background. Nor was she plagued with Greg's affliction, a futile long-held wish to be part of this mysterious set.

Greg however was clearly impressed and the conversation reinforced in him the power of money, causing him to ruminate on the cruelty of life. 'Oh how I would have benefitted from private schooling; if only I had been born into an adoring family who could afford to educate me properly, just like Tristan – and more importantly, love me enough to want to do it; or a well-connected Mother and a rich Uncle who conveniently died without issue, just like Amelia. What I would have achieved with that – but no. I was born into a poverty-stricken family of boneheads who said bath instead of barth and went to the lavvy or toilet instead of the lavatory or loo.' Greg sighed with envy and raging disappointment at his predicament of being born a silk purse in a dilapidated family trough of grubby, grimy, snorting pigs' ears.

"If you're feeling sorry for yourself again Greg – stop it. You've done okay for yourself and it's not Amelia's fault she came from a family with money – well, one half of her family anyway. Think about what she did have to put up with. Don't you think she would give anything to swap the money and the schooling, provided by her Uncle, which ultimately clashed with her parents' beliefs so they put a stop to it, to have had an ordinary upbringing with adults around her who encouraged her to grow up to know her own mind and who supported her in her endeavours rather than trying to mould her into a mini version of themselves? The elders were forcing her to believe exactly what they believed, attempting to clone her and very nearly breaking her spirit along the way I might add. And somewhere along the line her sister died, no one knows anything about it, not even Tristan, but there's something funny about all of that and why it's never discussed."

Lucinda warmed to her theme, "No, you think on. She was living in two different worlds. She's seriously disturbed at the moment and when you know her background you can understand why. Each time she meets someone she likes she starts to feel guilty, so the relationship is doomed before it begins, unless she were to marry at once and then it would be doomed sometime after; Well, knowing Amelia, probably rapidly after. For goodness sake, according to that religion, because she's never been married, she should still be a virgin!"

At the thought of Amelia the thirty-something virgin, Greg discovered that suppressing exploding snorts of amusement gave rise to a disturbance in the back of his throat. Pausing, he reflected upon Lucinda's words, contrition quickly settling. 'Lulu was right; blame could not be laid at anyone's door. It certainly wasn't Amelia's fault, and she was no pig's ear,' although not specifically directed towards Amelia, he still guiltily took it back. 'She above anybody, other than Lucinda of course, was a beautiful silk purse and had no need of money to make that quite obvious.'

"I know. Don't nag. I know what you mean and I agree. Unlike myself, Millie certainly likes the love, romance and roses around the door nonsense and for her, living in sin, to coin an old-fashioned expression, precipitates internal dissension and turmoil – again unlike myself."

"You're not so tough, Greg, you just hide your need for love behind a hard exterior. When you find the right person, you will be eternally faithful, I just know it." Lucinda smiled as she hurled another cushion at her friend. "Anyway, enough about you; let us get back to the urgent

Heaven is a Donut

topic of Millie. Fancy something stronger, a brandy maybe, as we talk?"

"Good idea, I could manage a snifter and I think it'll be a while before we get any sleep tonight. Hey, I've got it. I've got it!" Greg suddenly sprung to his feet with as much enthusiasm as his tired body could muster.

"Got what for heaven's sake?"

"It's something you just said, a few minutes ago."

"Me? What are you talking about? What did I just say?"

"Higher Being. You said, Higher Being. That's a HEB.

"No, that's HB. Which sounds more like a pencil to me."

"Very funny, no, I think HEB means Higher Evolved Being." Greg ended with the satisfaction and triumph of someone who had just stumbled upon the correct answer in a superiorly difficult crossword puzzle, of which no one else had been able to guess. "My God, no wonder she's depressed."

"HEB. Higher Evolved Being." Lucinda felt the need to repeat Greg's proclamation to make sense of it. "Are you suggesting our little Millie has been trying to be a Higher Evolved Being – and failing ingloriously?"

"Of course she's been failing; she's as Neanderthal as the rest of us. Hence the variance."

"Oh. Gosh, that's quite clever isn't it?"

"Now you've lost me."

"Millie said HEB was the opposite to your suggestion of Hereditary Evolution Bypass. I get it now. Actually really clever; she hasn't lost her marbles that much, has she?" Lucinda's face had become increasingly animated as she spoke.

"Exactly." Greg caught the change in mood. "No chance of becoming a HEB if you've had an evolution bypass and what's more, it's hereditary so it can't be helped. Amelia clearly feels she's had a bypass from the spiritual perfection she craves and probably believes that to be true of all mankind and therefore there is no hope, no hope for any of us. Poor little lamb cutlet, she thinks the human race is doomed."

"My God did you hit the nail on the head with that one or what?"

"Yes but I didn't know it. I wouldn't have rubbed her nose in her own and the world's failures so spectacularly if I'd known that was the meaning of it. I'm not *that* insensitive you know." Greg was clearly feeling the need for a bit of Godly compassion to come his way. "Mind you, you're quite right. I was pretty good - for a grammar school boy. One of my more enlightened moments, don't you think?"

"I think you were so enlightened you were blinding. Stop congratulating your own cleverness when it is clearly detrimental to someone else. That's no way to become a HEB you know." Lucinda scolded him lightly as she passed him the welcome brandy.

Greg thanked her for the drink and they remained thoughtfully silent as they clinked glasses.

"Here's to Amelia – she may be a misguided oddball but she means well. She wants the world to be a better place and no one can fault her for that."

"I'll certainly drink to that. Here's to all the HEBs in the world."

"To Hebbies everywhere." Greg smiled as he spoke, "It's a bit more-ish isn't it."

"What the brandy? You haven't had any yet."

"No, this Hebby lark. I'd love to be a HEB. In fact, I think I am already." Greg sighed again, this time with more than a little hint of satisfaction.

Meanwhile, Amelia lay upstairs, although supremely tired, rest shunned her. She cried for comfort, just as she had as a young child when hearing the subdued voices of her parents coming from below, turning the soothing sounds into a lullaby. She attempted to calm herself on the soporific knowledge that two of her dearest friends were downstairs solicitously discussing what was best for her. 'They will help me, help me, help me,' the sleep-inducing melody.

However, the ataraxia she craved proved elusive. She remained tortured. 'Go away, oh go away please, I can't stand it,' she cried woozily to her splintered self.

How right Greg and Lucinda were. Amelia needed help, quickly. Fruit and veg were the least of it. They knew it was critical, but the core, the depth, the remedy was way beyond them, clever as they were. As their murmurs from below brought comfort, she tried to still her thoughts and let the pills do their work. But she couldn't stop the echoes whirling around her head from drowning the placid sounds of her friends' whispers.

The sweet cautioning – '*Be good Amelia, be good.*'

The gruffer overriding command of – '*Get your own back Amelia. Fight like with like; people are evil, be evil back.*'

Mingled with the whines of – '*You're worth more than this Amelia; don't let people look down on you.*'

The unexplained shivers began; shivers like nothing she had experienced before in her life. She felt hot, she felt cold: she felt hot and cold. 'How can I be hot and cold at the same time,' she trembled. Her teeth began fortissimo clattering, adding to the confusing cacophony, a background noise of a disjointed drumbeat moving crazily to the fore. She endeavoured to rise but was deplete of strength; 'this isn't just a nervous breakdown' she sobbed. 'I've got something. The flu or some nasty little virus worming its way through me - the bastard. Explains everything, it's been coming on for days, if not weeks. Maybe that's why I've been feeling as if I'm going mad. Nervous breakdown? I'm delirious with the flu, that's my problem. I'm not burning out, I'm burning up.'

She called out to Lucinda and Greg but so weak had she become, her voice trailed to nothingness by the time it hit the bedroom door, curling to an invisible cinder at the thresh-hold. Her breath laboured, wheezing into short gasping sounds of desperation. 'Come upstairs Lu,' she concentrated fiercely on the thought in the hope to transport it telepathically to her friend. 'Come upstairs Luce, I'm ill - not sick. Or is it the other way round – I'm sick, not ill. I don't know, just come upstairs, please come upstairs.'

Lucinda, with no intention of going upstairs, was on her second brandy and oddly enough, not functioning on the same wavelength as the urgent vibes, sent by Amelia, swirling manically around her head.

"Did you hear something?" said Greg.

"No, she's gone off to sleep, I gave her enough to knock out a rhinoceros," she replied confidently, ignoring Greg's look of disapproval, "nothing else worked."

Amelia eventually began to drift into a restless erratic sleep, soaking the sheets with sweat as she turned fitfully in bed.

Eventually, Lucinda and Greg, equal in their, 'not drunk exactly but not quite sober either,' status, tiptoed tipsily upstairs.

"I think we should take a look at her before we go to bed just to check. It's been very quiet up here for the last hour or two." Lulu's whisper pierced the serenity of the landing air as she deliberated which was the offending creaky stair, in order to warn Greg who was zigzagging closely behind. She held her shoes aloft as she turned towards his words.

"Luce darling, for the last hour or two, we forgot why we were here - and we owe Millie a bottle of brandy, by the way." Greg retorted in a, not quite drunk slur but not quite his sober-precise tones, either. "Damn, caught the creaky stair." he added.

"We didn't drink a whole bottle, only two small glasses each. Ssh," she hissed messily, causing the giggles to threaten for both. "SSHHH."

"Who are you shushing, you can talk; the neighbours down the road would have heard your whisper. Come on, let's take a peek."

All was quiet. Amelia appeared to be in a deep pill-induced sleep.

"Ah bless, she looks like a little girl. Bless our little Millie-Merecat, our little Millie-Moo," said Greg in a wave of brandy-generated paternal love. "Looks a bit like a merecat from this angle doesn't she? She needs tucking up. I'll go that side and you tuck her up this side." he instructed Lucinda as he walked around the bed. "Good grief, this bed's a monstrosity, it's huge and, look, she's got steps to get up to it."

On realising he couldn't reach to pull the cover over Amelia, he climbed the small set of wooden steps, lost his balance at the top and tumbled into the bed next to Amelia, whose sleeping frame bounced gently as he fell.

"Oh, Oh Greg," whispered Lucinda, "are you all right? Don't wake her." Lucinda shushed him again. "Hey, that did look funny," she began to giggle once more, "you should've seen the look on your face as you fell; it was a picture. I'll try from this side."

With that, Lucinda hitched up her pencil skirt and clambered up onto the bed, balancing on her knees next to Amelia in an effort to make her more comfortable by plumping her pillows and pulling the counterpane around her chin.

Meanwhile Greg, perfectly happy with where he'd found himself; lay on the other side of Amelia as Lucinda administered to her. He stared at the canopied bed hangings above their heads. "Wow this is some bed." he repeated. He found a stray pillow and flicked it deftly across the sleeping Amelia at Lucinda.

"What is it with you and bombarding me with soft furnishings." she said, throwing it back.

"You started it." He threw it again, more forcefully this time.

"That's it, you're in trouble now."

Tiredness out – second wind in - the great pillow fight began.

Above and across Amelia's head, pillows were flying and feathers were fluttering in delightful skirmish. The more the pair strove to subdue their game, the more they could not contain themselves, the giggles became out of control breathy gasps of air as the pillows swished and bumped into each other saliently back and forth.

Greg, having lost all his ammunition, just managed to resist the urge to yank the pillow under Amelia's head in an effort to take Lucinda by surprise.

"Oh sorry honey child," he whispered to the now stirring Amelia, "sssh, Lulu ssh."

"It's not me. You're the one making all the noise and getting carried away. Oh now look what you've done, you've woken her. You're hushing is so shrill it's like a spitting viperous threat, like you were threatening me. You threatening me boy?" Lucinda grabbed a pillow and paused mid air to take aim.

"Who you calling b..." Greg stopped midsentence as Amelia spoke.

"What's going on?" she whispered hoarsely. She looked from one to the other, painfully turning her head in fatigued amazement at the guilty pair as Lucinda tried to hide the pillow turned weapon behind her back and Greg reached out and seized her wrist to take her temperature in quick pretence to sanction his presence on her bed.

"Hush baby girl" said Greg like a doting father. "Go back to sleep. We're just checking you're OK."

"OK? OK? Any fool can see I'm not OK. And I was better by far before you both came to check I was OK." If Amelia had a voice she would have been screaming at them, but all that was able to erupt from her mouth was a high-pitched rasp, much akin to scraping nails down a chalkboard and equally painful to the ear. "What are you both up to? Can't a girl die in peace for goodness sake?"

She sank back, exhausted by the exchange, both her hands fumbling to reach out for them. "Sorry," she whimpered, quieter now, "sorry, don't go, I love you both being here, please don't leave me. Lulu, I love you. Greg? Greg?"

Greg leaned his head close to hers.

"You know I love you don't you."

They retrieved the fallen pillows, plumped them up for comfort and covered her gently with her warm duvet and top cover before tucking themselves in as they settled down either side of her in the huge and oft-lonely bed. But for this night, bound by friendship and love for each other, solace and succour was brought to a troubled soul.

The following morning, her symptoms had worsened, informing them in no uncertain terms what they needed to know – Amelia was indeed desperately ill. Whatever else was wrong with her, of most urgent and in immediate need of treatment, and confirmed at the hospital later that day, she had fallen prey to pneumonia.

Chapter 27

The Hypnotherapist meets the Murderer

(If you're a really mean person, you're going to come back
as a fly and eat poop - *Kurt Cobain*)

Amelia helpfully sat herself up in bed as Lucinda walked
into the bedroom carrying her breakfast tray.

"Hey look at you, how well do you look this
morning? Better than me – I think it's me that should be in
bed."

"Sweet Lulu, you do look a little tired. I hope I
haven't been a demanding patient. I can't thank you
enough for how you've looked after me these past few days
since I came out of hospital. I'm sorry if I've kept you away
from Coten."

"She fully understands, she's planning a visit next
month, I'm sure you'll be up to it by then. Oh sweetie, only
you could time your nervous breakdown to clash with the
nastiest bout of pneumonia, not to mention the allergic
reaction to penicillin that appeared out of the blue. You've
been very ill you know – and it's been weeks rather than
days."

"I know but at least that gets the next 10 years of
ailments done and dusted. And I'll be fit and well for when
it's your turn." Amelia smiled back at Lucinda as she
added, "I told Tris yesterday of my intention to see a
hypnotherapist, he's beside himself with worry."

"He did mention it, I have to say. He told me he
doesn't like that sort of thing. I promised I was going with
you and wouldn't leave you no matter what. You'll be in
safe hands Amelia, I'll make the Hypno stop anytime I'm

not feeling comfortable with whatever happens and I'll be with you afterwards as well, just in case."

"I'm actually quite excited about it. I know I've got deep-down issues that bother me and I have some recollection; but it's almost as if the thought of getting it all off my chest by revisiting will make it less scary and somehow manageable. Does that make sense?"

"Yes sort of. But don't raise your hopes too much in case that doesn't happen."

The following month when Amelia was strong enough, they set off for her allotted appointment with her chosen, highly recommended hypnotherapist, Nigel Thomas.

Amelia settled nervously on the couch; sitting in a chair arranged to one side out of eyesight sat Lucinda, close enough to hear and see what was going on.

Lucinda watched in trepidation as he took Amelia swiftly and expertly back, peeling away the years until she became fully acquainted with her young self.

What transpired was to change Amelia's life ..... forever.

"How old are you Amelia? Amelia?"

"Yes?"

"How old are you?"

"Four. I'm four."

"What's happening?"

"I'm worried about my Mummy."

"Tell me all about it."

"I'm a big girl now. I'm at school. What's my Mummy going to do without me?"

Amelia fretted, worried her Mother may be bored or lonely without her, what could she be doing all day without her there to keep her company? Her concerns for her Mother were all consuming.

From day one at school, Amelia had made it her mission to find every scrap of play-dough she could find and lay them tenderly on top of the large warm radiator, causing sunny rainbow streams of smelly dough to surreptitiously drip and drool their way to the floor in a delightfully slow-growing puddle of sky-scrapers she called Colour-City. Her punishment then being, much to her dismay, to scrape away all remnants of Colour-City with a dull palette knife, making her very late and thus keeping her Mother waiting.

"Detention already." Her teacher had disapprovingly shaken his head. Amelia didn't know what detention was, but didn't like the sound of it and all in all, began to find the whole business of school very stressful. She didn't recognise it as stress, this was a new feeling, but she began to feel an uncomfortable gnaw inside her tummy, rather than the fun she had expected. This only eased when she was safely hand in hand with her Mummy, skipping and jumping all the way home as had been her custom since the daily long trek to school and back had begun and she had sought ways to help make the journey pleasurable, as only a child could.

"What's happening now Amelia?"

"I'm skipping of course and counting every crunchy leaf I can find to jump on. You've made me lose count now. I'll start again. One, two…three.. I'm a big girl now; I can count up to…."

Amelia fell silent. Lucinda looked sharply at Nigel, her face a question mark of awkwardness. She was finding the experience unsettling. To be present during such intimate moments in her friend's life sat uneasily within her.

"I don't like him." Amelia the child spoke.

"Who?" Nigel responded gently. *"Who don't you like Amelia?"*

After waging the great plasticine war and losing - finding the cleaning up process of her beloved Colour-City far too tedious, and ushering unbearable guilt affiliated with being a naughty girl rather than a good girl, Amelia settled into a life at school that had, in general, a very promising start. This was just the beginning and destined to change, had she but known. The salad days of Amelia's childhood experience at school were idyllic but brief. Her innocent and so far unchallenged belief that, adults know best and are kind and caring to children, was to change forever before she even made it to five years of age.

"Amelia, what is it? You look worried."

"He scares me. I don't know... I don't know. Oh what's happening?"

"Well Ladies and Gentlemen. Ladies and Gentlemen, may I have your attention please, I'm sorry to have to tell you this." commenced the stentorian autocrat. After a short pause to gain maximum anticipation, big scary voice, sounding gleeful rather than sorry, continued. "There is a murderer amongst us!"

A long, but hushed, intake of breath could scarcely be heard as the class of four year olds scanned the room in abject horror. Fear pounded in their heads mingled with burning curiosity and a childish belief that they were safe even though there was apparently a murderer amongst them; teacher was there to protect them.

In truth, they weren't entirely sure what it meant, what is a murderer? It was teacher's tone that created the stir. Teacher of infants knew how to make his small charges sit up and take notice.

They sat up and took very great notice.

Amelia was worried, not knowing why. She noted with relief to see her classmates reacting the same way; she somehow found comfort in a shared experience. They too, clearly puzzled and expectant, were equally unsure as to what was going to happen next. Certain of one thing only - something was going to happen and it was not going to be good. She felt the hairs on the back of her neck prickle. It was a feeling that was to become all too familiar for little Amelia as she worked her way through painful growing up in a harsh world of insensitive, callous, narrow-minded grown-ups. A feeling she grew very quickly to hate. She wriggled in her chair. She too looked around.

The children were not looking at her, again feeling relief. She could not see anyone who looked like a murderer. But then, she did not know exactly what a murderer should look like.

The comfort from witnessing the bewilderment of her classmates grew. That was what he said, "There is a murderer amongst us." She was not sure, but it must be bad. Oh gosh, yes it was bad. The tension mounted.

"Children," said self-important, over-inflated bigot, "Children do you know what a murderer is?"

"No Sir." The class whispered in quiet chorus.

"It is someone who wilfully takes the life of another. Takes the life! In a horrible way they make someone fall asleep in pain forever! It is a terrible crime. A sin God will never forgive. Murderers burn in Hell for their wickedness - forever."

Oh my goodness, that was bad, so bad Amelia was unable to contemplate the full implications. Who has fallen asleep forever in great pain? What does wilfully mean? No one spoke a word. She scanned the room once more to see if there was anyone missing. Wouldn't they have said it in assembly? Wouldn't Headmaster have remembered them in their prayers like they had done the other week when a teacher who used to work at the school had fallen asleep forever, she remembered he had explained it was called passing away.

Miss Jones has passed away he said, that meant she had fallen asleep forever and we were all to remember her in our prayers because she had gone to live in Heaven with Jesus. He didn't say she was in great pain though. How can you be in pain if you're in Heaven with Jesus, she thought anxiously? Why does a murderer making you fall asleep mean you're in great pain and if you're in great pain, you can't be in heaven with Jesus – or Miss Jones, surely? Amelia was still confused and her agitation was growing.

She did not care for his explanation of murderer, it did not answer her newfound questions, and then she began to worry that he would answer, but she would not like what she heard. Something inside Amelia told her she was not ready to hear such adult truths about life. She wasn't ready for this; she wanted to stay ignorant of tales of murderers who make people fall asleep forever in great pain.

She shifted awkwardly, her legs sticking to the chair. The teacher, purple self-importance bulging from his thick putrid neck, licked his lips with triumph at the affect he was having on his class of victims. He leaned his heavy overindulged frame forward towards the little ones he had captured with fear and excitement. The children mirrored his body language, looks of awe on their baby faces. He is about to tell us they thought, he's going to tell us who it is, who the murderer is. They fell silent in morbid expectation. Silence, oh so silent in that room.

Amelia's eyes welled with painful realisation. He was looking at her! He's looking at me, oh, oh, he's looking at me. Am I the one? Am I a murderer? I don't know, I don't know, I don't know. Or maybe I'm the one who's fallen asleep in great pain forever. Is this what it feels like? It could be. Oh I don't know. What have I done? She searched the room frantically with her eyes blurring, but not fast enough to shield her from the growing knowledge that the children were slowly trailing his piercing stare - to her. Oh, oh, she cried quietly inside, now they're all looking at me. It's me and I'm not asleep, so I am the murderer. I am a murderer!

Amelia felt her knickers dampening slightly and battled to control the fear flowing into them. Her throat constricted until she thought she was going to die. Is this what happens to murderers? Do they die in shame of wetting themselves and not being able to breathe the sweet air of life because of the heavy hands of guilt and disgrace strangling the life out of them?

"NO" Amelia was on her feet in defiance. Her small, four-year-old body outraged with indignation. "NO, not me. I am not a murderer!"

"Really?" sarcastically queried the cocky fifty-year-old bully masquerading as a teacher of children. Feeling very pleased with the deference he had managed to attain so quickly and skilfully, he haughtily viewed the tiny trembling creature in front of him. 'She's got some spirit,' he thought, 'I'll give her that.' The small bag of human bones known as Amelia was shaking furiously before him at such an evil accusation. He laughed. She shook all the more. 'Better take her down a peg or two now rather than later' he surmised, 'just being cruel to be kind. This one has got to learn her place.' He inched his heaving belly, quivering with expectation, down to Amelia's level, like an ageing hunter moving in for a rare kill. She could smell his rancid breath behind yellow, stained teeth.

She sprang back, away from the devil before her, hoping to find something or someone to support her, a prop, even if it was just a wall. There was nothing there. There was no one there. She had to return to her original place, now occupied by a monster, to steady herself on the table, clutching with both hands, she felt a fleeting relief at the one means of support offered by this inanimate object.

The monster before her eyes stated in exulted tones, "Isn't it YOUR parents who believe that God doesn't allow blood transfusions? Your parents Amelia, no one else's in this room, only yours. Your parents don't allow blood transfusions. Do you know what that means?" His voice rose to controlled fever pitch as the pleasure of someone else's pain rumbled through him.

"No."

"What? Speak up I can't hear you. Can you hear her class?"

"No Sir."

"No Sir, I don't know what it means." Despite the pain caused by her vocal cords coiling snakelike in a diligent suicide mission, Amelia made brave attempts to turn the animal whimpering emanating from her compressed throat audible enough to pass for understandable language, so that he would not order her to repeat herself.

"No Sir, I don't know what it means," he cruelly mimicked.

This isn't right. This isn't right. Amelia knew that in all her four years of long life and experience, she had not put anyone to sleep in great pain and it was not right of him to tell everyone she had. He may be her teacher, an adult, but he was lying, and lying is bad and nasty; thus heralding the slow beginnings of Lemon, with Reg hot on her heels, both too new to help. Grown-up Lemon would have protected her by telling her, *'he's just a pervy old man getting his rocks off by terrorising little children too young to fight back. Pervy old man probably has a hard on by now because he can't get one any other way,'* Lemon would have satirised him.

But young Amelia did not have Lemon or Reg to wreak revenge, or Sugarplum with which to forgive his gratuitous sin. She had no one to help her. She was on her own, clutching a small table to avoid collapsing, with the whole class glimpsing the wet patch on her knickers. She alone was fighting against injustice as only a small child could. She cried.

"Ah, that won't help. Tears don't help when you're dying and your Mother and Father say you can't have the blood that will save your life. You see what it means Miss hoity-toity Amelia; it means they don't love you enough to save your life. They don't love anybody enough. They love only their religion, which means they love only themselves; they think their religion will save them so they put it first. They would let anyone die. That makes them murderers. And it's your religion too. That makes you a murderer!"

The whole class of children gasped in horror at Amelia's cold heartedness. 'How could she?'

"How could you Amelia?"

"Ooh. No. No."

"What is happening Amelia?"

"No. I hate him."

Nigel turned to Lucinda, 'I'm bringing her back. She's had enough. She's closed herself off and there is something else, more to do with this man I fear, but she doesn't want to remember."

If there is any fairness in the world, four-year-old Amelia was, so far, unaware. Nevertheless, she began to realise that it became unnecessary to quake with fear every time she left the house to go to school; or hide when she saw his colossal bulk filling the school corridors. He no longer came to lead the petrified child into the dark privacy of the classroom cupboard. He was gone from her life.

There indeed came a day when she no longer had to run from the monster who had come to haunt her dreams, whilst squeezing her knees together tightly in attempts to calm the quaking bladder - he was no longer there. His crimes against children were many and loathsome; he had, at least, disappeared from her life. His whereabouts left unsaid. Who could possibly know how many little people had suffered at the tormenter's hands and what on earth had he done and gotten away with over the years.

That Amelia would feel better having her heartfelt belief ratified by a grownup - that he was truly evil - would undoubtedly have made it better for her. However, in true adult ignorance, forgetting all about him was considered the best course of action. Children after all are very resilient. They will forget.

Damage had been done, irreparably. Amelia would not forget, she would squeeze it into a little box marked 'Dangerous. Do Not Open.' and leave it in a crevice in her head labelled with a skull and crossbones. A warm and fanciful place to incubate Lemon and Reg who, emerging later, had time to acquire a deft and adroit purpose before their birth.

Chapter 28

The Tree

(No man ever believes that the Bible means what it says. He is always convinced that it says what 'he' means – *George Bernard Shaw*)

Tears beset Amelia's face as she lay on the couch in Nigel Thomas's treatment room. Lucinda, looking on helplessly, suddenly became aware of her own eyes stinging and tears dampening her cheeks.

Nigel cautioned her not to touch Amelia by arresting her hand as she reached stealthily out towards her.

"She's going to say something else, something is happening, please don't disturb the process."

"*What is it Amelia? Where are you?*"

"*At school.*"

"*How old are you?*"

"*I told you silly, I'm four.*"

"*What is happening?*"

"*Oh it's beautiful.*" Amelia's face grew into a wondrous smile as she spoke.

"*You are looking at something beautiful. What is it?*"

"*I don't know. I'm asking my Mummy.*"

Despite the virtuous morality dispensed to the loathsome creature now invading Amelia's dreams, the unintended abuse of innocent children continued.

One cold wintry day, shortly after the master of trauma and corruptor of innocents had been dismissed, Amelia, cautiously attempting to trust school once more and return to happy-self, skipped into the foyer, hand in hand with her Mother. She drew to a sudden halt.

"What is that? It's so beautiful; I've never seen anything like it before. What is it Mummy? Why is it suddenly there? Where did it come from?"

Feeling her shoulders give way in resignation, Amelia's Mother paused, knowing this moment would come. She silently and wearily acknowledged the time had arrived when she would have to answer her ever curious and demanding daughter.

"It's a Christmas tree Amelia. No, it's not beautiful. It is evil. It is from the devil. God does not approve of such things."

"But it is beautiful Mummy; you're not looking at it. Look. It's got stars on it. Did they fall from Heaven? God must like it if he let them use his stars."

"Amelia!"

Her Mother's voice was unusually harsh and Amelia did not know what she had done wrong. She loved the tree, and clearly, so did her classmates, currently gathering around with their Mummies, all saying how lovely it looked. "What a good job they've made of it this year, they've spent some money at last. It looks much better than the scrawny old thing they had last year," she heard them comment.

Amelia realised at once her Mother was mistaken. It can happen sometimes she was beginning to learn; adults did sometimes get it wrong - even mummies and daddies.

"No Mummy look, it's lovely and everyone is saying it. Jennifer's Mummy just said they do it every year. Why do they have a Christmas tree every year? What does it mean? Can we have one? She said they have one, they have one in their home and it's almost as big as this one. She said they have a real one. What does she mean, isn't this real? It looks real; I can see it so it must be real."

Amelia's arm was all but torn from its socket in her Mother's rush to leave the school - the building of evil and danger to her offspring, she now realised it had become. Amelia's admiration of a tree was deeply disturbing for her and she was out of her depth as to how to deal with it.

Amelia was sobbing now. 'How could such a beautiful thing that everyone loves, with the exception of Mummy, be evil? My Mummy. Why couldn't it be Jennifer's Mummy? Why couldn't it be Jennifer being tugged along like an old raggedy-rag doll with everyone sniggering at her?'

'Why can't I be the one watching downcast as my friend Jennifer's head bobs up and down looking silly; her quivering plaited hair looking silly; and she snivels her way out the door, looking silly. And there I am, still in front of the sparkly miracle called a Christmas tree, standing with my Mummy who's looking a little surprised and disapproving as Jennifer is marched off the property with all the dignity of a slug.' Amelia wasn't sure what dignity meant but new teacher had told the class last week that doing handstands up against the wall and showing your knickers wasn't respectable and one should always keep one's dignity. As Amelia had been the main instigator of this crime against dignity, she had been in very great trouble.

Respectable, her Mother explained, was, "being proper, decent and tidy." To be avoided at all cost and completely unforgivable, "being common." For example: "shouting, interrupting, laughing too loud, playing with the children from the local council estate and wiping one's nose with one's sleeve." None of which made any sense whatsoever, as being loud and shouting was good fun, the children from the council estate were nice to her, and using her sleeve to wipe her nose was jolly convenient. All-in-all, the adult world surrounding her was extremely confusing and certainly did not help her understand this particular misdeed. Amelia had ensured she had only done handstands when she was wearing, what her grandmother referred to as "highly respectable but ugly," green physical education knickers. This must surely make it an alright thing to do, she reasoned, because when it was PE lesson all the girls were made to wear a white PE shirt with special knickers the colour of sick, looking like balloons of horribleness billowing down to their knees. "I was respectable and kept my dignity – so why am I in trouble?"

"It's outrageous" she had fumed, (outrageous was another new word she had learned, this one from the congregation meeting; she had heard an elder say it and she loved the sound it made in her mouth and knew she would never tire of it and would use it frequently – relevant or not). "Outrageous - what's the difference between doing the relay race in your sick-green knickers in front of the whole school and wearing them when you do handstands up against the wall during break-time?"

Amelia, not for the only time in her whole life - was *outraged* at the unfairness of it all. Now new outrageousness was looming and shuddering its way through her body with waves of indignation, making her tingle with brittle tension.

She thought that Jennifer and her Mummy, Amelia and Jennifer's classmate Tommy, who everyone called the class clown because he kept doing silly things like falling over on purpose to make people laugh, on witnessing her Mother's mystifying behaviour, must have caught sight of her knickers as Mother raged out the school hall dragging her as she slightly stumbled, not much, she managed (quite skilfully she thought as it was a rather unexpected onslaught), to untangle her feet in time, but it wasn't without a little scuffing of her new shoes which upset her greatly.

That must have been when she lost her dignity, Amelia was certain, because she hadn't even been wearing her hated green balloons but her little white pair of which she'd almost outgrown and they may have observed this embarrassing witness of poverty. Oh and how she wished it had not been her - again.

"Why couldn't it have been Jennifer?" She sighed dramatically, turning it around vainly to cut free from the pain and distress of it all by giving it away. She had discovered recently if she willed hard enough, she could think it had not happened to her but to someone else. This for some reason she was unsure, always made her feel so much better. Yet, Amelia now felt guilty; she liked Jennifer and did not want to see her upset.

At which point, it helped her internal anguish to resolutely decide that it is all right to wish it upon Jennifer instead of herself, because she would be there to comfort her and say, "Don't worry Jennifer, that your Mother gave you the dignity of a slug, calling the dazzling wonder of wonders Christmas tree - evil Satan's tree, making you look silly. Or that Tommy the class clown and me saw your knickers and you looked silly. Or that we all heard a teacher call you a murderer - you looked very silly then when your face went all red and you started shaking and shouting at him, then you nearly fell over. But none of that matters - none of that matters dear Jennifer. I, Amelia, will still love you and be your friend even though you often look very silly and the other children laugh at you."

"Adults are so strange; they really get themselves in a mixed up pickle. Sometimes they don't mind when you do something and another time they start ranting and raving as if you've just murdered someone or shown your

304

knickers when they don't want you to. How am I ever going to know when it is all right and when it isn't all right," she thought intensely, "this is so unfair." With this cruel blow Amelia felt herself growing giddy as if being swept off her feet high into the sky, not fun like a flying happy bird, but hurling and swirling like a leaf torn from its family tree, not knowing or seeing where she would land. She reached out, clawing desperately with her mind to make sense of the senseless, but unable to yet steady herself with the biting finality that would inevitably dawn.

"Mummy, listen, just listen. Why is a Christmas tree evil? It isn't evil to Jennifer and her Mummy or the other mummies and children, or Tommy the class clown, or the teachers, or they wouldn't have put it there. Why is it there?"

"We don't believe God likes it Amelia. It's to celebrate Jesus' birthday and we don't celebrate anyone's birthday. Not yours, not our own and not Jesus'. God doesn't want us to."

"Why not?"

"He says we should celebrate Jesus' life not his birth and the celebrating of a birthday was started by someone who hated God, so we don't want to upset God do we?"

"Why not?"

"Because we should love him."

"Why?"

"He tells us we must. He demands it."

"Why?"

"He wants us to obey Him."

"Why?"

"So we survive Armageddon. That's God's war before you ask, and it's going to happen any day now, God's war on the devil. God will wage war with the devil.

God will win of course and all the people who worship God properly the way He wants them to, like us, will survive because He loves us, everyone else will die."

"Why?"

"They haven't obeyed Him."

"Why?"

"Why what Amelia?" asked a very agitated Mother.

"Why will He let them die?"

"Because they haven't listened to Him or to us and they should because we preach His message, we know the Truth. God wants everyone to worship him the way we do. Not go to their Churches or celebrate their own birthdays or Jesus' birthday, which they call Christmas. Nor do they use His name – Jehovah. We are the only people using His name and therefore, we will be saved."

"But Church's are beautiful, just like the Christmas tree - well not as beautiful, God hasn't given them His stars to decorate them with, but they're very pretty because I've seen them, we pass one every day on the way to school don't we Mummy? And I heard you say to Daddy once it's a very nice building, so I know you like them too."

"Amelia," her Mother replied rather wearily, not liking her relatively newly found faith impugned in this way. How was it everything the elders said to her made perfect sense until she was faced with the logic of a four-year-old; a stroppy argumentative four-year-old. They had none of this with Alice. Alice, Amelia's older sister accepted everything without dubiety. It made Mother irritable with Amelia and more determined than ever to fight her cause. They were right and Amelia must learn this. It may be a harsh reality at first, but Amelia must learn that they are not part of this world. That she must rise above "the world" and detach herself from worldly pursuits. People in the world will laugh at her, torment her, but she will be rewarded with her life when Armageddon comes - very, very soon.

She began again with firm resolve. "Amelia, Jehovah does not want people to go to these Churches to pray to Him - it is wrong. They believe in the wrong religion."

"Well, there's a lot of them that's wrong then. I saw them coming out the Church the other day, you saw them too Mummy, so did Daddy. There were loads of them. They can't all be wrong."

"Yes Amelia," (her voice rising slightly). "They can and they are."

"Will God punish them all then?"

"Yes."

"Well, that's not fair. It's not their fault, if they're all doing it. They don't know it's wrong. And anyway, they think we're wrong. They think we're murderers!"

"Yes Amelia, Mummy and Daddy know about that and I know he was your teacher and we told you always to obey your teachers, but he was wrong and it was wrong of him to talk to you in that way. We are very sorry he was so nasty to you. But that's what we're trying to tell you. People in the world are not nice and they will do things like that to hurt you. But you know better. You know that Jehovah will look after you. Mummy and Daddy and you and Alice are doing what He wants and they are not. There won't be people like him in the new system after Armageddon. Amelia, it's just around the corner, Armageddon will soon be here and then you'll be safe, but you must do as you are told. "

Amelia was puzzled. She really didn't want to hurt Mummy and Daddy but she was beginning to think they were being awfully dim about this. 'What does it matter?

How can it matter to God which Church people go to?' To Amelia this was all very stupid.

"Mummy?"

"Yes Amelia?" (Please stop soon).

"If God loves us - as you just said, He wouldn't make us die. That's going to sleep forever and if He did that it would make Him a murderer and that's a horrible thing to be. He's making someone go to sleep forever in pain. It's not fair to all those people, it's not their fault they've got it wrong by going to Church and He would be making an awful lot of people sleep forever in pain which doesn't make sense at all. Why doesn't He just tell them if it's so wrong? Just tell them. Anyway, I don't like Him anymore, He's not very nice and I'm not going to use his name, it's a dumb name. I hate Him!"

Amelia's Mother felt her eyes prickle with the pain of not being able to make her child understand all the things in the world which were, without doubt, going to reach out and scar her. She drew her little one to her as if to block out the world.

"It's not Jehovah's fault Amelia, don't ever blame Him, it's the devil's work. Jehovah will soon put it all right, very soon, even before you've grown up so you don't have to worry. You will never have to worry because this bad world will be over long before you have to live a grown up life within it."

She loved her child so fiercely, if she could spare her from discovering how cruel the world is as she grew up, she would do so. Her religion was the only way, the only way to protect her. 'How I hate this world and all those part of it,' she thought violently, 'it is vicious and spiteful and I can't wait for its passing.' "One day my little one, one day very soon God will bring about a beautiful new system and I want you to be there, you will live forever in peace and perfection, but you must do His will to be there, you must obey Him."

"You must obey."

Inlaid and buried in Amelia from these early experiences, adding to her confusing dread of a man who was supposedly there to nurture and cultivate, but ulterior stimulus proving to be self-serving impulses, another deep and terrible fear grew: fear of failing God; fear of disappointing her parents; fear of the adult world; fear of growing up. Therein lay the biggest fear of all – becoming one of them – a grown-up.

Lemon yawned and stretched within her womb, carelessly kicking the other occupants as she jostled for space with Reg and Sugarplum. Personalities were evident even at this early stage of development. Reg, elbowing for his spot with a fledging mewl of 'what about me?' Sugarplum, habitually winding her arms about him to placate and bring consolation. Lemon, the cuckoo in the nest, forever striving to push them both out, her own comfort imperative. Sunshine, where was she? Sunshine shivered in the corner, a newborn forever damaged by a multitude of pins thrust into her defenceless vulnerable body.

Amelia's sessions with Nigel the hypnotherapist, had dislodged latent memories that had not only unnerved her, but also her friend Lucinda.

"It's fine." Amelia had tried to convince her. "By recalling these experiences in detail I'll learn to cope with them. At last, I'll begin to understand how I developed into multi-facets instead of one big blob of self-conscious gloop."

"Don't joke about it Millie, I'm not sure it's a good idea. You were quite upset for a long while after the first session."

"Only because I felt sorry for myself, sorry for the little-Amelia who couldn't cope."

"Yes and now you're laughing at yourself – not sure which is worse."

"I know, I know. But I'm all right, honestly. I was upset afterwards, struggling to get my head around it. Basically, having a better understanding of why I've reacted in this way helps me make changes in the right direction; changes I need to make if I want to stop feeling so tormented. I need to not be so sensitive. I need to relax and not be so self-critical, not to mention critical of others. How about you? Are you okay to keep coming with me? I don't want you to be upset by all this, but I do appreciate you accompanying me."

"No, I'm fine, really." Lucinda lied. She had decided it was crucial Amelia had support throughout this although it was all rather perplexing: to witness someone experiencing almost perfect recall of their childhood, long forgotten incidents that make you and shape who you are and who you become. It was incredible, fascinating and extremely disturbing.

"You've been talking to God again haven't you?" Lucinda eyed Amelia suspiciously.

"No, of course not. No I haven't." It was Amelia's turn to lie.

Chapter 29

The perplexing question of Christmas

(Every religion is true one way or another. It is true when understood metaphorically. But when it gets stuck in its own metaphor, interpreting them as facts, then you are in trouble - Joseph Campbell)

"Dear God?"

"Yes Amelia?"

"Thank you for the lovely day. Thank you for my home. Thank you for my car. Thank you for my job. Thank you for all my friends. Thank you for my family."

"Hello Amelia, you sound very cheerful."

"I am. I love this time of year. God?"

"Yes Amelia?"

"Do you believe in Christmas?"

"Ah, that time of year."

"Yes God, do you? Do you believe in Christmas? Some people don't, they think it's wrong. They say birthday celebrations are of pagan origin and Jesus' birth is of no consequence. They say that it is what he did as a man, how he lived his life, the message he brought to the earth, Your message, that is significant and his death - how and why he died."

"All of that is true. This belief worries you Amelia?"

"Yes, I love Christmas. I look forward to seeing everybody, to spending time with my friends. I used to love my Christmas with Uncle Billy. For three years he had a lovely girlfriend, Ava, who moved in with us and we'd sing Christmas Carols and go to the late service on Christmas Eve, and then I would help them both cook Christmas dinner next day – it was the best time of my life. I mean, it was still good after they split up because Uncle Billy would invite family around, with the exception of Mother and Father and all their cult friends, so he could make sure I had contact with them all. But I did miss Ava, no idea why they parted – she went off to have babies I think because Uncle Billy didn't want any by then – too old he said."

Amelia tripped over her words to avoid the possibility of a Heavenly cessation. "Anyway, he had me and he did everything to make my Christmas memorable. Two years after Ava left, I was into my 2nd year at University and had met Greg, Lucinda and little Coten, Kitten as we called her then. Prior to that, Tristan had come back into my life as well. Gosh, we all had some fabulous Christmases. What was so sad, it was secretive so my parents didn't hear of it – and sadly, without dear Alice of course. I love it all you see, I love baubles and tinsel, trees twinkling at me, the carols, the food – I wished every year my parents would have a change of heart, sharing the wonderful times with us.

Amelia drifted abstractedly into her imagination of childhood, and then hastily scrambled back. "Most of all - I love presents. I love it that people have bought me nice things - I love nice things. What's wrong with that? Now, you're now saying it's wrong!" she sulked.

"How have I said that Amelia? There is nothing wrong with celebrating Christmas, nothing at all."

"But you've just agreed with the reasons people give for not celebrating. I'm confused."

"I do not pass judgement on those who celebrate Christmas or those who do not. I have said this before; mankind is free to make of life as they choose."

"So it's alright then, celebrating, with all that drunken nonsense going on and the getting into debt that goes with it?"

"Human beings do many bad things to each other and often in my name. War is raged in one country after another. Inconsequential disagreements give rise to bloody battles. Children are abused, neglected and starved. This earth could support you all but you appear hell bent on destruction. Destruction of each other and the world you live in, the world that feeds and sustains life. Therefore, why would I object to happy celebrations and people enjoying themselves?"

"Well I will then, I will celebrate Christmas - with knobs on!"

Amelia changed direction, "God, You sound weary."

"I have spoken many times throughout the ages, one day enough of you will listen. This world will change. Use this precious time wisely. Why would it matter to me how people choose to remember the birth of my Son? Enjoy life and do not be dragged down by the stresses of a temporary and corrupt system. The key is sagacious and loving hands to govern all decision-making, with love and forgiveness. Enjoy your Christmas with benevolence and laughter. Use it as a time to remember the Son of God with love and perception. There is no negative to that. Help each other, support each other, and love each other as self. If that is truly happening, there will be no anxiety to provide an expensive gift, thereby incurring the trauma of financial debt. The best gift in the world is being shared amongst you – love. "

The voice Amelia had come to recognise as God, continued with a spell-binding gentleness, "There will be no drunken violence towards oneself and others, nor angry jealous rages, because love transcends all distorted harmful thinking. It becomes a blessing of peace and contentment. When this happens, not if, the world's hungry will be fed. The suffering of the oppressed will cease. There will be no victims of violence or abuse. Separation of self will not exist. All is one. One is all."

"Wow. That's heavy …. I only asked about Christmas."

"No Amelia, it is exactly the opposite. It is light. It is enlightenment. Enlightenment is weightless. Enlightenment is Joy. Think of a world, a society of mankind living in harmony with each other all of your years not just one day; all society throughout the world."

"Christmas every day? Some would say that's impossible. People become angry, jealous, worried about what others think of them. They become anxious and frightened. Need I go on?"

"Amelia, it starts somewhere. It has started. When enough people understand all of what you have just said is ego driven, they can stop feeding it and see beyond it. See beyond ego."

"What do you mean, see beyond ego?"

"Ego is identifying only with self. This is a basic need for survival. To live, one has to win – says the ego. To shine and be successful, one has to outwit and pull down the other – says the ego. Ask yourself, does this work? I observe, ego dies when separatism does not take place; when people treat each other in accordance to their needs; when people find love in their heart for each other and can therefore forgive. Ego becomes obsolete."

The voice of her God pulsated mesmeric waves of wisdom. "Where forgiveness exists, no matter what the sin or the crime, real or imagined, a merging as one takes place, ability to function as one. People therefore do not turn on each other, fighting, blaming, hating and hurting. They nurture, help and comfort. They love; this makes them strong. Ego does not want to die so tries to stop people from seeing this truth, the bigger picture. Ego makes one seek attention. It says constantly, what about me? How dare you do that to me? That is not fair! I should have this, I should have that, I should be rich, and I should be famous. Everyone should look at me and admire me; me; me."

"Gosh, that sounds just like me."

"It sounds like ego and ego is inside every human being Amelia. Now you have the knowledge, what are you going to do about it? The world beyond ego is you, the real you, as for everyone. It is awareness. That is the power of the universe."

"But we're not One, are we? Society has always been unequal. Some people have very privileged lives and some people live in poverty. Some people are born into luxury and some are born with talents they use to better themselves, in some cases, this results in nothing short of hero worship, so-called celebrities, the world's crazy about them."

"There is nothing wrong with using one's gifts and talents. Why else would they be? Think about the intent. If the intent is to enjoy what you're doing, gaining pleasure from the moment, experiencing the present, then the sheer joy of singing and hearing beautiful music that also brings happiness to those around - is great blessedness. Living for, and enjoying the moment, when it is creating pleasure in a warm and positive way without bringing harm to others, is Love. But if the intention is to feed the ego, to say to the world look at me, I'm more deserving. In what could that result?"

"Surely the end would justify the means. Does it matter what someone's intentions are if ultimately they could make others happy with their talent or skills, or save lives in some way?"

"If the end result is to obtain peace, does that justify the endless wars and the mindless killing of millions that takes place in the name of peace? No it does not. Therefore the means is ego driven, to achieve an ego-boosting end, they then label peace. "Look at us" they declare, "we were brave, we conquered evil by destruction." What sort of peace is achieved by the suppression and killing of others? Of nations? Of cultures? Of races? How long will this peace last? How genuine is this peace? Has it worked before? Or, has it merely momentarily scared people into obedience, whilst whispering hatred and poison into the next generation, ready to leap into action at any time in history when they may temporarily feel stronger, and yet more vindictive with the passage of time?"

"America and Britain managed it. They were at war once, but now they are on the same side."

"Side! Yes they still take sides, just not against each other at present. Why may this be so? Who gains from this alliance and why? What does the western world want? Are these wants and goals achieved by consolidating effort with each other to overcome resistance? Is this alliance based on the striving for a worldwide peace? Or is there something else that these countries gain, something more sinister? How about money, power, status, the earth's resources, the supply of oil and fuel?

"Do you think that if Britain discovered all of these and kept it to herself, America would not turn on its new friend by declaring war once more? Do you think that if America achieved all of these things and kept it to herself, Britain would not join forces, finding allies wherever they could to snatch back what they want or need?

"Intent, Amelia, Intent! It is a natural desire to want to be praised for helping and assisting another in need. It can motivate a person even when things get difficult and the road is long and arduous and the burden is onerous. It is usual to be pleased with oneself when one has achieved a special thing. This is not sycophantic nonsense, nor is it foolhardy superciliousness. Everyone living has an aptitude, which they can either use for good or for bad.

"If a person acts for personal flattery, what happens when the flattery dries up and they are scorned? If someone does a good deed in order to be fawned upon and rewarded, what happens if the prizes don't come? Ego happens. Ego says with puffed up false pride, 'if you do not appreciate me, I will not help. If you do not love me, I will not love you. If you do not put me first, I will not give you any consideration.' Then where would the world be Amelia? Far better those who show the way without pausing for praise and for adulation. How much sweeter it is to receive gratitude when it comes in this mode, for it is genuine and a true reflection of self. Ego creates war. Lack of ego creates love."

Amelia slept fitfully throughout the following nights, her sanity branded with the words of God. 'Is God saying there is no hope for us all if we don't change?' She worried through the nebulous lonely hours until her days mingled into nights. She spent every moment she could, alone, trying to contact God. When she heard Him, she wasn't sure if she was asleep and dreaming or if she was awake and actually hearing a voice from Heaven.

Her wretchedness immobilised her. Initially, interactions with God nursed her into a calm and positive mood, but then, the anxieties would set in. She agonised about her ability to change and inability to identify what she needed to change; what state is the world in? She would ask endlessly, 'how shall we – can we - survive? What can I do? What of all those people committing horrors and crimes against humanity in the name of God? Or worse, hiding behind the skirts of decent and honest religious people in order to claim easy access to their chosen victims?'

"A pretty monumental task to be giving yourself," her Doctor said recently, in the hope she would see reason.

This all-consuming passion was the concern of her friends not just her GP, who was beginning to think he should try and call time on her sessions with Nigel Thomas.

Lucinda, worried about her relapsing into illness again, had also voiced her growing fear about the visits.

"Amelia, I'm not sure you should go back, I know you say that afterwards you feel better and the experience gives you explanations about yourself; but do you need any more? You become quite distressed at the time you know – it's hard to watch. Plus," she emphasised by repeating the word, "plus, it hasn't stopped you hearing voices – you know, all this God talk. Don't give me that," Lucinda raised a hand at Amelia's protest. "I know you're still at it and quite frankly, it frightens the life out of me."

"But Lulu, God only ever talks perfect sense."

"Don't you "but Lulu" me! It's your own voice talking perfect sense – it's called common sense, not God sense! You just don't believe in yourself enough to realise it. Not sure you can call some of it perfect sense though, come to think it. I think it's what you want to believe! You've always loved science fiction movies, now suddenly God is avowing aliens exist! You've always felt bitter about not having Christmas and birthday parties as a child, and now guess what? God is telling you it's okay! You've always felt at a disadvantage because of your disrupted education and now all of a sudden God's given you an important job as a Blue Angel? And now, you want to single-handedly bring down the might of a multi-billion dollar cult? Come on Millie, give me a break!"

"Wish I hadn't told you all that now."

"Well, I'm jolly glad you did. It all makes me realise that you're not quite yourself ...yet."

"I'm sorry Luce. I can't help myself. Look, if I promise to stop the God talk, will you come with me one last time to Nigel's? Only if it doesn't upset you of course."

"One last time?"

"Yes, one last time."

"And no more God talk?"

"Yes. No more God talk, I promise. In exchange will you stop talking in exclamation marks please, it's like being continually scolded."

Lucinda relaxed; Amelia retaliating to a reprimand has got to be a healthy sign.

Amelia had her own thoughts on the matter, and they didn't include doing as she was told. 'I must ask God about Hell next time I talk to him. If he doesn't do thunderbolts, maybe he does Hell, and I'll go straight there for lying and breaking promises.'

Chapter *30*

The Last Session

(Life and death are one thread, the same line viewed from different sides – *Lao Tzu*)

"Ooh, ooh, no, no. No. She isn't, she can't be. She's not dead; tell me she's not dead." Amelia's frail groan turned into pathetic tokens of misery as she lay writhing on the couch.

"Oh my God," Lucinda whispered urgently to Nigel. "This can't be safe, bring her back; bring her back."

He turned, "Just a moment longer. It's painful for you to watch but I believe this is the crux of the matter and will be good for her in the long run. Only a moment." he repeated with a promise, calmly returning to Amelia.

"Where are you Amelia?" He questioned in his polished professional manner.

"Sitting in his car. He's come to take me home."

"Who? Who's come to take you home?"

"Uncle Billy. My parents have sent him to get me from the police station."

"Why were you at a police station?"

"I ran away. Everyone's been out looking for me. I didn't know, I didn't mean to cause a fuss. I just had to get away; find him, find Tristan. Now she's dead."

"Who is dead Amelia?"

"Alice. My sister Alice."

"What has happened to Alice, Amelia?"

He raised a cautioning hand towards the ceiling to stop Lucinda who was desperate to call time. Amelia had never volunteered information into her sister's death and no one had ever dared ask. The emotional toll evident when anyone even mentioned his or her own sibling, or she heard the name Alice, Amelia would visibly withdraw into a closed shell.

"Uncle Billy says her car crashed. She was a passenger, her fiancé Richard was driving. He's only just passed his test. Alice and I were told by the elders that we didn't need to drive because it was a man's job. Alice said that's all right as her lovely Rich takes her anywhere she wants to go. But I don't like it, I want to drive when I'm old enough and they can't stop me. I want my own career, my own life. I want to go out with my friends, wear the clothes I want to wear; I want to make my own mistakes in life – not theirs. I don't want to go to the Hall and be preached at all the time, trying to make me someone I'm not.

That's why I ran away. They keep telling me what to do. They took me out of my school, the one Uncle Billy's paying for, because the elders disapproved. I hate them, all of them. Not Alice, I love Alice, but she's one of them, she accepts everything they tell her. I don't. That's why she was out looking for me. She loves me, she's worried about me; they were all looking for me, because I ran away. It's my fault. It's all my fault."

"How old are you Amelia?"

"Fifteen. Fifteen years old and I've just killed my sister." Amelia's voice was quietly twisted in anguish as the tears flowed steadily. She stiffened as her body awoke to a new truth, *"He was right. That fat bully, when he called me a murderer. He was right. I am. I am; I've murdered my own sister."*

"Amelia you know it wasn't your fault. It was Alice's choice to get in the car and look for you. It was an accident. What is Uncle Billy saying to you? He's telling you it was an accident isn't he?"

"Yes but I don't believe him, they blame me, the elders, I'm sure they do. Mea culpa. Mea culpa." Amelia turned onto her side and began rocking quietly as she lay there.

"Uncle Billy has never lied to you before has he Amelia? He wouldn't lie about this. It's too important. Listen. Listen to

him; it's not your fault. Amelia, you've been very upset, you didn't know to whom you could turn. You cannot blame yourself for what has happened to Alice. Alice doesn't blame you."

"Does she understand?"

"Yes Amelia, of course she does."

"Oh Alice, Alice. Why? Why did you have to die?" Amelia's cries were pitiful and this time Lucinda found her own tears silently streaming down her face.

"Stop it now, please stop this now." She whispered authoritatively.

"Of course. It's safe now. She'll be all right. I promise she'll be fine."

Much later, when they were curled up together on Old Faithful, Amelia was able to fill in the gaps for Lucinda.

"I met Tris during the school term leading up to the summer holidays. We spent a lot of the early summer months together. He fretted at first when he found out I only turned fifteen that summer, but I said as long as he was a good boy he didn't need to worry. And he was, such a good, decent boy. After all, there are only three years between us – but obviously at that time in our lives, an important three years." Amelia smiled at the memory of young Tristan and those happy months they shared: carefree children in love and innocently planning the rest of their lives together.

"No one needed to worry; he was a gentleman, always. Well, of course, my parents got wind of it and what with that and the school pressuring them to help me with my career choices, what followed was inevitable. Career! Well, I wasn't supposed to have one of those was I – a mere subjugated female. Uncle Billy was great; he did his best to persuade them to let me stay. He had paid for it all you know.

"He'd paid for Alice as well, but she was a good girl and didn't get into trouble all the time, unlike me, always arguing and rebelling. She just finished her time there, left as soon as she was legally old enough and then settled down to devoting the rest of her life to her religion and of course, after they met, to Richard. A waste of Uncle Billy's money if you ask me – wasted on both of us. Seven years I'd been there, a fantastic school, my home, and then I was gone – I left at fifteen.

"Anyway, they took me away from there and put me into the local comprehensive, just to finish my last year at school. It was awful. Looking back, the school and the children were all right. But I didn't fit in, I couldn't comprehend their ways, it wasn't what I was used to and I couldn't cope. I knew nothing, was green in all matters, compared to them. Not as green as Tris of course."

"No one could be as green as Tris was back then Millie let's face it. Bless him; he's come a long way." Lucinda smiled gently.

"True. He's a darling." Lucinda urged Amelia to return to her story.

"I could only stand it for three agonising months. Then I ran away. I was looking for Tristan, but didn't know where he was. It was him who found me about two years later; he knew my parents' address so it wasn't difficult. They were unsure about it, but figured as Tristan genuinely cared for me he couldn't make matters any worse. I was about seventeen when they supplied him with Uncle Billy's address, where I was living. But back when I was a fifteen-year-old runaway with everyone out looking for me, well, he knew none of that and they told him nothing.

"I wanted to celebrate a Christmas for the first time in my life. Be normal. Do what normal people do. Stupid girl that I was, thought I'd be taken in by Tris's parents' and would be able to live there, that they would love me as a daughter; then when I was old enough, Tris and I could set up home together."

"Well, there's a fair few fifteen-year-old girls with very similar dreams, honey."

"I know. But this story ends badly. No fairytale ending this time. Richard explained much of it to me later saying Alice had begged him to take her out in the car to look for me, she had an idea I'd be heading for Tristan, but she only knew as much as I knew, the area where he lived, not the full address. Richard was tired and said he wasn't sure he should be driving in London as he had only just passed his test and didn't know the roads. But apparently she insisted. He never forgave himself for that you know. He said to me many years later that he shouldn't have given in, but he could never say no to her, he really loved her."

"Where's Richard now?" Lucinda asked.

"I don't know to be honest. I heard he married eventually and had a couple of children, but I'm not really sure. Alice needed blood you see and at first was aware enough to refuse it. When she fell into a coma and couldn't speak for herself, my parents took in the disclaimer she signed years before, 'No Blood.' She was twenty years old, the staff couldn't overrule her own decision and my parents were her next of kin, not being yet married. In the end, Richard changed his mind about blood and begged them to let her have a transfusion, but they stood by their beliefs and tried to convince him she would have done so too; had done, when she was able.

"Discussions as to whether she would have died anyway were rampant; her injuries were too severe; transfusion or not, she may not have lived – we'll never know that one. The whole thing destroyed Richard. He'd lost his sweetheart and betrayed his religion. My parents probably know where he is, but I can't ask them now."

"How are you feeling now? That is, about, well, everything that's happened really?" Lucinda wasn't sure where to direct her question so allowed Amelia to decide.

"I feel all right - I think. I've always felt responsible for Alice's death. Always."

"And now?"

"Now? Now I don't – so much. Hypnotherapy has helped. It was as if I was able to go back in time and convince myself, "No Amelia, it's not your fault." I can talk to myself; heal myself, if that makes sense. The hypnotherapist helped me absorb Uncle Billy's words at the time. You remember my Uncle Billy don't you?"

"Remember Uncle Billy? Of course I do, he's an unforgettable legend, a wonderfully interesting man. I proposed to him if I recall." Lucinda laughed as she spoke. "He politely turned me down saying he would marry me in a heartbeat if he was thirty years younger, but alas, would never be able to do justice to a beautiful young filly such as myself, so he would just have to get by with dreams of what might have been and his memories."

"Well he's got a few of those I can tell you; had his share of beautiful young fillies in his lifetime. I do miss him. Not of the same religious persuasion as his younger sister obviously. He was married for a time but his wife died young and childless and I think that's why he took such an interest in Alice and me - his only nieces and no nephews. Ava thought the world of him, but he had been heartbroken when his wife died and he never met anyone else he felt the same way about - not even Ava – until you of course, but he decided you were off limits, being far too young."

Amelia smiled fondly as she acknowledged that her Uncle Billy had, undeniably, been very taken with a twenty-something Lucinda, but considered her twenty-two years far too young for a fifty-eight-year-old world-weary gent such as himself.

She continued, "But over the years he thought of us as his own girls. Unfortunately for him, his little sister, my mother, brought home a husband of rather humble origins compared to her, becoming more and more embroiled with his religion which discarded wealth, education and all things worldly with a careless wave of a sexist hand."

"Didn't stop the old fellow though did it?" Lucinda mused.

"Certainly not. He blamed himself though. He was tortured as to whether he should have interfered with our upbringing. Would I have been so unhappy and run away? Would Alice have lived had he not involved himself? You know all those 'what if's' nearly killed him at the time. Poor Uncle Billy, I never blamed him. I never fitted in with my parents' religion the way Alice did. He was my hero; he once told me there isn't anything I can't achieve if I work for it and believe in myself enough. My Ma & Pa's advice was to be patient and sit back and wait for God's new order, to be happy. That was never going to work. You can see the difference in parental guidance there can't you? I was never going to obey them, was I?

"Contumacious: that's how the elders described my behaviour to my parents and convinced them that I was a lost cause; I suppose they were right really. Well, to cut a long story short, Uncle Billy never remarried, and because he never had children of his own he left this house to me,

plus a substantial trust fund. After Alice died, well ..."
Amelia faltered, "I got it all you see."

"Adding to your burden of guilt no doubt."
Lucinda felt it now safe enough to state the obvious.

"Absolutely, now I feel very differently, reconciled somehow. What I've learnt about my guilt is, it's not mine, although I've shouldered it all my life. Alice died because that cult never gave her a chance to live. I ran away because of the sexist and abusive nature of their doctrines. They stripped me of all I loved and of what I wanted to be and become.

"You never used to call them a cult, but you use it now to describe them, Ams, what's changed?"

"Like a veil lifting from my eyes, Lulu, I stopped blaming myself and began to scrutinise what had really happened to me and my family. Everything they stand for and everything they do demonstrates cult-like behaviour. Firstly, they flatter and cajole people into thinking they have the Truth. Then once hooked, they instill fear in people by saying the end of the world is coming very soon, and everyone, not one of them, will die. They control aspects of people's life – medical treatment, relationships, work, schooling, what to wear and even what kind of sexual positions married couples are allowed to use. Their two-witness rule is a despicable disregard of children, or any other victim, cherry picking scriptures to justify their belief and throwing the victims out of the religion if they dare question them, or if the result of this abuse causes them to develop problematic behaviour. If people break their rules, they deliver the ultimate punishment; splitting families apart by shunning those who stray, which could be for something like, smoking, celebrating Christmas, or even just for questioning their policies as I have done. They are a mega rich organization even though they encourage their members to live for the organization rather than pursue monetary desires and, to cap it all, they are a registered charity - talk about hypocrites. They change their doctrine regularly, carelessly explaining it away as 'New Light.' Quite frankly, Lu, it's incredible what people will believe once they've been got at – more than incredible, it's downright frightening.

"I'm so sorry it was hard for you Lulu and I can't thank you enough for being there for me. He was right you know, Nigel that is, when he told you I'd be fine now. I do feel all right. Calm somehow, accepting of life. There is more, but to a degree, I've put young Amelia to rest somehow and feel able to redefine the here and now and the future."

"Millie, whatever else, you must set your mind at rest about these allegations regarding this religion. Tris is on the ball, and Chris and Greg are helping him. He's been in contact with others who are as equally aghast as us about all this, and are more able than you are right now to do something about it. The ball is irreversibly in motion, so rest easy on that one my friend. All of which means, you're able to keep your promise, aren't you."

"What promise?"

"No more God talk."

"Ah, that promise."

That reminds me, thought Amelia ..... something I want to ask God about… I'll have to wait until tomorrow, when Lucinda's gone home.

When Amelia awoke the following morning, rather than panic at what she thought she should be doing, or what she thought God wanted her to do; she made herself a cup of coffee, snuggled comfortably into Old Faithful again, and paused to meditate on all that had happened.

Lemon gave Reg a sharp kick. *'Stop your whining you inflatable fool.'*

'I can't help it,' sobbed Reg, *'don't you know what's going on? Did you hear all that God talk and then what happened with the Hipporapist? I'm doomed. Doomed I say and don't kick a man when he's down with all your name-calling, it's not fair.'*

'It's not as bad as all that,' Lemon retorted, *'think about it, I am in the same boat you know, all this love talk going on.'*

'But, but they want to kill me, how bad can it get? What could possibly be worse than that? They haven't talked about killing you.'

'Yes they have, if all they do is love each other all day every day, what am I supposed to be doing eh? Where am I in all this?'

'So why did you say it's not as bad as all that? Let me tell you, it clearly is.'

'Look, we waged our war didn't we, and lost. We've seen Amelia when she puts us all together, like we're supposed to be – and it works. We've felt the happiness she feels when we don't argue with each other. She figures things out without the trauma. She's happy, reasoned, doesn't suffer the headaches and palpitations. She makes good decisions. She's learning to like herself. We, rather than I – work. There is a place for you, just not as you know it yet. You can feel respected and enjoy the pleasure of achievement and compliments. You can give Amelia self-confidence, self-respect, self-belief - without the showing off and the pretentious haughtiness. That is your place. That is your job.'

Reg was agog, *'Oh. So I'm not going to die after all? I'll have to start practicing all of that – my new job. But what about you? I can't see much of a place for you with all this fluffy lovey-dovey stuff going on?'*

Lemon answered with great solemnity. *'I know. I've fought it for years, but I have to admit defeat. I have to admit I was wrong. I've been thinking very carefully and I know there is a place for me somehow. I can be the other side of Sugarplum. Without me, Amelia would be so damn naive her life wouldn't be worth living. People would walk all over her, I have to bring common sense and a worldly knowledge to her; otherwise Sunshine would be done for. Sorry Sunshine but you have to admit you couldn't cope without me. No, my place is to bring a calm, collected, logical and balanced understanding of life.*

'Sugarplum, stop squealing, you're a pain in the butt, I'm not wrong about that, I know your happiness is intense but give me a break. It's not going to be easy you know. We all have to make changes and that includes you Sugarplum. No one can be dominant otherwise Amelia won't be balanced. That's what's been the problem, all along.'

'Gosh Lemon, how did you get to be so wise?' breathed Reg in awe and admiration.

'Born with it,' Lemon smiled her reply at Reg, as Sunshine slipped one small hand into hers and the other into Reg's.

Amelia felt calmer, but there was still so much she didn't understand; so much she wanted to know. Was she able to stop spending all of her time in isolation talking to herself? If her other voices disappeared would God also? The thought panicked her - she had questions to ask.

Would she stop trying to contact God?

'Hell no........' Hell that is, as in, 'does it exist?' This had been eating into her, causing nightmares for years. "Does Hell exist?"

Well, does it?

Chapter 31

The Burning Question of Hell

(I long, as does every other human being, to be at home,
wherever I find myself - *Maya Angelou*)

"Dear God?"

"Yes Amelia?"

"Do you believe in Hell?"

"That is an unusual question."

"Why?"

"People usually assume I know the answer to that one and ask me if there is a Hell or not? In fact, most people assume I created Hell."

"Oh really? Well, did you?"

"No."

"No? How come? If people think you did?"

"Why would I create a place of evil that serves to punish and torture when all I hope is that humankind live in joy and love? God is not a hypocrite."

"But most religious people believe in Hell, in one way or another, just as much as they believe in Heaven. That's what they are taught. How do you keep them on the straight and narrow without the carrot and stick theory in place?"

"It is nothing to do with me Amelia. People live the life they choose to live. Why would there be a Hell waiting for anyone? Amelia, what does Heaven look like to you?"

"It is wherever You are."

"Which means what?"

"Peace, contentment, happiness, joy. Someone to talk to, someone who cares."

"How do you achieve peace and contentment?"

"By learning to challenge my thinking? If I think in a negative way, the outcome will be negative. If I think positively and have self-belief, insofar as I believe I can make the changes in life that I want or need, then the outcome will be positive."

Amelia paused; she knew there was more to comprehend. There are some things one cannot change, that are beyond one's ability to alter, no matter how positively approached. "I think it's about perception. If we perceive a situation in a certain way then we will react and feel in a certain way, that's where positive thinking comes in. But it's also about a kind of acceptance. As if one is saying to oneself, okay, this is what has happened, I don't like it, it's not nice, or it could be worse than not nice, it could be tragic, or immensely painful in some way. But if I empty my head of all negative thoughts, like self-pity, blaming, revenge, or sheer unadulterated anger - then I can formulate how to respond, how to survive."

Amelia paused again taking a deep breath. "It's rather like problem solving I suppose; think about where you are right now and where you want to be, and you have to make it realistic and achievable. But you're less able to do that if your head is twirling and spinning with angst and worry and woe is me stuff, which is what I always did. Take note, I'm using past tense by the way God. I know it genuinely works because I'm trying it."

"So heaven looks like a place where you can feel good about yourself? To know you have the ability and means to deal with whatever comes your way effectively? What about enjoying life? How do you achieve that Amelia?"

"I've learned to look around me. Like I did when I walked into town that day and bought the cards and ate a donut. Enjoy every single moment - quite literally - every single moment is so precious. I've looked back on photographs of myself with friends or family and thought, what a good day that was, but at the time, I didn't appreciate the moment fully. Life brings changes we have to deal with; my sister died a long time ago, tragically, and I never fully recovered. I know that now.

"For a long time God, I swayed between blaming myself and blaming you. But even that most painful of experiences and all the others in between - all mist over in time. The losses may stack up … but, if you look hard enough, so do the gains. I lost my sister and her death was very painful to us all, but now, outweighing that loss, I'm learning to see the happy memories. My anger at her death was blanking them out. I find a little bit of Heaven when I think about her. You have taught me this - look for the joy of her life by turning away from sadness and anger – not to mention the blaming. So I can find my little bit of Heaven wherever I am and whatever I'm doing."

"Which takes us back to Hell Amelia."

She voiced her thoughts slowly, "Hell does exist but not as a place of evil torture - that's what you're going to tell me isn't it? It's the opposite of You. It's negative thinking and you are positive thinking. It's bad reactions and you are good reactions. It's anxiety and worry and you are happiness and joy. It's retribution and revenge and you are forgiveness and compassion. It is selfishness and self-pity and you are empathy and consideration - isn't it?"

"Amelia, have you heard before, that God is Love? So, as it is, that I am Love, so it is, that Hell, is wherever I am not. Hell is the opposite of Love. God is Home. Whenever people are able to forget ego and forgive, and above all Love, they are Home: those who are vengeful, angry or arrogant, experience negative thinking and behaviour. That is not Love, therefore, they are not Home - they are in Hell."

"But some people are like that all the time. They don't know how to find Home, it seems so far away."

"I am never far away Amelia, I am right here for everyone. When people stop opposing this truth; that is when they find me."

"What about all the naughty people then? You know, the horrible people, who hurt and kill, start wars - and cults, and all that kind of evil-stuff? What do you do with them then?"

"What would you like me to do?"

"Burn them in Hell?" Amelia suggested hopefully. "Forever." she embellished.

"There is no Hell. That would not be free will would it? Amelia, life on earth is an experience, a journey. It is helpful if people learn about themselves as they go along, making appropriate changes as they see fit. Some, as you just pointed out, do not manage to do that. I am here, I am Home. Those who seek love, justice, forgiveness, and live their life by it – find Home. "

"So there's no carrot and stick then?"

"No."

"No, burning in Hell threats then?"

"No, definitely not Amelia."

"No fire and brimstone?"

"No. No fire and brimstone."

"Oh. Well that's good then. .... God?"

"Yes Amelia?"

"What's brimstone?"

"How about you go and find out."

"Oh... and I was doing so well."

"You are undoubtedly doing well Amelia."

"Thank you God."

"These are your changes Amelia. You are finding peace and happiness all by yourself. You have discovered that your happiness is not the responsibility of another; it is your own entirely. You have also realised, that anything that happens in life is nothing to do with me. Life happens in all its ways, all its twists and turns. I do not interfere, punish or reward. I am delighted to offer support when people call upon me in genuine need. That is all I do. It is up to them to listen, many do not. This you have learned. You should be feeling very pleased with yourself for such enlightened knowledge and making attempts to use it."

"Wowsers, of course it was to do with you God, don't be so modest."

"No Amelia, it is you being modest."

"God?"

"Yes Amelia?"

"Heaven is a donut!"

"Yes Amelia, and what else?"

"A walk in the park; or a delicious cup of coffee; a baby's smile; a vibrant burp; a healthy..."

"Amelia I think you are now heading unnecessarily into the realm of bodily functions."

"True though."

Amelia tidied up her silent conversation with one last thought, "And Hell is if you're not noticing any of it - the good and the bad, the big and the small, the ups and downs of existence that turn it into a life. Life is all of those things brought upon us, sometimes of our own making, sometimes by someone else's hand, and sometimes just because it happens that way. Hell is facing antagonists, uphill encounters and hating or blaming anyone in the way. Hell is swimming against the tide. Turn away, just turn your head to see, and you will find Heaven."

Heaven truly is a donut.

"By the way Amelia."

"Yes God?"

"I am not a He."

"What?" Amelia, frozen by the words, until a small but succinct smile erupted, rousing her into a frenzied dance of triumph around her kitchen table, through to Old Faithful, lunging with an athletic leap upon his worn cushions, three jumps, then pirouetted her naughty toes back into the kitchen.

"Hah! Hah – I knew it; I knew it, I *so* knew it. I thought You were a bit girly – talking about love and feelings, and stuff. I knew you were one of us. Hah, Hah!"

She continued to whoop delightedly round the room, until interposed by a persistent voice.

"Amelia? I am not He, nor am I She."

"What – oh. Star! So what are you then, an IT?"

"Yes Amelia, that is exactly what I am – IT."

"Sounds a bit rude to me, going around calling someone *It.*"

"That's because you are human Amelia. I do not take offence whatever people call me, or how I am perceived."

"Just as well considering some of the things you are called at times. I'm not sure I will always remember though, I mean if you think about it, the English language isn't exactly geared up for a third option is it."

"Amelia, if it helps, please continue to refer to me in the same way you always have; it will make no difference either way."

"Thank you God. I mean to say, the usual profanities just don't sound the same do they – 'OH MY IT' hasn't quite got the same ring to it as, 'OH MY GOD' has it? Oh no."

Amelia didn't feel guilty about breaking her promise to Lucinda. In fact, she was very pleased she had. 'One day,' she said to herself, 'I'll sit her down and tell her all about it. At the moment, I can't find the words to explain it properly and she might start arguing and become upset. Basically darling Lulu thinks my talking to God is a sign of increasing dementia, and I know it isn't. I know it's the opposite. I'm finding the answers to questions I've had for years. They're my answers. They satisfy ME. Make sense to ME.

I don't actually care if people think that it's just my in-built common sense or wishful thinking – and not the voice of God. Who cares? God certainly doesn't. If He exists. Funny that – takes me back to when I used to call him Cloth Ears. But now I know better. I'm beginning to learn how to be happy, contented. God it feels good.'

'I do have something else to ask Him. Something that's been really bugging me, for a long time…..'

Chapter 32

Suffering and Death

(The fear of death follows from the fear of life. A man who lives fully is prepared to die at any time - *Mark Twain*)

"Dear It?"

"Yes Amelia?"

"Why do you allow people to suffer?"

"In what way do I do that?"

"You said we've got everything we need to live and it's up to us and you don't interfere. But let's face it; some people really are dealt a rum hand aren't they? Not to mention a sporadic curved ball turning around to knock us off our feet like a frenzied boomerang, just when we think it's all going so well. You could in all fairness, God, do something about it, couldn't you?"

"What would be the point of my pledge to not interfere if I interfere? Amelia, this is hard for you to understand, of this I am aware, human beings have railed against this and blamed everyone but self for a long time. Think. What is the difference between suffering and pain?"

"God, I've never thought about it before and don't see why it's relevant, if you're in pain, you suffer - surely?" Amelia was beginning to think God was stalling, unable to find an answer that would satisfy her curiosity and expectation.

"Amelia, pain is a physical experience that is not pleasant and everyone has their own limits of endurance. It is nature's way of telling a body that all is not right and should not be ignored. Suffering is different. What is suffering?"

Amelia opened her mouth to say, "Trying to understand You." but shut it again quickly in a showing of latent – but hopefully growing - wisdom.

"Amelia, pain is objective: it is impartial and happens for a reason. It has purpose. Suffering is subjective: it is emotional, idiosyncratic and prejudiced. No one should suffer by staying in conditions that inflict continued heartache."

"What about an unhappy marriage? That can cause untold suffering. But some religions don't allow divorce and I haven't got enough fingers and toes to count the times I've heard the old expression, "You've made your bed so you have to lie in it." Probably one of yours, now I come to think about it. Well, Tosspots to that is what I say."

"Amelia, living with any situation, or past decision made, that makes one unhappy, is not the purpose of life on earth - the opposite is truth: to experience joy and happiness. I do not reward those who remain utterly miserable, shackled to the belief they are doing the right thing; when in reality, all they are doing is wasting their life, their many opportunities. Think about what feelings you want to experience and then create them. Do not react to them. *Make* choices; do not *permit* them."

"So some choices we make that become difficult; or depressing or upsetting in some way, we don't have to put up with?"

"If your current way of finding happiness and fulfilment is at the expense of someone else's, and creates suffering, this is not true happiness. Their welfare is paramount – as is your own. This is essential knowledge. What of your own happiness? Are you expected to be a martyr for the sake of others? What thin veneer of contentment is found if one person has to be miserable, in order to make the other person happy?"

"God, I understand what you say about the difference between pain and suffering. We can change the way we think and this will change our life. I get that bit. But what about suffering caused by pain, prolonged pain with the knowledge that it's never going to get better or go away? That's terrible, insufferable."

"Yes Amelia, it may well become insufferable. It is sad when life is thrown away, rather than used as an enjoyable experience. However, as you know, some people reach the point when they ask themselves if it is necessary to cling to life, if life itself has become intolerable."

"God, are you talking about suicide or euthanasia? Bit radical – even for You. Most religions disagree vehemently with it and class it as a sin. In a way, the biggest sin because you're not around to repent." Amelia's tones were hushed in honour of this most difficult of subjects.

"No Amelia, I am saying, humankind has free will."

A quiet subdued noise emitted from Amelia's mouth, which could pass for a prolonged "Wow." Was this any different to what God had been saying to her all along? 'Basically, that He doesn't interfere and He doesn't judge. He doesn't want us to suffer. He enjoys our peace and contentment. If that's not possible, we can find our own answers as long as we weigh up the consequences and don't be blind to the suffering of others.'

"God, You're being evasive. Are you saying euthanasia and suicide are acceptable?"

Silence.

She rallied, "I guess I'm left to make my own mind up on that one then God …. thought so! It's called 'passing the buck' if you ask me."

She still had her other question to be answered, possibly more than one if she was brave enough. Hardly daring to hear his response and, unsure if she really wanted to know the answer, she spoke with a small voice, "What about death? Why do we die?"

"Remember your dream Amelia. Death is development, progressive movement. Death is evolution. Humans find it exciting, exhilarating and natural, but only when they experience it. Prior to the experience, some worry and whittle with fear at the prospect."

"But the children, God; why do children have to die before they've had experience of life on earth?"

"It is their chosen path Amelia. They have chosen this to happen before they entered their physical status. For their own learning, or someone else's. They have agreed it. They go with joy to their true reflection. You all have this choice. "

"Oh. So... so we shouldn't fear death?"

"If you fear death - you fear life. Amelia, there is nothing to fear about death whatsoever. Embrace it when it comes. It comes when the time is right for it to come, and for you to move on."

"God?"

"Yes Amelia?"

"How is my sister doing?"

"She is doing extremely well Amelia. Living in joy. More so now you have accepted you are not responsible for her moving on. This brings her great happiness."

"And Uncle Billy?"

"An expression you may use - kicking up a storm."

Amelia smiled. For the first time in her life, she felt satisfied with the answers she had received.

She began to feel stronger, to feel she had tipped the balance. She felt she was truly winning the fight for peace within herself.

"I can do this, I can. Hey God, my *if* has become my *when*. God?"

"Yes Amelia?"

"I mean it you know. I've grown up an awful lot lately and it's been painful I can tell you. I feel all hot and prickly when I think of some of the things I've said and done in the past, it's very uncomfortable. Some things I can never put right or apologise for. But I feel sorry inside even if the person I've hurt would prefer for me to curl up and die, and certainly wouldn't ever want to give me the comfort of repentance and opportunity to say sorry to them. One thing is for sure, I don't need to attention seek anywhere near as much as I used to."

"Amelia, do not worry over mistakes that trap you in the past. Learn by them and change, when change is helpful. But you can only live in the present and it is only the present that can shape a future, bringing all that you may desire. That is what will come back to you. Be joyful and share that joy. That is the best atonement."

"Thank you God."

Chapter 33

Amelia makes the lunch

(Which of all my important nothings shall I tell you first? - *Jane Austen*)

"Lulu, when are you coming round? It's your turn and I haven't seen you in an age." Amelia spoke rapidly into the phone.

"It was last week darling, and I'll come round today if you like, I've got the afternoon free. We could go out for lunch?"

"Oh please let me cook something, I owe you big time and I fancy brushing up on my culinary skills such as they are."

"That should be interesting." Lucinda remembered some of Amelia's previous efforts in the kitchen. "1pm suit you?"

"Yes, come in a taxi so you can have a drink if you wish; go home whenever you're ready."

"That's fine by me, I'm not planning to see Coten until tomorrow evening – don't forget you're coming with me, she's expecting you. So I have every intention, my sweet, of drinking a good vino - if you're cooking. Amelia, nothing fancy, but something better than the packet of crisps and curling jam sandwich you produced last time you made lunch for me."

"Thanks for your confidence in my abilities – I'll show you then...... stay over," she added, "you don't need much of an overnight bag; I've got everything you need." Amelia laughed happily as she flung her phone down and scuttled off to poke around her kitchen cupboards; something out of a packet that was good enough to pretend it was home cooked, but not too good, otherwise Lucinda would guess it wasn't her own creation.

"That was tasty Millie," said Lucinda appreciatively after they had lunched, dabbing the corners of her mouth with the napkin. Your cooking has improved and served with a glass of delicious wine too – thank you."

"Well, I always knew I could do it, I couldn't be bothered in the main; I'm just learning it's worth making the effort."

"Yes, I suppose there is a bit of a difference isn't there. It's just good to see you back honey, to your old self. I feel so much better, seeing you like this now."

"Come on. Let's take our coffee through to Old Faithful. I've got something serious to discuss."

"Really, then why are you laughing?"

"I'm not."

"Yes you are, behind your eyes you are."

They settled down onto the sofa, Amelia explained, "I am aware I've been a little erratic lately and I'd like to thank you for your patience. I'd alienated myself from my friends and thankfully, you all ignored me and carried on as if nothing had changed. I wasn't myself – not by a long shot. Do you know, Tris had invited me to an event and I forgot to turn up? I had been really looking forward to it; bought the outfit and everything – even new shoes. New shoes!" Amelia still felt more than a little puzzled by that one.

"New shoes?" repeated Lucinda, "You forgot why you bought new shoes? Wow, that is bad."

"And, oh gosh, poor Tris - Did I tell you I packed Tristan's shoes in my suitcase when I went away for a week."

"I didn't know you'd been on holiday with Tristan recently, you dark horse, why didn't you tell me?" Lucinda queried.

"I haven't been on holiday with Tristan - just his shoes. I thought they were my hiking boots. Had no reason to think they were my hiking boots - they were still in the closet where I'd left them. I found a bag holding footwear in my car and for some inexplicable reason, believed they were my hiking boots – didn't think twice, stuffed them into my case and off I went. My, got to get away from it all, break. Remember?' Tramped all around the Scilly Isles in a pair of flip-flops with Tris's size 9s grinning at me every time I got back to the holiday cottage. Stupidly, I was the one who had put them in my car in the first place, and forgotten to return them."

Lucinda's mouth was twitching. She fought to subdue it into a look of concern rather than amusement.

"Not much of a get-away break then, not with that little reminder every day. You did return them to him didn't you?" Lucinda ended suspiciously, noting an evil glint lighting Amelia's eyes.

"No, I lobbed them overboard on the crossing back to Penzance. Cheek, ruining my holiday."

"Oh Amelia – that's so not fair, poor Tris." Lucinda wiped the laughter from her eyes not quite managing to achieve the disapproval she felt was due on Tristan's behalf. She settled for a genteel nose blow.

Amelia, ignoring the feeble attempt at championing Tristan, her story had imbued, continued. "Do you remember Ben, well, it wasn't just me that wanted to end it, I didn't tell you at the time, he was, well, ready to walk shall we say."

"What did you do?"

345

"He stayed over one night and I had to get up for work the next morning. Everything was good, we'd had a great time and I kissed him goodbye as he snuggled contentedly, very contentedly I may add, in bed and I told him to take his time, have some breakfast if he was hungry and just pull the door shut after him when he left."

"Yes?"

"I said goodbye upstairs and by the time I got downstairs – I'd forgotten he was there, so – I locked him in. Double locked the front door; he couldn't get out. He called me at work two hours later and I had to go tearing all the way home to free him. He always wore a pathetically suspicious look after that – began to vex me."

She paused again, realising Lemon would have called her a stupid retard by now. Sugarplum would be regaling sanctimoniously that she shouldn't use such anti-social language and think so unkindly of the poor man, whilst Reg would be smarting with self-pity at life's cruelties. Amelia then managed a very good example of her new skill, 'Positive Self Talk,' by imagining the wandering thoughts of her other selves were in a bubble. She visualised herself speedily bursting it between her two hands, flattening them with a slap. She then returned her thoughts to Lucinda.

"Am I as mad as a box of frogs? No, I'm completely sane - almost. I haven't got Alzheimer's have I? No. I've been through stressful times; a bit anxious that's all. Stress makes people forgetful you know. If I stop worrying about everything, these little distractions will pass. There is nothing to be concerned about."

"Are you going to let me speak?" Lucinda could hardly contain herself, but managed to make herself serious for a moment. "You're right. You have absolutely nothing to worry about and no you haven't got Alzheimer's. You've been working too hard, and don't overlook how stressful your job is, most of your peers have experienced burnout way before you – you should be proud of yourself. Plus, you've been upset over the situation with your poor Mum & Dad. Also, you don't know how long the pneumonia had been coming on either do you? This would have weakened you considerably." Lucinda had been enthusiastically banging her hand on Old Faithful in rhythm with her words. "Aren't you forgetting something though? What's all this about toothpaste? You hinted at it earlier but then didn't tell me - but vino veritas and all that." Lucinda's smile lengthened, sensing a story.

"Ah, yes, the pièce de résistance of my tale. Promise you won't tell anyone?"

"Of course."

"Well, the other night, when I was brushing my teeth… mmh, nothing to worry about? …..Okay, well, let's just say brushing my teeth with KY jelly wasn't the most pleasant of experiences, and leave it at that."

Giving Lucinda time to pinch the corners of her eyes with a desperate squeeze to stop the leaking inspired by her confession, Amelia's smile began to broaden as she contemplated her latest faux pas. The memory of the questionable taste still lingered, causing her to abstractedly smooth her tongue over her teeth in an absentminded, and futile, attempt to erase it.

"Hey," she nudged Lucinda, "good job it didn't happen when I locked in Ben, couldn't blame him for being a little disturbed over that one - may have panicked and jumped out the upstairs window."

"Oh Amelia you are as crazy as ever, please don't change." Lucinda eventually managed to gasp out her words. Here was her friend back on form. Mad, scatty, witty and as sane as she was ever going to be.

Amelia had at last recovered her interest in someone other than herself and pumped Lucinda for information on whom she had been dating and how it was going. She had wanted Lucinda to see her like this, to be able to show her improvement.

After Lucinda had updated her, and the evening shadows lengthened, Lucinda returned the conversation back to Amelia as she cobbled together a late supper for them both in Amelia's kitchen.

Amelia told Lucinda that all her life she had been searching; all her life feeling an overwhelming loneliness, never knowing why or how to fill her emptiness, looking in all the wrong places. "An endless search for – I didn't know what Luce, only what it wasn't and hurting myself and a lot of other people along the way. I found it in God. I found my inner peace. Lulu, do you know something – I know without a shadow of a doubt I will never feel lonely ever again."

"OK, I hear you, but what I don't understand Millie if that is the case, why did you become so distressed by it all. You worried us all silly for a while – if it's as good as you say it is, why did that happen? I can tell you one thing, you certainly were not exhibiting any positive reactions and quite honestly, lonely is exactly how it looked; you lost all reasonable contact with the outside world without appearing to find anything helpful from within. Amsy, you were lost and suffering and it was pitiful to watch; it very nearly broke my heart seeing you in such a state and not being able to help you."

Amelia covered her friend's hands in a gesture of love and appreciation for the friendship and support she had continued to show throughout her difficult time.

"I'm so sorry I put you through that – and thank you so much for being there for me, all of you. What would

I have done without my family? You and Coten, Tris, Greg, Chris and Gail - you're all I've got and you stuck by me. You'll never know how much I treasure you all for that. I think my upbringing was partly the reason; an enforced belief I was brainwashed into thinking was the truth. I challenged that and eventually, after a considerable mental struggle, rejected the teachings of my childhood. It left me, well, I'm not sure – hating myself. I was an adult who didn't know how to think like one. I didn't know who I was because I'd always been someone else."

As they talked, Amelia relived the experience: back when she had challenged her very core, heralding an unremitting dread ensuing from the entrenched thought that always snaked its way back to re-implant itself in the forefront of her brain, the home from where she had always wanted to evict Lemon, the conviction that stated God did not exist.

The birthplace of the equally damaging reminder of a tenacious mordant belief she had grown up with despite her constant endeavours to shake: *you will never be capable of having a loving relationship with anyone, not even God. They find you out soon enough, they see through you; you're not worthy of love; you're not decent nor courageous; not clever nor funny; not warm nor pleasant; not much of an individual at all really. Let's not even think about what a crackpot you are and how impossible you must be to live with. You're just a whole lot of irritating nothingness.* How Lemon's spite and Reg's self-indulgence asserted themselves above Sugarplum's cry of, '*Amelia, many people love you. Believe in yourself. Love yourself.*'

"But I didn't believe in, or love, myself, Lulu, that was the problem. I had no defence against the voices in my head, as I allowed Lemon to formulate cold judgements without the compassion she would show to a roving spider or lost bumblebee."

Amelia fell silent as she remembered her past warped reasoning. 'After all' she had concluded, 'if God can't even bring Himself to love me, how could I expect a mere mortal to be able to manage such a thankless task? Far better then, to agree God doesn't exist and then my worthiness to be loved by Him or anyone else won't be tested. Anyway, who needs nice? Sugar and spice is bland, boring and institutionalised. Stay safe, stay with what I know and who I am; change is scary. Be ugly, nasty and bitter.'

'Don't forget fat.' Lemon and Reg had chirped in to remind her, *'you can't possibly be worth loving if you're fat - you know that. So what does it matter? No one will notice or care, put self first, what the hell.'*

"Yet still I had waited Lulu, whilst encountering the worst relapse into self-loathing experienced for some time, I stood with a sliver of longing, hoping Sugarplum could rescue me. Hoping against hope God would come; that He had finally noticed the desolation inside me and had chosen to help. My belief in this seemed to ebb and flow like a vicious tide. Despite wanting to desperately cling to this dream, my expectations faded then returned; faded then returned, sending me mad with longing.

"At one point, it felt as if Sugarplum was valiantly going down with the ship, into the sea of rotten bubbling poisonous gases, leaving me helplessly jettisoned. I subconsciously fought it every step of the way; splitting myself in two, and more, as an internal argument raged back and forth. I had to learn who I was and learn to like who I was, before I could even think about whether God, or anyone else for that matter, could accept me and love me.

But it happened. Lulu, it is the most wonderful feeling; to feel supported by love, supported because it's all-powerful.

"It took a long time for me, because I had become so sceptical. It was a cloak of protection. I had to deal with that before I could move on. I had to deal with issues from my childhood; with feeling responsible for Alice's death and that I'd let my parents down so badly. Now I have come to terms with all that – or at least, the process is well on the way: it feels good Luce, it feels good. As I said, I never feel lonely. That gives me a strength I never knew I was capable of experiencing."

"Wow, Millie, that's powerful."

"It is. Yes it is and I'm so grateful; grateful and happy."

"There's something Millie, that has been bothering me. This woman at work – the one Greg has dubbed, Narcie. I know you said you used the situation to deflect from the real issues, but it was, and for all I know still is, a real issue. This mustn't be lost in all this Ams – you've still got to face it and deal with it. How's it all going?"

"I have to forgive."

"Bummer! That sucks Millie. Why should she be let off the hook, she needs stopping?"

"Oh, you dear thing. Thanks for your support. This is the way I see it - letting her off the hook and stopping her behaviour are two different things. Of course she should stop; anyone behaving the way she does should stop. How I was before, is, I wanted it to stop, but I also wanted justice. I wanted her to be faced, named and shamed, with her behaviour. I wanted everyone to know exactly who and what she is. I'm sure, that probably, anyone would react in the same way as I did at the time."

"What's wrong with that?"

"Even justice can become an act of ego. The quest for justice can be an excuse. All manner of evil acts have been perpetrated in the name of Justice; causing retaliation, revenge, wars, and eruptions of violence throughout history."

"Careful, you're getting a bit banner-waving. Personally I still can't see what's wrong with wanting justice. People have to stick up for themselves. Surely we have the right?"

"The real strength is in the collective, the collaboration of humankind. When more of us stand together, in love and acceptance, behaviour like hers become isolated. Reject the behaviour, not the person. What do we teach our children? To share: not to fight: not to be selfish: to play nicely with each other. Then what do we *show* them? What do adults do? I'll tell you what. We do the opposite. We don't share – think of the gap between the rich and the poor. We fight – think of war and conflict all over the world. We're selfish, selfishly hoarding what we've got - think food mountains. We don't play-nice – think of terrorist activity, governmental corruption, and not to mention the manipulative games played to control a population by whatever means – religion, culture, despotic rule, democracy. Basically Lulu, the human race is a raging mass of contradiction. We lust after power and control. No wonder our children grow up confused and damaged. We're monstrous."

"Well, when you put it like that, I see your point. But what's that got to do with Bitchface and you forgiving her rather than putting her in her place – which is being fired."

"Because she is accountable for her actions – not me. I just need to feel better. I can't feel better by trying to change her – not if she doesn't want to. But I can change my perception; the way I think will change the way I feel, and the way I react to her. In order to do that, I have to forgive. If I forgive, I'm not feeling hurt, or upset. I'm not ruminating by churning it over and over. I'm not bitterly and angrily plotting her downfall. In fact, I'm not thinking about her at all – what she has done is no longer affecting my emotional wellbeing. Everyone at work knows what she's like, they know what she is capable of, and I have built my own, and pretty positive, reputation amongst my peers. Therefore, I do not need revenge."

"I see. Impressive – but unrealistic surely."

"Exciting though Lulu. Just imagine if those principles were applied on a much larger scale – globally. Instead of one country saying to another, "you can't do that to us – that's outrageous: we must protect ourselves, so we're going to bomb you to smithereens, that'll teach you, and anyone else, to mess with this 'Great and Godly' country – hah!" And Luce, don't forget it's still a man's world. We need some peacekeeping women in charge for a change."

"Hey, now you're talking. When do we start?"

"Yes, but real women, not those with as much testosterone coursing through their veins as men. Women with communication skills; mothers who are sick and tired of living to see their dead sons; women who can be assertive; women who seek peace, not control, not power... well...I suppose to be fair – there could also be some men out there able to be like that."

"Yes definitely. Chris is, and Greg, and, I can't think of a better man that Tristan. He's such a good man Millie." Lucinda threw a sly sidelong glance at her friend.

"Stop – I know you're game." Amelia laughed, "But I do agree."

"Millie, what does it sound like? The voice of God?"

"It's not really a voice as such Lulu. I ask something and the answers come straight back to me. They are just there, in my head, but so strong, it's as if I've heard a human voice. Does that make sense?"

"No, well, yes, sort of. I'm kind of envious now, it all sounds rather wonderful."

"Try it my love. It won't hurt you I promise – as long as it's for the good. A request to hurt or bring troubles to another soul would not work, but I know you wouldn't do that anyway – maybe worth mentioning to Greg though, in case he fancies a try."

Amelia smiled with Lucinda as they both pictured their dear Get-a-Grip Greg attempting to weave magic potions of revenge and entering into all manner of promises with a God who would not be listening.

"Sorry, poor Greg – he wouldn't harm a fly really, he's too soft, don't tell him we know that though will you."

Amelia knew everyone had been worried about her mental health and were all at a loss to know what to do. Even Chris had broached the subject when he popped round to see how she was doing. Unlike the others, he knew what she had been looking for, and also knew in his wisdom that only she could unlock the clues and see for herself. He had been extremely worried as he took a backseat and watched her find her way, her own way Home. "She's finally there," he told Gail, with great relief, "she's made it."

Amelia realised that once upon a time, this thinking would have been an argument with Lemon raging in her head, who would have pitilessly laughed and belittled her with no mercy for her apparent idiocy. 'How about gambling with some empathy towards self? Allow yourself to be yourself,' she told normal-face, so she did. How good it made her feel. No put-downs, no retribution and no long-term niggling feeling of inadequacy to add to the once overflowing bottle of negativity.

Later that night, Lucinda had made her way to the guestroom, both of them laughing like schoolgirls as they first inspected her toothpaste before Amelia retired to the privacy of her own bathroom. She brushed her teeth before going to bed, she too carefully checking that she was actually using toothpaste. Remembering the conversation she had with Lucinda, she began smiling as she brushed, causing considerable dribble.

After the seriousness of her illness, they had laughed and joked their way through a wonderful afternoon together like old times. She deftly mopped up the trail of dribble and toothpaste (and yes it really was toothpaste) then purposefully walked towards the doorway into her bedroom, following her childhood habit of pacing out her steps silently, she wiped the spearminty drool on her silk pyjamas as she went.

With great solemnity, she counted to three before drawling a slow and long intake of breath. Steadying herself, she then performed a hop, skip and run, enough to make Hussain Bolt proud, in the general direction of her bed, thankful, if a little surprised, that she managed to judge the distance accurately on this occasion, as there had been many a time she had missed and winded herself with a thump and a splodge on the floor.

Triumph. She landed with some aplomb amidst the extravagant pile of feather pillows billowing all around her. She scrambled in excitedly, unsure why she was so thrilled by the prospect of going to bed alone, but nevertheless recognising that she wasn't at all dismayed and that had to be a good thing. She snuggled and stretched before turning over to arrange herself comfortably: she thanked her friends for being there for her; she thanked her Angels; she thanked Jesus; she thanked God. She thanked Him for her sanity, deciding that if she assumed she was sane then everyone else would follow suit, including God. Last but not least, "Good night Uncle Billy, see you in the morning." Amelia then fell contentedly asleep.

Chapter 34

Friendships

(We are all in the gutter, but some of us are looking at the stars – Oscar Wilde)

Amelia's Lemon had vanished some time ago. Despite her original doubts, Lemon was not missed. The transformation was complete. Amelia was complete. She finally realised and accepted that she didn't need to split herself in two, or three, or even more. She could cope with all that she is; all that she isn't; all that she will never be and all that she could be.

Lemon of course would never truly disappear. She had merely found her proper resting place. She was a component of Amelia as all the parts and sides of a personality that had been unjustly shrunk-to-fit. She had been the fractured fraction. But slowly over time Lemon found her own spot, her own location inside the mind of the mixed up human being. She had discovered a place where she could nestle happily inside the hiding places of Amelia's mind and heart. She had found Home. She gathered her companions and as Amelia learned to thaw her mistrust of all things human, Lemon, Reg and Sugarplum had softened and liquefied into the corners of the soul they had been cruelly ousted and barred from so long ago.

What of little Sunshine? She accompanied them to the Enchanted Hall – the place of safety and faith and of love. What delights to uncover? What little nuances of behaviour could Lemon now be drawn into, without vilification and backbiting denigration? How Reg could grin happily without worrying about disrespect or taking pleasure from humiliating another. How Sugarplum smiled wisely, knowing peace and contentment. And Sunshine – how she danced. Now, everything fitted neatly together like an assembled complicated jigsaw puzzle.

Well - that's how Amelia's fanciful brain liked to view it. Her friends thought otherwise.

"Enchanted Hall?" said Greg, when they were all gathered outside in the pub garden one gloriously sunny day, hunched over glasses of lemonade and crisp packets, "Enchanted nutcase more like. Get a grip Millie-Moo."

Having listened intently as Tristan outlined his findings, and agreeing the next step was to join forces if possible and contact action groups already operational in their determination to identify loopholes in the law that unwittingly assist any religious group or organisation's ability to hide sexual predators, Greg was keen to temporarily change the subject. Easing the topic of conversation away from the concern they were all feeling and lighten the theme - such was the scope for fun at Amelia's expense, he managed with great success.

"Leave her alone Greg. It helps her to think of it in that way and I quite like it." Tristan attempted to come to her rescue, much to Amelia's irritation, as his voice held a morsel of patronising goodness, reminiscent of her own Sugarplum.

"No you don't," she argued, "I can tell, you've got your Father's look on your face."

"Yes you have a bit," said Lucinda, "you know that 'Dense but Tense' look."

"Dense but Tense?" Tristan queried, without the surety he really wanted to hear the answer.

"Yes, you know, it's the, 'I inhabit a different world and I really don't understand the workings of the lower classes, however, I'll mask it with an expression that suggests thoughtful, intelligent consideration, so as not to upset the plebs.' look."

Anyone else would have ensured "the look" fastened an even tighter grip on Tristan's face. However Lucinda, being Lucinda, was instantly forgivable such was the light, well-meaning humour with which she spoke.

Tristan smiled ruefully, "Am I ever going to be forgiven for being born into a family of nobs?" he challenged.

"No." They all chorused.

"Sorry Tris," Amelia was smitten with guilt; gaining Tristan the contrived success he anticipated with his purposeful self-deprecating air.

Greg interpolated, "Is that nob with or without a k?" he quipped.

"Definitely both." wisecracked Tristan swiftly. "The nob is a Knob – as in thick as."

"Tristan, stop it now; don't play up to him. He's just jealous." Amelia cast a sardonic look towards Greg, who skilfully parodied her expression.

"Okay, Okay, 'tis true, Tristan. We know you're not a knobby nob and yes, I'm jealous. I would love to be. Well, not the thick or dense bit of course - that could never be - but how I'd love to have been born a nob. Anyway Dearheart, we love you madly, but don't humour Amelia over this business. She's been acting like a fruitcake and that's all there is to it. She's had the invasion of the fairies and the goblins for far too long. They have outstayed their welcome – bloody squatters." Greg turned, confirming with satisfaction that all of them were earnestly nodding their agreement in Amelia's direction.

"So," Greg, satisfied their assent signalled the veneration he constantly craved, walked his fingers authoritatively across the garden table, "so, my love, all your little people gone away, pitter-patter, off they frolic to the Ench..."

"Stop it, meanie." Amelia was laughing now, they were all laughing. "I know it sounds very stupid, but it's how I feel. But I haven't got little people in my head anymore."

"That's because they've moved out - to the Enchanted Hall," exclaimed Lucinda.

"The important thing is that you're feeling better Millie." Chris as ever, wishing to placate.

"Absolutely," Gail agreed with her husband, "you look and sound well Millie; I'm so relieved to see you so chirpy."

"Thanks Gail, sorry I've been a pain, but I feel pretty good now, I've been thinking about how beautiful life is. How capable human beings are and always have been, of living a wondrous life. We will evolve because the alternative is extinction." This will happen Amelia knew with a surety never before experienced.

"Surely," she continued, "a species evolves not by choice, but because it has to; death being the only option if it doesn't." Amelia's lively imagination caught onto the theory of life beginning as fish in the sea. "Think about fish."

"Fish?" They all repeated synchronously, trading looks of exaggerated disbelief.

Amelia was not to be put off.

"Yes, fish. This is how it goes, right, are you listening? They were forced onto land because of a threat to survival in their murky waters."

"By what? How do you know the waters were murky? And who's they?" questioned Greg.

"The bloody fish that's who, and I don't know by what – your ancestors probably. The fear of the uncharted, balanced precariously by the threat of extinction. How brave they were, the few who made it safely out of their customary habitat to face whatever menacing danger of the unfamiliar mysteries that lay ahead. How many would have baulked against the very thought of leaving the sanctuary they had known for maybe thousands of years, and how many died in battle protecting that sanctuary, that fragile house of cards? That was all they had known so they tried to honour their history, their heritage."

"Calm down Millie-Moo, you're getting a bit carried away. I don't think fish think too much about their history, bearing in mind they only have a memory span of two seconds or whatever. That doesn't make much of a heritage does it, if you think about it. Now, son, remember your birthright, now son …. who are you anyway? Who am I?"

"Where am I?" added Tristan.

"In the murky waters apparently," suggested Lucinda helpfully.

"I will ignore your mockery; you know what I'm trying to say here."

"Yes, you're trying to convince us that fish – that would be *fish* – are opening up heritage centres and museums so their little spawn don't forget where they came from; their roots."

Undeterred, Amelia ignored their rising hilarity at her expense and pressed bravely on. "Chris, Gail, back me up here, you both surely know what I'm trying to say - it's an example, an analogy. They wouldn't have *known* anything, that's my point; they would have just tried to protect their territory instinctively. But if they had been able to see the bigger picture, they would have known that so many of them didn't have to die, but just get on with the business of evolving. And we're just the same. We are just the same." She presented triumphantly.

"What, like fish?"

"Yes."

"I can't breathe for long under water. I think they must be more highly evolved than me." Tristan informed them.

"No, stop it." Their laughter was infectious and Amelia was at pains to remain serious. "The fish wasted time, and lives, fighting their corner. Are you following?" Amelia bit back the laughter, "Eventually, when they realised that they had to move on or they would become extinct, they stopped fighting each other and allowed evolution to take place. That is, they evolved into a species able to co-habit in a better setting, a new world. That ensured their survival.

The theory being, that's where we come from. So far, history has been repeating itself: that's exactly what humans have always done; fighting and squabbling over futile territorial rights and not seeing the bigger picture. They will come to know; there is nothing to be done other than to move forward into a new world order on earth. When they stop fighting each other, they will see it is not scary; it is life as they already have it, only better."

Amelia had to stop to draw breath, enabling Greg to seize his chance.

"What's all this *they* business - talking about human beings as if you're not one yourself? You're not a Hebbie yet you know." insisted Greg.

"Neither are you."

"Don't be too sure about that my little cute-nosed friend."

"Look to the future Greg. Look and see the life we have, the life of survival. The life of success is not war; nor arguments with each other; with religions; with race; with politics. Nor is it about status; power and control; land and who owns what. The life of success has none of these powerful instruments of Ego. Look beyond these human failings and see the dazzling horizon."

"Hey, I'm with you on that one sweetie," said Gail, she turned to her husband, "how about you Chris?"

"No shadow of doubt as far as I'm concerned, grinned Chris.

"Wow," said Lucinda, "I'm dazzled just thinking about it."

"Your eloquence knows no bounds Amelia," added Tristan with moot admiration.

"That may be so, but the only thing that's dazzling me right now is the sun; and the need to top up my pint. I'm going in. Amelia?" Greg ended with a question as he rose.

"Yes Grip?" Amelia waited for the next onslaught of sport at her expense with resigned patience.

"I like your style. I may mock, just to hedge my bets really – but I do think there's something in what you say, you know. So when are we entering this new phase? When are we to become much more spiritually aware and nobody fights each other and stuff?"

"Oh." This sudden allegiance unseated her. "I don't know. Soon I guess. In the meantime, I'll have another one of those please." She glanced at her empty glass.

"Me too," echoed Lucinda, "Got to keep my strength up for when I turn into a Hebbie."

"Yes," Tristan spoke thoughtfully, having wrestled manfully to keep his Father's look off his face throughout the exchange. "I guess I'll be out of business when all this happens; no need for barristers when everyone's a Hebbie. I'll have to think of something else to do."

Greg spun on his heels. "Hold on a minute." They all turned to stare at him expectantly. "What about Adam and Eve?"

"What?"

Obliterating his usual face proclaiming distaste of the word 'what' as a one entity, Greg startled them with his reply, "You're going on about fish; how we started out as fish and then evolved onto land. What about Adam and Eve, is creation a fable? What does God – your God - have to say about that then?"

All eyes were now on Amelia. Lucinda, privately acknowledging that Greg had raised an interesting query, felt unsure as to the wisdom of discussing it. She worried about Amelia hearing any voices; even though so far, the voice of God (or IT as Millie had assured her) was pretty impressive, Lucinda agreed. Sure enough, Amelia responded with the words that unsettled her.

"I don't know. I've never asked Him. I could ask Him."

"Thought He was an It?"

"Given up on that one, it's too much like hard work remembering, and sounds ridiculous anyway. I tried referring to God as a She, but I can't make it stick in my head. No, I'm staying with, He/Him, because it doesn't mean I believe God is a man or male, thank goodness, it's merely habit, and to return to the topic lest we forget, I'll ask *Him* for you – about Adam and Eve. It is a bit of a mystery isn't it."

"Didn't Adam and Eve wear fig leaves? I've never seen a fish in a fig leaf." said Tristan dryly, in the hope of leading the subject away from discourse with God.

"Shut up Tris." Amelia said pleasantly. "I mean it, I could ask Him."

"Now, there's a thought. Adam and Eve were fish; explains everything. Tris is right. Perhaps they could have a display of 'Fig Leafs through the Ages' at their heritage centres." Greg, realising that he had slipped Amelia back into a dangerous world of forbidden voices, ignored her words and latched onto Tristan's theme.

"The changing world of Fashionable Fish." King of quips, Greg continued to move Amelia's thoughts away from God homilies.

Tristan nodded his head with implied perspicacity, as if together, they had discovered the meaning of life.

Lucinda was glad with relief the subject had lightened once more and turned away from, 'the voice,' which she feared Amelia may become embroiled. However, Lucinda had been forming a secret desire to hear God herself. She felt in her heart that hearing the voice of IT had been a bumpy journey for Amelia because she was made that way. 'But now she's listening properly and getting it right, she's never been more at ease, more comfortable.' They could all see it growing within.

'I'm going to try it.' Lucinda decided, 'won't tell this lot though – don't want them all clucking with worry, chewing the cud and gossiping in corners the way they did with Millie. Well, OK, I have to include myself in that – but we *were* worried, couldn't see it ending well. But, it seems, we were wrong.' Bringing herself back into the conversation, Lucinda giggled her response to Greg. "All very well, but this little fish is dying of thirst."

"The things some people do to dodge buying their round. Come, old boy get a move on. These little fishes must be fed – they've got legs to grow and I've got a new career to plan. Not to mention we are about to meet

Lucinda's new beau, so move it." Tristan's words spurred Greg into moving towards the pub again. Walking backwards so he could still see them and waving the empty glasses in his hands as he went, they laughed light-heartedly with each other.

"Yes and I don't want you all frightening him off on the first meet, and he's not my beau, we've been out on a few dates that's all. I'm beginning to feel sorry for him already. God knows what you'll all do to him, the poor man, with all that 'God versus Evolution' talk. And don't walk backwards whilst carrying glasses, it's dangerous." Lucinda frowned as she decided it was *such* a bad idea to go to the pub first, before introducing the new man in her life to her friends.

"Not quite as sophisticated as a 'God v Evolution' debate is it really? Welcome to, 'The Murky Waters and Fish Growing Legs' discussion," corrected a receding slowly from sight Greg, raising his voice as he edged, still backwards, towards the pub door, "Not to mention Amelia's frigging Enchanted Hall."

"Quite. Best not to mention any of that. He'll think I keep the company of lunatics." Lucinda urged with a smile that attempted to cover up growing concern for how the coming meeting would turn out. "And just repeat that a little louder Greg, I don't think everyone in the bar quite heard you."

"Oh ha, bloody ha to the lot of you. Where's my lemonade?" Amelia smiling at them all one-by-one, tentatively reached out for Tristan's hand as she spoke. She silently promised herself to ask God at the very next opportunity about Adam and Eve - and fish.

Heaven is a Donut

Epilogue

"Daddy, what does The End mean?"

"Really? No, I don't believe you – that's outrageous."

When

When I see the faults in others, *are my faults too being same*
When I learn of such humility, *not giving nor receiving blame*
When I learn to live in present, *a space that's whole and vast,*
I shall learn I'm not a victim, *nor trapped in turbulent past.*

When I learn to sit harmoniously, *with peacemakers of good heart,*
When I share my wisdom, with a child - *to nurture and impart*
When I learn to not give others, *my worries and my stress,*
I shall kiss them with a promise - *this life here on earth will bless.*

When I learn the life of heroes, *crying out in lonely pain,*
When I see their death a calling – *they shall never die in vain.*
When I see the path, so humbly trod - *to show each and all the way,*
I can light the road for others; *this price is so small to pay.*

When I see which things are trivial, *and all those that truly matter*
When I see the clarity of God, *with lives not ending in tatters*
When I see the world around us, *is transient and fleeting,*
God's evolution triumphs proud, *too precious for a cheating.*

When I recall insanity, *edging to man's dysfunction*
When I learn of earth's sweet reason, *I halt my own destruction.*
When I learn of all good truthfulness, *humankind shall soon become,*
To end their pandemonium, *oh yes and Thy Will be Done!*

When within my life's short story, *I but see the need to change*
When I can open wide my eyes, *to the distance and the range*
When I learn scope, of all there is, *with guidance, truth and spirit,*

Heaven is a Donut

I learn of better ways to live, *with all goodness I shall sit.*
When I change the final ending, *of accumulated need*
When I find the peace within me - *that soothes and stems the bleed.*
When I see who that I am not, *and so all that is a sham*
That is only when I can learn - *who it is I really am.*

Heaven is a Donut

Acknowledgements

I would like to thank Mike Somerset, for helping open my eyes to the existence and love of Spirit, thereby enabling me to reacquaint myself with God - which has become the most beneficial relationship of my life. Thank you soul-friend.

I would also like to thank all of my family, friends and acquaintances who, without mockery, listened and absorbed my inner changes with calm and loving acceptance - if some bemusement.

Likewise to thank all of those (actually there are not so many) who at some time or another, have caused me angst, done me wrong, or acted without consideration towards me, or my loved ones. You have granted a very great favour. I have learned through trial and error what it is I don't like about myself and have found the inner peace of walking in forgiveness, empathy and compassion; for me - no easy journey, and one I remain doggedly, if at times unsteadily, intent upon.

I would like to offer my heartfelt apology to all of those (I hope again there are not so many) who at some time or another, I have likewise caused angst, done them wrong, or acted without consideration.

I mention here my children, for their patience, love and understanding. I love you unconditionally.

To one close to me (you know who you are) who continues to support my endeavours – even whilst not quite understanding my love of Heaven or agreeing with my beliefs in, or about, God.

To all those who helped me reach publication. I thank my friend, the author Peter Morrell, who succeeded where all others had failed, to kick-start my determination to publish this book, by ousting me from the plateau of apathy I had self-indulgently rested upon and for whom the poem When is written. Thank you.

The biggest thanks go to my very great and wonderful friend, Jackie Fitch, who in the face of debilitating illness edited the first draft of this book tirelessly, with love and diligence, and without question, brilliant advice. You have never let me down. You are still with me. Thank you my friend.

I finish with something I do every day of my life:

Thank you God.